UP IN SMOKE

Hannah R. Conway

ISBN: 0692945636

ISBN-13: 978-0692945636

To the Military Spouse, this one's for you.

You're stronger than you know.

Up in Smoke, a novel

This book is a work of fiction. Names, characters, places, and incidents are either the product of the author's imagination or are used fictitiously. Any resemblance of actual events, organizations, places, locales or to persons, living or dead, is purely coincidental and beyond the intent of either the author or publisher. The characters are productions of the author's imagination and used fictitiously.

Some scripture quotations or referral are courtesy of the King James Version of the Holy Bible.

Some scripture quotations or referral are courtesy of the New King James Version of the Holy Bible. Copyright 1979,1980, 1982 by Thomas-Nelson, Inc. Used by permission. All rights reserved.

This book was produced in publication with Jessica Kirkland from Kirkland Media Management.

The cover art is from Jennifer Zemanek of Seedlings Design Studio.

ACKNOWLEDGMENTS

Where do I start? Words truly do not seem sufficient enough to express the love, gratitude, and appreciation I have for those who have helped make this novel possible. But I have to try.

To my husband, Stephen. *Wink*. I love you, babes. We did it again. Book three. Thank you for continuing to have my back, and find a way to make all my dreams come true. The love and appreciation I have for you grows every day. You've endured scribbled on notepads all over the house, manic bouts of writing, talking about fake people and strange what-if scenarios—and you haven't had me committed yet. Bless you! But seriously…thank you.

To my kiddos. Oh how I love you both. You are a source of joy in my life, a blessing that is hard to describe. Thank you for loving me, and thank you for understanding when Momma had to drink gallons of coffee and hide away for hours to write. I'm now free to play outside more!

Thank you to Daniel & Wendi Ufford who invited our family into their home for dinner and answered my many strange questions on law and custody issues in order to help make this novel possible. Any stretch was made for the sake of fiction. Any false information or mistakes are to be blamed on me and not on Daniel's expertise.

To Shannon and Cynthia who were my writing partners back when I was calling this book "The Deal". Ladies, you're lovely!

Sara Turnquist, my friend, writing partner, sounding board, and partner in crime. We work well together my friend! Thank you!

Jessie Kirkland, with Kirkland Media Management, the most amazing agent on the planet with endless creativity. Thank you for all that you

2

do, and for listening to my crazy voice texts. I love being on this writing journey with you!

To Clarksville Christian Writers, a small but mighty group of writers that know how to sharpen skills. Thank you for listening to my scenes and giving thoughtful feedback.

Thank you Dr. Larry Robertson and Bro. Tim Munoz from Hilldale Baptist Church for their incredible insights into God's Word that weaseled their way into these pages. You've been a blessing to our family in so many ways.

Jenny from Seedlings Cover Design Studios. WOW. This book cover is breathtaking! Thank you! You've been a pleasure to work with.

To Amanda Stevens, my editor. I feel like I should apologize for making you work so hard. Really, anything awesome about this book will be because you are an incredible editor. Thank you!

Conway's Convoy…my tribe! My people! May cheer team! Y'all (Can I say y'all here?) are a constant source of encouragement and passion. For some reason you love me back! Hugs to each of you!

A huge thank you to my Advanced Copy Readers and Reviewers. You took time to read and give me valuable feedback. Thank you! You've made me a stronger writer.

Mom, Dad, Luke…I love you guys. Thank you for being who you are, and for always having my back.

And God…I'm arching a brow now with a sideways grin just saying Your name. Thank You for never giving up on me, for speaking to me through Your Word, for always putting those story ideas in my head, and pulling me out of bed at the crack of BEFORE dawn to get stuff done. You're my savior, my friend, and the best writing partner ever.

I acknowledge that without these individuals, and even more than I am surely not mentioning because my brain is fried after writing this novel, I would not be here…there would be no Hannah R. Conway —author.

Thank you. From every part of me—thank you.

CHAPTER ONE

LEANNA WILSON COULDN'T seem to shake the chill from her bones, and it wasn't because of a lack of warm bodies filling up the funeral home parlor. She cupped her hands around her nose and mouth and breathed in and out, in and out, warding off the next panic attack.

The hills of Kentucky called her home, but not in the way she expected. Why hadn't she returned like promised? Before this?

She longed for the warmth of her parents' kitchen. The savory smells of comfort wafting about the air. Vegetable soup. Fresh bread.

Echoes of their laughter danced throughout her memories.

Laughing. Mom and Dad always laughed. Leanna attempted a smile. Unable to stand any longer to greet the mourners, she sat in the front row on-looking the twin caskets, supported by a rickety wooden white chair. Its cushion, well worn, matched the color of her sister's tear-stained cheeks.

No nine-year-old child should lose so much. Leanna consoled her sister, one arm holding her close, though her attempts were as foreign as her relationship with Brie. A seventeen-year age difference did nothing to decrease the gap.

Brie was still pasting Band-Aids on her body as stickers by the time Leanna graduated college. Back then they were close. Visits during summer breaks and holidays included piggy-back rides, finger painting, and braiding Barbie doll hair.

Leanna tucked her chin, face warming with the memories bittersweet. Yes, she and Brie had been close, but back then, Leanna considered herself close to all her friends and family. Much had changed. Too much.

Brie neither stirred nor stiffened when Leanna squeezed her small hand, but sat, slumped forward. Her soft honey curls veiled her face but couldn't hide the sobs, or the tears that dripped from her cheek.

The cries twisted Leanna's heart, the burning sensation almost too much to bear. She clamped her bottom lip between her teeth, eyes closed. Why hadn't she returned sooner?

No reason came to mind, only pitiful excuses.

Lamenting sobs, like nails driving into the layers of grief and regret in her soul, echoed around the room. How many more hours did they have to endure this? And tomorrow, the funeral.

Another hand touched her shoulder. Another. Then another. So many people, compassionate people, offering condolences. Their words she could not hear. Their faces, familiar, but indistinguishable. Her hand trembled at her side against the black burdet dress—a gift to herself from a trendy boutique during her travels in Europe.

Europe. Leanna rolled her neck, breathing in the memories of that summer, but the cobble stone roads, rainy days, and ancient castles of Europe couldn't hold her focus. Tattered carpet, thick air saturated with a floral scent, and twin caskets took precedence in her mind.

Leanna held to the soft coal-colored fabric of the dress meant to be worn at cocktail parties and other social elite events in New York, never at her parents' funeral. Her throat constricted. She swallowed, but the tightness remained, and the chill returned. Leanna shook, and the diamond on her left ring finger hung loose. It caught on the threads of the cushion. She tugged it free and moved the engagement ring into place, but the stone sent a series of shivers through her body.

Marrying William had also been in the plan, but not anymore. He could keep his daddy's money and expensive apologies.

Why had she not taken the ring off yet? A year apart, six months since the breakup. It was she that ended the relationship, but the ring still sat in place, like a bad omen, or something chaining her to him—a man she'd tried to rid herself from for over a year now. This time it was for good, permanent, like death. This time she'd hold her ground and refuse to return to him.

Leanna slid the rock from her finger, glanced at it once, and then let it fall to the bottom of her purse. It was time to start fresh—start over. But here? Back home in Lebanon Junction, Kentucky?

Mom and Dad were gone. They'd left her to mourn—and Brie too.

And now, Leanna was alone, helpless, and...

Hopeless.

The word scrolled through her mind. As she surveyed the room and the child at her side, hopeless fit.

Why weren't her parents alive? Alive so she could apologize, hug their necks, and bury her head on their shoulders.

Leanna blinked, and a fresh tear raced down her cheek. She swiped it away. No crying. Not now. Her stomach turned, and her chest grew heavy, threatening to crush her. She couldn't raise her eyes to meet those of the funeral guests any longer, and instead focused on her parents lying there, lifeless, still.

They could be sleeping. If only that were true.

If she could only wake them. They'd welcome her into their arms, laugh, and beg to hear all about New York. They'd help her figure out her path in life, which until now seemed so clear—something both comforting and terrifying.

It was clear she'd graduate law school, and she did. She'd been lucky to secure a paid internship at a firm in New York, and now with close to a year of experience under her belt, the firm offered her a solid position. A position full of promise, and more money than she'd seen this side of the Appalachians. She readily accepted a month ago, but now?

Life seemed so uncertain. Leanna held in a breath, and pulled Brie closer.

She rubbed her hand up and down the length of Brie's arm. The motion steadied her perhaps more than it consoled Brie. A low familiar tune deep within her memory worked its way forward. Leanna let the low melody slip from her mouth in a hum—a hymn her mother once sang. Brie stiffened but soon melted against Leanna. She swung her arm around Leanna's waist and held tight.

Leanna pressed her lip into a fine line, and tucked her chin. She never should have left for New York. Kentucky had plenty of great universities, but unlike the dullness of the funeral home and the rust-covered buildings of her hometown, New York sparkled and called. It promised a better life, more money, and happiness. Was it her, or New York, who had lied?

"Shhh, Brie. We're okay." Leanna kissed the top of Brie's wavy blond hair and hoped her words were true. "We're going to be fine." She pressed her cheek atop Brie's head and breathed her in. Brie smelled like home. Honeysuckle, soap, something baking in the oven.

Leanna closed her eyes. Her heart ached.

Brie whimpered. Leanna winced at the heart-piercing sound, and steadied her breathing.

She pushed Brie's hair back, and pulled her closer. "We'll get through this."

Brie lifted her head. Her eyes, once curious by nature, held only uncertainty. How much she had grown. Her rounded cheeks had begun to lengthen. She no longer wore Band-Aids as stickers, or swung her legs to the beat of a tune in her head. Did she still demand sprinkles on her toast, or read Christmas stories all year long?

A lump rose in Leanna's throat. Yes, they were sisters, but right now they were strangers. It had taken the death of their parents for this realization.

The weight of Brie's stare forced Leanna further into the chair. The child staring back needed so much. Much more than what Leanna could offer.

"I love you, Brie. And...and I'm going to do my best to take care of you."

Brie tucked her lip under her top teeth, eyes shifting to her hand. She hadn't uttered a word since the car accident, and bore the gash across her forehead in silence. The doctors said she was still in shock, and rightfully so. It could be days until Brie found her voice, but even in her silence, she said so much.

Well-wishers held tissues to their noses and dabbed at their eyes as they passed in front of the caskets. They stopped patting both Leanna and Brie on the back with pursed-lips too full of sorrow.

The funeral home director, arranged the flowers at the front of the room. More arrived. The sweet floral scents repulsed her. She swallowed back the bile.

As a child, she and Dad stopped along the roadsides to pick flowers, relishing their fragrance. They brought them home to Mom, who delighted in making them the centerpiece at the dinner table. A Mason jar and wildflowers.

Leanna buried her teeth into her bottom lip.

There weren't any flowers on her parents' table today—only on their coffins. She held her breath and shut her eyes, embracing the burning sensation growing in her lungs. Her lashes fluttered open as she sucked in a gulp of air.

She scanned the room through blurred vision. Fragrant blooming bouquets lined the side walls and filled the front and back of the ever-shrinking room. But one bouquet gave her pause.

A bright bundle with buds beginning to droop, stuffed in the corner, made her stomach pinch. Scrawled handwriting, too familiar for comfort, poked from behind a red bloom.

William.

No sight of him, but the flowers? Those were from him, for sure. He'd sent the same arrangement to her door countless times. Well wishes, but mostly apologies she'd stupidly forgiven, and now, he sent condolences.

Her heart was too numb to care.

Leanna puffed her cheeks and wiped at her forehead.

She scanned the room once more. No sign of him. Maybe he finally took the hint and moved on. Then again, the flowers suggested not.

Perhaps starting over here would prove more difficult than she hoped. Leanna cradled Brie close and kissed her wavy hair. Where else was there to go? Taking Brie to New York and away from the only home she'd ever known wasn't an option. Right now at least.

God help me.

Would that count as a prayer? It had to. But was God still listening?

Leanna rocked side to side and fought to keep her hum steady, but failed.

CHAPTER TWO

LEANNA AWOKE GROGGY and, like most mornings, with a faint headache.

Six A.M. The digital red numbers on the clock were mesmerizing. Funny how time stood still for no one, and for no occasion—not even for the death of her parents.

She'd bury her mom and dad today.

A tear soaked into the pillow, and a yawn pushed its way out. She breathed a heavy sigh and rolled to her side. Brie slept on, curled in a small bundle, her head on the pillow next to Leanna's. She could be an angel. Leanna brushed back a strand of hair from Brie's cheek and planted a gentle kiss.

For the first time since the wreck Brie slept soundly, and for that, every part of Leanna was thankful. If only she would talk. Time would help. It healed all things, right?

Leanna stretched and stood. The hardwood floors were cool against her feet, much like the concrete floors of her New York flat. That room was filled with the finest furnishings. Leanna glanced around her bedroom. This room overflowed with better things—things money could never buy. How had she forgotten that?

Swim meet blue ribbons and academic achievement awards hung on the wall and surrounded her dresser. Mom and Dad had preserved her room like a time capsule. An evolution of paintings and drawings hung on the walls like a timeline. Her work spanned from the toddler years to the oil paintings of backwoods and barns that landed her admission to Columbia as an undergraduate.

Leanna pressed her fingertips against her lips. She stepped closer to the painting as if she could fall in and turn back time. Shades of green and trees of different heights hid an abandoned home on an old farm down the road. Barefoot children ran past.

A scene from her childhood where she once played 'house' with friends in the crumbling home. Leanna tilted her head, the painting taking on a new life. It wasn't merely a scene, or memory, but a foreshadowing of how things crumble. *Homes. Friendship. Life.* Yet, the scene was beautiful, and much different from her current work that lacked depth, warmth, and story, or so said a vendor at an art gallery close to her firm. But who had time to paint with soul when working eighty hours a week, and when her soul no longer saw color?

The clock on the wall chimed at the half hour, bringing her back into the present. She rounded the room, tired legs shuffling past rock band posters, stuffed animals, and rows of photos of friends and family.

Leanna brushed the frames with a hand. A family photo, taken the day she earned her Bachelor's degree. She'd been the first in her family to graduate from college, so of course her parents were proud.

She pulled the frame from the wall and held it close to her face, drinking in their smiles. This was the way she wanted to remember them. Leanna squeezed the picture to her chest and slipped out the door, careful to contain the creaking. She tiptoed down the hall and stopped in her parents' doorway.

The room was tidy. The bed made. A patchwork quilt lay at the foot. Leanna forced herself forward. She skimmed her finger across the quilt that had once made tents in the living room and bundled her family close during storms. The Bible lay open on the nightstand. She touched the highlighted verse, Romans 8:28, yet found no comfort in the words. Instead, the empty space inside her heart grew.

Alone. Yes, that emotion held her hand too tight. Mom and Dad would've encouraged her to find rest in God's Word during this struggle, but they weren't here, and nothing about their religion sounded comforting. A list of *do's* and *don'ts*. She'd spent most of her life checking off the boxes but somehow coming up short. What was the point?

Leanna wandered from the Scripture and leaned against the wall.

Dad's slippers sat near the closet. Mom's ancient fluffy floral-print robe hung from the bathroom door. It looked as if they had just stepped out of the house to run errands.

"I love you, Mom and Dad." Could they hear? Leanna turned, face downcast, and walked back to her room. She climbed in bed with Brie, pulling the sleeping child close. It was too early to get up anyway.

Brie was her responsibility now. There was no way around that, nor would she choose to escape that responsibility. But how could she provide for her sister in this town?

Working at William's firm wasn't an option. Under his thumb was bad enough, but under the hand and eye of his family, too? They practically ran the town.

She'd find work somewhere else. Anywhere.

Teaching was an option, but school let out in a month. Crap.

And teaching required a license. That took time and money, both of which came up short. Her bank account all but echoed. Even if by some miracle she were to be hired, she wouldn't start until August. Leanna squirmed and fought with the covers.

What could she sell to get quick cash? Her mind ran blank, but then ticked through options. That dumb engagement ring would surely sell well. Maybe Dad had scrap pieces of copper left in the barn.

Those things could put a little quick cash in her pocket, but what about health insurance? Life insurance? Utilities?

Her head now throbbed.

Even though they weren't married, William had been her primary income source. Why she ever consented to being entirely dependent on that man, she'll never understand. Regardless, leaving him had severed her ties with free-flowing cash. An occasional painting sold to the gallery, and the internship barely allowed her to make ends meet on her own.

It was going to take money, lots of money to raise a child. Maybe moving to Louisville or Lexington, or tutoring until something better came along could work.

Leanna buried the side of her face into the pillow and clung to Brie. At least they had a house. Perhaps Mom and Dad had enough life insurance for them to get by for a while.

The thought brought some comfort. Leanna breathed in the sweet smell of Brie's curls and smiled. They'd make it somehow. Some way.

CHAPTER THREE

LEANNA FOLDED HER arms, hip jutted to the side. This was the last place she wanted to be a week after her parents passed, but this was the only firm in town, and the location of her parents' will.

"It's good to see you, Leanna, just not like this." William's eyes were cool. He maneuvered around his desk as if playing a strategic game of chess. A game he'd lose. Leanna stepped back, chin high.

"I don't want to take up any more time. Let's clear up a few things so I can get going." She lifted a brow, working to keep a stony expression.

"How's the flat in New York?"

She wet her lips and sighed. "I'm letting it go." Her life was here now. A new dream. A strange dream.

"And all your stuff?"

"You mean, the stuff you purchased?"

"I bought it for you."

She scratched at her arm. "I've got to find the time to get back up there and box it all up."

"I'd like to help with that. It could be the thing we need—"

"William, please, let's focus."

She knew that look, and that silence. William wasn't one to relent, but considering the circumstances, he must've caved. Leanna kept her composure but sighed inside.

William let out an audible groan and resumed the legal jargon. She spoke the terminology well, but he made little sense in his attempt to shed light on the components of her parents' will.

The office, though the largest building downtown, shrank with the rising tension. Its furnishings, finer than much else around town, did nothing to lighten the conversation. Leanna pressed her fingertips against her temple and chewed on the inside of her lip.

William stared out the window for some time, looking at what, Leanna was uncertain. He turned, eyeing the gun cabinet to his right. "Your dad and I hunted for years. Good folks—both your parents. Saw them a few days before..." He ran a hand over his face, color drained. "Terrible. Just terrible."

And for once, he seemed truly moved, compassionate even. Leanna relaxed her stance and focused on the toes of her heels.

She shifted her weight, aware of how the sorrow of each resident pressed against her. They sent cards, flowers, and home-cooked meals. Just this morning she stepped onto the front porch and found a basket of fruit and a box of chocolates. Their grief may have matched her own, but they could not understand the guilt that plagued her. She'd left them—Mom, Dad, and Brie.

Leanna cradled her face between her palms, and then squared her shoulders. "Again, I have other pressing matters." Like selling a bunch of junk and finding a job.

"I've known your folks a long time—"

"William—"

"How's Brie?"

Leanna eyed the glass door. Brie sat outside the office, gazing at the tile floor.

Leanna let her arms fall. A heavy sigh followed. "We're both here."

William nodded, not lifting his eyes.

She took a seat, legs sticking to the leather, and steepled her fingers over her nose as if in prayer. "You've never been one to avoid a conversation. If there's something you're trying to say, then say it. If not, I need to go."

He coughed and sat, knees working a nervous pump. "I wish things would've ended different between us."

Us?

"I'm not here to talk about us. My parents are dead, William, and I'm here to make sure I have the immediate means to provide for Brie. If you can't help with that, then I will drive however far it takes to find someone who can."

Where was this newfound nerve? She'd never spoken so harshly to him, even when she broke off their relationship.

His jawline hardened. He adjusted his tie and opened the file on his desk.

A few moments passed before William spoke. "It's not what you're expecting."

"Guess that depends on what you think I'm after."

What was she after? A place to raise Brie, and the funds to do so. A chance to start over and be the person that would make her parents proud.

William let out an exasperated breath. He sat, fingers interlocking and outstretched on his desk.

"Here's a copy of the will for your records."

Leanna reached out turning the two-page document over in her hand.

"There's nothing, Leanna. They have nothing to leave you."

She froze.

"And," he continued. "There's nothing here giving you custody over Brie."

The news was simple, but nonetheless devastating—and even more life altering than the death of her parents.

Leanna pressed her back against the studded chair. The air left her lungs.

There must have been some mistake.

Brie. The child who'd been through too much. The sister she barely knew. The same girl Leanna promised to care for.

"Who? Who will take care of her?" The limp words fell from her mouth.

"I'm sorry, Leanna."

"Who?"

William ran his hands through his hair and closed an overstuffed file in front of him. He shook his head. "There's more we have to talk about. Your parents' finances—"

"I want to know who." A furious heat rose and rumbled from within.

"We can contest—"

"William, stop it." Leanna smacked her hand against the wooden armrest. It stung and throbbed with a beat that mimicked her pulse.

"Your aunt and uncle."

"Cindy and Dale?" Her chest caved. She shook her head. "I won't let that happen."

"I know they weren't always the best kind of people."

"You think?"

"They're different now. If you —"

"I want Brie. She's my sister. My responsibility."

"How are you supposed to care for her?"

And he was right. He was all too aware of her financial situation.

No career in this town. Little money. Maybe in a few months when she got back on her feet, but not now.

"I'll find a way. We can't be separated."

What judge would deem her suitable right now?

William lifted the heavy manila file and slid it across the desk toward her.

"You've inherited a mess."

She titled her head, lips parted.

"Every penny of the insurance money is going to go toward paying for your parents' funeral, and their debt."

"Toward their debt?" Leanna swallowed and cowered back into the seat. William's eyes took her in, like some kind of prey he pitied, or a caught animal.

"Your parents kept a detailed record of their finances. They came to me before, well..." He rapped on the folder with his knuckle. "Hearts of gold, your parents." He opened the file and flipped through a few pages.

A numbing sensation climbed the length of her body and wrapped around her throat. Leanna jerked free from its grip.

"They didn't want you to know, but now..." He handed her the file. So many pages. "We never got the chance to sit down and figure out this mess." His face paled with some shade of genuine concern. He appeared almost ill, but not as sick as she felt.

"Are these...?" Leanna held the papers in her hands. "These are..."

"From Columbia. And several credit card statements. Letters from a mortgage company too."

The room spun. Leanna sank into the leather seat. She scanned each letter, each payment stub and bank note. "What is this?"

He shrugged. "Looks like they borrowed until they couldn't borrow anymore, and then they borrowed against their home. There are two mortgages now."

She shook her head. "Their home was paid for. I had a scholarship." A partial scholarship. Not once did she consider the cost of an Ivy League education. Not once had her parents mentioned the burden. "This can't be. It's a mistake." She flipped through the pages. "Have you looked through all of these?"

Maybe some reasonable explanation lay between the bills.

William nodded. "It will take a few more days to really get through all of this."

"My parents would never –"

"They did. You're holding the proof, and they hid it from all of us. There isn't enough insurance money to cover this amount of debt." He placed his hand on her shoulder, and she was stuck, held in place by him once more. "Everything is going to have to be sold."

Everything. The word sank deep.

"The Scoop?" Her parents' life work and ministry. It was more than a soup kitchen—at least to them.

He nodded, mouth turned down. "Just the property."

"The house?"

Another nod.

This was all a misunderstanding. The house couldn't be sold. "How much are we talking?"

His brows furrowed. "Around $160,000. Maybe more."

"Even after the insurance?"

He nodded.

The file in her hand became a weight.

Her parents had ruined themselves financially in order to help send her to the school of her dreams. Leanna bit her tongue to keep from shouting. How ungrateful had she been? How selfish?

"This is my fault." Brie would suffer because of her. One, two, and then a multitude of tears raced down her cheeks. "Why? Why would they have done this?" She knew why. They loved her, wanted to make her dreams come true. She'd heard them say it a thousand times.

"I'm sorry, Leanna. I really am." William choked back tears of his own, but what kind of tears, she could only imagine. "You didn't need to hear any of this."

She stared at the file until it blurred as unclear as her thoughts.

If she could fix the financial aspect of the situation, she'd have a fighting chance at gaining custody of Brie. A court would have to be stupid to hand Brie over to Cindy and Dale.

Leanna dried her eyes, her burden lessened at an obvious but twisted solution.

William.

Could she crawl back to him, beg for help? Of course he would oblige, but at what expense?

No. She could no longer live in his world.

But he had money.

There had to be another way. She'd work two, three, or four jobs if she must.

"There's time before things have to be sold. Grant it, not much time, but some." The tone of his voice sounded more like some sort of proposal. One she didn't want to contemplate. "Don't rush into anything...foolish."

Wise words from someone so foolish.

"How much time with Brie do I have?" But she knew the answer.

"Cindy and Dale live a few miles down the road."

"Don't do this today, William. I can't lose her right now." She read about custody cases. The Courts would side in the best interest of the child.

"My hands are tied."

His hands were never tied. He and his family held the keys to the town. Leanna stood with the folder tucked under her arm and headed toward the door.

"Don't go. We may be able to work out something."

She paused, and refused to turn. "William, I don't know what you have in mind, but—"

"I can help. That's all I've ever wanted to do—take care of you." His voice stalled. "We, we—"

"We were, and now we're not." Leanna spun on her heel.

"All I'm asking for is a few dates. A few dates, and it won't hurt to wait a while to notify Cindy and Dale."

"You do know I'm a lawyer too."

"Not in this state." He shrugged.

He was right. She'd have to be admitted to the bar for this state if she wished to practice nearby, and with William's ties, he'd probably make that a difficult task as well. That would cost her more than a few dates for sure. Truth told, a career in law was the furthest thing from her mind. Brie was priority. Yes, Brie. And William wanted a few dates in exchange for more time.

Leanna pinched the bridge of her nose. "This is illegal."

"It depends on how you look at it."

Leanna swallowed. She narrowed her eyes twisting her lips. Why was she even considering him? "Or I can go see Judge Sinclair. I'm sure he'd like to hear about our conversation, and afterward I'm positive he'd grant me temporary custody—"

"He's my uncle."

Her chest sank. Leanna folded her arms, fingernails digging into her skin. Yes, William's family held more than the keys to the town. They had the entire county at their disposal.

"Look." He pointed around the room, eyes pleading. "I'm sober now."

No decanters anywhere. Leanna walked over to the tree in the corner and dug around in the bottom of the wicker pot. None hidden there.

"C'mon, Leanna. There's no way you can take care of Brie alone right now. Not until you get back on your feet." His smile was devilish, and convincing. "I can help. Just a few dates."

She lifted both brows. "Bye, William."

"I'll pick you up on Tuesday," he called out.

She paused. "I don't want a penny from you. Just more time to figure out this custody thing."

"Done deal." William made an X across his heart.

God help her, but what else could she have done?

***

The Family Dollar parking lot— what a stupid place to cry. Leanna hit the steering wheel and bit her tongue to keep from cursing. Not in front of Brie. Crying in front of her sister was bad enough.

She breathed into her hands until the tightness in her chest dissipated.

Brie kept her head lowered, hands folded in her lap. Sweet Brie. She deserved so much more, so much better than what Leanna was, and what she could provide. But not with Cindy and Dale. No one deserved to be raised on that side of town. Even if William was right and they had changed, Brie still deserved better.

How could this be happening? Any of it.

The death of her parents was difficult enough, now coupled with this, this web of financial insanity. What was she going to do?

Freaking out wasn't helping, and being angry with her parents didn't make it better either. But how could they have done this? There was no one to blame but herself. She'd put the pressure on her parents to pay for a college education they couldn't afford, and never once said 'thank you.'

Who am I?

The answer sickened her.

Leanna wiped her eyes and nose, and rustled with the Family Dollar plastic bag. Sitting around crying wasn't going to help the situation, but selling her car would.

She pulled out a For Sale sign and jumbo marker and pinched the cap between her teeth while she scrawled.

2013 Lexus 350.

53,000 miles

$15,000 OBO

For Sale by Owner.

What would William think of this? Who cared? He'd bought it for her, and it was hers to sell.

Leanna held the marker over the offer. Adding 'must go' sounded too desperate, and asking for a couple grand more may be greedy—she'd been too much of that already.

She left the sign as it was, jotted down her cell number, and then taped it to the back window.

CHAPTER FOUR

GARRISON HELD EZRA'S hand as they walked from the graveside. Too many of those he loved now rested in this place. Tiff's and now Mr. and Mrs. Wilson's headstones lay a row over from his mother's. Picking up his pace wouldn't keep the memories away, though throwing out the bad meant getting rid of the good.

The Army had moved him all over the nation, but something about being stationed close to home didn't settle well inside Garrison. Perhaps it was the memories of his past ruffling against moments of the present, keeping him from the promise of a future.

And now, he'd heard, she was home. He'd seen the lights on in the Wilson's home.

Even saw a Lexus with New York plates parked a bit ago. Had a for sale sign in the window. That was a car too nice for most people in these parts, figured it was hers, and he'd jotted down the cell number. Calling couldn't hurt anything, but then again...

A cool wind, too cool for summer, danced across his face. He wasn't certain of the time or place, but was certain at some point he needed to make peace with Leanna just as much as he needed to make peace with all the layers of his past.

Garrison straightened his tie. Next time he came, he'd bring fresh flowers for them all. The professional, big bouquet kind.

He continued forward and squeezed Ezra's hand three times — code for *I love you*. Ezra responded with four squeezes —*I love you too.*

Ezra glanced over his shoulder toward the cemetery. "You think Momma would like my report card this year?"

Garrison held back tears. "I know she would."

Most kids Ez's age wanted to go to a theme park, skating rink, or out to eat on the last day of school, but not Ez. For the third year in a row, Ez begged to come to the cemetery to visit his momma. Garrison gave Ez's hand another squeeze and kissed the top of his head.

"Dad? You think Meemaw and Mr. and Mrs. Wilson will like the flowers we picked for them?"

Lilac and hydrangeas bundled and tied with honeysuckle. "They would love them."

"Hey, Dad?" Ezra kicked at the ground as he neared the pickup.

The sun made it difficult to see, but Garrison couldn't miss the house across the street, or forget it. His childhood home. "Yeah, bud?"

Garrison peered down at Ez, and then back at the house. The lawn hadn't been mowed in months, if not longer. The boarded windows and chipped yellowed paint gave the illusion it had been abandoned, but Garrison knew better. His father, the old drunk, was home, sitting in filth, and murmuring to himself.

Ezra tugged on his arm. "Do you ever have a hard time remembering Mom?"

Ezra was six when Tiff left. No matter where they were stationed, they'd made the trip back to Lebanon Junction for the past three years. Garrison expected Ezra to forget some things, but wasn't ready for the pang in his heart each time he asked.

"You know, bud, I knew your momma longer than you." Garrison crouched to eye level with his son. "I remember more, but that's okay, son, 'cause I can help you remember."

"Like you help me remember Meemaw." Ezra nodded and lifted his big blue eyes to Garrison. Sometimes he swore he was looking at Tiffany. So many things he wished he could say to her, but she never gave him the opportunity.

"Dad, do you think we'll ever find a new mom?"

"Maybe." Garrison dated here and there, but nothing more. "If we can find the right woman." He stood, knees popping as he reached for the door handle. Cracks and pops were a side note of the Army life that he had earned well.

Ezra slid into the passenger side of the beat up Chevy. He struggled to roll the window down.

Garrison scratched his head as he pulled the door shut with a thud. He brought the truck to life and let it idle in the parking lot.

"How 'bout we pick up some ice cream?"

Ezra wrinkled his forehead. "Only if I can get a double-scoop this time."

"Done deal. I bet Aunt Mary would like some too."

"Ha. For sure." Garrison pulled Ezra close and planted a loud kiss on top of his head.

***

Garrison knocked once and then opened the Commander's door. Commander Jones stood from behind his desk, both hands wrapped around his lunch. Bad timing. Garrison grimaced and considered turning back.

"Burke."

No turning back. Garrison closed the door behind him and held a salute until his superior saw fit to return it — which was taking longer than normal.

Commander Jones took another bite. Sipped his drink. Reached for a fry. Garrison kept his hand up, salute still in place. No rush. Not like he had inspections in half an hour. Hopefully his soldiers would pass.

He arched a brow, but Commander Jones kept right on eating. Garrison held in a smile. He deserved such a response for interrupting the man's lunch.

Garrison kept still and silent and allowed his eyes to wander about the room.

Nice office. A few ferns decorated the corners. Unit portraits and historic battle paints clung to the walls. The place was roomy too. Garrison shared a space the size of a janitor's closet with three other soldiers, and though he was certain they had more fun working together than the Commander did in solitude, it must've been nice to have all that elbow room.

One more giant slurp from his cup and Commander Jones saluted back. Finally.

Garrison dropped his arm, thankful to move.

He swallowed the last bite of his burger, dabbed the mayo from the corners of his mouth and gestured for Garrison to approach.

Though brave enough to go to the Commander, Garrison dared not to speak before spoken to. Such disrespect to authority made him shudder. He kept his legs shoulder-length apart, hands on the small of his back. Chin up. Eyes forward. Commander Jones eyed him. Nothing menacing. More of a *here we go again* look.

Deep lines spanned from the corners of his eyes, and Garrison was thankful to have a Commander with both vigilance and a sense of humor. Patches of gray hair peppered alongside his receding hairline. Not that Commander Jones was old, more like weathered. The Army does that to all. Garrison's back, legs, and shoulders, and most of the rest of his body, attested to such.

"I'm almost afraid to ask why you're in my office." Commander Jones sighed and locked his arms.

"Sir, I'm here —"

"I know why you're here. First Sergeant just left before you got here." First Sergeant knew him well.

"And?" Garrison kept his chin high.

"Why do you have to make things difficult for yourself?"

"I'm trying to perform my sworn duties, sir. I'm ready to deploy again, sir." He swallowed as the Commander circled.

"You're ready, huh?"

Garrison nodded. The time of mourning had passed. He'd stayed behind the last two deployments to care for Ez, but it was time to join his men in battle once more. How could he be a leader and not lead his own men?

"Just so you know," Commander Jones stopped and held up a manila file. "I've read over your family care plan."

"And, sir?"

"Martha Weathers, your Aunt Mary, will be caring for your son while we're deployed?"

"That's correct, sir."

"And she's in the early stages of dementia?"

"Yes, sir."

He slammed the file on his desk. "I think you're the one with dementia."

"Sir, she's quite capable. She practically raised me, and she's been living with us since my wife passed."

"Burke, we're deploying for nine months. A lot can change with dementia in that time. I'm pulling you off this deployment."

"No, please." That would be career suicide. Garrison shook his head.

"I know you love your country and your troops. That's why you've always been an exemplary soldier—duty first, but you've got a lot to consider." Commander Jones rubbed at his forehead. "That's why First Sergeant wants to put you on Rear D. You can stay behind, push papers while we're away, and you'll be home to take care of your son and your aunt."

"My other options?"

"Maybe it's time to consider another career outside of the Army?"

Garrison lowered his head for a moment. He'd dreamed of a life outside the Army, but that was after he'd put twenty years in.

"If getting out isn't in the cards, then you need a family care plan that I can approve."

Garrison nodded. Suitable care. In his town?

"So, First Sergeant says you've declined Rear D. That right?"

Garrison swallowed. "Yes, sir."

"Then you have two options remaining."

Chaptered out of the Army or suitable care. Both made his stomach turn, but he already knew the choice he would make.

He balled a fist. Oh, if his pride only allowed him to choose Rear D and stay behind.

Garrison relaxed his stance.

"I assume you'd rather update your family care plan."

Garrison nodded.

"Well, then, my hands are tied. First Sergeant was trying to protect you, but you seem bent on making your life more complicated." The Commander let out an exhausted groan. He shook his head, arms folded. "You should know we deploy sooner than projected."

"Sooner?"

"The last week of August."

"In thirteen weeks?" Much sooner. Not in December like they'd been planning.

"Burke, you're on the advanced team."

Garrison's heart stopped. He knew what that meant. The Commander didn't have to say another word, but he did.

"You leave in ten weeks."

Garrison did the math. The first week of August. When school started.

He cupped his hands over his nose and chin. News like this never used to startle him. He expected the unexpected, but back then his life had been stable.

"I'm giving you thirty days to submit a family care plan I can sign off on. If not, I'm forcing you on Rear D, or forcing you out of the Army. You're dismissed."

Garrison turned and left.

Thirty days.

CHAPTER FIVE

THE DOCTOR'S OFFICE hadn't changed since Leanna could remember. Same pale green walls, and Harvey, the Skeleton, still hung out in the corner. Their family doctor decorated Harvey according to the seasons, and today he flaunted shades and a Hawaiian shirt. Leanna smiled as the doctor made Harvey's sunglasses bob up and down. Brie smirked too, but then tucked her chin. She dangled her legs from the side of the exam table.

"Yep." The doctor shook his head, graying eyebrows drawn as he checked Brie's heart, then eyes and ears. "There's something wrong with her. I knew it."

"What?" Leanna's heart quickened. She grasped the armrest, and the doctor chuckled.

"Looks like Brie's got a case of cat-got-her-tongue."

Not funny. Leanna stood sighing relief. "I'm trying to be serious."

"May I talk with you for a moment? In private?" He lowered his voice.

Leanna nodded and he gestured toward the hall. She turned offering Brie a gentle smile before the door clicked behind her.

"Leanna, I know you're concerned."

"She was in the crash and hasn't talked since."

"And we've checked her out head to toe. Have you let her return to school?"

Leanna shook her head, and rubbed at her arms. "Figured it would be better to rest. School's almost out anyway."

"I think that's a smart move. Brie is one lucky child."

And she was. Those on the scene of the crash could barely bring themselves to talk about it. Mangled bodies, and the blood—Leanna shivered and shook the thought away.

"In all my years I've seen only a handful of miracles, and Brie is one of them. God was looking out for her."

Yes. Leanna lowered her lashes. Why hadn't God looked after her parents? Leanna moved her hair over one shoulder. "I don't know what to do."

"Give her time."

"It's been almost a month."

"She's nine, and quite frankly, what she's been through, what she saw," he paused, and Leanna swallowed hard. "Grown adults would have issues with it. I believe she's experiencing symptoms of post-traumatic stress disorder."

"PTSD? A child can have that?"

Leanna worked to process the possibility. Anyone could have PTSD? Guess that made sense. She'd studied cases of abuse, neglect, and trauma during law school. Trauma was not concerned with the age, gender, or race of a victim.

"Anyone with a traumatic experience can have PTSD. Which reminds me." He folded his arms, and his chin doubled. "This has been a stressful time for you too. How are your panic attacks?"

She blushed, and held on to her purse a bit tighter. "Really haven't had any issues."

Just a partial lie. To be honest, she hadn't experienced a full blown attack in years, until the night Pastor Jay called with the news about Mom and Dad. Leanna sucked in a breath and smiled.

"I can't help if I don't know."

"Right now I'm here for Brie."

He pursed his lips, fine lines and crevices forming. "If this continues, we can look into counseling and medication if necessary, but right now, Brie needs to be loved and supported."

Which she'd continue to do by keeping Brie from Cindy and Dale. Her stomach pinched. How long could she keep these dates up with William before he expected more? Eventually, she'd have to confront the situation head on, even if that meant having a chat with Cindy and Dale.

***

Counseling. At what point should Leanna consider that option for Brie? And who to go to? The conversation earlier in the day with the doctor played through her mind.

Smells of supper drifted from the oven. Leanna sat at the kitchen table reading over her parents' will one more time. Wills weren't the final say in the Courts. If she could find a similar case with a ruling close to her preferred outcome, no judge, even William's Uncle, should argue. However, custody was only one issue. She flipped through the stack of bills. Figuring out this mess was quite another issue. Her head throbbed and her chest began to pull tight.

Leanna moved from the kitchen to the back door. Lights were on in the old house behind hers. She tilted her head. No one had lived there for quite some time, since Garrison's Aunt moved in with him. *Garrison.* Now there was a name and face she'd prayed to forget, yet, her heart never quite let go. Leanna leaned against the doorframe and strained to see, but the fence blocked much of her view.

The doorbell rang and Leanna jerked back.

William. Here for their weekly date.

They'd have dinner again.

Brie would paint or color or play something on her tablet.

The night would be over, Leanna would hate herself, and the cycle would continue.

Leanna made her way through the kitchen and into the living room. A handful of flowers greeted her as she opened the front door.

"These are lovely."

William kissed her hand and entered. "Smells wonderful."

"Just a casserole."

"You'll be eating those for a while."

She smirked and turned back toward the kitchen. Her parents' church family kept she and Brie stocked up on casseroles and baked treats.

Leanna pulled the casserole from the oven and let it cool. Brie preferred to eat alone, and Leanna didn't push the issue, especially with William present.

"You look beautiful."

"Thank you." Leanna shuffled food around on her plate dodging the meat. The vegetables were nice and tender, and much more interesting to look at.

"I ran into Cindy and Dale today."

Her head shot up, fork clanging against the plate.

"Don't worry, I didn't say anything." He smiled.

How long could she keep doing this? He was toying with her. A sick game.

"What is it you want William?"

"You." His laid the napkin on the table, one hand nearing hers. "I've always wanted you."

"What we're doing is wrong. I can't keep doing this."

"You're not even trying to see if we can make things work again."

"I'm trying to keep Brie. We're over, and we have been for a while."

He shook his head. "You're wrong. You and I are meant for each other, and you know it. We're alike."

Her stomach twisted.

"I think you need to leave." Leanna stood.

William paused, his face reddened. He wiped his mouth then pulled away from the table. Leanna kept her chin high. She'd stooped low enough agreeing to these little dates, the least he could do was be respectful.

"You want me to leave?" He smirked. "What you say, and what you mean are often two different things."

She stepped back but he yanked her catching her waist with his arm and hooked her body to his. Before she could protest William kissed her, one hand locking her in place, the other searching down her backside. Leanna jerked and stomped on his foot and he stumbled back laughing.

"Stop it." Leanna swiped a hand over her mouth and straightened her shirt. How dare he?

"See you next week," he said with a wink as he turned.

She held herself steady, palms gripping the edge of the kitchen table. This couldn't continue.

***

A month had passed, but missing her parents had not.

School was out, but Brie hadn't seemed all that excited. At least she was still here. A few dinner dates with William bought more time before Cindy and Dale would be contacted, but he'd get in touch with them sooner or later. Especially after the other night.

Agreeing to the dates cost her dignity. The way he groped and kissed her. Her skin crawled at the prospect of him asking for more, and she shoved William and the bribery dates from her mind, turning her attention to the open tabs on her laptop. Custody laws, outdated wills, and now hiring sites. An eclectic search combination that mirrored the insanity of her life.

At least her final check had come from the firm. However, they included not so much as a *sorry for your loss* or *thank you for busting your butt for us* card.

Leanna rolled her eyes and huffed. She tapped a pencil on the kitchen table as she scanned her bank statement and makeshift budget. She'd been able to keep the banks and businesses at bay while working to sort through the mess, but selling would be inevitable. If only that stupid car would sell, but no one in these parts could afford to buy the silly thing. The thought of lowering the price made her eyes cross.

Finding a job, or several, was a must.

Her phone lit up in an angry buzz. Another 800 number for the billionth time today. Bill collectors were ruthless creatures.

She dismissed the call and turn the screen face down.

Please, God. Help. I'll take any job. Did that count as a prayer? She hoped.

Leanna pulled away from the kitchen table and closed her laptop with a click. Twenty online applications filled out and submitted—including the school system that wasn't even hiring right now.

She sighed, and the burst of breath tossed loose strands of hair from her face. There were simply no jobs in the area that paid enough to make ends meet.

A nanny position about an hour north. Janitorial staff at a Family Dollar nearby. Handful of waitressing gigs. Farm hand. Maid.

A degree from Colombia, and here she sat applying for positions with no degree required. If it wasn't so sad, it would be funny.

With a groan, Leanna stood and rounded the table. She patted the manila file folder from William's office, silently vowing to examine each paper starting tomorrow. Right now, sorting of a different kind was needed.

Fruit baskets, baked treats, canned preserves, and casseroles of all kinds lined the counter tops. Enough food to keep her and Brie full for more than a month for sure. Leanna wrapped and labeled each meal, storing many in the freezer. Most had meat, but nothing she couldn't pick around. She grabbed a piece of broken chalk from the catch-all drawer and scribbled out a menu on the kitchen chalkboard.

Tonight, lasagna, thanks to a member from Mom and Dad's church, and fresh greens from Mom's garden.

Tomorrow?

She chewed on her lip, scanning over the meal selections. Brie entered the kitchen, eyes red, holding a bundle of flowers. She extended the arrangement.

"Someone else drop these off?"

Brie nodded.

Goodness. This community sure knew how to show support. Smothered in kindness. How could she repay them? Sending a card seemed so insufficient, but maybe a verbal 'thank you' would work. "Anyone you know?"

Maybe continuing to ask questions would get her talking, but Brie shook her head.

"You can set them on the table." Leanna huffed. "Not sure what to do with all these flowers. Any ideas?"

Leanna waited, but Brie never took the bait. Still nothing.

"Would you like garlic bread with the lasagna tonight? I can make it extra buttery. Add cheese on top too. Sound good?"

Brie arched an eyebrow, one hand wrapped across her body. She nodded, but that was all. After a few moments, Brie skirted past and out the back porch door. Leanna watched through the kitchen window as Brie took her place in the tire swing and swayed.

Time would help, yes, but how would she ever be able to connect with her sister when she wouldn't talk?

Leanna rapped her nails on the sink, until the flowers on the table caught her eye.

William again.

She'd give him one thing—the man was relentless.

***

Leanna pulled the covers off Brie. "It's summer break. We should be doing something. Anything."

She'd made it to Louisville earlier in the week and consigned some of her trendiest most expensive clothing items. Three hundred and fifty dollars in cash, up front. She should've gotten twice that amount, but couldn't turn down the offer. Besides, Brie needed to have some fun this summer. Water parks, movies, maybe even a camp.

"It's noon. Get up."

Nothing but a groan.

"You're nine, not ninety. C'mon, Brie, I'm trying. Help me. Meet me halfway."

Still nothing.

Leanna crawled into the bed, and slid under the covers her face close to Brie's. "The doctor said you're okay."

And he had, insisting seeing her parents die was traumatizing for Brie. The thought of Brie between their mangled bodies made her stomach twist and turn. Leanna wrapped an arm around Brie and kissed her cheek.

"Want to paint?" They both shared a love for art. "It'll be like the old times. We can even add glitter." She tickled Brie, but Brie neither laughed nor smiled. Leanna sighed and slid from the bed.

She crossed her arms. "I'll just do some yard work. Maybe we can go for a manicure or something later." Anything to get out of this house for a bit. Anything to make Brie smile or talk again.

Leanna pulled her hair into a quick ponytail and headed for the door, eyes stinging.

She hurried to the garden—a place to vent. Leanna knelt, hunched over, and yanked each weed from the garden, her frustration seeming to grow with each root pulled from the soil. Sweat pooled over her brow and she wiped the beads with the neck of her T-shirt.

Stupid weeds.

Stupid garden.

Stupid everything.

Leanna gripped a clod of dirt and launched it across the yard. It hit the wooden fence and exploded.

"Oh my." A small voice sounded from across the fence. "Are you okay, dear?"

Leanna stood, shifting her weight, face aflame. "Aunt Mary?"

"Yes, dear." The top of her gray head popped over the fence.

"I...I didn't realize you were home." Or still lived there, for that matter. That explained the lights.

The old woman chuckled. "Where else would I be?"

Not here. With him—Garrison. Her heart raced at the memories from nearly a decade ago, and how it all ended—how they ended. She tucked a strand of hair behind her ear and worked to find words.

"I uh, um, didn't know you had returned, that's all."

No response.

Leanna stood on her tiptoes, hands in the back pocket of her jeans. "Aunt Mary? You okay?"

Faint humming faded in and out. Aunt Mary's shadow walked the fence line, and then stopped in front of the gate connecting their yards. The old rusty latch lifted, and in she walked.

Her hair was a mound of gray formed into a bun on the back of her head. She walked with a certain waddle, and never once in Leanna's twenty-six years of life had she seen her in anything but a handmade dress. Aunt Mary outstretched her short arms, and Leanna smiled.

"Come here, child."

And Leanna obeyed. How could she ever say no to a woman who played a pivotal role in her childhood—to someone who took on a grandmotherly role to anyone breathing? No, she wasn't kin to Aunt Mary, but that mattered little. In their town, friendship ties were just as binding as the family kind.

Leanna wrapped her arms around the old woman's back, and rested her head.

"Come sit." Aunt Mary ushered her toward the log bench by the garden, and they sat at first in silence. Minutes passed, but soon Aunt Mary smoothed out the apron tied to her waist and bent to pluck small blooms of clover. Leanna watched, amazed. Aunt Mary tied each bloom together until they created a long chain. Her fingers, slow and steady, joined the chain. "For you."

Leanna smiled, and lowered her head as Aunt Mary slipped the lovely necklace around her neck. "Thank you."

Leanna lifted the clover to her nose. A sweet scent—better than any expensive perfume.

The old woman giggled through a tight-lipped grin and patted Leanna's knee. "It makes my heart happy to see you here again, but I'm sorry that you're home for less than perfect circumstances."

Leanna nodded. She dusted off her jeans at the knee. "It's...It's an adjustment."

"And how are you, dear?"

The question went below the surface. Leanna lowered her head, eyes fixed on the green grass below. She pinched the bridge of her nose and shook her head. How was she? The answer, well, went deeper than words could find. One would have to suffice.

"Struggling. I'm struggling."

Aunt Mary rubbed circles on her back, and kissed her cheek. "Hang in there, my dear. Things have a way of working out."

Always the optimist. Leanna nodded. "How's, um, how is..." Did she dare ask? And why bring him up now, after all these years?

"Garrison? Oh, he's well."

"That's good." She cleared her throat. Coming home brought back so many memories—good and bad, but mostly bittersweet.

Aunt Mary shaded her eyes. "This sun is too much for me, and Ginger needs to be walked before it gets much hotter."

Leanna nodded, thankful for the topic change. "I can't believe Ginger is still alive."

"That makes two of us." Aunt Mary chuckled and eased from the log. "She still doesn't care too much for most people."

"Mom always said Ginger was a good judge of character." Which could have also been Mom's way of saying William wasn't the one.

Aunt Mary smiled. "I'm glad you're home, dear. It's been too long."

And it had. "See you soon?"

"I know where the gate is, and so do you." She grinned. For a woman her age, her eyes were filled with so much youth. Leanna waved as Aunt Mary waddled back to her side of the yard.

Yes, this place brought back so many memories, and for a second, she was twelve, passing notes through the fence with Garrison.

***

Two missed texts from William. He bounced from apologies, to begging, to taking back every gift he'd ever given. Whatever.

The phone buzzed.

She eyed the phone number—not a bill collector, awesome.

Leanna jabbed the weed puller into the ground, scrambled to clean the dirt from her hands, and answered.

"May I speak with Ms. Wilson?"

"This is she."

"We're calling about a recent job application you submitted online."

A job. Her heart leapt.

"Thank you for calling me."

"We are in need of assistance, but you hold a law degree, and that seems a bit…"

"Over qualified?"

"Well, yes, ma'am."

She stood and paced the yard. "I don't mind. I'll take whatever's available. I'm sorry, what business did you say this was?"

"The Scoop."

Oh.

The Scoop, the Soup Kitchen. Part of the mess she'd inherited.

"I don't remember applying." Yet, she'd submitted too many applications to count. "Ma'am, do you do know that my parents— "

"That's part of the reason we're excited to talk with you."

So they were aware.

Aware that her parents left her the place. Aware she was nothing like them. Aware everything must be sold.

The voice on the other end of the line was way happy to offer a part-time janitorial, and part-time tutoring service positions. Two twenty-hour-a-week positions added up to forty full-time hours.

And how would that work anyway—working for a place she now technically owned, and planned to sell?

"When do I start? Yes, today is perfect. Right now? Um, sure, but I have Brie—oh, she can?" The woman said Brie could come too. Even better.

Maybe that's what Brie needed—to be around a familiar setting. Mom and Dad practically lived at that place. Surely going back would bring some life back into Brie.

"Thanks again. I'll be right over." Leanna grabbed the garden tools and headed toward the back porch. "Hey, Brie," she called out. "Put some shoes on. Time to go."

Leanna raced through the kitchen and ran to the bathroom. Whoa, she was a hot mess. A shower was a must. And what should she wear? Surely knowing she was the rightful owner would keep her from doing any of the actual janitorial work.

Yes, an owner should look the part. Leanna settled on a cute business outfit before hopping into the shower.

CHAPTER SIX

TOILET DUTY? LEANNA rolled her eyes. Yes, she was way overqualified for this position. Did complaining count as a prayer? Her sigh echoed throughout the tiled room. *All I wanted was to talk to the person who runs this show. Get a financial update and maybe stick a For Sale sign on the property.* At least while she was in the mood to get rid of all things frivolous and unimportant. Inheriting a life-sucking, money-draining business fit the bill —even if it was a soup kitchen. There was simply no way to keep it running.

But no. Instead, Leanna got zebra striped plastic gloves with hot pink feathers glued to the arm opening. According to Macy, a staff volunteer, and the local pastor's very pregnant wife, those hideous rubber atrocities were supposed to make her feel pretty. With her hands deep in some strange person's waste? Well, it wasn't working.

How many bathrooms and broken toilets could an old schoolhouse-turned-soup-kitchen have?

Too many, for sure.

Maybe if the place stopped feeding these people so much, the toilets would stay cleaner. Leanna worked her jaw from side to side, and continued to scrub. She held onto the toilet rim with one hand, and worked a rather short and worn brush with the other.

The smell.

Ten dollars an hour. Ha.

All the chemicals. Toxic. Her eyes burned. Leanna coughed, wearing the neck of her shirt like one of those surgical doctor masks.

This place may be feeding people but they were killing them, and the environment, with fumes. Just one more thing she'd talk to the manager about when she got the chance.

Leanna groaned as water splashed up and inside her glove. So disgusting. Didn't the place have hired help for this sort of work?

"I didn't go to Colombia to clean a toilet." She gritted her teeth, continuing her little chat with God. "Especially for ten dollars an hour." But it was the best The Scoop could do. She jerked her head up, her face losing the protection of the shirt-mask.

A feather broke loose and attacked her nose. Leanna fought back, but more toilet water joined the battle and found its way to the bottom of her glove. Ick. Ugh. She waved her hands, stepped back and slipped, bottom landing in a pool of dirty water on the tiled floor. Soaked, and sure to be bruised, Leanna tucked her chin.

"Fine. Real mature." If that's how God wanted to answer, then whatever. Leanna slumped against the stall door. "I'm soaking in a tub of sanitizer tonight."

She eased back onto her knees with a grunt. Thankfully no one had seen the incident.

Leanna mopped up the water. Four stalls finished. She rested her elbow on the hand dryer. The place didn't look so bad now. Actually kind of clean, though a fresh coat of paint would help. Maybe some pops of color here and there, and where was the baby-changing station?

Never mind. She had more important things to tend to besides bathroom decor. For starters, drying off. Soapy, toxic, bodily waste water spotted her favorite button-up shirt, and soaked the hind-end of her pressed pants. Not a good look. She leaned against the solution mounted on the wall.

Coated in rust, the metal push button created resistance, but Leanna pushed with all her might until the hurricane winds began to blow. She maneuvered her body beneath the air with ease until most of the spots dried, but not much grace could be mustered when drying her rear via a bathroom wall dryer.

Bent over, rear in the air, her hair brushed against the floor. She gathered the locks in her arms and shifted her weight around as the heat from the dryer amplified the cotton pants fibers.

Leanna alternated frowns and chuckles as she jumbled around like a participant in some strange game variation of hot-potato. Thank the Lord no one would ever have to know, or see how ridiculous she must look.

The bathroom door swung open with a whoosh. A burst of bleach-filled air smacked Leanna in the face before she could hold her breath or move from beneath the dryer.

"There you are. We, wha..." In walked Macy, Pastor Jay's wife.

Great. Leanna let her arms dangle. No need to hide.

Macy giggled. "What are you doing?"

No witty comment came to mind.

The dryer stopped just as Leanna stood and smoothed her hands along her backside. "Pants are dry now."

"That's one way to do it."

Leanna nodded, face warmer than wind from the wall dryer.

Macy stood on her toes and peered past Leanna. She scanned the room with wide eyes and then a smile. "You've done a great job."

Hmph. Did that surprise her? Leanna bit her lip, but smiled. "Is the manager able to meet?" Please, Lord, please.

"You really should've worn work clothes."

"Didn't get the scrubbing toilets memo." Leanna popped off the zebra gloves and gave them a fling toward the bucket. They missed, of course, and landed inside the closest toilet. Really? Leanna shook her head and shrugged.

"Your parents were right; you are funny."

"I'm a hoot." Leanna fished the gloves from the toilet with the stubby brush as Macy laughed out loud holding the sides of her belly.

Dear Lord, please don't let the woman's water break. Cleaning up amniotic fluid would cause a mental breakdown for sure. Leanna removed the gloves with success, and placed them in the bucket. She stiffened as Macy hugged her.

"We appreciate all the help you and your family have given. Because of your parents, this place ..." She dabbed at the tears in her eyes. "Well, we love all of you so much."

She ended the bear hug with a giant squeeze. "I haven't seen the bathrooms look this good in Lord knows how long."

Leanna nodded and stood a bit straighter. They did look rather impressive.

"Only three more to go."

"Three?" Leanna swallowed. Three bathrooms equaled twelve toilets. Tears threatened. "I really do have a lot of other things to get to today. If the manager can't meet, then—"

"Honey, you are the manager."

Oh, her heart totally stopped. Leanna couldn't even stutter. "I'm? Me?"

"You run this show now, but my husband will be here in a bit. We can give you the grand tour. Your parents have helped to transform this place. Did they tell you about all the new things?"

She couldn't remember.

"You okay, Leanna? Look a little pale."

"Do I?" She wiped at her forehead, watching her eyes gloss over in the bathroom mirror. Wow, she was a mess. Her dark hair frizzed out in all directions.

They always had some service project going on. The usual— helping people who can't help themselves. "Really, we do need to go. Brie is with me, and –"

"She's having a blast helping around here. Hasn't been on her tablet once."

Good to know. At least Brie was having fun. Leanna rolled her neck and pinched the bridge of her nose. Sweat, or toilet water, trickled down her forehead.

"Finish up the bathrooms, then Jay will come by and we'll all go on the grand tour." Macy smiled, her chubby cheeks pushing her eyes to an almost close. "You're just gonna love it." She swatted the air with a hand. "The tutoring center, GED program, family center, gardening classes. Oh, I just get teary-eyed thinking about all of it."

Leanna's eyes filled with tears for quite another reason. Twelve more toilets.

"Look at us getting all emotional." Macy embraced Leanna. "You're just as precious as your parents."

Hardly.

Macy released her hold and wheezed a sigh. "Sorry, my hormones are insane right now." Macy pointed to her stomach. "Baby number four. Pregnancy zaps the brain."

Leanna nodded. "I'd say having that many kids is enough to zap a brain." Did she say that out load?

Macy laughed and snorted, thankfully un-offended. Her belly shook as hard as her cheeks. "You're spot on, my friend."

Friend? They'd known each other for five minutes.

"We're having a few staff members and volunteers over at our place for dinner. We'd love for you and Brie to come."

How could she get out of this? Leanna's mind went blank. "We, um—"

"We insist." Macy pursed her lips, then smiled.

"Not sure where you guys live."

"Brie knows the way. We are literally maybe half a mile from you guys."

"Oh." Joy. Leanna wet her lips and lowered her head for a moment. Macy was kind and genuine. Sigh.

"We'll see you at five. Best get back to work now." She giggled and smacked at Leanna's arm. Macy gave one last hug, then flitted out the door with a quick wave.

Leanna's shoulders slumped. She pressed her back to the wall, and then slid to the floor.

Dinner tonight and toilets today.

Leanna eyed the cleaning bucket, staring at it until the color blurred with the tile backdrop. The gaudy zebra gloves and twelve more toilets called her name.

Mom and Dad made all this service and sharing stuff look like a breeze. Sigh.

***

Her fingertips pruned. Bottom ached. Nails broken. Rust marks from creaky old toilet seats stained her favorite shirt. Totally selling this place. Surely she'd make enough to pay off all, or nearly all, the debt.

What her parents got out of serving others she'd never understand, now, for sure.

Leanna made her way down to the supply closet at the end of the hall and rid herself of the cleaning caddy — best moment of the day.

Twenty-four toilets in all. She'd have nightmares about the day for weeks to come.

Not one thing accomplished on her to-do list. Not one.

She should have left, but something kept her there. The Scoop was a place her parents had poured their life into. Being there, even if to clean toilets, made them seem alive. Leanna smiled at the thought.

Pastor Jay walked her way, Macy tucked on his arm like they were on some kind of a Sunday stroll. "Ready for the tour, boss?"

Boss. What kind of boss spends the day scrubbing toilets? Leanna tried to control her face but it begged to contort.

"You wanna freshen up a bit or something?" The way he flinched at the sight of her, then scowled — it didn't settle well. Leanna stared, no, glared at him. Her lips drew into a pinch. After hours of experiencing near forced labor, Pastor Jay wanted her to freshen up?

"I think she's fine, dear." Macy tugged on his arm. "Just fine."

Fine. Fine? Leanna focused on breathing. Fine for now. "Let's get the tour going before this whole day is a total waste."

"Right this way." Pastor Jay walked ahead, Macy at his side holding that huge belly.

Down the hall and to the right. Through double doors and into the gym.

Gleeful shouts rang out as kids chased one another, tagging and dodging. Brie was among the playful group. Leanna waved, but she was too preoccupied to notice.

"Look how happy Brie is." Macy yanked on Leanna's arm. And she was.

Pigtails flying, smile bright.

"She's looking like that more and more every day." Leanna's chest tightened at the sweet thought. "I'm ready to hear her voice again."

Pastor Jay nodded and squeezed Macy's hand before stepping ahead. "This is part of our summer program. During the school year we do an after-school program. Snacks are given over there." He pointed to the far corner. "Tutoring and homework assistance are through those doors and across the hall. Teachers volunteer from surrounding schools to come in every day to staff that program."

Wow. Leanna followed, through the gym and out the double doors. Classrooms, occupied, filled with teachers and students.

"The classes on this side of the hall are specifically for our high school students."

"For tutoring?"

"That, and college entrance exam classes."

"Unbelievable. This place is doing all of this?"

"And more. So far, we've seen a ninety-five percent college admission rate for the students who've come through this course."

Leanna slowed her steps to take in every class. This was incredible.

"Keep up." Macy chuckled and walked past. "Down this hall, there's more."

More. Wow. Leanna followed along. Gardening courses outside where those in attendance learned to produce and harvest their own food. Parenting classes met in room 401. Bible study three doors down.

"We're using the old administrative offices as the counseling rooms. Right now we do family, marriage, and individual counseling, all from a Biblical perspective of course. Interview and resume building skills can be found on the floor below along with professional clothing." Macy's voice was so proud.

"The clothes?" Leanna turned to Jay and Macy.

Macy nodded. "Those are for when they land an interview and need something a little extra special to wear."

A knot lodged itself in her throat. Another formed in her chest. She sneered at the homeless in New York, passing them by, while her parents worked a thousand miles away giving them the tools to succeed.

Giving.

That was the issue. These people hadn't earned anything.

Leanna swallowed the lump and held her head high. "And how do they pay for this stuff?"

"We never turn a person in need away." Pastor Jay shook his head, releasing a small breath, disappointed for sure. Did he see a handout wasn't helping these people?

Macy looped her arm in Pastor Jay's, her smile never faltering. The woman really was kind to the core. "We're a nonprofit. And those who come to our classes earn points. Points they can use in the food, supply, or clothing stores here."

Wow. So it wasn't exactly a handout.

"And they come? To the classes? To earn spending points?" Leanna arched both brows.

Macy nodded. "From all over. As far as two hours away."

Pastor Jay kissed Macy on the cheek and directed his attention to Leanna. "We serve, feed, teach, equip, disciple and send. That's what we're about here at The Scoop."

Leanna kept her lips pressed together and arms tight across her chest. She finished the tour in silence and soaked in the scene, the rooms, the people, and the classes, all of it. Amazed.

The more she watched, the more she saw. This place didn't smell like poverty, but like opportunity. Like hope.

"My parents did this." She managed a whisper.

Macy reached for her hand. "And now you are, if you'll accept the position."

Leanna closed her eyes. Her parents once owned this property, and now it was hers. How could she ever put a For Sale sign on something like this?

CHAPTER SEVEN

WHAT TO WEAR to this dinner invite thing?

And why was she even going?

Because of how kind Macy and Pastor Jay were. Because of how much fun Brie had playing with all those kids today. Because socializing a bit actually sounded fun. Because it's what her parents would want her to do.

She huffed and stared into the abyss known as her closet.

Still full even after consigning a third of the items. She gazed at the fine fabrics.

More clothing articles, furniture, and fine art filled the walls of her New York Flat. When would she ever see that stuff again? Honestly, she didn't care. Not anymore. In his last text, William threatened to box it all up and send it away. Fine with her.

Brie's reflection showed in the closet mirror.

"Hey, honeybee. Come in."

Brie walked forward, one arm folded around her waist.

"Want me to braid your hair?"

She nodded, and Leanna's heart leapt.

"Here, have a seat." Leanna patted her bed, and they both hopped up, folding their legs criss-cross.

Leanna leaned and reached for a brush and hair tie perched on her night stand. She ran the brush through Brie's waves, hair much lighter and finer than her own. It would have taken two hair ties to hold her dark hair. And soft—Brie's hair was so soft.

Brie rested her hands on the sides of her knees.

"You know, you look a lot like Momma."

Brie nodded.

Light skinned, thin, freckled. Fairy-Princess-like really, especially with those aqua blue eyes. Leanna took after Dad's side, where the Cherokee showed more. Higher cheek bones, darker hair, darker skin, and eyes that looked more a like a muddy pond than the Caribbean sea. Genetics were a funny thing.

Though she did have freckles like Brie's dotting along her cheeks. Even more splattered on top her shoulders. And according to Dad, both she and Brie had a warrior's spirit unique to their personality. Brie—the warrior firefly, and she—the warrior wildcat.

Leanna smiled and parted the top portions of Brie's hair in three ways. "Momma taught me to braid when I was just a bit older than you."

She weaved the hair with her fingers, one strand over the other, adding in new pieces of hair with each layer. "I saw how much fun you were having today at The Scoop. You know all those kiddos?"

Brie nodded, and Leanna continued to braid.

"Mom and Dad were kind of rock-stars there, huh?"

Brie bobbed her head once more. When would she talk?

Leanna weaved in another strand and another. "I could tell you loved that place as much as Mom and Dad. And I can't believe all the changes." All the good—no, great changes.

Selling it would be...complicated.

Her phone lit up at her side. Bill collector. Again. Yay.

Maybe it wouldn't hurt to accept the boss or whatever position at The Scoop. It paid. And maybe it would keep them afloat awhile longer. Enough to catch up on the second mortgage and credit card bills? Worth a try.

***

"Let's go, honeybee." Leanna called out to Brie as she stepped onto the front porch. A high pitched whistle rang out.

William.

"Where you going looking like that?" He walked toward her, flowers in hand, dressed in a suit. "Makes me wish we never broke up."

She raised a brow.

"What's it to you?" Leanna tugged at her denim shorts. They didn't look that short in the mirror, and the V-neck sleeveless top was modest by any standard.

"Well, I'm hoping you're dressed for our date tonight."

Leanna threw him a sidelong glance. After their last date what made him think they'd ever go out again?

"I mean, I was thinking something a bit fancier, but I'm up for something different." He winked and she frowned.

"Something's come up."

"I'm sure it's nothing you can't reschedule."

"Actually—"

Brie skipped out the door and paused at Leanna's side. William waved at her, and offered her the bouquet. She took the flowers from him but kept to Leanna's side.

"Hey, honeybee, how 'bout you go swing in the backyard for a second." Leanna smiled and gave a playful tug on her braid. Brie nodded and made her way around the house.

"Brie seems like she's doing well." William stepped closer.

"She is." Leanna inched backward, but William stayed near. His eyes lingered on her too long for comfort. She crossed her arms over her chest. Maybe she should put something on with sleeves—like a turtleneck.

"Heard you've been to The Scoop. And they hired you."

He seemed surprised.

Leanna nodded. This town was too small, and he had too many eyes. Just another reason she'd ended their relationship. "I accepted the position."

"And you still want to sell it?" He arched a brow, smile widening.

She didn't answer.

"Bet you haven't told them yet."

She couldn't respond or even meet his gaze.

He laughed, throwing this head back. "You're more hardcore than I thought."

"It's nothing I'm proud of." Leanna shrugged. "And it can't be helped."

This time William shrugged, and Leanna prayed to God he didn't offer to solve her problems. She'd rather scrub toilets for the rest of her life than to take anything he'd offer.

But wasn't she under his thumb again?

She tucked her chin. This was different. She had to keep Brie.

"Heard you applied for a position in the school system too." Nothing about his tone was conversational, but prying, and threatening.

She locked her eyes with his. Yeah, he knew too many people in this town—too many people willing to have their arm twisted by him and his family.

"Any position you're interested in?" He traced her shoulder with the tip of his index finger. "I'm sure I could pull some strings."

Or cut them.

"Just considering all my possibilities." She moved to the side, and he smiled.

"Don't consider too long."

Her skin crawled. They were no longer talking about job positions.

"So," He closed the space between them, and Leanna forced herself to stay still. For Brie. For Brie. "You ready to get out of here?" His hand clasped to her waist, then inched its way down her hip.

Her stomach turned. "I...I don't have a babysitter for tonight."

"My parents will watch Brie."

Over my dead body.

"Besides," he continued, "I won't keep you out too long." He snaked his way to her neck and planted a kiss.

Too much. Too far.

She pushed him away and his eyes flashed. "You never used to pull away."

Leanna slunk back. She'd been so stupid to think she could keep his advances at bay. William always expected more. And now it was more than she was willing to give.

"We can't do this...this...whatever this is. I'm serious, William." She leaned on the porch railing. Her head spun. What was she saying? He could have Brie taken away.

But she couldn't give herself away like this. A kiss or touch tonight would only leave him expecting more later, and she'd given him too much of herself already— no way would she give him all.

William straightened his tie and turned, back to Leanna. She steadied her breathing.

"Do you know how much I'm risking for you?" His tone was rushed and frantic. He faced her, biting at a balled fist. "My career is on the line so you can keep Brie from her rightful caretakers. But do you care?"

"I care about Brie, and what's best for her."

"And that's you? A selfish brat?"

Leanna raised her hand, but thought better of slapping him. She turned, and he snatched her arm in a tight grip.

"What have I ever done to make you want to leave me? All I've ever done is love you."

"Have you been drinking?" But she smelled no hints of alcohol. No, this was William angry and sober—she could handle this William. "You really don't know why we couldn't work out? Let's start with all the women." She hoped her words bit.

He rolled his eyes. "How many times do I have to apologize?"

That's the point. Once was too many.

Was he that blind? So much like his father with mistresses too many to count. And so much like his mother who couldn't care less about those things.

"I gave you so much." His breath was hot against her face.

She tugged but he held her arm. She bit her lip, refusing to let him see her wince. "All you had to give were gifts. Gifts you threatened to take away. You control, and I can't be that anymore."

"I let you hang out with friends. Let you go to New York for college."

"You let me?" She sneered. "Gee, thanks."

He twisted her arm tighter and she yelped. "Let me go."

"You may want to start packing Brie's bags now."

"You're hurting me, William."

"Now you know what it's like. To want something and not get it. To love someone who won't love you back. It hurts, Leanna. You hurt people."

He was at least partially right. She'd hurt him. Used him to fund her bank account, much like he was now using her to satisfy his need to control. Leanna twisted but couldn't loosen his hold. He pulled her closer.

"I'd take your hands off her, now." The voice, familiar, called from the front yard.

William jerked his hands away and spun around. He paused, then let out a small laugh. "Ha. Of course."

Leanna rubbed at the handprint on her arm, then peeked around William.

A man in uniform, dress blues at that. She sucked in a sharp breath, hand against her mouth.

Garrison. Her lips parted.

William stepped from the porch, hands in the air, and then dropped them to his side. He bumped Garrison's shoulder as he passed giving a sidelong glance at Leanna before climbing into his car. He winked before driving away.

Garrison followed William down the drive with his stare. He turned his attention back to her.

There he stood, like a ghost. A memory from her past, but he was very much in the present.

Oh, Lord.

Now Aunt Mary's return to her old home made sense.

Leanna plunged her hands into the front pockets of her shorts.

"You're back." *Way to state the obvious, Leanna.*

"So are you." He smiled, his eyes just as deep and green as she remembered. Cut short, his hair was still as dark as hers. His bottom lip pouted, fuller than the upper lip. Once upon a time she stood on her tippy toes to kiss those lips.

This town really was too full of memories — good and bad.

She lowered her head. The sunlight reflected off the top of his black shoes, as spit-shined as the medals on his chest. At this angle she could see bits of her distorted reflection.

Garrison scratched his short haircut, Army hat in his hand. He looked handsome—no, striking—in his Army dress blues.

"Thank you," Leanna managed to mumble.

He nodded. "I see William hasn't changed much. You okay?"

He eyed her arm and she moved it from his view, giving a half-shrug.

"Guessing you two are no longer a thing."

"He's harmless."

"If you say so."

"He's just ticked off. Long story." Not really. Leanna grimaced. How could she explain the situation without it sounding just as weird and twisted as it was? She settled on another shrug. "It's hard to move on sometimes."

"Agreed." Garrison tucked his hat under his arm and gestured toward the driveway.

The conversation lulled.

Garrison cleared his throat. "Aunt Mary said she saw you the other day, and just thought I'd, we'd, you know...see how things were."

A mess. "Thanks."

"Ez and I are going over to Pastor Jay's dinner thing. Thought you guys might want to walk over with us."

Leanna tilted her head. "You work with The Scoop?"

"We volunteer a lot."

"Oh. Um. Sure. That's where Brie and I were headed to."

"Good timing."

The best. Leanna rubbed at her arm again, willing the stinging to subside. Garrison watched but didn't respond, and for that she was grateful.

Ez and Brie came from around the house walking side by side like old friends. Surely she and Garrison had appeared that way during their childhood. They all started down the gravel drive, Ez and Brie trailing behind, giggling at something on the tablet.

"You guys been back for long?" Mom and Dad hadn't mentioned them returning, but then again, given Leanna's rocky past with Garrison, they never mentioned him much.

"Early March."

Not too long ago.

Garrison slowed his pace. "It was easier to live in Aunt Mary's old house than to try to get in on base. It's been good being back. Glad we had a little time with your parents..." His voice trailed. "I'm so sorry for your loss, and

I'm not going to ask how you are."

Her stomach pinched. "I don't think I'd have the words to answer."

"I get that."

Leanna nodded. She lifted her chin and stared ahead, keeping one foot in front of the other. "I don't feel like myself right now." Not all together a bad thing.

"I get that, too."

She didn't deserve the gentle smile he gave. He knew her pain better than anyone. "So, you're stationed at Knox. Here in Kentucky. Funny." She tried not to smile. "Looks like neither of us got too far away for long."

Garrison got a head start on his journey away from home being a year older than she. They'd been inseparable in their adolescence. Leanna shrugged the memory away. Her gaze fixed on the gravel road.

"It's really good to see you again, Lee."

Lee. She hadn't heard that name come from his mouth since...since the day she went away. But then again, he was part of the reason she had to leave.

She nodded.

"How was New York?"

She rubbed the fabric of her shirt between two fingers. How *was* New York? Loud. Fast. Disappointing on so many levels. "Living the dream."

Silence settled between them.

"Sounds amazing." His words probed deeper than his eyes.

Leanna focused on the hem of her shirt between her fingers. No sense in hiding the truth. "I think I may have gotten lost in all my big city living." Garrison still drew out her most honest inner thoughts.

"Nah. You're not lost." He flicked her shoulder, like old times. "You're right here."

"Where I'm supposed to be?"

"Maybe." He shrugged. "Look, I've got some time off soon. Maybe you'd like to..."

Like to what? Hang out? Pick up like the past nine years never happened?

Garrison squinted up at the sky and then back on the gravel drive. "Maybe we could take the kids somewhere. It's good to see Brie in her element. She and Ez were in class together."

"I didn't know that." Leanna squinted, and glanced back. Ez held a tablet for both him and Brie. They snickered, watching some sort of YouTube video and walking absentmindedly along the drive. Leanna smiled.

"Aunt Mary says she's not talking much."

"More like not at all."

"Thought about counseling? It's helped a lot of my soldiers who come back with things like that."

Leanna nodded. Maybe. The Scoop offered counseling services. Maybe it was time.

"It takes time." He'd know. "You both will be okay." His tone was soothing but distant, as if he was reaching into his past to speak to the present.

She forced a smile.

"So, how have you been since...?" Leanna froze, her face growing hot. "I'm sorry. I shouldn't have said..."

"It's okay." Garrison stood a little taller and cleared his throat. "Tiff's been gone three years now."

That long. Leanna let the memory settle. She crossed and uncrossed her arms.

His laugh was short. "Ez is growing fast. He looks so much like her. Acts like her too."

The silence, familiar as an old friend, returned.

Leanna eyed his wedding ring finger. A pale line marked where his band had once been. He must have worn his ring a long time after Tiff passed. The thought pulled her eyes shut for reasons Leanna decided not to explore.

Garrison touched the empty space on his finger as if aware of her stare. He stopped walking. "Lee?"

Leanna snapped her head up, meeting Garrison's gaze.

His eyes searched hers. What did he see? What would she let him see? She lowered her lashes.

"I can't believe they're gone." Garrison's voice was low. He cleared his throat and wet his lips. "Your mom and dad meant more to me than my own parents."

Layers of truth rang from his statement. As a child, Garrison frequented their home for days at a time, often sneaking back over in the evening to escape the turmoil in his home. Mom and Dad never complained. They only cared for him.

So had she.

"They gave all they had to everyone and never asked for anything in return."

She nodded. Her parents cared for the community, maybe a bit too much. They'd spent their life savings operating soup kitchens and shelters, but then, what had she spent her life doing? The thought caused her to shiver.

Were do-overs possible? Lord, please say so.

"I'm sorry I wasn't able to attend their funeral, and ..." He ducked his head, then looked back down at her. "I'm sorry for so much more—"

"Garrison—"

"I jotted down a number from the Lexus."

"The For Sale sign?"

"I've been meaning to call, but—"

"It's okay. We don't have to have any of those conversations. No apologies."

Not now at least.

Tears stung her eyes. Her breaths grew unsteady, her words almost inaudible. "You know, I hear Mom and Dad. I hear their laughter in my head, and I miss it."

She trembled, and Garrison steadied her with a hand. He folded his arms around her, a gesture as comforting as from their childhood.

Their embrace ended like it had a million times before, and they continued on, nearing Pastor Jay's home. Good thing he had plenty of acreage. Looked like the whole town showed up.

"Guess we're neighbors again?" His laughter sounded nervous. Rightfully so.

"Please come by the house a little later," Leanna said, arms swinging at a slow pace. "I know Dad would want you to have some things."

Before it all had to be sold.

He nodded and smoothed out his uniform jacket.

She offered a smile.

"I'd appreciate that. Mind if I bring Ezra with me? He may be able to help." Garrison gestured toward Brie.

Having another child seemed to benefit Brie.

"You're both more than welcome to come." Leanna tilted her head.

Macy and Pastor Jay waved from their front yard. Their tribe of children and plethora of guests huddled in patches playing lawn games or were engaged in some loud conversation. Music boomed.

Leanna giggled.

"I think you should've brought a change of clothes." She eyed him for a moment.

"Had a thing at work and didn't want to be late."

"I'll say." Well, he looked nice. Nice enough to make her look twice. Maybe more. But look only.

Garrison hollered a hello to Pastor Jay and Macy. His lopsided grin made him appear youthful, as if he'd never once experienced loss or pain.

"C'mon, Lee. Let's go have a little fun. I think we both deserve that."

Yes, after the day she'd had, fun was a must.

***

Seemed Pastor Jay and Macy invited the entire town to The Scoop. Leanna scanned the room holding her plate of food in one hand and Brie's in the other. Not too many seats remained.

"This is what they call a few staff members and volunteers?" Leanna soaked in the scene.

Light-hearted, friendly conversations filled the air followed by bursts of warm laughter. Her heart smiled. Mom and Dad would have been right in the mix. Seeing such fellowship would have warmed their souls. A few children with painted faces ran past, and Leanna held the plates of food above her head.

"Careful." Garrison laughed.

Music played a foot tapping tune. The worship team from church performed on a trailer set up by the barn. Long tables lined the front, back and side yard. Macy had covered the tables with red and white gingham tablecloths. A carved watermelon served as a centerpiece for each table.

"They look like baskets," Ez said as he leaned over to grab a piece of melon and popped it in his mouth. "How did she do that?"

Leanna shrugged eyeing the melon sculptures. "Impressive." All of it.

She made her rounds shaking hands and hugging necks mindful of the food in her hands. Garrison followed suit not far behind.

A few of the older ladies whispered as they walked by, but Leanna paid no mind. Whether good or bad, the town would talk, and she'd given them plenty to talk about in years past.

Garrison chuckled and waved over at the white-haired ladies. He leaned over, his grin wide and mischievous. "Do you think we should hold hands for them?"

"That's all I need." Most of the town was still in shock hearing she'd broke off her engagement with the area's most eligible bachelor. Seemed like many of her choices shocked them. Dating Garrison, the poorest boy in town, was probably the most baffling to them. The two whispering the loudest had been the first to say 'told you so' when Garrison up and married Tiff. Now here Leanna was, nearly a decade later, walking in with Garrison. Ha. Leanna hid a smile.

"This seat looks open." Garrison ushered past the tables and gestured for her to sit.

"Can we eat with the kids out back?" Ez scrunched his face, and Leanna couldn't blame him for making such a request. Surrounded by elders must have felt like a punishment.

Garrison sat. "Lee, you okay if Brie goes with him?"

"You can go if you want to." Leanna toyed with Brie's ponytail. Brie nodded, and Ez scooped up Brie's plate and carried it with his. "Great kid."

"Thanks. I'd take all the credit but that wouldn't be fair."

"True." She grinned and took a bite of salad and wished she had added more dressing. "But you were always a gentleman."

Garrison kept his eyes down and picked through his food with a fork. He smiled.

Leanna watched Brie and Ez weasel their way between the tables like a maze. Ez led the way. "Can't believe how much they've both grown. How are they both nine?"

"It happens fast."

She was seventeen when Brie was born. The day after Christmas. Brie was a surprise to her parents, but a blessing nonetheless. Two days later Tiff gave birth to Ez, and Garrison became a father at eighteen. So young.

Leanna shook the thought. "So why are you so dressed up? For this?"

"Got a ball tonight. Have to be there at seven."

"A ball?" She'd heard of those before. Fancy gowns and dancing. Sounded like a good time. "On a Tuesday?"

Garrison grinned. "Doesn't make sense to any of us either."

"And you're taking Ez?"

"He likes to go. The soldiers love him. Besides, we never stay too long. "

"Celebrating anything special?"

Garrison smirked. "We're going on leave for a while here soon, but the Army uses any excuse to celebrate."

"Work hard, play harder."

"Seems to be their motto." He winked, and her heart fluttered.

She smiled and tucked her hair behind her ears. Leanna crossed her legs at the knee and tugged at the fabric of her shorts. Maybe they were too short. Eyes watched them. Leanna ate in small bites careful not to turn to the right or left, or even to lift her head. Locking eyes with Garrison may cause her to unravel. Locking eyes with the folks surrounding them, well, no telling what would happen then.

"You, um, you want to go out back for a bit?" Garrison broke the silence.

"Please." She laughed, head still down.

"After you." Garrison stood and lifted her plate. Always the gentleman. "Finished?"

Leanna touched her stomach. "I think so."

"I hear ya." Garrison scooped up one more spoonful of beans before tossing their plates into a nearby garbage can. They eased through the rows of tables.

"I'm so glad you could make it. Both of you." Macy's voice was unmistakable and held elements of curiosity. Leanna gave her a quick hug but said nothing, only stood with Garrison, holding food, stomach pinching. Macy gave them a quick once over, but was tugged in two different directions by her youngest children. "We'll catch up later."

Leanna was sure they would. Macy scooted off, kids in tow.

"That woman." Garrison shook his head.

"Yeah."

"Get the feeling people are talking?"

"Guess there's not too much to talk about in this town. Glad to provide the entertainment."

"Well, we did give them quite a story."

Leanna sucked in her bottom lip. Funny how hundreds of memories could fill a second.

They walked alongside the fence line, ducking past an overgrown Rose of Sharon tree. Children played out back, chasing one another. Brie and Ez had found solace on two old tire swings feet reaching for the sky.

"Look at them." Leanna laughed out loud, her soul relishing the sight. "They look so free."

She'd felt that way once. All of them—she, Garrison, William, and Tiff. Back then life was simple, and sweet. Intentions were innocent.

Leanna settled in on the back porch. Two striped cats purred, and wrapped around her ankles. She petted them and watched the children while Garrison propped against the railing. What was he thinking?

"I could watch them all day."

Leanna nodded in agreement.

He turned, jawline slack, eyes heavy. "I'd say being back hasn't been easy for you. Me neither, but really, Lee, it's good to see you."

He'd said that already.

She kept the toes of her shoes pointed, dug into a small gap between the wooden slats of the porch floor. Leanna bent, running a hand over the largest cat's back, and lifted her eyes. She swallowed. "It's good to see you too, Garrison."

His name. Their past. The memories. The hurt. But here they were. What did it mean? What did any of it mean? The passing of her parents, the custody issue and financial mess?

Maybe nothing, only serving to prove life wasn't fair, but then again, maybe something more. Something better.

Garrison checked his watch. "I, I'll have to be heading out of here in a bit."

How long had they been here? An hour or so? Time passed too quickly.

"Ez can stay with us. I mean, if you're okay with that. We'll be heading home soon. Might stop and get some ice cream."

"He'd like that. Sure you don't mind?"

"Really, it'll be good for Brie." Leanna glanced over at the two kids. Brie was smiling again.

"Promise it won't be too late."

"I'll be up." She stood, but the toe of her sandal caught in that dumb gap. The cats tangled their way around her ankles. Leanna screamed and fell forward hands grabbing for the air. One palm caught the rail sent a sharp pain up her arm. The other arm fell over Garrison's shoulder. He held her steady, her eyes wide. She froze.

The children quieted and then resumed their play. A few adults ran to her aide and Leanna waved them off pulling from Garrison's embrace. She smoothed out a few wrinkles on her blouse and tugged at her shorts. What that must have looked like to them, her pressed against Garrison? Ha. Leanna held a hand over her mouth, shoulders shaking. The hilarity of the moment struck her.

"What's so funny?"

Leanna chuckled. The cats found her ankles again purring in circles.

"Get." Garrison shooed the cats from the porch, one arm still around her.

Leanna steadied herself and freed her shoe. She shook her hand, her palm stinging. Just a scratch. "I must've looked ridiculous."

"Let me see." He took her palm turning it over in his hand, and wiped away the small streak of blood with his thumb. A small smile growing on his face. "Get some medicine on that. You okay?" He gave her elbow a quick squeeze and released her hand.

Leanna nodded, and stifled another laugh. "I'm good. Just need to learn to walk. You need to get going."

"Let me make sure you get down from the porch in one piece."

"Funny."

He saw her safely down the steps. "I'm gonna tell Ez bye." He turned. "See you tonight?"

"We'll be waiting."

He walked off, and she released an audible sigh. Having Garrison around felt like old times—the good parts of those days. Yet, the thought gave her heart pause. Good times often soured quickly.

CHAPTER EIGHT

GARRISON PULLED AT his white T-shirt and ball cap. Much more comfortable than the dress blues. The ball had been fun, but he'd been ready to head out the moment he arrived. Commander Jones made sure to remind him of the family care plan due at the end of the month. *Still had a little over three weeks.* Avoiding that man proved a challenge. While others danced with their spouse, Garrison hung out in the corner counting the minutes on the clock. Now here he was, sitting with *her*. Of all the impossible scenarios.

Fragile wasn't a word Garrison would use to describe Lee, but leaning against the back of the porch swing, she fit the description. Frightened even. He rubbed a hand over his jaw.

"How's your hand?"

She smoothed fingers over her palm. "Just a scratch."

Her hands. They were worn and scraped. How had he not noticed them earlier? What had she been doing?

He cleared his throat. "Food was good tonight. Nice of Pastor Jay and his wife to invite all of us over."

She nodded but didn't stir. She gazed toward the field to the side of the house.

Garrison cleared his throat. "Wanna go fishing?" Lame question. "It'll be like old times." Even more lame.

She fixated on the rickety boards beneath her feet. "Dad's got poles in the shed."

Stated as if he were still alive. Garrison nodded.

"Glad you changed into something more suitable for fishing."

Lee stood, arms folded as she followed him out past the house, toward the tree house—their tree house. Garrison gave it a once over. The

56

branches hung low over the river. Boards still in place, though grayed and splintered with time. He shoved a hand in his pocket.

The crickets were out. Frogs too. Each took their turn singing out of tune. Brie and Ezra stalked along the hillside, Mason jars handy, waiting for the lightning bugs. A bit too close to the water's edge. His heart raced.

"Ezra, don't go near the water."

Leanna looked over her shoulder, but said nothing.

Ezra waved and ran up the hill, Brie trotting at his side. Good kids. Garrison wiped a bead of sweat from the back of his neck.

"We've got life-jackets in the shed, you know, in case..."

"Not sure how he'd feel about wearing one on dry land." He laughed. "Though I'd make him wear one all the time if I could." He reached for the shed door. The rusty knob turned with ease.

Dust particles filled the shed. An angry hum buzzed overhead. Wasps hung out in their nests. Leanna hunkered down. Still afraid of them. Couldn't blame her though. Garrison hid his grin.

"Your pole's right over there." Lee pointed to the corner.

"I remember this one." He picked up the old fishing rod from the corner and bounced it in his hand. Memories.

Lee held the old rod and reel, and smiled.

Garrison grabbed the sturdy tackle-box from beneath the workbench. "Still remember how to do this?"

She huffed and smirked.

"Guess that's a yes." He nodded toward the door. "Ready?"

They walked in silence.

Garrison cast his line into the water and tightened the slack. The water rippled around the bobber.

They sat, riverbank beneath them.

Ezra and Brie swung on the tire swing at the top of the hill. One on top of the tire, one inside it.

He laughed and shook his head. "Brie looks like she's having a good time."

"I'm glad Ezra is here to help."

"She'll be okay, Lee."

Lee nodded and pulled a blade of grass from the ground.

The sun continued to sink.

She toyed with a strand of her hair. She needed to tighten the slack in her line, but he figured she didn't care. Nothing seemed to be biting anyway.

He stole a glance, then another. This was real. She was real. And they were here, back home, together. Sitting like old friends, not fighting—yet.

Garrison swallowed and stole another glance. Lord, she was beautiful.

Where others saw plain, he'd always seen unique and spirited. Her hair had begun to fall from a loose braid, and the sun had tinged her high cheekbones. He cleared his throat and focused on the water, but the fading sunlight cast a glow, and Lee's skin shone. She crossed her legs at the ankles and Garrison followed the length of the glow to the tips of her toes. He pried his eyes away and reeled in his line a bit.

"I'm ready to listen if you're ready to talk." Who said she wanted to talk? Maybe she didn't.

Her lip quivered. A quiet sob escaped her mouth. "I don't think I'm gonna make it." Her voice was numb. He remembered that plaguing sense after Tiff passed. The normal part of grief.

"Hey Lee, you're gonna be okay. It just takes time." Not that it stopped hurting, though he figured best to leave the obvious unspoken.

She shook her head, dark eyes piercing. "I've lost Mom and Dad, and now I'm going to lose Brie, and our home." Her shoulders slumped.

Garrison drew back. Losing Brie? Their home? "What are you talking about?" He propped his pole against a tree stump and turned to her.

A few tears escaped as she explained the whole tumultuous situation— a challenge to believe. All of it but William's extortion. He'd always been a jerk.

She hung her head and picked at another blade of grass with her free hand. "So, I'm working at The Scoop." That explained the roughness of her hands. Wow. "Figure that's a good place to start until I can find a way to fix this and keep Brie."

Short of running back to William.

Garrison's throat tightened. No one would take Brie from her family if he had any say in the matter.

Leanna gazed over her shoulder at Brie and Ezra on the hillside, then back at the blade of grass between her fingers. She sighed and wiped away a tear. "How do I say goodbye to our home?"

Funny. She spent years running from her home and her life here, but now? Garrison tugged at the bill of his ball cap. He peered at the three-bedroom, two-level home in the distance. A mini Cape Cod perched on a slight hill. Nothing specular in appearance, but overflowing with the best of memories.

He held his breath. Moments passed, but the lapse in time produced no solution or consoling thought. Lee would lose it all.

He balled a fist hard against his knee. "We'll fight this."

Leanna loosened her grip on the fishing pole. It bounced around on top of her knees. "I'm sorry, Garrison. These are my problems, and I know you've got your own—"

"No way."

"But—"

"Yeah, we've got a lot of junk in our past." That was one way of putting it. "But I care, Lee. I've always cared."

She kept her eyes downcast.

Garrison glanced in Ezra's direction for a split second. Nowhere near the water. Good.

"I'm scared, Garrison. For the first time in my life...I'm scared." And rightfully so. So much weighing on her. Leanna turned to face him with a crushing look of despair. "I went from working in a prominent law firm, to barely making ends meet stuck back in the place I wanted to get away from." She huffed. "Ironic."

Garrison fumbled through a few responses in his mind but decided silence was best for this moment. He rubbed the knuckle of his thumb over his bottom lip. If only he could make her worries go away—fix her, fix this.

How?

No clue.

Instead he settled on what he could solve—listening to her. And so he did.

***

Garrison hid a yawn, and walked past soldiers leaving morning formation. Four cups of coffee was not doing the trick, but exhaustion was worth being there for Leanna. He'd done so little of that in the past.

Their conversation from last night continued to play through his mind. Leanna tugged at his heart and interfered with his life. And that could be dangerous, even if he and his men were only training today. His men rested, worn out from today's land navigation. Still hours ahead of them until they'd made their way back to camp. A few minutes and some grub would do them all some good.

Garrison leaned forward, perched near the tree line, forearms on his knees.

"What would you do different?" Nelson, his battle buddy, pried more than Aunt Mary's million questions after he'd returned from Pastor Jay's shindig.

"What would I do different? Why you wanna know that?" Garrison gnawed on a cracker from his MRE. Not the tastiest lunch, but it did its job. Better than tree bark.

"Figured you'd do something different, 'cause all I've heard about for the past three hours is 'Leanna this' and 'Leanna that.'"

"Hmph." True. Garrison bit off another piece of cracker and launched the rest at Nelson. He took a swig of water from his canteen. The cracker scratched its way down his throat. Nelson's question rolled through his mind. Where to start? "I'd have apologized sooner to Leanna. Years ago. Both Tiff and I should have apologized sooner." They'd tried. Halfhearted attempts. A few letters in the mail, but nothing more.

"That it?"

Hardly. Garrison worked his jaw from side to side. He pinched off another piece of cracker and decided against eating it. It fell to the ground. Birds could have it. "If I could change things... Well, what does it matter? I can't."

"How you'd do things differently may help in how you do things from now on."

"Like?"

"Like pursuing her, man." Nelson landed a punch in Garrison's shoulder. "C'mon, this ain't hard to follow."

"Date her?"

"Or at least get to know her again."

"Why?"

"It's obvious, dude. The two of you are together again." Nelson groaned, his tone sarcastic.

"Far from it." Garrison scrunched his face. "And I'm still not tracking."

"You need someone you can trust to take care of Ez and your aunt while you're away."

"No."

"You're on the advanced team."

"No." Heat raced to Garrison's face. The air became thick.

"Think about it, man." Nelson hung an arm over his bent knee. "You two know each other. Trust each other."

"Trusted. There's a difference."

"She's already looking after her sister. She's in a bind right now. You help her, she helps you. Winner winner chicken dinner."

"You're insane."

Nelson shrugged and leaned against a tree. "People do it all the time."

He was right. Garrison knew of several soldiers who hooked up with women to take care of their affairs while deployed. But hooking up? So immoral.

"Wipe that look off your face. I'm not saying marry her."

Marry her. Garrison's heart stopped. Why was he even contemplating the thought? *Now I'm insane.*

"All I'm saying is, she'd make a great caretaker, and you could help ease her financial burden."

"What about helping her keep Brie?"

Nelson frowned. And that's where his plan unraveled.

Garrison checked his watch. Few more minutes and they had to get moving.

Nelson stretched. "Maybe her aunt and uncle aren't bad people."

Garrison tilted his head, one shoulder lifted. "They have a past."

"We all do."

True. "And they live on the wrong side of the tracks, so to speak. Poor. More crime. That kind of stuff. Not many people make it out of that place."

"You did."

"'Cause of Aunt Mary." Garrison grunted. His father still lived in squalor and seemed content to do so.

"Look, man, the way I see it, you've got three options." Three was better than the two Commander Jones left Garrison with. Nelson lifted a hand, and counted with his fingers. "One: you chapter out."

Garrison grimaced. "Not an option right now."

"Two: crawl back to Commander and beg to be put on Rear D."

"Fat chance he'd do that after the fight I put up." Wouldn't stoop so low as to do that anyway.

"Three: help Leanna out while helping yourself out. Present Commander with a family care plan that makes him smile."

Garrison rubbed a knuckle over his chin.

"And who knows," Nelson continued. "Maybe you could have a chat with her aunt and uncle. If they're as poor as you say, maybe it would be a burden for them to take care of Brie anyway."

True.

Garrison considered the thought. Lee as a nanny. Ha. Though she cared for Brie like a mother—that much was apparent. Was working hard at The Scoop to earn a few bucks in order to provide.

"Just get to know her again."

It was something to think about, at least. But overcoming their mountain of a past? Could it be done? Ugh.

"Nine weeks." And less time to turn in a family care plan to Commander Jones. Garrison swiped dirty hands over his face.

"You better take it slow as fast as you can."

Yeah. Real slow, real fast.

***

Duty called. He was with his men, training for war, and shouldn't be contemplating how to take it slow real fast with Leanna. He shook his head, clearing his thoughts, and moved from the tree line.

They'd finished the land nav portion, and now honing combative skills was all that was keeping them from a warm shower and sleep.

Garrison signaled his men into the clearing. They held their positions until he waved them on, and his soldiers, all twenty, stalked the makeshift plywood buildings, covering one another as they searched for invisible insurgents shooting only at the appropriate target.

Excellent.

Tactical procedures, the ones they lacked only months ago, they now owned. Yeah, those young men were battle ready. At twenty-seven years old, most civilians would consider him young, but not in this line of work. He had experience; experience he now gave to the young men, and prayed it would serve them well. Garrison folded his arms across his chest, stance wide. A sense of pride washed over him.

The sun beat down, and the visor of his army cap provided little shelter for his eyes.

"Looking good." A raspy voice sounded nearby. First Sergeant approached. Garrison kept his expression tight. No need for another disagreement. First Sergeant mimicked Garrison's stance. "You've done well with these boys."

Garrison nodded. They'd come a long way for sure. "We're combat ready." So a little verbal jab never hurt.

First Sergeant squinted and gave a nod. "We look out for one another." He slid his hands in his ACU pockets and released a tired breath. Days in the field were long, and even longer for the older soldiers. "You understand what I'm trying to say?"

"Is that an apology for trying to force me on Rear D? Threatening to have me chaptered out of the Army?"

"I know you. Know all of you. None of us quit. We answer the call, but sometimes it's the wrong call."

"My country needs me."

"So does your son. These men out here—"

"I took an oath. Duty first."

"Duty to who? Or what?"

Garrison's stomach turned and twisted. He'd always served. Loyal to his country and his family. Tiff never asked him to stay. Though her eyes pleaded, she understood. So did Ez. Why was First Sergeant the only one not tracking?

The soldiers motioned orders with hand gestures, scaled fake buildings, and rounded corners. They worked well together.

"My men know me. They need me." Garrison stood taller.

"Your family needs you too. There are times when you have to go. You have to deploy. Have to serve. But, this time, you have a choice."

"Commander Jones made it pretty clear we're all deploying." Soon. Too soon.

"Commander Jones is waiting for you to ask to stay behind."

Garrison clenched his jaw. "This some kind of a test?"

"Not for us."

Then who for? Him. Garrison bobbed his head. Too many things all at once.

"Most guys would jump at an opportunity like this."

"I'm not most guys."

"We're aware." First Sergeant lowered his voice, sounding half frustrated. "Think about it. Enjoy the next few days off."

Think about it. He had many things to think about, and the First Sergeant added more.

***

It was late. Finally home. Garrison yawned going over the day's events. His mind and body ached. Half days at work would start soon—a nice pre-deployment gesture before their block leave started. Just the rest he and his men needed. What about Ez? What did he need? For Garrison to stay home like First Sergeant suggested?

Garrison took off his ACU jacket and let it drop to the floor. It landed with a soft thud. He stood in the living room and watched the moonlight draw shadow figures on the wall.

What *did* Ez need?

A home, and all that it entailed. Though he never thought Lebanon Junction would feel that way, he had to admit it felt more and more like it as each day passed.

Garrison scanned the room. Pictures of his family hung on the walls and greeted all who entered. Tiffany's smiling face, lips pressed against his cheek, holding a pudgy Ez in her arms.

Time stood still in this house—the place they'd visit on block leave, and any time the Army had given him off. He closed his eyes and it was as if Tiff were in the kitchen, or down the hall working on a scrapbook. He'd call out to her, and she'd run into his arms. Her kisses tasted of strawberries or some strange smoothie she'd concocted and begged him to drink.

But tonight, just like the others since she'd passed, the kitchen was silent. No music playing. Her clothes in his closet no longer smelled of her scent. He no longer found strands of her long blond hair on the pillow or clinging to his uniform.

She was gone.

And he'd let her go, time and time again, but letting go of someone you'd fought hard to keep, someone who'd fought just as hard to do the same — well, it proved challenging. He'd always miss her. She'd always be a part of his life, but as he picked the photo from the wall and held it in his hands, he knew it was okay to let go and reach out for another. She'd want this for him and Ez. Garrison sighed. Even if it was for the woman he'd wanted to marry the first time around? *Lee.*

That truth didn't negate his commitment to Tiff. He'd proven his love for her over and over.

How many times had he and Tiff fought over this? Even on the night she died. That ugly insecurity hadn't shown up in years, and it took him by surprise when she spat the accusation once more. Garrison closed his eyes, wishing so much a quarrel hadn't been their last time together.

Tiff had been the one with the New York dreams. The one who wanted to get away, do something with her life. At first the hate between Tiff and Leanna was mutual, but in the end, Tiff tried to reconcile. In the end, Tiff promised she was happy - content with her life. God had worked all things for their good, even when they had made ungodly life choices.

She'd learned to embrace a new dream, and Ez benefited. So did he. Garrison rubbed a thumb across her image, letting his mind drift back in time. The woman who once demanded so much gave all, even forfeiting her education to raise their son while he provided, and served in other ways.

He kissed the picture and placed it back on the wall.

His mind scanned the years of their marriage. The deployments. Countless days spent in the field, away. How many times had he wished for a chance to stay home with his family, even when duty called? Now the opportunity stood before him, and he fought it. Was it pride? Was it the dueling loyalties within? Or was it easier to deploy than to stay?

The thought caused Garrison to slump.

He swiped a hand over his face, the roughness of his five o'clock shadow scratching his palm.

How did the puzzle pieces in his life fit right now? Time. He needed more time to figure it out, but time was in short supply. If he was going to deploy, he needed a home for Ez, and Lee could help. Would she? And why would she even want to?

Whatever Garrison's plan, Nelson was right, something had to be done slow as fast as possible.

***

Saturday morning already. He'd spent most of the early hours tossing over Nelson's suggestion, Lee's predicament forbidding him to rest.

And William. Garrison gripped the steering wheel. He'd have half a mind to walk into that punk's office and break his jaw. The thought brought a smile to his face. Spending a night in jail would be worth it, though the Army may not think so.

"Are we staying long today?" Ez said as they neared The Scoop.

Garrison pulled into the parking lot.

"Not today. Two hours tops."

"Good. I want to play with Brie today."

Aunt Mary smiled, and Garrison ignored her pointed stare. "It would be nice to see Ms. Leanna again too, don't you agree, Garrison?"

"Mmm, hmm." He parked, still ignoring Aunt Mary. She giggled, and he shook his head.

"You two stay out of trouble. I'm gonna go see Pastor Jay."

"You do that." Aunt Mary ushered him away and shut the door with a heavy thud. Ez bounced off toward the entryway, and Garrison followed behind.

Garrison walked through the double doors and down the hall to the right. He knocked on Pastor Jay's doorframe. "Got a sec?"

Pastor Jay looked up from his coffee mug, and a stack of books. "For you? Of course. Have a seat."

Garrison sat. "Lee's back in town."

"Yep."

"And she's got a lot of stuff going on in her life."

He nodded. "Yes. Yes, she does." Pastor Jay stood from his desk and faced Garrison." "We're glad to have her here though."

"I'm not one to give up confidences."

"I know that about you."

Garrison slumped, working his knee in a pump.

"Garrison? Anything specific I can help you with?"

"I'm thinking of helping Lee."

"Helping?"

"You know my situation, but you also know my past. All of it. Even the part involving Lee."

"It's quite a story."

"You helped me get through Tiff's death, deployments." He scratched his head and rubbed his palms over his knees. "PTSD, childhood abuse."

Even his faith had grown since he and Pastor Jay had become friends. Though there was definitely room for more growth. "Thank you, Pastor Jay. I'm just not sure where I'd be without your guidance, and friendship."

"That means a lot Garrison, and you're welcome, but how are you thinking of helping Leanna?"

Garrison scooted forward, both feet now pumping. "I'm not quite sure, yet, but thanks for listening."

"Um. Okay. You're welcome. Not sure I helped."

"You did. Always. Thank you."

"Garrison?"

Garrison turned, hand on the doorframe.

"Will you let me know when you figure it out?"

"Come again?"

"When you figure out how to help Leanna. We'd like to help too."

"Sure thing." Garrison rapped his fingers on the wall and headed down the hall.

"Garrison?" Pastor Jay called, his voice echoed in the hall.

Garrison spun. "Yeah?"

"Don't do anything…impulsive."

"Me?" Garrison grinned and then laughed. "Never."

"Uh-huh."

Asking Leanna to be a nanny wasn't impulsive, just not quite well thought out, yet. A few kinks remained.

CHAPTER NINE

A DAY OFF was a blessing. Working at The Scoop kept her hopping like her internship at the firm, but in a good way. A way in which Leanna couldn't quite place. She sipped at her water bottle, Brie at her side as they walked toward the nail salon. Girl day. Maybe a picnic later. Wonder what Garrison was up to this Saturday morning? He and Ez might want to come along. Brie stiffened, and clenched at Leanna's wrist. Leanna halted.

Cindy and Dale walked their way. Had they come from William's office? Her throat dried, warmth spreading up her neck.

Leanna held Brie's hand as the couple approached. They hadn't changed too much. Cindy's hair, speckled with grey and white now matched Dale's beard. Dale appeared fuller around the middle, while Cindy was still small, skin wrinkled from years of smoking. She resembled her sister, but Mom carried herself better, and had a certain glow about her. Cindy did not. But to anyone else, Cindy and Dale might seem like a sweet old couple. Leanna knew better.

"Leanna." A sad smile shone on Cindy's face. Dale wrapped an arm around Cindy. "It's so good to see you. Look at you. All grown up."

Leanna forced a smile. "It's been a while." Try twenty years.

"And Brie. Sweet girl." Cindy bent, hands on her knee.

Brie clung to Leanna's hand. Her eyes fixed on Cindy and Dale for a moment, and then she hid her face, cheek pressed into Leanna's arm. What was this response? Though, Cindy and Dale were probably strangers to Brie, and truly, not much more to Leanna.

"We're so sorry." Dale's voice was sincere. "The loss of your parents. It's too much." He shook his head.

Cindy lowered her head. She'd lost a sister, but then again, their relationship had been severed after years of drug addiction. Mom and Dad would help Cindy and Dale out. They'd get clean for a while, and then one morning, they'd be gone again until the family got word of their arrest or drug affiliation.

They stood on the sidewalk, an eternity passing between them.

"If, uh, if you and Brie need anything," Dale said hands now deep in his pockets.

Cindy chimed in. "Yes, please, let us know if there's anything we can do."

Leanna nodded. "We're making it work right now, but thank you."

Cindy opened her mouth as if to speak, but must have thought better.

"I'm glad we bumped into each other," Leanna lied. "Brie and I are having a girl's day."

"Maybe we will see each other soon?" Cindy's eyes seemed hopeful, a promise of a second chance shone behind her slight smile. "There's a lot to catch up on, and we have some things we'd like to discuss. Family things."

Things? Her heart squeezed inside her chest. Things like custody? Leanna kept her breath steady. Did they know? Had William told them, and what was he planning?

"Maybe we should get together." And maybe not. Leanna raised her brows and considered the option. There would be no getting to know Cindy or Dale better until the custody issue had been handled. Whatever William's scheme, Leanna needed to stay a step ahead—get her own plan together. She'd start with a visit to Judge Sinclair's office. Risky for sure, but it's what she should have done the moment the issue arose.

Dale cleared his throat. "We'll let you two enjoy your girl's day."

Leanna offered a smile and watched for a moment as the two walked away. They talked back and forth, but nothing Leanna could make out. Yes, she'd see Judge Sinclair on Monday, and arrive at The Scoop a bit later. Macy would understand. For now, Brie deserved every bit of a girl's day.

***

The bell jingled overhead as Leanna pushed open the door and ushered Brie in first. Place looked nice. Updated. Very spa-like with cool shades of blue and green. Soft sounds of water played in the background. Wow, Lebanon Junction was moving on up.

Chatter ceased once heads turned, and they whispered as Leanna neared the counter.

Oh, how this town talked. And what were they saying?

Did they pity her and Brie? Did they know about the money issues? Wonder why Leanna had stayed gone so long? Or perhaps they chatted about all the reasons she was a fool to break up with William. Maybe they were wondering what she was going to do now that Garrison was back in town. And maybe she was wondering the same thing.

Or maybe she was giving herself way too much credit for being the source of their chatter. But with smiles and sparkling eyes that stared her way, maybe not.

The woman at the counter greeted her with a nod. "How may we be of service to you ladies today?" Her accent was like syrup. Leanna's friends back in New York would have loved hearing this.

"Two pedicures, please." Manicures made no sense when scrubbing toilets, floors, walls and whatever else could be deemed scrub-able. Leanna counted out a portion of her consignment money. The rest would be used for half-priced tickets to Kentucky Kingdom. Brie loved theme parks, and she deserved to have some sort of an adventurous summer. Maybe an adventure Garrison and Ez might want to join in on?

"You can pay after." The woman smiled, sweet and Southernly. "Right this way."

She wiggled while she walked, which seemed stereotypical of women in the beautician world. "Pick out your color, ladies." She gestured to the wall of rainbow-hued polishes.

"I bet you want the usual." She aimed her statement at Brie, who smiled and shook her head. Brie had a usual? Leanna tried to hide her surprise.

"Been a while since we've seen you in here, Brie. Good to have you back." She gave Brie a full-on hug and lifted her from the ground with a hearty twist and shake before letting go. "Here you go, sweetheart."

The woman plucked a shade of pink and rose-gold sparkles from the wall and handed them to Brie. So Brie liked sparkles? Leanna smiled and faced the wall of colors. It would be nice if she too had a usual. Definitely cut down on the selection time. She opted for a happy shade, similar to Brie's, minus the sparkles, and followed behind the woman.

She ran the water in the pedicure tubs, and she and Brie relaxed in their cushioned chairs. Ooh, a massage button. Yes, please.

Two older ladies sat close by, both craning their necks.

Leanna waved, and they continued their chatter. Low at first, and then just plain obvious.

"Garrison has turned out to be quite handsome," one said. "Though he's lost that boyishness."

"War does that," the other added.

Brie reached in Leanna's purse, pulled out the tablet and earbuds. Leanna watched as she put them snugly in place, and sighed with a tinge of envy.

Probably a good thing Brie was otherwise occupied, considering the conversation.

Leanna closed her eyes, feet soaking, the tension leaving her neck.

"And he's raising that boy on his own. So sad about his wife, but I have to give that man a round of applause."

Leanna opened an eye. Nope. She wouldn't bite.

"Well he hasn't done it all on his own, Grace," one said.

"True. True. But Mary, bless her heart, she's getting worse."

Worse? Leanna peeped through a slitted eye.

"Mary is a wonderful woman, bless her heart, but there's no way she can look after that boy in her condition."

Condition? She seemed fine.

"And now he's deploying."

Deploying?

The salon sighed in unison.

Leanna pulled her feet from the woman with the sea-salt scrub. "Excuse me, ladies, but how do you know all this?"

They stared as if she were stupid, or undignified for interrupting their loud conversation obviously meant for her to hear. The older of the two women spoke. "Honey, we put the prayer line to good use."

"Aunt Mary is in their Bible Study," said the woman with the scrub.

"Oh."

"Now sit back, relax, and just listen," the woman chuckled. "We all do."

Leanna closed her eyes, and their chatter continued.

"Life has dealt that man some serious hard times."

"But his father seems to be getting his life back on track."

Finally.

"God works in mysterious ways," said a woman from across the room.

"He sure does."

The salon "mm-hmmed" in unison, but Leanna kept her eyes closed, paying them no mind. This pedicure was heavenly. And Garrison would let her know what he wanted her to know, what the Old Daisies in this salon deemed pertinent.

"One thing's for sure," the woman closest to Leanna said. "We haven't see that man smile like that in quite some time."

"Like what?" Her eyes shot open. Did she say that out loud?

The woman with the scrub arched a brow. "Like the way he did over at Pastor Jay's. You know, Leanna, when you were in his arms."

Leanna gasped. "I fell. He caught me. End of story."

The ladies grinned, and the salon "mm-hmmed" in unison once more.

***

Sunday morning was a blur. After church she and Brie scooted on over to

Elizabethtown, where tofu could be found.

"Hey, Brie," Leanna called over an armful of groceries. "Could you grab the bags with fruit in them? Then you can play for a bit."

Brie nodded and hoisted a few bags over her shoulder fingers spanned in front of her face grinning at the polish.

The gravel drive clicked and popped, a car horn honked.

William.

Leanna held in her grimace and set the groceries on the porch swing. Better to greet him now and get it over with.

He rolled the window down, arm resting on the door. "Passing through. Got a client to meet out this way."

"On Sunday?"

"Your nails look nice."

"What do you want, William?"

"Man, Leanna," He shook his head. "You sure do make it hard to apologize."

She kept her comments to herself, and not one word of Cindy and Dale. He could play a little game all he wanted, but she wouldn't give him any leads. "You want to apologize?"

"For how I acted the other night."

"Well don't let me stop you."

He worked his jaw. "I'm sorry."

"Thanks. Well, I've got groceries to put away."

"Saw you at church this morning. Sitting by Garrison and his boy."

"People go to church on Sunday, William. Glad you tried it." She folded her arms.

William clenched the steering wheel and broke eye contact. "The town talks. Heard the two of you were getting friendly again at Pastor Jay's."

Leanna huffed, and rolled her eyes.

"It's not like that, William." She kept her arms tight across her waist. "Today I sat by an old friend at church. End of story."

"Garrison was never right for you, and you know it. You chose him, and he chose her."

Tiff. Leanna held in a sigh.

"I think it's time for you to go. Thanks for apologizing." She offered a grin hoping he read sarcasm well.

"We could start over, you know. Get us right this time."

"Thanks for stopping by, but Brie's inside, and like I said, there's groceries to put away."

"Guess nothing's new, huh?"

"Bye."

"You're making the wrong decision."

"I'm not making any decision."

"Maybe you should." With a flick of his wrist, William launched an envelope her way.

"What's this?"

"Court date."

She turned, palms sweating as she opened the letter. "June twenty-seventh." Leanna scanned the letter. He'd beat her to the judge.

Leanna spun on her heals, letter bent beneath her grip. "A custody hearing?"

"I'm only doing my job." He shrugged. "There's still time to change your mind."

"I'd rather die than be with you again."

His expression darkened. "Maybe you'll get your wish."

Leanna shivered, then turned and gathered the groceries leaving, William in the drive.

She kept close to the window and waited for at least five minutes before the man finally backed out of the drive.

William...the definition of persistence.

***

No point in seeing Judge Sinclair. Not right away at least.

Leanna scrubbed dishes at The Scoop, her frustration growing. *William. Who did he think he was?* Leanna pursed her lips. William's threat to take Brie away and Garrison's gallant entry into her life still played in her mind.

What to make of it all? Had William contacted Cindy and Dale? She huffed—of course he had or at least would. Cindy even said she wanted to go over 'things'. What else would she possibly want to go over? Maybe Leanna should call her. Ugh. The thought turned her stomach.

And Garrison was deploying? Leaving again. That part of their past seemed to repeat. No wonder he hadn't called or come around since the dinner, minus seeing him at church. He'd been silent though.

Her thoughts blurred, and more dishes came.

How many plates had she cleaned? And forks — too many to count. "This place always busy?"

"Day and night. This is just the mess from the breakfast crowd." Macy folded her hands on her pregnant belly, hand towel thrown over her shoulder.

"You guys serve three meals a day?" Leanna reached for the next pan to scour.

"In the summer. When school's out and we want to make sure the kids are fed well."

"And how many people does it take to run this place?"

"Most volunteer." Macy tilted her head, lips pinched and twisted. "I'd say around fifty people, but we can get by with half."

Leanna nodded and set the pan to dry.

Fifty people. How many were paid? Maybe she could cut staff positions to save money. Or shut down part of the facilities. How to choose?

"By the way," Leanna rinsed a few cups out and set them in the drainer. "I never thanked you for inviting Brie and me over."

"Looks like you guys enjoyed yourself." Her smile was scheming "Didn't know you and Garrison were such good friends. From what I'm hearing, there's a story there."

"One for another day, that's for sure." Leanna flicked a water droplet Macy's way for good measure. Macy batted it away with the dish towel. "And a pastor's wife shouldn't listen to gossip. Tsk. Tsk."

"Saved by grace, and honey, it ain't gossip if it's coming from the choir."

"Oh, those beacons of truth."

"You know they all call in on the prayer line just to make sure they have their information accurate."

Leanna tossed more water Macy's way.

She laughed, belly shaking. "Your folks said you were a lawyer."

"Corporate law. Mostly advising businesses, reviewing contracts. Interned with a firm for almost a year in New York."

"That's impressive. Miss it?"

Leanna shrugged. "Yes and no. I thought I wanted to be a lawyer. Part of me still does. Just figuring things out right now." She reached for the next pan and scoured the surface until all food particles were gone. "Guess I have, or at least had, big dreams."

And now? Now keeping Brie and staying afloat were the only things that mattered.

"Did you ever think your dreams maybe weren't big enough?"

"That was the problem. They got too big, and things fell apart when Mom and Dad died."

"I'd say things were falling apart long before your parents died."

Her words smacked at Leanna's face. Truth had that effect. Leanna lowered her head, arm around her waist.

"I'm sorry." Macy came close, her voice soft. "Sometimes I need to be careful with what I say."

She didn't mean any harm. Leanna swallowed hard and lifted her head.

"As painful as it can be, I'm happy to know someone who will be honest."

"Will you be honest with me?"

Leanna blinked. Macy was more direct than she imagined. Did she trust her enough to be honest? Leanna folded one hand in the other, her thumb scratching a circle in her palm. With more than a leap of faith, she nodded.

Macy smiled, and raised a brow in return. "Are you going to sell this place?"

The room shrank.

"You know how to ask a question." Leanna forced a laugh from her throat, face growing hot. She rubbed her gloved hands along the sides of her jeans, not minding the dishwater.

"Jay and I were wondering what would happen to the property."

"I…I planned on selling the land, but now…"

"We're a nonprofit. The community funds The Scoop, for the most part. We've got a nice balance of paid employs and volunteers. Not much of a reason to sell."

"It's so much more complicated." Leanna slipped her hands from the soapy water and took off the gloves. "There's this financial mess from Mom and Dad. It's not making sense, and the numbers aren't adding up, but, ugh…" Leanna groaned. She shouldn't be talking about any of this. Especially with someone she hadn't known long. "Part of me wants to sell everything to get rid of this debt." Leanna shrugged. "I've been over the numbers in my head a few times, and it's not adding up." Not much added up lately. "It's like I'm missing something."

Macy stepped closer, her mouth curving downward. She laid a hand on Leanna's shoulder.

Leanna shook her head. "I don't understand how Mom and Dad ended up owing so much."

"Have you talked to William?"

Leanna scrunched her nose. "Let's say, he and I've had better conversations."

"So he's part of the problem."

Leanna avoided the answer and instead shifted her weight to one leg. There seriously had to be some other lawyer nearby to look things over.

"Jay and I, and the church, will do anything we can to help."

"You guys have been so kind." How could she return the favor? Leanna clicked her tongue. "How about all of you come over."

Macy opened her mouth, probably to object.

"Trust me." Leanna lifted a hand. "We've got a surplus of casseroles, and honestly, there's food in the freezer and fridge we need to use up." Use up. Remaining pieces of her parents began to fade whether or not she wanted them to. But to keep items stored away, preserved, when they could help or bless others … no, her parents would never want such a thing. Her throat tightened. "It'll be like Mom and Dad making everyone one last meal."

"Please don't cry."

Leanna dabbed underneath her eyes with her forearm, soap dripping from her rubber gloves. "Ugh, I'm such a mess."

"We're all a mess. A beautiful mess."

"How about five-thirty?"

"Done. I'll bring sodas, and don't try to stop me."

"You think there's time to invite others from the church?"

Macy raised a brow, eyes wide.

"Yes, there's enough food."

"Then I'll send out a text."

Pastor Jay scooted through the kitchen, stole a cookie from a nearby tray, and kissed Macy on the cheek. "Hi, ladies. Bye, ladies. Gotta go shoot hoops with the kids."

"Brie okay?"

Pastor Jay shook his head. "I'll let you decide that. Looks like Ez is here today." He wiggled his eyebrows, and Leanna frowned. He left before she could throw a snide remark his way.

Leanna toyed with her fingernails and then plucked at her apron strings. "Ez come here often?"

"You mean, does Garrison come here often?" Macy teased.

"Definitely mean Ez."

"In that case, yes. Garrison drops him off a few days a week while he's at work. Gives Aunt Mary a break." Macy rubbed her belly and stretched. The woman looked miserable. "Besides, all the kids love this place. Finger painting, sports, weird exploding science projects, and silly songs. Better than summer camp."

Yes, it was.

But all summer camps came to an end.

Leanna huffed and plunged her hands back into the dishwater.

"Hey." Pastor Jay popped his head around the doorway. "If you're okay with it, I'd like to counsel Brie. You're more than welcome to sit in, and no charge for anything."

"I…I…that's really nice of you." Leanna played back the conversation she'd had with the doctor a couple weeks back. Do you think it's time?"

"Do you?"

What did her gut say? "I'd give anything to hear her talk again."

"We've had a lot of success; all God's doing, of course. "Brie's been through a lot. These things can take time. Anyway." He gave the doorframe a quick rap with his knuckles. "I have an opening tomorrow at ten."

"We'll be there."

Pastor Jay smiled, eyed the cookies, then glanced over at Macy.

"No more," Macy said with a sly grin, hands on her wide hips. "Now go shoot some hoops before they all come looking for you."

Leanna shook her head. All the kindness and love, yes, this was evidence of faith. Wasn't that a verse somewhere in the Bible? They will know you by your love.

She eyed the clock. The morning vanished, now lunch time crept close, and more dishes to follow. Geez.

CHAPTER TEN

LEANNA SPENT THE early morning hours packing bits and pieces of her parents' items, but it was too soon to let them go, so they sat in the closet underneath the stairs. With other treasures.

She propped her feet up on the patio table and sipped her coffee. A few birds played a game of chase, and then the singing started. Aunt Mary. Leanna smiled.

"I love that song." She stood and made her way to the fence.

"So do the birds." Aunt Mary tossed up grains of bird feed. Leanna laughed at the woman. "I'm surprised you're awake at this hour."

"Why's that?"

"Garrison was out here in the backyard for hours. Figured you were with him."

Leanna pursed her lips and leaned against the fence. "Nope."

What had that man been doing out there?

"Hmph. Guess I was wrong. Well, I'm going to walk Ginger."

"You do that." Leanna laughed and headed back to the porch, but a faint glimmer caught her eye.

She knelt down. At the base of the fence, tucked under a mound of lifted dirt, there it was. The old Altoid can. Rusted. Bent.

Leanna covered her mouth.

He remembered.

So this was what Garrison had been doing.

She lifted the tiny tin and opened the lid. She was twelve again, passing notes to Garrison between the fence that divided their backyards. She unfolded the small letter.

I can't tell you how good it was to talk to you again. I'm sorry about everything going on. I'm here for you. Always. Love, Garrison.

She held the note to her heart.

Love grew in the strangest of places and in the strangest of circumstances. She'd come home, broken from life, dreams deflated, never expecting to find healing...hope, or second chances.

Perhaps she and Garrison could be friends again. And down the road, years perhaps, maybe more?

She let the thought linger.

***

The notes continued, morning, afternoon, day and night over the course of the week. The tin passing from one fence to the other.

Have a good day at work. ~ Lee

Scrub dishes and tutor well, my friend. ~ Garrison

Do you remember when we tried to make sushi from the catfish we caught in the lake? ~ Lee

And the visit to the emergency room that followed? Good times. How's Brie? ~ Garrison

She's good...better...I guess. Sigh. And Ez? Want to take the kids to the movies or something? ~ Lee

Sounds like a plan. Think I got someone who wants to buy your car. Call ya later. ~ Garrison

Good news on the car. Anyone I know? So...deploying soon? ~ Lee

My First Sergeant says he's interested. Praying you don't know that crazy man. And, yes...deploying. ~ Garrison

What about Ez? Aunt Mary? You know we can text, or call, or meet in person? ~ Lee

Yeah...we need to talk. Important. Meet me at the playhouse tonight. ~ Garrison

Leanna held the tin can and laughed. What were they, children?

CHAPTER ELEVEN

TIME RAN FROM him. Half-day schedules now, but he, like the rest of the men lived for the weekend. Garrison raked a hand over his head. Not too much longer until a revised family care plan needed to be turned in to Commander Jones.

The Scoop had closed an hour ago. Garrison had spent most of his Saturday painting and shooting hoops with area kids. Not a bad way to spend a Saturday, but Ez ditched him to hang with Brie and Leanna. Definitely not a bad way for Ez to spend a Saturday. Still, he missed his buddy.

Garrison walked down the gravel drive, hands in his pockets. Nice thing about being back home, one could walk pretty much anywhere. Good exercise, and a good way to clear the head. And his head was full.

He would ask her tonight.

To be Ez's provider while he was away.

The thought made his stomach clench.

"Need a lift?" A voice called out from behind him.

Garrison turned. Great. William trailed him in his car.

"No thanks." Garrison waved. "I'm good."

"Never thought we'd see you back in these parts."

"Trust me." Garrison kept walking. "Never thought I'd be back."

"And Leanna, huh? From what I hear you two got cozy at Pastor Jay's house."

Not surprising. Garrison stopped and leaned over. "Maybe you should stop listening to hearsay."

"Watch yourself. This ain't high school anymore."

Garrison sneered. "Bye, William." And he walked on.

William spun gravel, leaving Garrison in a cloud of dust.

What a jerk.

***

Garrison dialed the first few digits, then blew out a burst of air.

"Dad, I'm ready. Can we please go?" Ez slumped over the sofa, pool towel covering his face. "You're taking forever."

Could he call? Should he call?

It was just an invite to the pool. He'd see her tonight anyway, at which time he would ultimately end up asking her to assume all responsibility for his son while he left her alone for the duration of a combat deployment to care for two children and an aging women with dementia. No. He couldn't call.

"Dad. Come. On." Ez tugged at his arm.

"K. Almost ready." Far from it. Three weeks left to turn in this family care plan to Commander Jones. Garrison picked up the papers from the coffee table and scanned through the checklist for guardians. Qualified, reliable, and stable. A person about whom he had no reservations entrusting the sole care of his son. Yes, yes, yes, and yes, but would this person be willing to care for Ez?

He shook his head and stood. "Okay, bud, let's go."

Garrison pulled Ez over the couch and tickled him, wrapped his arms around the wriggling boy. He squeezed three times.

"I love you too, Dad."

Those words melted his heart.

"You invited Ms. Leanna and Brie, right?"

Garrison sighed.

"Scared to call?"

"Me? Scared? Ha."

"You act weird around her."

"How? We've hardly been around each other."

"All smiling and stuff."

"Oh, that's very descriptive. Hey bud, I need to talk to you for a minute."

Ez grabbed a pillow and placed it on his legs. "And then can we go swimming?"

Garrison nodded. "You know I'm deploying soon, right?"

Ez nodded.

"Like sooner than we thought, remember."

"I know, Dad." Ez rolled his eyes. "Aunt Mary's gonna take care of me."

"Yeah, bud, about that." Garrsion explained the situation, and Ezra shrugged.

"Ms. Leanna."

"You'd be okay with that?"

"Duh."

Garrison paused. Well, that was that.

"So what's the issue? Call her and ask. You scared?" Ez teased.

Garrison sank into the couch. "Yeah...something like that."

CHAPTER TWELVE

HE KICKED AT the blades of grass, wet with dew, slapping against the hem of his jeans. "It feels like we're in middle school again."

Leanna snickered and climbed into the playhouse. "So, you're deploying."

"It's a lot to process."

She nodded. "Looks like we both have our own set of issues. Now I've got a custody hearing."

He swallowed. As if it had a mind of its own, his hand extended out to her. At least he could offer. She took hold. Her small hand in his. Dainty and strong.

She kept her head lowered and continued to walk almost hunch-backed, as if wounded. As if holding his hand kept her moving.

"Lee." He squared his shoulders. She turned to him, sad eyes searching his. He swallowed the rising lump in his throat. "I. I'm sorry. I really am."

She looked at him sidelong, her eyebrows pushed together.

He bowed his head. No. He needed to look her head on. "I've apologized before, but more needs to be said." Words swirled through his mind. What to say first? "I never meant to hurt you."

"Garrison. That was years ago."

"No. Please." He gave her hand a squeeze. "I can't and won't apologize for marrying Tiff. Ezra was the best thing that happened to the both of us."

The corner of her mouth lifted.

"But I'm sorry for the way it happened."

The moonlight drained any hints of sun from her skin. Her lashes skimmed the tops of her cheeks. She kept her hand in his.

Garrison blew out a burst of air. He felt her worry and it panged his heart. How could he help her? He had some cash stored away. Maybe he could buy the house. "There's got to be a way I can help you and Brie out."

"There's nothing you can do." She shook her head. "There's no way out of this mess."

"There has to be." He could testify on her behalf at the custody hearing. He could—Ezra's words flickered through his mind. His own son recommended Lee as a mother or caretaker. His mind played through the possibility once more.

After what he'd done to her in the past, Lee would never go for it. But he could hope. Maybe he could make things right.

"Lee, I know I can help you, and I...I need your help too." Garrison held her gaze as her eyes widened. "I need a safe person to take care of Ez. And look after Aunt Mary. And I can think of no one better than you."

"Me?"

"Ez thinks so too."

He fumbled with his thumbs and waited. And waited. "I'd pay you."

Would she ever respond?

Garrison swallowed. "I know you're worth more than what I could pay —" Oh, Lord, that sounded all wrong. "I mean, paying for your service—" He bit his lip. Geez, that was worse.

Lee laughed, thank goodness.

"You've always had a way with words. Thank you, Garrison." She chuckled again, folding her arms over her knees. "Would a judge give me custody over Brie then? If I was a caretaker?"

Was she considering his offer?

He tugged on the bill of his hat and sat up a little straighter. "I don't think so."

The deal sounded slightly one-sided in that light. She'd still not have insurance, and the job was just for a short-time. This deployment would only be nine months.

Garrison closed his eyes and let his shoulders relax. "I know another way." Was he insane? He had to be. "Leanna, marry me, and you'll have a solid way to keep Brie, and your home."

Did he even hear himself? His heartbeat pounded in his head. What kind of insane idea was spilling out of his mouth? But he couldn't stop.

"What's mine would be yours. You'd have insurance, benefits. Brie too."

Her lips parted, but no sound came.

Garrison placed his hand on top of hers. "I'll even find a way to pay off your parents' debt. We can do this. Together."

She sucked in a sharp breath, drew her hand from his, and stood. "You're out of your mind."

Yeah. They both were.

But this could work.

CHAPTER THIRTEEN

"Insane. You've always been insane." Leanna's cheeks blazed. What nerve. "Marry you? Ha." She kept her arms tight at the side of her body, fists clenched.

"Think about it." Garrison reached for her. Right now his cool demeanor agitated her like none other. "Lee, I'm sorry for everything, but I'm offering a way to help you."

"You mean help yourself, right? You just want to use me—"

"Come on, Lee." Garrison thrust his thumbs through his belt loops. He shrugged and shook his head. "I won't lie. I'm in a predicament too."

"Only thinking of yourself. Taking what you want, without thinking of anyone else."

"You're not being fair—"

"I'm not being fair?"

"Just say it. Say what this is really about."

Who did he think he was, spouting off to her like that? Leanna jabbed a pointed finger in his direction. "You. Have. No. Clue. What I've been through."

"No?"

Leanna stepped back, steadying herself as she nearly stumbled over a tree root. He did know. At least some. He'd known so much heartache and sacrifice. Even if he'd brought a lot of it on himself.

She stared at Garrison. What was she searching for?

"Go ahead, Lee. It's been brewing long enough, right? Or do you plan on keeping a grudge for your entire life?"

Did she dare? Fine. He asked for it. "Would you have ever told me you slept with her?"

There. She'd said it.

Garrison filled his cheeks with air. He shook his head. Honesty could be cruel.

"Would you have married her if she hadn't got pregnant?"

***

Garrison's heart thudded inside his chest. She never took her eyes from his.

He raked his knuckles over his lips. He'd asked himself the same question a million times. "I'd like to say yes. Yes, I would have told you. Yes, I would have married her anyway."

"But you can't say that, can you?"

He shook his head. His eyes stung.

Years flooded between them. Garrison felt them all. The good, the bad, the mundane.

He searched for words. For excuses.

Her eyes watered. "Wasn't I worth waiting for?"

"Lee." A whimper escaped his mouth. Garrison forced his body not to crumble. Her words were more of an unbearable accusation than a question. He closed his eyes, head lowered. "You were and have always been more than worth it."

"Then why?" Her voice strained. Desperate.

He shook his head. "I wasn't worth the wait."

There.

He said it.

The ugly truth that still stalked the corners of his mind. There to accuse. Confirm his worst fear, fulfill his father's words that he might actually not be worth it, or anything for that matter.

Her fingertips touched his for a moment. "You were worth it to me."

"And I never understood why." He inched forward, pushing aside the darkness between them. "Me? Of all the guys." He shook his head. "Knowing..." He sighed. She knew all. She'd seen the bruises and cuts on his body as a child. The demeaning way his father spoke. How poor they were.

"None of that mattered to me."

"And now?"

Leanna lowered her head, concealing her expression. Garrison lifted her chin. No need to hide.

She swallowed. Her expression hardened. "Why are we even talking about any of this?"

Garrison winced and dropped his hand. Good question.

"Lee, I know I messed up. I know I hurt you, but I'm here now." He moved his hand close to hers. Did he dare reach?

***

Leanna stomped off. Garrison and comments, like exhuming a grave best left alone.

"Lee."

Leanna threw darts with her eyes. He matched her pace, then took a double step and positioned himself in front of her. Always blocking her path.

"Move." She held balled fists at her sides.

"Why are you running?"

"I'm not. I…" Maybe he was right. She bit down on her bottom lip, brows drawn tight. "I'm right here. What else do you want from me?"

"Say what you want to say—what I know you want to."

She kept her jaw drawn tight. "I hated you both. Is that what you wanted to hear? Happy now?"

"Keep talking. Get it out. This is good."

Good? She huffed and swiped at her burning eyes. Get it out? So he wanted her to spill it all. Her chest burned. Where to begin?

The air grew thick and swirled around her at a suffocating speed. All the regret. Loss. Wills. Custody. Bills. William. She managed a few short breaths. "Just leave me alone."

Garrison caught her elbow as Leanna turned to run. "Don't do this, Lee. Don't run."

She squeezed her eyes shut, willing her legs to stay in place. The urge to break free thrashed throughout her body. Leanna dug her heals into the ground. No running. Not today.

"I loved her, just like a sister." She spun toward him, her mind still reeling. "Yes, I was angry, but I never wanted anything to happen to Tiff. Or you." A large knot lodged itself into her chest and threatened to climb her throat. "I...I...still can't believe she's gone. Or my parents. They're...gone." The realization never ceased to smack her across the face.

Garrison lowered his head, pressing his forehead to hers. He held her shoulders in his steady hands.

Leanna breathed in his earthy scent. The spinning settled, but the ache in her heart remained.

Garrison squeezed her shoulders, and then wrapped his arms tight around her like a shield. They stayed that way for a while. No words. A simple embrace sufficed. Why did he have to do that? Make it seem as if all problems had solutions. As if things would get better. So far, life continued to grow exponentially more complicated. Sparks of hope followed by chaos.

"Marry me, Lee." Garrison pulled away and tapped her chin with an index finger.

***

I'm insane. Leanna dug her fingers into her crossed arms.

But he had a point. Stable income. Insurance. A two-parent home. Marriage was an option. An option the Courts might like. Like enough to give her permanent custody of Brie? She sighed.

They'd marry and then what? A judge would then need to grant custody to her.

She weighed the offer through clenched teeth while Garrison stood in white T-shirt, ball cap, and worn jeans. Not much different from high school, but still—changed. How long had she waited for him? To be his. To do life together. Now he proposed marriage, but for all the wrong reasons.

But if it meant a way to provide for Brie…

The night sky cast a blue hue over the landscape.

"And this would be for how long?" She kept her eyes narrowed.

Garrison lifted his eyes to hers as if taken aback.

"What? Did you think this little arrangement could be anything but temporary?" How cold had her words come out?

"Until." He cleared his throat. "Until I return from deployment?" His hands fell from his waist to his sides and back into his belt loops. "Until you and Brie are settled. As long as it takes. Long as you need."

Leanna allowed a nod. Her fists unclenched as she ran her palms down the sides of her denim shorts. Brie could never be happy with Uncle Dale and Aunt Cindy. Mere strangers with a rap sheet longer than the Appalachian mountain range.

She stared past Garrison and at the house. If she said no, the house could be sold. Homes were sold every day. It wasn't the end of the world. Then again, if she said no, how long would she be able to keep Brie? And meet Brie's needs?

But to marry Garrison for the sole purpose of…of financial support, seemed sickening, and screamed against what remained of her ethics.

"I'm an educated woman."

"In a pretty tight bind."

"Are you blackmailing me?"

A disgusted huff rumbled from Garrison's throat. She knew better. Garrison wasn't like that, like William. Not like William. At all.

Leanna shook her head. "I can't think clearly." She pressed her fingers into her temples and paced along the riverbank. Another way out of this conundrum existed. Some other way. Any other way.

Think.

"Couldn't I just be some kind of live-in nanny?"

"I wouldn't be able to extend health benefits to Brie that way."

A sob rose from within. Leanna held a hand over her mouth, but the sobs refused to cease. Her life, reduced to this. Her shoulders quaked with each sob. She doubled over, her palms on her knees.

"Leanna." Garrison stepped closer. Too close. Not close enough. His eyes pleaded. For what? Forgiveness? Someone to fix his situation? Or perhaps...no.

No.

Years of pain and regret, coupled with waves of grief, flowed between them. Some bridges were meant to stay broken.

Her sobs lessened and then loosened their hold. She stood, back straight. Her eyes followed a distant lightning bug until it floated toward the house. The dining room light shone from the window almost as if Mom and Dad were home. She wiped the tears from her cheeks.

What would they say about this arrangement? A marriage of convenience?

Love is kind? Love is patient? Love endures all things? Marriage is forever.

Well, sometimes it wasn't.

Her legs trembled. She tugged at a strand of hair stuck to the corner of her lip. "I loved you." A knot, too large to swallow, rose in her throat.

"I —"

"Don't say you loved me too." Leanna swatted at his words. She shook her head and stepped closer to him.

"I. I'm sorry, Lee."

Her face warmed. She tucked her chin.

"Do we have a deal?" Leanna extended a hand.

"Is this what we're calling it?" His face grew solemn. "A deal?"

Marriage should be more. They should've been more. Leanna kept her hand outstretched, her chin squared. "I don't know how it could be anything else."

***

Garrison pressed his lips into a fine line as he shook Leanna's hand.

A deal.

Not much different than his marriage with Tiff. Well, up until the last few years. And then...

He sucked in his bottom lip. No need for Lee to see it shake.

He blinked a few times, and cleared his throat. "What now?"

Leanna shrugged.

"Courthouse?" He managed a laugh. "Been there before."

Leanna frowned. Her eyes watered.

"I'm sorry, Lee." He rubbed a hand over the back of his head. "I'm sure you never planned to get married in a courthouse."

She shuddered, her gaze settling over the river.

"We can find another way." Garrison let the silence settle. "We don't have to get married. Not like this." No response. He dared to step closer. He'd take the risk of getting punched. Right now, more than anything, she needed someone to simply be there. He could do that.

Garrison wrapped both arms around her. Lee didn't flinch. Her body, warm and trembling, melted against his chest. He stared with her, over the river. If not for the moonlight, the waters would go unnoticed. He sighed. "It's okay to cry. Let it out."

"I won't stop."

"That's okay too." Garrison held her close. She'd stop crying. Eventually. Grief came in waves.

"How do we tell the kids?"

"I think that will be the easy part."

"There's so much that needs to be done." Her breath caught in her throat.

"Let's focus on one thing at a time."

She nodded beneath his embrace. "And what do we do right now?"

"Sit here." That got a smile out of her. Garrison held out a hand, but slid it instead into his back pocket. He wouldn't demand to hold her hand. He'd asked too much already.

Marriage. Hmm. People married for more than love. Not that he didn't love her. He flinched. He didn't know her. Not like he used to. But then, he'd changed too. For the better. But what about Lee? She'd changed, that's for sure. But for the worse? No. Not worse. Only emotionally unavailable to him, but with Ez, she clicked, and that's what mattered now.

Leanna bumped her shoulder against his. She kept her arms hugged around her waist.

CHAPTER FOURTEEN

A MARRIAGE LICENSE on a Tuesday, and the next, she was getting married—the definition of insanity. Leanna's stomach churned with force. She focused on each breath and counted when her lungs would stop.

Breathe. In. Out.

Just breathe.

Her knees rocked beneath her as unsteady as her insides. One foot in front of the other up the courthouse stairs. Her wedding day.

No William. No veil. No white lace dress. No, it wasn't even a fall wedding. Leanna squinted as she peered into the sky. The summer sun blazed down. A Wednesday wedding.

She laid a hand on the necklace lying flat against her chest. So many things about this day were wrong, but the pearls, they were right. Her mother's pearls.

Momma. She should be there to help with something old, new, borrowed, and blue. To kiss her cheek. Leanna's eyes stung. And Dad. He should be at her side, walking her down the aisle, giving her to a man she loved and intended to spend the rest of her life with.

They were taken too soon. Too much left undone. And for what? Why? Her heart cried. Why had God let this happen? Why on earth were they on those back roads that time of night anyway?

Leanna sighed and continued up the steps. She blinked back the tears.

Brie held tight to her side, elbow locked with hers. A calm, quiet child, the personification of innocence. Leanna swallowed the tightness creeping up her throat. Brie was worth this. She deserved to be taken care of. So did Ezra.

He walked at Garrison's side and stole an occasional glance at Leanna. Her heart hurt, but his eyes held hope. An expression that longed for a mother, someone to stick by his side, someone she could never be.

Her face warmed. She wrung her hands and smoothed them over a sheer layer of the peach knee length dress that clung to her body almost as tight as Brie did. Leanna welcomed the affection despite the tension surrounding the situation. Brie hadn't objected to the news, though she said nothing at all. Ez on the other hand had knocked her over with a hug.

Garrison cleared his throat. His eyes focused straight ahead, hands deep into his front khaki pockets. Leanna refused to let him wear his Army Dress Blues. It seemed inappropriate, considering the arrangement—a marriage meant to die. Even so, Leanna was grateful he decided to dress nice for the occasion. White button-up shirt, and a tie to match her attire.

She slowed her steps, one hand against the pearl necklace. She lifted a brow.

His second marriage. She shook the thought aside but it held on. Her throat tightened. Another marriage that would end for him. Her shoulders sagged. Would he remarry? And to whom? The air thickened.

Her heart thudded an irregular beat in her head. She stopped, pressing a hand to the closest marble column. No time for a panic attack. Her nostrils flared, but no air entered. "Breathe." Garrison grabbed her shoulders and spun her around. "Look at me and breathe." He inhaled. Exhaled. "Match me." She tried, but failed. Her chest screamed in protest. "Focus, Lee."

Leanna dug her nails into the palms of her hands. Of all days to panic. Of all moments. She gasped. Still no air.

Ezra hid his face behind Garrison. Brie stared, not shocked, hands now at her side.

Leanna sucked in a short breath, hands now cupped over her mouth. A small cry found its way out. Another breath.

"Keep going." Garrison shook her. She coughed, and a few tears seeped from the corners of her eyes. "Don't take your eyes off me, Lee. Breathe."

Short breaths mimicked his. In. Out. His eyes, fierce, never left hers. Thank God.

She'd thanked God. Leanna winced.

"I said don't look away." His hands pressed into her shoulders and held her steady.

Breathe. Leanna coughed once more. The veins in her neck relaxed.

A small hand slipped into hers and gave a slight squeeze. Brie. A second hand slipped into her free hand. Small fingers intertwined with hers. Ezra. Their skin was smooth. Untouched by years and difficult decisions.

Air filled the bottoms of her lungs. Another breath. She smiled and inhaled once more.

Garrison swiped a hand over her forehead and let out a sigh sounding much like relief. He crouched down, hands holding fast against his knees.

Leanna pressed her back against the marble column. The coolness of the stone sent a welcomed chill through her body. She tipped her head back still holding the hands of the children.

"We don't have to do this." Garrison ran a hand over his face. Sweat dampened his hair.

No, they didn't, but no other way remained that she could see.

Ezra and Brie stood quiet, listening too close for her ease. Leanna swung the children's hands in hers. "People will know all this was because we love these two kids more than ourselves." The truth. Leanna inhaled and closed the distance that draped between her and Garrison. "They'll know we love these kids more than anything, even any plans we may have had for our lives." The painful truth. Leanna swallowed. It hurt, watching her dreams of becoming a successful lawyer dissolve. She winced. Silly dreams. Selfish dreams. Perhaps a new dream awaited. Somewhere. Someday.

Brie and Ez gave a satisfied nod, then scampered after each other up the stairs ahead of her.

Garrison tilted his head. His stare seemed to size her up. Read her thoughts. She squared her shoulders as he tightened his jaw.

"You can look at me like that all you want." She stiffened and lifted her chin. "This isn't wrong." Right? She nodded. "It's not."

Garrison stared on, never releasing her. This couldn't be easy for him either. He rubbed a knuckle over his mouth.

"How is this wrong?" She swallowed, pushing the question to the bottom of her gut, and prayed it wouldn't surface again.

He turned away and headed up the stairs.

Leanna narrowed her eyes. "That's it? No answer?"

Garrison stopped mid-step. Leanna's stomach cringed as he faced her. Had he changed his mind about their impromptu marriage?

"Marrying you isn't what's wrong, Lee." His words were low, even, and sad.

What did he mean by that?

As if she didn't know.

She rubbed one hand over the other.

No, marriage wasn't the issue. Divorce was.

But could he honestly think she could ever love him again? She pushed the lump in her throat down where it belonged. In the pit of her stomach. Yes, divorce was the issue here, but it couldn't be helped. It was part of the deal—their deal, and Garrison had agreed.

Garrison held the courthouse door open. A lady and gentleman walked out arm in arm, perhaps newly married, and in love? Good for them.

Leanna kept her posture straight as she walked over the threshold. She blinked as the dim lights wreaked a moment of havoc on her vision, but then the signs were visible.

SECURITY SCANNER AHEAD.

CHECK-IN FOR LICENSE AND CEREMONY.

She tucked in her bottom lip, head held high. No turning back now.

The clicking of her wedge shoes echoed in the corridor. They walked in through the scanner without an issue. Ezra asked to examine the metal-detecting wand, and the officer obliged with a nod-grin combo. Brie watched Ezra with wide eyes, but as usual, no words. Ezra swung the wand as if in an epic galactic battle. Garrison smiled, and Leanna allowed herself a laugh. The mood lightened. A welcome moment.

"C'mon, Ez." Garrison rubbed Ezra's hair until it looked a mess. "Thank you, Officer."

"Have a good day there youngun's." The officer tipped his hat, and they were off, down the hall, to the left.

The Ten Commandments hung on a wall to the right.

Leanna choked back any reservations. God hadn't offered up any other way to help in this situation. Or maybe this was His way?

No. Probably not. She bit at the corner of her lip. Who knew what His way was? Not her. Not anymore.

Ten years ago, marrying Garrison made the top of her prayer list. Begging God to be his wife. She tugged at her bare finger. It would hold a ring soon. Garrison's ring.

She rolled her eyes. The irony in it all.

She steadied her breathing, pushed pack the rising tension in her chest and counted the clicks of her heels.

Seventeen. Eighteen. Nineteen.

Another panic attack or not, they were getting married. Today.

Twenty-five. Twenty-six. Breathe.

Garrison cleared his throat from time to time, hooking his thumbs in his belt loops. If only she had the ability to read his mind like he could hers. He seemed calm. Resolute. Or perhaps she'd mistaken his silence for peace. Inner turmoil could look outwardly calm. She'd know.

Thirty. Thirty-one. Thirty-three. Her heartbeat steadied. Thirty-four. Breathe.

There were perks to getting married. She lifted her chin higher, if that were possible, and smiled to herself. A marriage license would shut William up, and any judge would have to give her custody of Brie. She pressed her lips together and squeezed Brie's hand. Brie peered up, meeting her stare. Those eyes. Those rounded rosy cheeks.

Leanna held in a sigh and bent, placing a kiss atop her sweet, wavy curls. "You look beautiful, honeybee."

"What about me?" Ezra jerked on his tie, sending it swinging over his shoulder.

Leanna reached for his tie and caught it mid-air.

"Hey." He yanked it from her with a playful laugh.

"You, sir, are incredibly handsome."

"That's right." Garrison tucked the tail end of Ezra's shirt into his pants and gave his bottom a quick pat.

"Not in public, Dad."

Garrison shrugged and held open palms in the air. Still the same Garrison. After all he'd been through, he could smile, and play, and laugh. His crooked grin worked a number on her heart. She pressed a palm to her chest to steady the uneven beats.

A door opened and closed with a thud as they passed through the hall. The air threw a whiff of Garrison's aftershave in her direction. She breathed in the woodsy scent and closed her eyes.

"We're here." Garrison cleared his throat.

Leanna opened her eyes. What an idiot she must've looked like, walking, eyes closed, inhaling.

Her face warmed.

The three of them stared at her. She touched her hair. Had the earlier panic attack left her appearing disheveled?

"What?" Leanna tried to keep her gulp as inaudible as possible. "Is there something on my face?"

"Just making sure...." Garrison's voice trailed as he lifted a brow.

"I'm still sure." Leanna picked at the material of her dress, face ablaze. "I'm not changing my mind. We're doing this. Today."

Garrison held the door open, his gaze paralyzing her for more than a moment. Her throat dried. She managed a nod before entering the quaint courtroom.

She turned to face him as he shut the door. Ezra and Brie scooted off to the front of the room, finding a seat on a wooden bench.

"Garrison." She forced the words from her throat. Her heart pounded. "You understand our arrangement. You know my intentions...our intentions are not to stay married." It wasn't a question, but a fact.

He nodded, stepping into her personal space. "I'll let you go, if that's what you want when the time comes."

She leaned back, wrapping her hand around the back of a long bench, but he leaned forward. The man had lost his sense of a personal bubble. The woodsy scent of his aftershave filled the short space between them.

Garrison tilted his head. Leanna shifted her weight. Cold feet didn't warm up by standing around. He stared at her as if searching the most direct way to say what was on his mind.

No words. No comebacks? Or snide remarks? Her mind went blank. Maybe that's why Brie didn't speak. She had nothing to say? Her mind was blank?

No. There were no words to express her thoughts. That's why she didn't speak, that's why Leanna couldn't speak.

Leanna clutched the back of the wooden bench. Garrison made himself clear, while she stood, knees shaking, rendered speechless.

And then he kissed her cheek.

How dare he!

"Meet you at the altar." His voice trailed behind as he walked down the aisle toward the officiate.

Leanna kept still, body numbing. What had she gotten herself into?

***

The kiss on her cheek? His face warmed. What sort of boldness grabbed hold of him, and where had it gone? The only thing Garrison managed to do now was adjust the window visor. Didn't help the sun situation much as he drove back to the hills, but it offered something to fill the awkward silence in the car.

He swallowed, and eyed the paper lying on the console between him and Lee. A marriage license, signed and dated.

Wow, how the course of his life had changed in an instant.

What would his Army buddies say? Garrison gulped. The level of jesting at his expense would be unprecedented. Though Nelson may prove a source of encouragement. And what about Aunt Mary? She'd be the easiest to tell, and the easiest to accept, but Pastor Jay, Lebanon Junctions's most beloved pastor and Garrison's confidant?

Garrison tugged on his collar and loosened his tie. Pastor Jay would flip over such a rash decision to marry, and then flip again when he learned the conditions.

Confidence level sinking lower.

The gold band on Garrison's left finger cut into his skin as he tightened his grip on the steering wheel. His lips dried and cracked as he pressed them together. What would Tiff think about this marriage? The thought raised gooseflesh along his neck and arms.

In fact, he'd moved on, or rather, was forced forward by life and responsibilities. It took being forced ahead to pull him through a two-year fog, a life of mess-ups, and countless apologies.

His eyes watered and burned. Ezra had a mom now. But for how long?

He cleared his throat.

Tiff would approve. Yes. Even given the history. Lee was someone they both knew…loved even.

He bobbed his head and ran a hand over the edge of his chin. No, the situation wasn't ideal, for sure, but what in life was? He had a chance now to right past wrongs. A do-over. Who gets that?

"Can we listen to the radio?" Ez's voice carried over the backseat.

Garrison reached for the dial, his hand colliding with Lee's. Her slim fingers recoiled to her side. He caught a glimpse of the ice in her eyes as she turned away. He shook away the chill and rolled the window down, welcoming the warm breeze as it flooded the car.

A sigh pushed its way from his mouth. Stubborn woman. Resistant and guarded.

For as much as Lee and Tiff grew to hate one another, they sure shared many similarities. Couldn't Lee at least pretend to be a bit excited—for the children's sake?

"Country okay, bud?" Garrison twirled the dial between his fingers until settling on a station. A good one that played the classic country hits. Not the new stuff which sounded a bit too hip-hop for his taste. "Fishin' in the dark. Now that's a song we can sing to."

He nudged Lee with an elbow, but she didn't respond, only looked on out the window as if in a daze.

She'd come to.

Garrison glanced up at the rear-view mirror, able to see Ez playing an air guitar to the beat of the tune. Brie watched him. Such sad eyes for a little girl, but she smiled as she watched Ez strum the air.

Yes, Lee would come to, and so would Brie.

Maybe it was time to talk to Aunt Mary about this whole situation, and its many limbs. Garrison turned up the music. Ez bounced in the back seat, now openly singing. Though a bit out of her mind at times, Aunt Mary was a praying woman. Her prayers worked, and those were the kind of prayers he was going to need.

CHAPTER FIFTEEN

MOM AND DAD had been in a car, not all too different from the one in which she now sat. Leanna rubbed the leather material under the windowsill. The texture differed from the silken fabric inside her parents' coffins. A thought too morbid for her to continue.

Leanna shivered, adjusting the seatbelt as it closed in on her throat.

"Slow down a bit." She pushed invisible brakes on the floorboard of the passenger seat.

Garrison nodded and turned down the radio as if the volume affected his speed.

Had her parents slowed down on the curve, then...well...

Leanna glanced back, and then returned to her almost slouched position. The passenger mirror provided an innocuous way to observe the kids. Brie seemed quite content watching Ezra lip-sync to the tunes on the radio. Their sweet little faces exchanged knowing smiles. He poked at her leg with a mischievous laugh. Brie poked back. A smile crept up on her face.

Leanna wet her lips, unable to look away.

I'm a mother.

A jolting thought.

Her heart must've stopped. She sat up and clutched the purse at her side.

Calm. In control. She closed her eyes, drawing in a hearty breath, and released her hold on the purse.

Garrison kept to the road, but jerked his head in her direction for a series of double takes. Geez, that man worried way too much. Focusing her attention out the window would be her best bet. Less to worry about.

"Wanna talk about the panic attack at the courthouse? Didn't know you still had them."

She answered with a glare.

"Just asking."

"I'm fine." Or at least she would be. Yet their recently increasing presence did give her pause, if only for a moment.

"Hey, Ez, turn the sound down on that game." Thankfully, Garrison turned his attention elsewhere. "Kids and their electronics. There's an app for everything nowadays." He smiled and the high-pitched computerized game music faded in the backseat. Leanna smiled in return.

The roads began winding. Leanna ignored the ring on her left finger and Garrison's occasional worry-filled glance. She gave her attention to the scenery. Green grass, freshly cut. White fences as far as the eye could see. Slender, toned horses grazed and galloped with such pride she had to stare. How free they were. Unbridled and free. For now at least, until racing season. She tucked in her bottom lip, eyeing the wedding band that now bound her much like a racing season bound a horse, but not for long.

Time ticked at a steady beat on her wristwatch. The mile markers passed by in streaks. The hills, however, took their time. She couldn't deny the beauty of the land. How it flowed to the point, if not for their green hue, one would swear the hills were waves. Not only waves, but a song beckoning one to sing along—a siren's tune. Trapping anyone dumb enough to stay behind and get sucked into the poverty, become an unemployment statistic, dependent on welfare and eventually end up in some sort of drug ring that screwed up everyone's life in some form or another. Should be a country song. Probably was.

Familiar small crumbling towns grew distant in her passenger mirror. How many miles had she spent traveling up and down this road? Family outings. Church trips. Some mission project her parents had coordinated.

"Your car drives well." Garrison hugged a curve while oncoming traffic blurred past.

His attempt at breaking the iceberg? Leanna loosened her seatbelt and tightened it back in place before deciding to hold onto the door handle. Extra support. "Yeah, well, let's hope it sells well." She raked her fingernails along the handle.

"This car doesn't suit you anyway."

Like he'd know.

"You're more of an old Ford truck girl. Refurbished." He tapped his chin. "Blue. No, a charcoal gray. Or." He tilted his head, voice curling. "Maybe some kind of classic, like a '68 Mustang. Silver. Fast. Down to earth, all American, and wild."

So maybe he knew. A little.

"But if I'm a Ford, and you drive a Chevy?" The corner of her mouth lifted, shoulders in a shrug.

He paused, and she laughed.

"Maybe, Garrison, that's not the kind of car I am anymore. Maybe I'm a Rolls Royce. Some kind of Bentley. Benz even."

Garrison nodded with a smirk. "If you say so."

"You'd be..." Leanna scrunched her nose. "Don't tell me." She swatted away his attempt to respond. "It's hard to peg what you'd be."

"Now c'mon, Lee. Don't act like you don't know what kind of car I am."

"You could be a car or truck."

"Fair enough." He shrugged. "Car?"

"You'd never buy a brand new car right off the lot, and definitely not a high society ride." She narrowed her eyes and frowned. Something loyal. Something reliable, yet fun. "Something like…" Wait. He hadn't been loyal or reliable—not to her. She wet her lips and let her hands fall into her lap. "I can't think of something that suits you."

His shoulders sagged.

Leanna sat back. Why couldn't she just let it go and stop being so hateful?

"Well." Garrison smiled. "When you think of the right car or truck, let me know."

He rounded another bend. Leanna held fast to the handle as if tuck and roll were an actual possibility. Garrison appeared oblivious to her movement. "I was thinking the kids might want to go out to eat. Celebrate a little."

"Celebrate?" Did she say that out loud?

He rubbed the back of his head, keeping one hand on the wheel. "It's no honeymoon, but shouldn't we have a little fun?"

Honeymoon. Her face burned, mouth growing as dry as some far off desert land she never intended to travel.

"We, uh, you know, not like we'll have a real honeymoon." Color tinged his cheeks. Garrison all but gulped. "'Cause, well, we're not like that. I mean, we could." He stared ahead. Leanna scouted his knee working a nervous pump. "You know what I mean."

Leanna nodded and let her hair shield her face. How could he think they could do or be...that? Ever?

"So, um, leave starts soon."

"Work." Her shoulders hitched. Leanna smacked both hands over her face. "I've got to call them back."

"You work?"

"Took a leave of absence, but I haven't even called them to let them know I won't be back." Two months home had flown by. She rambled through her purse shoving item after item aside. Where was that phone?

"You have a job. That's impressive."

"Of course I have a job. For about a year now." She threw a hard glance in his direction. "Actually, a career."

"Oooh."

Jerk.

She clasped her phone pulling from the depths of the designer bag by her side. Another gift from William. What did she own that wasn't gifted to her from him? She slammed the purse into the floorboard. Dumb thing.

She scrolled through missed messages and calls. One from work. Better than a hundred.

She scrolled down. A text. She'd know that number anywhere.

William. Leanna deleted the message. She didn't care what he had to say.

"Everything okay?"

She nodded.

Garrison's knuckles whitened as he held onto the steering wheel. He could always tell when she was lying.

"Just some friends from New York." Such a liar. "I'll call work tomorrow." Leanna slid the phone into her purse and pressed back into the seat.

Ezra shoved his way in between the front seats. "Can we have a honeymoon in the treehouse?" He bounced and the leather seat squeaked with each squirm. "I've always wanted to stay the night there."

They both stared at him.

"Sure, Ez, now sit back." He tossed Ezra a smile. "Adult conversation going on up here."

Leanna tucked her hands under her knees. The seatbelt pushed back as she leaned forward. "What were you saying about leave? That's when you've got so many days off, right?"

Garrison nodded and rubbed at his chin. A simple question, but no response.

"Hello?" She tightened her lip, head tilted, tone way too harsh. Leanna pinched the bridge of her nose. Why, why, why was she so mean? Garrison was only concerned for her, for Brie. A good man. A great father. The man even served his country. And here she was serving up a warm dish of rudeness.

If only she could run home to Mom and Dad. They always knew how to help, whenever she decided to grace them with her presence, that is. Now where would her help come from?

Leanna rubbed a hand over her face. Sleep. She just needed rest, and then her head would clear. Things were looking up.

"Yeah, sorry. Mind wandering a bit." He checked the rearview mirror, one hand on the wheel. "We get thirty days off before we deploy."

She let his response settle, and then the questions swarmed like some kind of Old Testament plague. Could she handle military life? How difficult would it be to care for the kids and Aunt Mary? Could she and Garrison hide their deal from Brie and Ez? When William found out, he'd surely go to Cindy and Dale, if he hadn't already, but it would be okay. She'd be able to keep Brie.

"I can almost hear your thoughts." Garrison's smile was almost too carefree.

"I'm fine."

"I'm sure you are."

How was it possible for this man to be so kind one minute, and then so smug the next? "You're telling me you're not concerned about some of the details surrounding our..."

"Marriage?"

Leanna gulped at the word.

"We'll work it out." He extended an open palm. A peace offering?

Did she dare accept?

No words. Just his hand. It hovered over the gearshift shaking slightly with the jostling of the car.

Whatever the circumstance, no matter the feelings, complicated or not, she and Garrison were at least one thing: a team.

Leanna slid her hand into his.

"I'm here for you, Lee." He pressed his lips together. "Always remember that."

She nodded. A lump rose in her throat. Just the other day he confessed to feeling not good enough to be with her. Oh, how she related. She didn't stir when Garrison interlocked their fingers. She sat watching the hills roll by, one fingernail rested on the corner of her lip. The phone buzzed in her purse on the floorboard below, then shook, notifying of a voicemail.

Stupid bill collectors. She'd be happy to pay off her parents' debt, if the funds were there.

"Let's grab a bite, get back home, then we'll swing by William's office." Garrison gave a short laugh. "Bet he'll be shocked."

Leanna lifted a brow. Yes, shocked, for more than one reason, but with the marriage license in hand he'd back off for sure, and Brie would be safe and sound with her.

"Thought you and Brie might want to come over and have dinner with us at Aunt Mary's." He winked. "I'm grilling."

"That actually sounds nice." She'd rather not spend too much time in her parents' home today anyway. Fewer memories to face. Her shoulders pressed into the leather seat. She leaned her head against the neck rest. "It's been a few days since I've seen her." Sweet woman. Kindest lady in the community, aside from her family. "Your Aunt Mary is a special lady." Her lashes skimmed the tops of her cheeks. "Does she still remember—" Leanna paused. As if he wanted to divulge the ins and outs of his aunt's illness.

"Hit and miss what she recalls, really." Garrison chewed on his jaw. "Most often she forgets the little things. Car keys. Phone numbers. Stuff like that. Yesterday it was like nothing was wrong." His Adam's apple dipped. "This morning, a different story." His shoulders lifted and fell. "Guess that's how life goes sometimes."

Leanna nodded. Life seemed to hand out an unfair amount of unfairness.

"The woman still prays." He kept his eyes on the road. Leanna eyed the signs for Louisville as they sped by. Cute town. Been a long time since she'd been there too.

Garrison released a breath. "Her Bible is falling apart. All marked up. Thought about getting her a new one, but she's content with that one."

Leanna rubbed a thumb over Garrison's hand. Her parents' Bible sat on their nightstand, opened, marked up, and highlighted. Her own Bible, who knew where it was? Tucked away somewhere. Had she ever underlined a single verse? Made a note?

"You guys are married now." Ez bounced in the backseat, smile wide. "What house are you going to stay at?"

"Mine." Leanna's face warmed.

Her face grew warmer by the second. They'd have to work hard to make sure the kids thought this whole marriage was real.

"We're all on this new adventure, huh?" Garrison bobbed his head as if marking off points on a mental to-do list. "Work. Living arrangements. Kid's school. Insurance."

He reached for her hand and gave it a squeeze. "Nervous?"

"No." She swallowed, finding her voice. "You?"

"Never."

"Must be the soldier in you. Ready for anything."

"Yeah. Anything. Ha." He paused, and Leanna wondered about his thoughts.

"I thought I saw my dad yesterday." His low announcement was startling. Guess getting married makes one think on their parents.

"At The Scoop?"

He nodded.

"Pastor Jay and Macy—"

"Yeah. Your folks told me he doesn't get outa the house much, just to get his meals at The Scoop during the week. Stopped coming in on the weekends. Guess cause we started volunteering."

Leanna held tight to Garrison's hand. Why her parents continued to serve his father she'd never understand.

"Aunt Mary checks in on him here and there— just to make sure he's still breathing. Ha. He keeps on living. Funny, huh? Tiff's gone. My mom's gone. Lost several good buddies in Iraq. Your folks...well, just not fair, huh?"

Her mouth dried. She shook her head.

"When are we eating?" Ez groaned from the backseat.

Leanna's stomach rumbled. "Hold tight buddy." She pressed her free hand to her abdomen. For once in the past two months food sounded appetizing. "We're stopping soon. I'm sure of it, kiddo."

"You bet we are. Got just the right place." Garrison clicked on the turn signal and glanced at the rearview mirror. "We'll get us a big, fat, greasy cheeseburger. Fries. Largest chocolate shake on the menu."

Ez cheered and Leanna grimaced.

"City girls don't eat like that?" Garrison bumped her arm with an elbow and slowed the car.

"I don't really eat meat anymore."

His eyes widened like those of a cartoon character. "No donuts. No bread. No meat." His lip curled into a smile. "Who are you? What's left to eat? Paper?"

"How about vegetables."

"If they're breaded and fried."

Leanna pushed a heavy sigh from her lungs. "Hopeless."

"Here we are." Garrison pulled into the parking lot.

"Little Rick's Neighborhood Bar & Grill." Her mouth hung open. "Can't believe this place is still here."

"How's this for a honeymoon lunch?" Garrison laughed and unbuckled his seatbelt. He high-fived Ez and Brie.

"This is so redneck." Her cheeks warmed. She shook her head, reaching for the door handle. "We're dressed up, you know."

"They'll bring us lots of napkins."

Great.

Garrison bounded from the car and around to her side to open the door. She stared for a moment. William never got the door for her. Always rushing her here and there. She eased out of the seat, working to remove the sneer a restaurant name like Rick's Bar & Grill seemed to force upon her face.

"Smile. I'm sure they've got something leafy and green for you."

"And swimming in grease, gravy, and dressing."

"Mmm. Mmm." Garrison patted his stomach.

Ez helped Brie from the car, and they both raced for the long front porch of the restaurant to find a home in the rocking chairs. Garrison reached for Leanna's hand. The place had a certain quaint, homey appeal. Sort of. In a backwoods country sort of way. If someone liked that sort of thing. Which she didn't. However, wafts of home cooking rolled through the front door. That, she liked.

Garrison leaned over just as they walked inside. He pointed at the house special sign hanging in the entryway. "Veggie platter."

She smiled, tucking her hair behind her ear. "If I get grease on my dress, I'm sending you the bill."

"No doubt."

The conversation was fun and lighthearted. Leanna laughed at Garrison's silly jokes, and even launched a small paper wad through a straw at Ez. Brie giggled, and Garrison's eyes were wide, surprised even.

"What?" Leanna smirked, straw in hand.

"So unrefined." Garrison joked.

Ez rolled tiny paper wads creating his own arsenal. The server waltzed their way, plate of onion rings and milkshakes high above her head. Ez lifted the straw, shooting a wad Leanna's way. Leanna dodged with a hand, and met the waiter.

The waiter screamed, but there was no way to stop the food flying toward Leanna.

Leanna flinched, and the milkshakes smacked against her neck, chest, and arms. The onion rings, hot grease and all, landed in her lap. She stood, hands outstretched, mouth open, as the restaurant sounded in a collective gasp.

The waiter covered her mouth.

Ez and Brie froze. Garrison's eyes were huge.

"Don't you dare smile." Leanna warned all of them, and made her way to the restroom, milkshake dripping from her arms.

What. A. Day.

***

Garrison decided it best to place a to-go order after the fiasco. He did his best to hold in the snickering, but her facial expressions were too much, and he caved—more like busted.

So now they sat, driving back home.

The kids kept quiet in the back seat, minus the occasional rustling of paper from their Styrofoam containers.

No need for the radio. No need to speak. Nothing to be said, at the moment. Garrison held tight to Leanna's hand and listened to her muffled sniffles.

They rolled into Lebanon Junction. Not too much to see, but it was home. He passed an old factory. Remnants of an abandoned general store. Many homes were small, and falling in on themselves crouched behind cracked sidewalks.

This town wasn't so different from Lee, himself, or the rest of the world for that matter. Broken, tired, lost, and in need— of so much.

CHAPTER SIXTEEN

JUNE TWENTY-FIFTH. Two days after her wedding. And the honeymoon? Making clay creations from the riverbanks, and grilling out. Honestly, she hadn't laughed so much in years. The time almost made her forget about today. Almost. Leanna blew out a burst of air and stood on the courthouse steps. She held onto Brie's hand, Ez close by.

"Thank you for being here with me today, Garrison."

"First Sergeant's a good guy." He reached for her hand and she didn't object. Not now. No way. She needed the added support. "Besides, I wouldn't miss this for the world." He gave her hand a squeeze. "I, um, I called Pastor Jay."

"Did you tell them?"

"Just that today was the custody hearing. They're praying."

No mention of the wedding. Relief rushed over her. "We need the prayers."

"You ready?"

"Do we have everything?"

She'd checked her folder three times, and now ticked off the paperwork in her mind.

"Paperwork ready on my end. Just need the judge to sign off and we can get Brie enrolled with DEERS."

"Deers?"

"Defense enrollment eligibility enrollment system."

"Oh. That's a mouthful."

"It's how I'll get you guys set to go with insurance and stuff." He chuckled. "We'll go on base soon and get ID cards, and enroll you in DEERS too."

Right. Ugh. This was happening.

They walked up the steps. She stood near the entryway, hands clasped at her waist, holding tight to the marriage license. Garrison stayed at her side, body at an angle, surveying the area in a near militaristic way.

The courtroom was her element, but today it felt foreign, almost malevolent. She wiped her palms on the side of her skirt and entered. Cool air greeted them floating down from the ceiling vents. Leanna welcomed the chill and its nerve-calming effect, but it soon faded at the sight of William. He smiled as if he had the upper hand. *Not today.*

William was slick, she'd give him that, but twisted and at times, downright narcissistic. How would he react, and what would be his next move?

Aunt Cindy and Uncle Dale sat at the edge of their chair, knees together, holding hands. They offered a smile.

It wouldn't hurt to smile back. Leanna forced her lips to cooperate. If it appeared fake, well then, it was the most sincere form of fake she could offer.

"Make yourself comfortable, Leanna, Garrison." William waved them in from behind his desk. "No lawyer? Representing yourself today?"

Leanna nodded and her throat began to tighten.

"You guys sit here." Leanna spoke to Brie and Ez, and pointed to the bench behind the railing in the courtroom. "Brie?"

Her eyes lifted, and Leanna's heart melted.

"Brie, I love you." Leanna knelt gathering Brie's hands in hers. "I want us to be together. And I don't know what's going to happen today, but I love you, and I'll fight for you."

Tears stung in Leanna's eyes. She leaned, planting a kiss on Brie's soft cheek and Brie wrapped her arms around Leanna's neck. Leanna held on tight, hands in her sister's curls. She kissed Brie's forehead and then stood, wiping her eyes. *Please Lord, grant me custody.*

Garrison placed a hand on hers. "I'll be right here if you need me." He sat beside Brie and Ez, arm extended around them both, and her heart swelled at the sight.

Leanna pulled her shoulders back.

William pressed his fingertips together. His eyes plotted.

Cindy and Dale sat still, hands still intertwined.

An officer stood to the right of the Bench, another near the exit. Leanna peered over her shoulder. A CPS officer stood in the corner.

The Judge entered the room, and took his seat. *Judge Sinclair.* Leanna's heart sank, but she kept her head lifted. She had a good chance, even if the man was William's uncle.

Judge Sinclair cleared his throat. "We're here today to determine the legal guardians of Brie Ellaine Wilson. Is that correct?"

"Yes, your Honor." Leanna nodded.

He leaned forward, the leather of the chair creaking. Judge Sinclair lifted a stack of papers and scanned them, head bobbing. "Looks pretty clear. Your parents wished Cindy and Dale Thorton to be the legal guardians of Brie."

"But your Honor." Leanna stood, fingers pressed to the table.

"You object? And believe yourself to be a better fit?"

"Yes, your Honor."

He skimmed through a few more pages. Leanna strained her neck. What was he looking at?

"And why should I grant you custody of Brie?"

"She's my sister, your Honor. I'm old enough now. I'm working, and I'm sure given more time will be able to begin career nearby. Your Honor, I hold a degree in law from—"

"If I may," William chimed in. "Ms. Wilson barely makes above minimum wage, and currently she has no way of providing insurance. This child is used to a certain standard of living."

"Excuse me, your, Honor. Mom and Dad were hardly wealthy, and I'm no longer Ms. Wilson, but Mrs. Burke." Leanna glanced at Judge Sinclair and then over at William. His face flushed and she hid a smirk

William stumbled over his words, working with this tie. "This is absurd. You're...you're married? To him?" A vein protruded in his forehead.

Leanna palmed her hip, and held up the marriage license in her other hand. "I can take care of her. We have a home. Insurance soon enough. A steady income. I'm a suitable caregiver, and her closest living relative."

William's face soured and hardened. His brow folded. Cindy and Dale kept silent, eyes lowered. Couldn't even look at her. How dare they try to take Brie.

William held up a hand, sweat now appearing on his face. He shook his head. "There's no getting around this. The will—"

"Is old," Leanna said to both the Judge and William. "It was made when I was a teen. When Brie was a baby. I'm sure the Courts will take the age of the will into consideration."

William shook his index finger as if he were some sole authority. "The two of you may be married, but Garrison, you'll have to adopt Brie before she's entitled to any of your military benefits, including insurance."

"We're prepared." Garrison called from behind in a matter of fact tone.

William seethed, face reddening. He unbuttoned his jacket and gnawed on his bottom lip. "The fact the two of you married in order to get custody of this impressionable young girl proves your incompetence."

Leanna rolled her eyes. Like he cared an ounce about Brie. "Think whatever you want William, you always do."

"Enough." Judge Sinclair spoke up. "I'd like to hear from Cindy and Dale. What do the two of you have to say about this?"

"Leanna." Aunt Cindy lifted her head. Her weathered skin and dry hair aged her unfairly. She wiped tears. Leanna's breaths labored as the room grew small. She didn't care about her aunt, uncle, or anyone who tried to take away Brie.

"You look so much like your Father." Aunt Cindy's dull gray eyes fixed on Leanna's face. What did she see? "We love you. We love Brie, and we're sorry that we haven't been much of a part of your life." She smiled. Leanna had to admit there were good memories. A few, and then, none. "Let us be a part of your lives."

Leanna tilted her head. "I can't let her go."

Cindy's lips parted, then pressed back together. She nodded. Her eyes drifted from Garrison to land on Ezra..

Ez didn't seem to notice, but Garrison folded his arms as if to take the whole thing in.

Cindy's gaze hovered a moment longer over Ezra before turning back to Leanna. Her eyes told of strife, maybe struggles too numerous to count.

Judge Sinclair groaned. "Sounds like the two of you are okay with raising Brie?"

Leanna's ears rang. *No. No.*

Cindy and Dale nodded.

"Mrs. Burke," Judge Sinclair said. "In my opinion running off and getting married in what seems to be some scheme to gain custody proves to me that you are currently unfit to care for your sister. I agree with William."

No. The room spun.

He continued. "Brie's been through a lot."

Leanna steadied herself and found her voice. "Forgive me, your Honor, but handing over custody to former drug addicts is somehow better?"

"Former is the key word, Mrs. Burke. They've been clean for three years, and do watch how you speak to me."

"Yes, your Honor." Leanna lowered her head.

"Leanna, we all have Brie's best interest in mind." William's words were sickeningly sweet. "Maybe we could revisit the custody issue at a later date, but I believe Judge Sinclair agrees with me that Cindy and Dale should have custody."

"No." Leanna said, fist tight. He wasn't going to do this. "You won't take her."

"Won't?" Judge Sinclair gave a sidelong glance. His eyes darted from hers to William's. They were in this together. Plotting.

Frozen. Leanna couldn't even swallow. She wet her lips, preparing a defense, but none came.

She narrowed her eyes at William.

Cindy and Dale kept quiet. At least they weren't butting in again. Leanna tore her eyes from them.

"Look." William held outstretched hands. He tilted his head. "We all know you love Brie. We do too."

"Don't speak her name." Leanna shouted.

He ignored her and continued. "The fact is, she hasn't spoken a word since the accident. She needs stability, Leanna. Therapy even."

"She's in counseling," Leanna said.

William continued palm extended. "You're in quite a financial bind, and making irrational, life-altering decisions that affect Brie's wellbeing."

He was sickening.

Leanna's bottom lip quivered then turned to stone. Her legs shook, but not for long. To give her sister up—unthinkable. Never.

William continued. "You've conjured up some kind of marriage with a soldier—"

"Sir." Garrison widened his stance and used his hand to point at William like a target. "You don't know anything about us, or our situation."

"I know you need someone to look after Ezra while you're gone. I know she's in quite a bind, and now the two of you are standing here in front of me married. Maybe that's the kind of behavior I can expect out of a grieving young woman, but from an American soldier? Tsk. Tsk. Although…" William lowered his voice, a slight smile on his face. "I would expect this from someone with a family like yours."

Leanna held in a gasp.

Garrison's expression hardened. The corners of his mouth fell flat, and his eyes steeled. Leanna pried his fingers from a clenched fist and slid her hands in his.

William folded his arms and arched his back, appearing rather smug.

"That's enough." Judge Sinclair smacked the Bench with a gavel.

William leaned on the side of the desk, crossing his feet at the ankle. He rapped his fingers in a rhythmic beat.

The room went still.

Leanna tucked her hair behind both ears. It seemed as if he'd already made a decision, but she had to try. "Your Honor, if I may?"

He nodded.

"I'm sure my parents would have been upset about some things I've done, but I know they'd want Brie to be with me." Leanna tried not to tug at her wedding ring. She squared her shoulders. "They'd be proud that I'm fighting for her...that I...I..." Her voice trembled. She drew in a calming breath. "That I'm finally looking after someone other than myself." Not easy to confess.

Her plea, her confession—were they not enough to convince him? Or was he that cold?

A clock outside the office door chimed two o' clock. The dual clangs struck at her heart like a gavel.

"Please." Leanna's words fell from her mouth as a whisper. "Judge Sinclair...it's me you're talking to. Please, don't take Brie from me."

"The Courts have to decide, but for now..."

"No." Leanna's fingers curled.

"Brie will have to go home with Cindy and Dale, today."

"No. No. You can't."

"You do not want her to be taken into state custody." Judge Sinclair spoke through a hardened expression. The Judge gave a nod and a CPS officer walked toward Brie. Brie stood, her face pale, void of any expression. They couldn't take her.

Leanna gasped, cupping hands over her nose and mouth. No need when no air would come. She scanned the room gaze split between Brie and Aunt Cindy and Dale. Cindy spoke to William in a frantic whisper, her face reddening. Dale lowered his head. Cindy's tear-filled eyes caught Leanna's. Why was she crying? She'd got what she wanted. Leanna snapped her head away, but she couldn't run from this. Brie needed her to be strong. Leanna drew in a breath until her lungs threatened to burst.

The fan overhead blew a cooling burst of air her way. It swirled around her, the unseen presence nonetheless comforting, like the prayers of Pastor Jay and Macy. A strong, but gentle hand cupped her shoulder, and gave a squeeze. *Garrison.*

"Please, your Honor." Leanna found her voice. "We can work something out." She pointed to Cindy and Dale, and they nodded.

"Perhaps working 'something out' should have taken place before this hearing." He leaned forward, jaws sagging. "It's interesting that we're just now meeting about custody—two months after your parents died."

Very interesting. Heat flashed across her face. Leanna kept cool as possible, willing her chin to lift, hands clasped in front of her. "It's been a difficult time for us."

"And I am so very sorry for that." His eyes spoke the truth. "For now, I'm assigning custody to your Aunt and Uncle. We'll meet again in thirty days, July twenty-fifth, ten a.m. for a permanent ruling."

Thirty days without Brie, and the possibility of losing her forever. He cracked the gavel to adjourn, and her heart crumbled.

***

Her body trembled from head to toe, as if cracking. She'd gotten good at suppressing her feelings, trying not to feel or process the weeks past, and perhaps the past several years, but now her defenses crumbled, and no will remained to stop the waves of violent cries that flowed to the surface.

The tears fell in sheets down her cheeks. Her chest quaked. Leanna willed her legs to walk down each step of the courthouse.

Garrison held one hand, and Ez held her other.

Quick steps followed behind, and then halted. "Did you think you'd really win?" William laughed. Leanna closed her eyes. If she faced him, no way could she restrain herself right now.

Instead, Garrison turned. "Hey Ez, meet me at the bottom of the steps."

Leanna opened her eyes and watched Ez walk down, glancing back once. She gave a smile, and he gave one back.

"What do you want?" Garrison's voice shot in William's direction.

"Guess I should be congratulating you two. I'm impressed Leanna. Well played. Looks like you'll use anyone to get what you want, but this time it didn't work. I'm the winner. Again."

Leanna balled her fists until her nails dug into her palms. She turned, eyes narrowed. "This isn't a game, William." *Not anymore.*

"Come on, Lee, let's go." Garrison tugged at her arm, but she stayed planted.

"I can't believe you chose him again," William said. "History repeats itself, especially with this piece of white trash."

Something snapped inside, and before she understood what has happening, her body lunged toward William. He shielded himself from the blows, but to no avail.

Garrison's arms wrapped around her waist. Her high heels flew from her feet. "Lee. Stop it. Do you want to get arrested?"

He tightened his grip. She stomped on his feet, but he didn't budge. "Lee, calm down. You're not helping your case right now. We still have a chance."

He was right. Her shoulders slumped and shook. Garrison held her tight

William wiped the sweat from his head and neck. "Don't think this is over."

"Get out of here, William," Garrison said.

Leanna crumbled on the courthouse steps, the concrete scratching at her ankles.

Garrison sank beside her. He rocked her, humming a series of shushes as she cried.

***

"Breathe with me." Garrison smoothed back Leanna's hair, wet with tears. They'd made it back to the house hours ago, but Lee's sobs were nowhere near ready to subside. She clung to Brie's teddy bear. He rocked her back and forth as she cried, breaths heaving from her body. Her shoulders quaked with each wail. A broken woman, no longer angry or stone, just completely torn. He pressed his cheek to hers, closed his eyes and hummed.

What was that verse Aunt Mary quoted to him more often than he wanted to hear?

A Psalm.

A broken and contrite heart—these, O God, You will not despise.

Yes, that was it.

Lee qualified, and so did he. Garrison held in a sigh. If God still listened, like Pastor Jay told him months ago, now seemed as good a time as any to start talking.

But how? Garrison swallowed hard, and continued to sway with Lee. Aunt Mary prayed out loud, like she was talking to the wind. How silly it looked, but wow, it moved mountains. He'd seen the evidence in his and Tiff's life, countless others' lives, and in the community.

He nodded. Here went nothing.

"God." Garrison squeezed his eyes as tight as they would go. "We need you."

CHAPTER SEVENTEEN

LEANNA HELD TIGHT to her parents' pillow. How long would their scent linger? Forever, she hoped. An inconsistent stream of tears trickled down her face and soaked into the pillowcase.

How had William and Judge Sinclair been so cold to pull Brie from her only home? And why had Leanna let him?

Mom and Dad would be so disappointed.

Shadows of leaves, cast from towering trees outside her parents' bedroom window, clung to the wall. Their limbs stretched and reached farther into the room as the daylight faded. Leanna closed her eyes, willing the dark claws of the branches to leave, or take her as quickly as possible. Deeper she sank into the bed, the old mattress hugging her body. She kept still in its embrace, letting her mind and muscles rest. Darkness, bent and twisted, crept closer.

Leanna stayed put and filed through her thoughts—any good memory, something to light up the room. She gathered a bit of the top quilt in her hand and brought it up to her face. The cotton fibers, worn with time, kissed her cheek. Years ago she had helped make this quilt. Echoes of laughter-filled memories flooded her mind, and Leanna smiled.

As a child, she'd jumped on this bed. Bounced for fun and dodged a barrage of pillows as they swung in her direction. Dad would fake a fatal blow. Mom chastised the noise but never failed to laugh along and deal a few fake fatal blows of her own.

Leanna traced her fingers along the pillow edge stitching, some parts cruder than others. No matter how she tried, she couldn't quite get her stitching to match the flawlessness of her mom's. Though it never prevented her from practicing for hours upon hours at a time.

A soft knock at the door pulled her to the present. She kept the pillow close and wiped a hand over her face. Her voice cracked. "C...Come in."

Garrison poked his head into the doorway. The soft light enhanced his features—the slight, natural lift of his brow. The straight slope of his nose contrasted with the roundness of his eyes. So handsome. Always. And now, her husband?

What had she done?

His lips pressed into a frown as he walked across the room. The door fell open and hit the wall with a muffled thud. He looked back, then continued forward until taking a seat at the edge of the bed.

The added weight lifted Leanna's body from the hold of the mattress.

For a moment they stared at one another. More than a moment. His eyes, fiercely green but as inviting as a meadow, held her attention until she could no longer stand the way her heart raced and ached.

She let her lashes fall. "Where's Ez?"

"Playing checkers with Aunt Mary on the front porch." He scratched his head and let his forearm fall to his knee. "Hope you don't mind me bringing her over."

"She's always welcome."

Garrison nodded, no words added. So much between them needed to be discussed, and even more now that Brie was gone, but he didn't push.

"Pastor Jay stopped by with a few more freezer meals and a hot chicken casserole. Smells good." He lifted a brow as if surprised. Leanna mimicked his expression. "I picked the chicken out of it in case you're hungry."

Her breath caught. This man. The lengths he'd gone to in order to help her, to show kindness, when she'd been cruel for years.

"Said their doing church service at The Scoop this Sunday. Thought we could go."

"The Scoop." Leanna smacked her forehead. "I didn't go in today."

"It's okay." Garrison smiled, fanning a hand. "I explained everything."

"Everything?" Her mind raced. "Even…"

"Even the marriage."

Leanna groaned and fell back into the pillow.

"Chill." He inhaled and rounded his fingers, inviting her to breathe along. "We don't need another panic attack."

True. Her chest ached enough.

She dared to smile, and her worries lessened their grip. His calm presence worked against the frenzy building in her insides. The leaf shadows flickered against the walls and began to fall into an easy sway, as if lulled by the serenity of the room.

"What did they say?"

"Well," he puffed his cheeks running a hand over the back of his head. "After they put their eyes back in their head, it went, well, it went okay. I guess."

"You guess?"

"I mean, they think we're crazy, but we already knew that, right?" His smile was sideways. He stood and bit at his thumbnail.

"Did you tell them about…about…you know?"

"The deal?" Those words made part of her soul wince. He nodded and sat on the footstool, head lowered.   Garrison sighed, then stood, hands deep in the pockets of his pants. "That's the part they took the hardest."

She figured. But they weren't their judge. These situations are complicated, and sometimes divorce can't be avoided.

"Lee," Garrison said. "Why can't we stay together?"

"Because we had a deal. Because too much has happened between us."

Because I'm too proud to forgive, and too scared to love you again. The thought pierced her heart.

The discussion ended, and silence filled the room.

She followed his gaze as his eyes skimmed over the pieces of art hanging on the wall. Custom paintings and pencil sketches she'd created throughout the years. A decrepit barn, a swirl of bright colors and patterns at odds, and actual bent and reshaped antique silverware. Each piece added a unique eclectic flare to the homestead décor of the room.

His body shifted to the side as he turned. "That one's my favorite." He nodded toward the largest piece over the mantle. A circle of holding hands near the lakeside. A photograph she'd enlarged, smudged, outlined, and texturized. Dad helped to craft the frame from pieces of old barn wood taken from out back.

The summer she'd turned sixteen. A summer of firsts.

Garrison smiled. "Your mom wanted the picture. You all circled up…"

"Then Dad yelled for you and Tiff to join in. William snapped the picture." Mom and Dad made everyone feel a part of their family.

"All of us camped out that night near the treehouse. Remember?"

She nodded. Her face warmed. Seven years had not erased the memory of her and Garrison, and how that first kiss felt.

The last perfect summer.

Leanna shrugged. "Thank you."

"For?"

"Where do I start?" She huffed a grin. He'd gone above and beyond the call of duty. "For starters, you kept me out of jail today."

"You'd never survive behind bars." He nudged her knee with an elbow, his grin growing more crooked by the second. "A wildcat has to be free."

She rolled her eyes but didn't try to hide her smile. "Being back here changes me. I'm someone totally different in New York. Refined, smart, elegant, skies the limit..." She lowered her head at the sound of her confession. All those things were true, until her relationship with William soured.

"You're all those things here too, Lee." He leaned forward, face pinched.

"Here I'm just some redneck girl from the hills, looking for a fight."

"There's nothing wrong with being from here, or—" his Adam's apple dipped— "giving your life to serve others, like your parents did."

The words stung. No, nothing wrong with a life of service, but to undeserving people in the community who seemed more like leeches, than someone working to better their situation? Yet, how was she any different? Allowing William to act as her financial host even after breaking off the relationship. A leech—she too was a leech undeserving of anything, yet, so much grace, love, and kindness was offered by many. She nodded and tucked part of her bottom lip under her teeth.

Leanna buried her face in her hands, then raised her head to Garrison. His eyes, they cared so much. "Thanks for holding me earlier. I must've looked like such an idiot. I...I didn't mean to fall apart like that."

"You needed to."

She pressed her lips together. "And thank you for praying."

"I wasn't sure what else to do. Should've been the first thing I did."

They sat. Leanna tugged on pieces of the quilt. Neither mentioned Brie or what their future, no matter how short, would hold. Perhaps he remained as uncertain as she?

Garrison rested his elbows on his knees. His T-shirt stretched tight across his broad back. Leanna averted her eyes.

"You're going through a lot right now." He rubbed the back of his head. "I don't know if loss ever stops hurting." Garrison gazed at the floor beneath his feet. "And I don't think you ever stop missing them. I mean, I wouldn't want to." His voice grew soft, thoughtful even. "But at some point, the tears go away, and you smile again. You learn there are so many reasons to live, and...love." He moved closer, his eyes now focused on her. Leanna swallowed. His face, so serious, so caring. "Sometimes living and loving again looks different from what you ever imagined."

She nodded, unable to speak, wanting to believe the best in him, that everything would work out. Could she dare to dream again, smile, laugh, and love? Even with Brie taken away?

She lifted her chin. There had been smiles since her parents' deaths, glimmers of hope, but...

She let her chin fall. "It seems unfair to laugh again. To love. To even move on." Leanna scooted and inched herself from the bed's embrace and into an upright position. She gathered her knees to her chest.

Garrison nodded. "It seemed that way to me for a long time."

"And now?"

"And now." He tilted his head. "It's like living in hope, and not just wishing for it."

What did that mean? She squinted and pressed her back into the headboard.

"For the first time in a long time, I'm doing that—living in hope. So I should be thanking you, and our crazy lives." He grinned.

Garrison paused, and several beats passed. "Do you miss him?"

William.

"Not at all." The quick answer slammed against her. "What does that say about me?"

"It says you're being honest with yourself."

The real question: how long had she been lying? She sighed and ran a hand through her messy up-do. "I've always had plans, and seen them through. Achieved my goals, and nothing ever got in my way."

"You mean you've always had to be in control."

Yes. Control. It felt secure and warm as the quilt in her hands, but in reality, what could she control? Leanna wet her lips. "Getting my life back on track has started off rocky and on a path that's pretty unclear."

"That's the only kind worth taking." Garrison laid an open hand on the bed at her feet.

She stretched, and placed her hand in his. It became easier to do, almost natural.

CHAPTER EIGHTEEN

IT WAS LATE Sunday night when Garrison crossed the tracks. He had made sure Lee, Ezra, and Aunt Mary were asleep. He had a plan.

Garrison pushed back a yawn. After the day he'd endured first at the courthouse, watching Brie walk away, and then holding Lee while she fell apart, this task seemed a lot easier to deal with.

His truck idled in front of the rundown trailer, and he thought better of knocking at the door this late. Could be dangerous in these parts. But it couldn't be helped. He crossed the yard, and knocked.

A small end window lit up, and before long, the curtain in the doorway was pushed aside.

Garrison waved, and Cindy opened the door.

Her eyes were sad and heavy.

"I think I know a way to help us all out. And I think you want that too."

She nodded, and Dale stood at her side, rubbing sleep from his eyes.

"You guys up for a move?"

They offered a sidelong glance and invited him in.

This had to work.

***

"Lee." Garrison squeezed her palm in his. "Lee, wake up."

She stirred, hair a mess, lying in the same clothes she'd worn yesterday, but still breathtaking. His wife. Garrison swallowed and focused. "Lee, we need to talk."

She sighed and worked herself into a half-sitting position, eyes still asleep.

"Lee, you're going to get Brie back."

Her face scrunched. She rubbed a hand over her forehead as she woke up.

"She's on her way over now."

Leanna jolted from the bed. Her bare feet planted on the hardwood floor with more force than he expected. "How?"

Garrison stood, hands in his pockets. He rocked back on his heels. "Cindy and Dale are moving into Aunt Mary's house. Brie will be next door now."

She jumped, wrapping her arms around Garrison's neck. In all the excitement, her lips skimmed across his. A current rushed throughout his body. Leanna stumbled back. Silence pushed its way in. Light played across her face with no indication of embarrassment. No shock. No uncertainty. He knew what he wanted. Her.

Leanna gathered herself, smoothed out the wrinkles from her skirt and blouse.

The corner of Garrison's mouth lifted. "Let's get some food in you, and I'm sure Ez is ready to work on the campsite already."

She nodded.

One thing for sure, that accidental kiss felt nothing like the peck on the cheek used to seal their vows.

Garrison rubbed a hand over his mouth. Leanna rushed in front of him, down the hall, and disappeared into the kitchen.

That thing. That spark. She'd felt it too. How could she not? Why else would she hurry away?

He hadn't planned on falling for her this fast, but now...he welcomed the fall.

Garrison made his way to the living room, boots clicking on the hardwood floors with each step. He eyed his wedding band, then smoothed his hand over his head and smiled. Somehow, some way, he'd reach her. He'd win her heart, and nothing would stop him.

Nothing but a deployment? Garrison shook his head. Nine months away from her. From Ez. And there was always the possibility of never returning. Tiff had worried herself sick before each deployment. His stomach turned.

A breeze trailing from the front porch passed through the window screen. It played in the living room curtains and carried Ez and Aunt Mary's laughter. Garrison shouldered his worried thoughts aside.

Aunt Mary was good today. Bright-eyed, remembering most things.

"King me, again." Ez's voice squeaked, floating through the window screen.

Garrison stepped over to the window and leaned his forearm on the ledge, careful not to be seen.

"You're getting too good for me, young man." Aunt Mary folded her hands in her lap and rocked in the rocking chair.

"I'm gonna teach Brie my battle strategy when she gets here."

Ha. Battle strategy. Spoken like a military child. Garrison held in a laugh. Ez focused on the checkerboard, his tongue peeping from his lips.

Aunt Mary chuckled. She leaned over the board, glancing at the pieces and then up at Ez. "Aren't you afraid she'll beat you once you give your secrets away?"

"Nah." Ez crinkled his nose. So much like Tiff. "Just makes the game better. You can't be afraid to even the playing field."

Garrison nodded. A lesson Aunt Mary had taught him as a child, one he'd forgotten to apply to his own life until of late. A lesson he'd strived to instill in Ez. It worked. What a boy. Tiff would be proud.

"Smart of you, young man." Aunt Mary's eyes danced as she ruffled Ez's wild hair. "Whenever you get a chance to make things fair and right, always do so."

A chance to make things right. Garrison let his sight gaze past the front porch, over the tree-covered hills in the distance. He'd made things right with Tiff. A rocky marriage, built on a have-to situation. Ez and Aunt Mary's chatter dulled in his ears. No, he hadn't loved Tiff at first, and she knew it—felt it, for years. But he evened the playing field, chose to love her, built a relationship, and they were happy. A bright future ahead, until...

Garrison pressed his forehead to the back of his hand. He closed his eyes.

Tiff would want him to move on, love again, and provide a wonderful mother for Ez, but with Lee?

He pinched the bridge of his nose. Tiff loved Lee. Loved her like a sister, but it didn't stop the jealousy. Lee, his first love, the one he wanted to marry. Garrison's stomach twisted. He forced his eyes open. Why did his boldness to love Lee waver? One moment ready to pursue her for life, the next terrified to do so?

He pushed from the window edge. Best get the campsite ready while daylight remained.

"I got a new mom."

Garrison stopped, his heart thudded at almost deafening volume as he reached for the door handle.

"How do you feel about that?" Aunt Mary's tone held no hint of surprise.

Garrison pressed himself close to the wall, intent on hearing, perhaps fearing the worst response.

Checker pieces clicked together.

"I don't think she knows it yet, but Ms. Leanna is going to be a great mom." Ez continued. "Brie thinks so too."

Ez, the most optimistic child in the world.

"Is that so?" Aunt Mary's laugh carried a slight wheeze—an aging sound.

"That's right. She told me so."

Garrison held his heart in place. *Brie talks. To Ez.*

"Well, that is something."

"She's told me a lot of things."

The breaking news kept coming.

"Like what?" Aunt Mary said.

"Like they were coming home from her Aunt Cindy and Uncle Dale's house the night they crashed."

"Oh. That is news."

Did he dare interrupt their conversation? Garrison reached for the doorknob.

"No. Wait." A whisper.

He turned to see Leanna near the living room entryway, eyes wide. How long had she been there?

Leanna poised a finger over her mouth, making a quiet shush. He let his hand fall to his side. Gravel cracked and pop. An engine came closer to the house.

"They're here." Ez's voice grew loud. Chairs scooted on the front porch.

Garrison froze. He kept his eyes locked with hers. She broke their stare and ran past him through the front door. She bound from the porch toward the drive, arms open. Garrison followed behind, keeping his distance, propped on the porch railing.

The reunion scene unfolded, and he found it difficult to look away. Pure joy on Lee and Brie's faces. Ez's too. Even Cindy seemed moved.

Funny how life unfolded. Aunt Cindy, by coming, had offered an olive branch. Brave. Sometimes peace treaties worked. Then again, sometimes, like in the case of him and his father, only a ceasefire could be arranged.

"Something to see, huh?" Aunt Mary slid her frail arm under his and locked at the elbow.

Garrison nodded, lips pursed.

"Let's hope she heard all the conversation, like you did."

He flinched. Aunt Mary knew he heard—knew Lee had been there too?

"I may be old and senile, but my hearing hasn't gone yet."

"Ha." Garrison kissed Aunt Mary on top of her silver head.

"I'm rooting for the two of you." She squeezed his arm.

"Me too."

"And no matter the conflict inside you..." He couldn't hide any strife from Aunt Mary, ever. She laid a hand over his. "You know where to find peace and guidance through the storm."

It wasn't a question, but a statement. A fact. The peace, the answers, would come from God, and God alone.

Garrison nodded. "I talked to Him today."

"That's the place to start."

"And the next step?"

"His Word, young man." She smiled. The wrinkles on her face only added to her wisdom and gentle spirit. Proof of decades filled with God's unfailing presence and provision in her life, come what may. This could be his life too, if he'd allow.

Yes, he'd allow.

CHAPTER NINETEEN

THE FLAMES DANCED higher among the stack of crackling logs. Soft glowing embers raced upward and faded from sight. The perfect night. Brie was back. The world was right, but Ez's confession to Aunt Mary created more thoughts and questions to occupy her mind. Brie talked to Ez. And Brie had been with Mom and Dad at Cindy and Dale's house. Why? From her understanding their relationship had been severed at Cindy and Dale's request.

Leanna shoved the thoughts aside and rotated a marshmallow on the end of a stick until the edges began to brown, just the way Brie preferred. She yanked it from the heat and blew out a small flame. A sliver of smoke swirled into the evening sky. Faint flashes of lightning lit up the clouds on the horizon. No thunder, just evidence of a storm miles away. Beautiful to watch.

"Here ya go, honeybee." Leanna slid the gooey mound onto a graham cracker, careful not to entangle her fingers. "I can't believe you don't like chocolate on your s'more."

But it was good to learn these new things about Brie.

"More for me." Ez chomped down on Brie's portion of the chocolate bar, cheeks a sticky mess. Leanna laughed aloud.

Garrison shook his head. A smile, much like the curve of the crescent moon, strung across his face. "Good thing vegetarians can eat dessert."

Leanna threw a marshmallow at him. He caught it with one hand and popped it into his mouth. Such a pig. She rolled her eyes but smiled. "I just eat the chocolate. Marshmallows may have pig and horse ingredients."

"Eww." Ez spit the marshmallow onto the ground, wiping his tongue with the bottom of his shirt. Brie giggled, and Leanna's heart jumped.

"Well by all means then, toss me another." Garrison threw his head back and Leanna launched the marshmallows in his direction. He caught each of them in his mouth. The man couldn't miss. "Mmm, pig. Mmm, horse."

The kids' laughter echoed all around. Silly giggles that caused them to double over. How beautiful Brie was, laughing along. Her eyes did more than dance.

Leanna soaked in the moment. Strange how full her heart felt. How right this scene seemed to unfold, like living in hope. Garrison's earlier statement found meaning in her heart.

"C'mon, Brie." Ez hopped to his feet and darted toward the tree house.

"Be careful, guys." Garrison strained his neck. "That thing's old." Ez waved at his warning. Such a cautious dad. Caring. Funny how his rough upbringing pushed him in an opposite direction.

Brie hopped to her feet. She had their mother's eyes, their father's square chin. A real mix, while Leanna bore all recessive genes, other than her mother's creamy skin tone. For a moment, Brie's lips parted, and Leanna braced herself to hear the sweet sound of her sister's voice. Nothing. Nothing came. Brie nodded, and lowered her lashes as she followed behind Ez.

Time was healing, and soon, she and her sister would be close again.

What would Brie talk with Ez about tonight? Leanna couldn't be upset, but why hadn't she come to her yet? And what if the courts took Brie's inability to talk as some signal to take her away forever?

At least she was in counseling. Pastor Jay allowed her to color during their time together instead of talk. Small steps.

Leanna rocked to her side and crossed her ankles. She flicked a pebble from the ground, sending it rolling past the campfire. Garrison swatted at the small stone and gazed back up at the tree house.

Clouds overhead parted, revealing an array of stars sure to put Van Gogh's rendition to shame. Up on the hill, the guest bedroom light clicked off. Aunt Mary prepared for bed.

"You sure it's okay if Aunt Mary moves in too? Ginger will be with her." Garrison nodded toward the house. "She can wake up disoriented. Never know what decade she'll be in." The corner of his mouth lifted, then fell.

Dementia humor. She shouldn't smile. Leanna pinched her lips between her thumb.

She sat straight. "I can help look after her, and Ginger. The kids love Aunt Mary and the dog."

"Look at you, serving others like your mom and dad."

"I. I." She was nothing like them. Who knew if that was a good or bad thing? Mostly a bad thing for sure. Her parents were saints.

"I never thought about it when I was younger, but it must've been hard for you growing up with Mr. & Mrs. Wilson always opening up their home to everyone." Garrison rubbed a knuckle over his bottom lip. "Gone all the time, serving the community, dragging you around with them. I always assumed you wanted to be there working with them. Did you?"

Leanna set her jaw. She swallowed the tightness creeping up her throat. No. She hadn't wanted to tag along.

"You never really had a lot of alone time with them, huh?"

She folded her arms over her knees. Garrison's words twisted deep, at an uncomfortable depth, and stabbed at some dark place inside she'd almost forgotten existed.

She gathered her thoughts and ran a hand along the length of her ponytail resting over her shoulder. "Some parents are gone every night running their kids here and there, or working a hundred hours a week." She dragged her teeth over her bottom lip. "We were always a family, always together, it's just …" She focused on the flames as if they could cauterize emotions. "Everyone was our family. Sometimes others had needs greater than mine…ours." She shrugged. "Being selfless was kind of ingrained in us." Until it morphed into resentment, discontentment, and rebellion.

The fire cracked and popped. Laughter floated from the gaps in the walls of the tree house as the kids wielded their flashlights. Garrison tossed a few twigs into the flames and fanned away moths. Leanna twisted her hair around her fingers and rested her chin on her knees. Her wedding band glowed under the light of the campfire. She closed her eyes and listened to the lull of the rural melody.

"I'm glad you want Aunt Mary to stay with you while I'm gone, but know her condition won't get better." Garrison's voice forced her head up. He sprawled on his side on the ground, pulling up blades of grass. They bent between his fingers. He tossed one into the fire. It withered before hitting the flames. "Ez has baseball practice, piano lessons. School starts in a little over a month."

Leanna's head spun. Brie would start back soon, too. No way was she ready to go to school, especially if she wasn't talking to anyone but Ez.

The glow of the fire highlighted the beaded chain peeping from Garrison's shirt collar. Dog tags. Her heart stopped. "I'm an Army wife." The words slipped past her lips in an almost whisper.

She couldn't interpret much from the pinched expression on his face, but it looked as befuddled as she felt.

Neither responded to the statement. No need. It was too big to process. What did being an Army wife entail? Or any sort of wife, or a mother? She let her head fall to her shoulder. All of these questions she should've considered more thoroughly before marriage. Too late now. Tomorrow she and Garrison would sort out all the fine details of what the next year or so of their life would hold. Oh, what fun that conversation would be. Lessons in marriage: Compromise 101. Ugh. Leanna cradled her chin on a fist.

She scanned the area, anything to switch the gears in her mind.

Lightning bugs put on a show with no signs of stopping, and in the distance, a lone figure walked the riverbank. Aunt Cindy kept her distance. She stared out over the river as if lost in thought. That happened easily enough these days. Too many thoughts to get lost in. Perhaps after the kids fell asleep, she and Cindy could talk, or Leanna could at least listen.

Leanna drew in a slow breath and pushed it out as she folded her legs to the side. Grass tickled at her ankles.

Despite the craziness of the day, the week...ha, her life… the rest of the evening played out like a sweet song. She closed her eyes. Crickets strummed a nearby tune. Frogs from the river chimed in. The water added its own soothing melody. The tune, familiar as a childhood lullaby, differed from the incessant horn honks and engine sounds of New York. She had frequented Central Park and found solace in the rural surroundings, often contemplating climbing high in the trees. No sophisticated person would ever do such a thing, so she stayed put, on the ground with William at her side. He didn't care much for the park. Nor for art. Nor for anything else she liked, but then again, she was someone else with him.

She tilted her head, turning her attention to the flames and their angles, but through the fire, Garrison stared. That look again. Serious, focused, and intent. She couldn't turn from him, nor did she try.

No. She couldn't fall for him. Wouldn't fall. This thing, whatever they were, expired whenever he returned from deployment—end of their story.

But what if he didn't return?

Leanna's face warmed. The thought brought tears to her eyes.

Garrison cleared his throat. "So what's New York like?"

Leanna forced a grin shoving the grim thoughts of war from her thoughts. Her mind flooded with off-the-wall shops, historical landmarks, and the sounds of a city that never slept. "A place you'd like."

"Excellent description. As long as there's pizza, I'm sold."

"You're in luck."

Garrison toyed with bits and pieces of sticks. He snapped a few more and laid them on top of one another in a grid-like fashion. He called out toward the tree house, "Game of tic tac toe, anyone?"

"Can we swim instead?" Ez poked his head from the doorway and crinkled his nose. Goodness, he resembled Tiff. Sounded like her too.

Garrison pointed to the makeshift game board equipped with rocks and snail shells for game pieces. "Tic-tac-toe is way cooler than swimming at night."

"Nice try." Leanna huffed a short laugh. "No one's buying that."

"Aw, c'mon." Ez's voice squeaked an octave higher. "You said you used to do it."

"That's different." Garrison's tone hardened.

Leanna frowned. "I didn't know you could ever be a dud."

He rolled his eyes, much more like something she'd do than he.

Ez huffed and folded his arms. "We never get to go swimming anymore."

"It could be fun." Leanna rocked back into an upright sitting position. "We've still got the old swinging rope up."

Garrison's expression tightened. He licked his lips. "I said no, Ez. It's safer in the daytime."

Leanna's stomach knotted. Garrison's face had filled with fear. Fear that Ez would drown like Tiff. Leanna pushed herself up and walked over to sit at his side. She held out a hand and waited.

He placed his palm in hers.

"Life jackets are in the shed." She squeezed once. "I'm sure Dad's got some of those big ole' spot lights in there too. We can light up this whole place."

Garrison swallowed.

"It's okay." Leanna squeezed again.

"I can't." He ducked his head. "Not right now. Not tonight."

"It's been—"

"I know how long it's been." His voice strained. "Please don't push this. Not now."

Leanna pursed her lips. She gave a short nod and squeezed his hand once more. "Tic-tac-toe it is then."

***

What a wimp. How weak he must've seemed to Lee. Garrison smacked a hand against his forehead. He lay on his back, peering up at the tree house roof, listening to the sleeping sounds of his family. Ez and Brie lay cuddled close between him and Lee. Her arm rested across their little bodies, her slim fingers inches from his. The early glow of the horizon seeped through the wooden slats. His eyelids hung half-mast, but sleep escaped him.

He should've let Ez swim. He should've jumped in first. Instead, he'd let fear get the best of him and put a huge damper on the rest of the evening.

129

Some way to start off winning Lee's heart.

But Tiff died in the dark.

Her bloated body — Garrison sat up and threw the thought from his mind. He sucked in a deep breath and carefully maneuvered up and over his family — his new family. Fresh air called.

The ladder creaked under his weight. Garrison held tight to the wooden slats, rough edges and all, as he made his way down. He planted his feet onto the dew covered grass and filled his lungs with the crisp morning air. Fog hovered over the river and drifted over the treetops. How had he ever dreamed of escaping this place and the beauty of these hills?

He lifted his eyes to the tree house. He'd wake them up soon. Maybe make breakfast. Scramble some eggs — that he could do pretty well. Did vegetarians eat eggs? Garrison shrugged a shoulder and rounded the tree, moving a low-lying branch from his path when he saw it. The initials. Their initials, G & L, encased in an etched out heart. Still there after all these years.

He'd found someone to look after Ez while he deployed. Found someone to love again, but it was the same someone he always wanted to love — to marry. His first choice. Did that lessen what he and Tiff had built?

Garrison raked his fingers over his head and blew out a burst of air.

Leanna woke. She stared at him, a million questions in her eyes.

He answered them in his mind. *No I won't leave you. Yes, this marriage is real. You're more than a deal.*

She closed her eyes as if unwilling to hear his heart.

He sighed, their gaze now disconnected. Maybe the walls around her heart were too tall to jump, but not too high to scale.

CHAPTER TWENTY

EARLY MORNING LIGHT played through the off-white lacey curtains, and Leanna watched as a few birds played a game of tag outside. She rested in the corner chair of the living room and gathered a pillow into her lap. Sleeping bags, and empty bags of marshmallows, graham crackers and chocolate bars littered the living room floor—remnants of a night of camping. A wonderful night. Brie was home.

Familiar kitchen sounds of plates, forks, and the sizzle of bacon widened her smile, and brought comfort to her heart. Sounds of home. The aroma of fresh brewed coffee filled the air. Aunt Mary had outdone herself. Leanna sat up, and rubbed her eyes.

"Good morning."

Garrison's voice gave her a start. He stood in the doorway, crooked grin on his face, and a plate in his hand. "Hungry?"

"You made breakfast?"

"Surprised?"

"Kind of."

"It's not breakfast in bed, but...breakfast on the couch?" He laughed at his own joke and covered the length of the floor in two strides. "Don't worry about the stuff on the floor. The kids and I will cleanup."

"Nice." Leanna pushed back a yawn and patted down her hair. She crossed folded her legs under, and reached for the plate. It was beautiful. Fresh fruit, and a veggie egg-white scramble. "Wow." She eyed the picture worthy dish. "Thank you."

"I'm hoping you eat eggs."

She nodded, still absorbed in the meal. "You cut the strawberry like a rose?"

"You're into art." He sat on the ottoman in front of her. "Figured you'd appreciate food art."

She stared at him and then back at the plate.

"Eat." He rested his forearms on his knees. "Coffee will be out in a minute."

"The kids?"

"Already ate."

"Of course they have. Probably outside playing." Kids had endless energy. Hers was dependent on, well, maybe sleep and coffee?

"Aunt Mary's with them on the back porch…teaching them how to make slime." He quirked an eyebrow. "That'll be fun to cleanup."

"Good memories though." Aunt Mary had taught her, Tiff, and Garrison how to make slime. The gooiest kind.

"I've got to go into work for a bit, but will be back around lunch time." Garrison scratched at the dark stubble on his jaw that only accented his green eyes. Her pulse raced, and she tore her eyes away.

Leanna lifted a bite of the scramble to her mouth. The savory combination melted her taste buds. "Oh my goodness." It was delicious. Was there anything this man couldn't do? Defend the nation, raise his son, come to her aid, and cook. She took another bite and watched as his face lit up. "Garrison, this is seriously the best thing I've ever eaten."

The man was near perfect. And here she was, someone like her, married to him. Leanna lowered her lashes, and pushed the food to the side of her mouth. A glint hinted in his expression, and she paused, the realization too obvious to ignore. Garrison was working to win her heart. She couldn't let him. She chewed slow and swallowed.

"Everything okay?"

No. Everything was not okay. Eventually she'd end this marriage, and hurt him. Entangling their hearts only made things more difficult.

"If it's about last night, I'm sorry, I uh, I get a little worked up when Ez is around water."

"No, really. I can't imagine what that must be like for you."

He cleared his throat, and grinned, but the smile couldn't hide the sadness in his eyes. Leanna fought the urge to reach for him, to help or console him in some way, just a fraction of how he worked to care for her.

"So, um," Garrison said. "Figured I'd help Cindy and Dale get moved in later today."

Them. Leanna held her fork a bit tighter.

"Lee, I think they really want to help. I mean, they're leaving their home so you and Brie can be together."

"They're jumping at an opportunity to get out of the slums."

"And what's so wrong with that?"

She stiffened, fork glued to her hand. What was so wrong with that? Garrison grew up in the same area with limited opportunities.

"It's a win, win for everyone."

He was right. Again. Grr.

"Anyway, Pastor Jay, and my Army buddy, Nelson will be helping out. Got any plans for the day?"

She shrugged. "Not really other than digging through my parents' file. Going over to The Scoop later. Guess I can help move too."

"Sounds like a plan. Cindy and Dale will like that."

Leanna hid a frown.

Garrison stood. His back gave a pop. "I don't remember sleeping in the tree house ever hurting this bad." His crooked grin lightened the mood. "Not even thirty and already aching."

"Guess the Army will do that to you." She'd never asked about his career, or any of his deployments for that matter. Might be painful to discuss. He stood with his back to her, one thumb in his belt loop. She hoped his uniform had loops for his thumbs. Leanna smiled and continued to eat savoring each bite. He scanned the living room from one end to the other, until his gaze landed on the far wall. Without a word he walked to the old piano, dragged out the bench, and took a seat.

"It still works." Leanna tucked her chin and lowered it into the pillow. The fibers brushed across her nose. Garrison lifted the lid and slid his fingers along the keys. Leanna pressed her lips together. Did he remember all the songs they'd sung? How the family had gathered around? How Mom and Dad danced to his tunes? Garrison flipped through sheets of music he never learned to read. He only played by ear.

"Sing for me, Lee?"

Did he still believe one could sing away a worry. Problems didn't go away at will.

"Please." He glanced over his shoulder.

Maybe he needed her to sing. Not to make a problem disappear, but to lighten the journey.

Leanna rose, arms folded.

His fingers, long and lean, found their place amongst the rows of ebony and ivory. First soft and low, then the familiar tune rose.

She rubbed the chill bumps from her arms and tucked a lock of hair behind her shoulder. Of course this song. The one he'd played for their entire family, and then again when they had stolen moments alone. It held dual meanings, he once told her. She huffed and rolled her eyes. "Still playing old songs."

"The new ones lack depth."

Leanna lifted a brow. Her art professor had said the same things about her work. Rotten old man. "There's nothing wrong with the new ones."

"I think there's a problem when things are written to sell and not for the soul."

Leanna flinched, a protest caught in her throat. Yet he made sense. So maybe her work lacked a smidgen of depth or soul. Whatever. This wasn't art class anyway.

He stared ahead, not needing to look at the keys.

She inched forward and bumped his shoulder with her elbow. "There's a saying about living in the past, you know?"

"And there's plenty to say about the present songs that skip from one trendy, fast, computer mash-up to the other. No class or technique."

Ha. Class. Leanna caught her laugh. Such talk coming from Garrison, the backwoods boy who used to sneer at school work. He'd always loved music, but to hear him talk about it like this… no, she never had before. Her face warmed.

Garrison played on and swayed a bit to the melody. "To be honest, little true talent exists in the mainstream today. Though some newer artists impress me." He held up an index finger while the other hand continued to play. "But it's only because they incorporate musical elements from the past."

Leanna wet her lips and sighed. "Maybe they've found a middle ground."

"I'd say they have." He offered a sly smile over his shoulder and never missed a note.

"We're talking about music, right?"

"What else could we possibly be talking about?" Garrison threw a wink in her direction. Arrogant man. Leanna bumped his shoulder once more.

Maybe a middle ground existed for her art. For her future— a mix between backwoods and city? What about a middle ground for her and Garrison?

He glanced back around with a playful smile stretched across his face. "Now sing."

Leanna grimaced and tilted her head. Really, did he think he could boss her around?

"Please."

"Fine." Her stomach knotted. Stage fright. Performance jitters. Leanna shook her hands out. She swallowed, and closed her eyes. The room stilled, and the calm came. As if her parents were alive, and Brie talked non-stop.

As if she'd never hated Garrison or Tiffany, or even left home.

Just sing.

The words came. They pulled from a distant memory, and took on a new life, a new meaning. Stand By Me. Sung by Ben E. King.

Leanna continued to sing, the words massaging her heart. But her parents *were* gone. And Brie *wouldn't* talk—to her. And she had hated Garrison and Tiffany. Maybe still hated? No. No. Not now. Oh, why had she not forgiven both of them sooner? Hate had fueled her flight from home. Her chest tightened, but the words pushed forward. Leanna's eyes stung. She let a tear free fall.

Garrison's baritone voice blended with hers. A familiar sound that caused her heart to ache.

Chill bumps raced up her arms and down her back. She kept her eyes closed and kept singing. No, their problems hadn't disappeared, but the journey seemed much lighter sharing a song — this song. Their song.

The music stopped.

Garrison scooted from the bench, and his eyes met hers. Leanna swallowed but didn't move as he closed the distance between them. He held out a hand and bowed with a smile. "May I have this dance?"

Leanna ran her fingers down the non-existent wrinkles in her T-shirt, then along the sides of her sweatpants. She must've looked a mess. No makeup.

As if it had a mind of its own, her hand lifted and slid into his. His arm snaked around her waist, then found a home at the small of her back. She held her breath. Better not to breathe than to make some crazy embarrassing gasp. He pulled her tight against his body, and she held onto his shoulder, fingertips dancing across the back of his neck and over the beaded edges of his dog tags.

Garrison took the lead, left foot first. She followed his step, mouth dry, and still unable to breathe. Did he feel her heart? Or hear it?

He lowered his head and pressed his cheek to hers. He hummed first, then sang. She allowed one breath then sucked it in again as he lowered her in a slight dip. He never missed a beat.

This man...her husband. Tingles from her head to her toes...

Leanna stopped, frozen, and rigid in his arms.

She couldn't do this. Not now. No, they were only a deal. She forced her eyes shut.

"Lee?" His kind tone begged her eyes to open. His nose hovered millimeters from hers. Lips closer. "I can love you. Let me love you. Give us a chance to be more than our past — our regrets."

Tears bit at the corners of her eyes. He offered a future she never imagined to exist, a future she never considered. A future without the big city lights, and a high profile career that proved she'd succeeded — made something of herself. Yet she couldn't deny what Garrison offered...felt, well, did she dare say, full and good and right?

But how?

She shook her head. "I want…" She managed to clear her throat. "We want different things."

"You're wrong." Nothing harsh echoed in his voice. He cradled her jawline in the palm of one hand. "Let me love you."

Leanna released her breath. A small sound escaped her mouth as her shoulders slumped. Her mind screamed yes, yet her mouth refused to open. She only stared, terrified her pounding heart betrayed her.

A slight smile played on his face as his eyes searched hers. What did he see? Whatever he found must've caused his smile to fade. "I'm scared too."

She winced at his confession. Garrison, scared? Maybe for Ez's safety, but in pursuit of her heart? He seemed the opposite of fearful.

"We can be scared together." His thumb smoothed across her cheek. "But let me love you, and—" He leaned in—"consider the possibility of loving me. You can choose to love me."

"I." *I want to choose you.* Her mouth parted. She wanted to?

Footsteps sounded. She pulled from his embrace as a frail but giddy voice called from the hall. "Please play Christmas songs." Aunt Mary shuffled toward them, her hands clasped around a mound of red slime. Her eyes smiled.

Leanna and Garrison shared a glance, then shrugged in unison. Their moment, and whatever electricity had filled the room, dissipated, yet a spark remained. Leanna placed a hand over her heart as if to snuff out the ember, but it refused. No, she'd choose to let it stay. For now.

"Christmas songs it is." Garrison lowered his head and plopped back down at the piano. His shoulders hovered over the keys and he swung into a spirited version of "We Three Kings."

Aunt Mary danced along. Precious woman. "I love Christmastime," she sang out.

Leanna watched Aunt Mary pet Garrison's head as he played. A grin, as content a one as Leanna had ever seen, grew on the woman's face. And Garrison, so willing to please her, no matter her condition. What more could Leanna want in a husband? Loyal. Loving. A man who owned up to his mistakes and did the right thing, no matter how difficult the choice. A man who wanted her, to love her, to be her husband. He had prayed with her, for her…

Leanna tugged at the hem of her T-shirt. She needed to apologize to him once more. To put their hurts behind and grow together. Yes, she could love him. Already loved him? Her heart thudded faster. No. She pushed the thought aside.

Brie and Ez peeked from behind the doorway, unable to hide their giggling presence.

Leanna waved them over, setting her inner chaos aside for the moment. They joined in, pulling and looping their own globs of red slime between their hands. The living room was filled with laughter, camping gear, red slime, and the sounds of Christmas music in summer. She stepped back, arms folded, taking in the hilarity of the scene. Mom and Dad would've joined in, singing right along, dancing too. Even Tiff would've taken part.

"C'mon." Ez yanked on her arm. Leanna groaned, but Ez kept at it and hung from the other arm.

Leanna hunched under the weight of Ez's attempts to draw her in, and Brie's pleading face.

Why not have some fun?

"You win." Leanna tickled his sides and belted along. She sang louder and swung Ez and Brie up and around — the few swing dance moves she remembered from way back when. Leanna flaunted jazz hands. Brie and Ez mimicked her motion.

"Where you going?" Leanna called out over the bellowing piano.

"We need a Christmas tree." Aunt Mary shrugged, hands out to her side.

Leanna laughed out loud. "Good idea."

CHAPTER TWENTY-ONE

GRASS SCRATCHED HER ankles and fell beneath her feet. Leanna stared ahead and kept walking the length of the field. She toyed with her ring. Married. What would the town say? Pastor Jay nor Macy had said much today, but then again, helping Cindy and Dale move took up a lot of time. And Leanna may or may not have presented herself too busy to talk.

"You worked hard today moving all those boxes." Garrison walked at her side.

Her stomach pinched. "Excited to have Brie back."

"Cindy and Dale seemed appreciative."

Leanna nodded, lips drawn. "Your Army friend was kind. Nelson?"

"Good guy." And for a moment Garrison's eyes were distant, looking further than the field. "Been through a lot together."

"Deployed together before?"

He gave a slow nod, but offered no other information, nor would she pry.

"You, um, know what date you'll be leaving?"

He shook his head. "Just a time frame." He bent plucking a weed and waved it at his side.

"You know," he rubbed the back of his head, and halted. Leanna turned toward him. His eyes appeared sad. "If, if something happens to me while I'm gone —"

"Don't say that."

"I need to know Ez will be okay. That Aunt Mary will be cared for."

Leanna folded her arms and followed his lead through the field and past the old barn.

Storm clouds threatened in the distance. No shade to shield them out in the open field, but no matter, Leanna welcomed the warmth. She drank in the sunshine, letting it dry her eyes, then exhaled. The thought of Garrison deploying was hard enough, but to consider him never returning... unimaginable.

He turned for a moment, revealing tight lines stretched across his forehead. His mouth opened then closed. He shook his head. "I'm serious. If something—"

"I'll take care of them both. Forever."

Garrison smoothed a hand over the back of his head. "It can get a bit rough over there, but we train hard. The last time—"

"You don't have to talk about this, any of it, you know."

"I want to." He kept walking, eyes on nothing specific, as far as she could tell. "The town thinks I'm some wounded warrior now."

"Are you?"

He smirked. "War changes a person for sure. But wounded? Maybe."

She listened, shoulder bumping against his on occasion.

"I like to think that any wounds I have help me to grow stronger, and help me to help others along the way. Like Nelson. Like the young ones deploying with us."

"You helped Nelson?" Leanna pulled her hair over her shoulder and tucked a hand in the back pocket of her jeans.

"We've helped each other." Garrison sighed. "The last deployment, well, it's hard when civilians are killed. Kids, and women. Babies. It's, it's not easy to deal with."

Leanna shuddered at the thoughts.

"Nelson had a hard time coping afterward. Guess we all did, and it cost him his marriage."

"That's really...sad." Devastating.

"When Ez and I moved back to Lebanon Junction, everyone looked a bit scared of me. Like I was going to snap." He laughed a bit. "You know how the town talks."

She did. Small towns talked, good and bad. Leanna braved a question. "So, how did you cope? With the war, and...everything?"

"Being around people with similar experiences. Helping out at The Scoop." He scratched the top of his head eyeing the sky. "Talking about it all a little. Pastor Jay's a good listener, and he helped me to see how my faith had wavered over the years."

"And when Tiff passed?" Oh, why did she ask?

"I thought I was going to die with her."

She shivered despite the heat. Mom and Dad nearly fell to pieces when Tiff died. Bringing up the details never fared well, but questions burned inside. "Why, why was she down at the boat by herself anyway?"

Garrison's brows lifted, then fell as if he'd asked himself that a million times. He folded his arms and eyed the grass beneath his bare feet. "She went down to get the picnic basket."

"That's it?" A simple task that ended Tiff's life.

He released a lengthy breath and gave a short nod. "We set up the campsite. Your parents helped Ez put marshmallows on sticks." Her parents often hung out with Garrison and Tiff when they had a chance to come home. Something she tried not be jealous of, but failed. "I should've walked down with her." His eyes glassed over as the story unfolded in a distant, even tone. Leanna shuddered and jumped as thunder clattered above. The storm neared. "She'd been gone too long. Thought maybe she ran into some of our friends down at the dock." He shook his head, eyes fastened on something, perhaps memories playing in his mind. Leanna was grateful his thoughts remained unseen. The image of Tiff dying...

A chill jolted Leanna's shoulders, and a loud clap sounded overhead. She glanced up at the tumultuous gray clouds. A drop of rain fell from the sky and splashed into her eye. Even the heavens cried as Garrison told this story.

"I found her body...but," his voiced quieted. "It was too late."

Leanna kept one arm around her stomach, steadying herself.

Another drop fell from the heavens.

"She'd slipped. Hit her head." Garrison eyed the clouds through squinted eyes, then focused his attention on Leanna. His face, expressionless. Almost too eerie. "Tiff and I fought earlier that day. Before we took the boat out. Only a handful of people knew she and I fought had fought. Most of them are now dead except me and—" He stumbled over his words— "William, and my father."

William and Garrison's father?

Her knees weakened.

"William heard we were in town, and came to visit just in time to catch the argument."

"Of course he did."

Garrison continued. "Tiff invited my father, but I refused to let him come. Told him to leave. She wanted us to reconcile. She never knew her parents, so it was important—" he groaned, and swiped a hand over his mouth and chin. "But she didn't know him like I did."

The wind picked up and swirled around them. The grass now slapped against her feet at a steady pace.

Leanna lifted her head. "Tiff had a kind heart, but people aren't always what they seem." Like William. "Too many secrets." Like her parents' financial situation.

"People like me." His eyes watered.

"Not like you. I'm so sorry, I didn't mean—

"But I did hurt you. My past—

"Is the past." Yet the past still stood as an obstacle to her heart.

Was there an end to his love for her? An end to his kindness and compassion? She prayed not, and prayed to be even a tiny bit like him. *Please, Lord, help me. Change me.*

Leanna huffed, half disgusted with herself and the person she had been.

Tiff's death still tormented him. Easy to see. Leanna swallowed hard. "Garrison, I'm sorry." She forced her mouth to move.

He nodded as a misty rain now fell from the sky.

Years and hurts may have passed between them, but she knew Garrison. Yet he'd changed...no, she'd changed the most, and for the worse.

He stepped closer. The rain fell harder. "I've asked you to let me love you, but there's a wall between us Lee, and I'm not sure how to get over it. If there are still questions between us..." He outstretched his arms, then settled them at his side. "Ask me anything."

Anything.

Did she dare? Did she want to know? Maybe.

So many unknowns surrounded her life at the moment. Perhaps knowing the one thing that plagued her for years would allow her to move forward. To move on and maybe start a new life, a new dream, with Garrison. She closed her eyes, seeing Brie and Ez—their smiling little faces drowning out her desire for a law degree and fat paycheck.

Leanna wet her lips, but despite the downpour, they dried. The corners of her mouth stuck together, too tight to move, but she forced them. "What happened that night? The night you cheated on me with Tiff?"

***

"Do we have to have this conversation here?" Rain fell in sheets. Garrison shook the water from his head and tugged at his drenched shirt.

"The barn?" Lee kept her arms across her chest. She took off over the hill, and Garrison followed along, careful not to leave her behind. The two ran from the storm, side by side, until they made it to safety—well, as much safety as an old, rickety barn could provide.

The rain beat down on the tin roof in a rumbling, rushing sound that would have been soothing on any other occasion. Not so relaxing when confessing the details of one's cheating ways.

Lee watched him for a moment, then stared out at the storm passing overhead. She wanted an answer, and after all these years, she deserved one. Where did he even begin?

Garrison scanned the barn. No place suitable to sit for a conversation sure to be too long for them to stand.

A couple of cinder blocks. A fallen rafter. Hmm.

He chose the barn wall with the least missing planks, and placed the cinderblocks three strides apart. The rafter, though old, felt sturdy enough to hold their weight, so he laid the board on top of the blocks.

"Nothing fancy, but it'll do." He rested his hands on his hips. Lee kept her arms tight around her body, the corner of her mouth lifting as she neared. Her hair, dark and wet, fell over her shoulder, several pieces clinging to her neck. She kept her chin high as if ready for whatever he had to say.

Garrison gestured to the bench, and Lee sat curling her knees up under her chin. Her bare feet were covered in grass and mud. So were his. The dirt barn floor beneath his feet felt as hard as cement, though not as dry as one could hope.

Lee waited. No smart comments. No mean looks or stubborn remarks.

"You sure you wanna hear this, Lee?" Garrison stretched the collar of his shirt. Wet collars had a choking effect. Lee nodded, though she appeared unsure. He swallowed and sighed. "I went out with some guys after homecoming. You were sick that night. Figured I'd hang out with them instead."

Lee nodded again. Good. They were both tracking.

"A few of them were drinking. Gave me a hard time about dating you, and bet I wouldn't take a drink."

He paused, waiting for commentary, but Lee kept quiet. If only he could read her mind, gauge her expression. Nothing. He continued, first sitting on the bench, then standing again. "I was young and dumb, Lee. Wanted to show them I could break the rules. That's all church was to me back then. A set of rules. And you and I followed them like they were some kind of check list." He kicked at the dirt floor with the ball of his foot. "One thing led to another, and Tiff and I, well, it was one time, Lee. One time." He shook his head.

"She knew I loved you." Lee's words spit out like venom. "She knew I wanted to spend the rest of my life with you."

"That made it all worse." How to tell her the rest? Garrison sat next to her, and the rafter shifted slightly beneath his weight. "She…" He lowered his eyes. Could he say it? Tiff would've wanted it all, the whole truth to come out. Garrison nodded. "She used me to hurt you."

Lee's eyebrows lifted. No gasp. No look of shock. As if she'd known this bit of info all along. "And it backfired."

"That's one word for it." Garrison smacked his hands on his knees, then crossed his arms. "She and I ended up hurting more people than we ever thought."

How could he continue? But he had to.

"I didn't even know about the pregnancy until…" His stomach flipped inside. A sick feeling slithered its way from his heels and up into his throat. Lord help him, he couldn't say it.

Leanna turned away. "Until the failed abortion."

"You knew?" Garrison's heart sank to the pit of his stomach. He sprang up from the bench and paced the hard floor.

He waited for her response, his heart racing at a deafening pace.

"I knew Ez had…had…a twin." Lee's voice cracked and started out as a whisper. He kept his eyes fixed on her. "Tiff came over, hysterical, frantic. Mom made me leave but I overheard enough to know what happened." She gazed at the barn floor as if reliving the memory, and then stared back at him. "At the time, I assumed you had a hand in it."

"No wonder you hated us so much." He laced his fingers behind his head, eyes closed. Digging up the past hurt. All the people he and Tiff hurt. A death sentence carried out upon the most innocent of victims—their unborn child. Ez had no idea. How could he ever tell him?

Garrison covered his face and smacked at the tears. "Like I've said before." He cleared his throat. "I'm not sorry I got Ez. That kid is more than a blessing. But Tiff and I fought for every shred of happiness we could muster, and when we made it to the top, started dreaming of a future, a real future…she died." He sat and leaned back against the wooden slats of the barn wall, palms pressed against the bench. "For the longest time I kept waiting for God to take Ez away, like he took Tiff, and my buddies in Iraq and Afghanistan. To punish me for having sex before I was married. For all the things I've done wrong."

"God's not like that." Or at least she didn't think so. Lee reached for his hand, cradling it between her palms. "Junk just happens."

"Junk and plenty of it." He nodded. "So I'm kinda glad God's in the business of taking that junk and making some kind of awesome art piece out of it."

"Me too." Lee smiled, her nose crinkling.

The rain showed no sign of letting up. He watched Lee for a moment. Her lashes lifted and fell. She kept still. They both sat quietly, their thoughts loud enough. He raked a hand over the stubble on his face. Tomorrow he'd leave for work.

Give them both time to process the whole conversation. Move forward.

But what did moving forward look like now that he'd unearthed the ugliest parts of his past?

CHAPTER TWENTY-TWO

IT HAD BEEN a week—a week of marriage. An intense week for sure.

No sign of the sun. Leanna sat on the front porch step and watched Garrison throw his duffle bag into the bed of the truck. She hadn't seen him in his regular uniform, the one without all the medals and shiny buttons. Though this uniform was without all the metals and shiny buttons, and more along the lines of some sort of digital printed material, her face warmed. She turned for a moment, thankful Garrison was too far away to notice the heat on her face.

He offered a quick salute. "We'll be in the field today."

What did that even mean? Guess she'd have to learn at least some military speak. He smiled at her, opened the heavy door with a metallic creak, and slammed it shut with an echoing thud. The engine roared to life, and he made his way down the long gravel drive at a snail's pace.

That's how he leaves?

What else to expect? Leanna grimaced, resting an elbow to her knee. A hug? A high five? Fist bump? She sighed. He was too much of a gentleman to kiss her goodbye. Not that she'd let him.

He continued to ease down the drive. At that rate he'd never make it to Ft. Knox on time.

She toyed with the wedding band on her finger. Somehow it didn't feel like a shackle today. She allowed a small smile and cradled her chin between her palms. Though she'd miss him while he was gone... Wow, she'd miss him. Ugh. Her stomach fluttered at the revelation.

She drank in the morning air and combed a hand through her hair. Yes, she'd miss him, like one missed a friend, that's all. She fidgeted with her ring again, swallowing hard, then decided it best to sit on her hands.

Her knees bounced of their own accord. All right. Think of something else. What else? Her fingers wiggled beneath her weight. Ah, got it.

Make cookies. Paint. Camp out. Swim. She tapped her toe on the pebbled sidewalk beneath the porch step and crafted a mental list of all the fun she and the kids would have while Garrison was away. Good for Brie. Good for her too. Get to know Ez better.

The taillights lit up as Garrison's pickup stopped near the end of the gravel drive. He stuck his head out the window, motioning her over. Her legs leapt from the step more eager than she anticipated. She steadied herself, remembering to keep composure, and tiptoed along the drive mindful of her bare feet. Oh, the pain a pointy rock could cause, but the childhood memory was not painful enough to keep her from shunning shoes. Freedom from heels was worth it.

"You used to run across those rocks," Garrison called out, arm hanging from the door window.

"The city's softened me." So had he. Good grief, she needed to get control of her thoughts. Leanna shook her head and offered a crooked smile as she neared.

He returned the same and continued to grin as she tiptoed across the gravel, holding her arms to the side.

"You wouldn't be smiling if I broke an ankle." She reached the side of the truck, hands on her hips.

"I'd make sure you were okay before laughing."

"Thanks." She snorted, cradling one arm in the other. "Want me to get the kids up?"

"Let 'em sleep." Garrison leaned forward and filed through his wallet. "Here." He handed over a card.

"We're fine." Leanna narrowed her eyes as her face heated. "We don't need any money while you're gone." Did she look like a charity case?

"You're my wife." He poked her forearm with the edge of the card. "You have access to all things mine now."

Leanna opened her mouth, but Garrison interrupted. "Just take it. It's too early to argue."

She plucked the card from his fingers, making sure he could feel her dissatisfaction. "Better?"

"Now you have the power to financially ruin me."

"'Cause there's so many places around here to do that." Leanna rolled her eyes. "Shopping spree at the Family Dollar."

Garrison laughed, the contagious kind, and his smiled reached his eyes. Leanna chuckled too.

"Come with me. All you guys. You can drop me off and pick me up later.

Got to get your military ID sometime."

An ID made it even more official. The thought should've made her want to run. Leanna cradled her arms closer.

"Next time." She twisted her lips and brushed the hair from her face. "I really do need to head over to The Scoop. See what's going on there. I'm sure Macy will be calling soon anyway."

He nodded, face pinched in a pout of sorts.

"Lots of other things too. Got to start sorting through Mom and Dad's things." She sighed. "Find a lawyer to help get me custody of Brie, figure out Mom and Dad's bills." She tallied off the to-do's on each of her fingers. Too early for a mile-long list. "And probably a few other thousand things."

"Just so you know," Garrison tapped on his car door, and focused on her. "We're not selling the place. We're buying it. Then we're gonna pay off any remaining debt."

"Garrison." She crossed her arms, hip jutted to the side.

"It's how it is, Lee."

"It's not your job to save this place."

"I'll work as hard as I have to, but we're not losing our home."

We're. Our home. Of course he considered this place just as much his home as hers. Leanna relaxed her stance, getting rid of any sass. They locked eyes, his decision unwavering. The man was just as stubborn as she —not a bad thing.

No changing his mind, even if divorced in a year or so. She bobbed her head. His generosity knew no limit. "The numbers are a bit insane."

"I'll be back tonight. We'll have a fun date night crunching numbers together."

Leanna lifted a brow. A date night and numbers. "How exciting."

The corner of his mouth lifted.

The low hum of the engine purred at a steady, even tone. Garrison stared at her, but she broke the connection. He'd divulged so much of his past yesterday, the ugliest parts, at her request, the least she could do was look him in the eye. Yet the weight of his confessions gave her pause. Much to consider and process, but a longing to know more, to be more to him. Why wouldn't the longing subside?

His fingers dangled over the side of the truck window and gave a soft wrap on the metal door. "About yesterday. Kind of heavy, huh?"

Heavy. Yes, that described it. Or perhaps a painful exhaustion. An abscessed boil being lanced open. She drew in a slow breath, then released it, cradling her arms against her chest. Maybe healing could begin. "My mind's kind of full, you know?"

He nodded. Of course he knew.

She gnawed on the inside of her jaw, shifting her weight from one foot to the other.

"You can ask me."

"Huh?" Leanna lifted a finger to her bottom lip.

"The question I see forming in your brain." His smile was soft. "I'll answer anything."

"So I've learned." Though, at the moment, she wasn't sure how much more truth she could handle, or even what to ask.

Garrison's phone chimed and he glanced at the screen by his side. "Missed call from a buddy at work." He held the phone in his hand for a moment. "And a text from Pastor Jay."

Leanna nodded and watched as Garrison read the text.

Garrison cleared his throat. "Says my Dad is down at The Scoop this morning."

He tapped on the steering wheel and then placed the phone in his lap. "Guess at some point I'm gonna have to see him, huh?"

Who was she to offer any advice, especially when it came to his father?

How Garrison managed to survive living under that man's roof was a mystery.

It made complete sense why her parents opened their home to the community – to people in need like Garrison, like Tiff. But then, why in the world had her parents ever agreed to serve such a despicable human like Garrison's father? Baffling.

An owl hooted in the distance. The dark, early morning clouds began to lighten.

"The more I think about it." Garrison cleared his throat and tapped on the steering wheel. "The more I don't want to."

She understood and gave his arm a squeeze.

"I don't have answers." Leanna shrugged. "But Aunt Cindy's here. Dale. Aunt Mary. Me, you, Ez and Brie. Something new and wonderful is happening around us." Something healing.

"Don't leave Ginger out. Poor old girl. Dogs need loving too."

"Better get going. I'll hold down the fort."

"Could be quite an adventure. Adventures of Backwoods Barbie turned Army wife."

Leanna flinched. Not ever had she wanted to be some Barbie doll, let alone from the backwoods or an Army wife. She rubbed at her arms, chin tucked under.

"I didn't mean it like that, Lee." His eyes lost their sparkle. Poor guy.

"You're an educated, sophisticated woman."

Educated and sophisticated, maybe, but generous, loving, and selfless? Not yet, but prayerfully soon.

"You better get out of here before this educated, sophisticated, backwoods Barbie Army Wife introduces you to her right hook."

"So violent. Always admired your spunk."

She rolled her eyes but smiled.

Garrison tilted his head, his expression shifting. "Seriously though, if you need anything, call me. It's kinda hard to take call in the field, but—"

"We're fine."

"The fact that you're saying that makes me concerned."

"Go before the Army fires you."

"Ha." Garrison threw his head back and started to pull away again, but stopped, turning his head to hers once more. "Lee..."

She met his stare this time, not letting go. So much worry there. So much to say, but words often failed.

"We'll talk more." Leanna stepped forward and placed her palm on his cheek. She smoothed her thumb over his cleanly shaven skin. He looked more like a soldier today. "I'll see you soon."

He kissed her palm, cleared his throat, and drove away. She watched the taillights fade before making her way back to the house.

***

Breakfast, dishes, a quick game of hide and go seek with the kiddos. How Brie managed to tuck herself into the dryer with such ease qualified for some episode of Ripley's Believe It or Not. Aunt Mary spent most of their morning in the garden, picking and pruning, which took some time in a garden that size. Seemed like Mom and Dad quadrupled the space as if it were their intention to start a farm. Keeping the house was one thing, but the gigantic garden? Thank goodness for Aunt Mary.

Ez darted into the living room just as the old grandfather clock struck eleven o'clock. He nearly slammed into her. "Lunches are packed. Is it time to go yet?"

"Almost. A few more things." She should've been out the door an hour ago. Leanna held the marker cap between her teeth and scribbled labels on a few of the boxes. Some of these books might be useful to the summer school students at The Scoop. Dad's encyclopedia and history book collection knew no end. "You guys can head on outside. I'll be right there."

"Can we bring our tablets?"

She twisted her lips. "I guess so."

Ez fist-pumped the air and ran down around the house, telling Brie the good news. Kids and their electronic devices, though she shouldn't say too much. Her parents' death seemed to be the only thing that could pry her away from the World Wide Web. All those social media posts. Status updates, friends of friends of friends. Over two thousand virtual friends, yet not one had checked in on her. A testament to them, or more likely, verification of the person she had been. Leanna sighed and looped her arm through her purse. Unplugging from the world felt...nice, and surprisingly not lonely.

"We're off." Leanna called out to Aunt Mary. Leanna lifted the box with a hmph and did a sideways hop on her way to the door, stretching for the roll of tape, to-do list and notepad on the coffee table.

The screen door screeched, then clapped closed behind her. Leanna smiled up at the heavens and then hopped from the porch step. A beautiful day, like the beginning of a new start.

***

Garrison pushed back from First Sergeant's desk. "You can't do this."

The soldiers musing past the open door quieted. How could First Sergeant do this? After everything they'd been through?

"It's done. You'll be staying back on Rear D when we deploy. Spend time with your new wife and family."

"But I have a family care plan now. Commander Jones said –"

"And I'm telling you Commander Jones is putting you on Rear D, unless you want out of the Army?"

This wasn't right, or fair. "Are we done here? I've got work to do."

"Make sure you and your men are ready for the field. We're staying a week now."

"But what about leave?"

"You'll be off in time for the fourth, fireworks and all that hoopla."

"America's birthday is hoopla?"

"Watch it."

"Got it." Garrison clenched his jaw. "Anything else?"

First Sergeant shook his head.

Just like that he was being forced off a deployment, and a day in the field turned into a week without warning. So goes Army life. He turned, more than ready to get out of First Sergeant's office.

"Burke."

Garrison stopped, sucked in a deep breath, and did an about face.

First Sergeant stared, bushy brows close together. He tapped a pen on the edge of his desk, then tucked it behind his ear. "Putting you on Rear D wasn't an easy decision."

Garrison slapped his Army beret against his thigh. "This is ridiculous and you know it. My men know me. We've trained together, and now what? You're pulling me out 'cause I got married?" Complete insanity. "How's that fair to them? To me?" Not that war was a joyous occasion, but it was part of his duty. "I took time off when Tiff passed. Didn't deploy the last time, but I'm ready now." Ready as any soldier ever is.

First Sergeant's face folded into a scowl that matched the mood of the room. He leaned back in his chair, fingers laced in front of him. "What are your plans?"

"Come again?"

"Your intentions with this woman and her situation."

"We've been over this, First Sergeant."

"You're one heck of a soldier, Burke. Impeccable leadership skills. Battle tested. Yet..." His voice rose an octave. He tilted his head, eyes squinted. "This woman seems to have caused you to have some serious lapse in judgment."

Garrison held his tongue. No need for an Article 15 today. He kept his hands gathered at the small of his back in parade rest pose.

First Sergeant let out a grumbled breath and rose from behind his desk. He slammed the door shut and stood eye level with Garrison, broader in the shoulders, but at last grapple not stronger. "You can't blame me for being concerned." His voiced softened. Those strong eyes filled with sadness.

Garrison kept his composure. "My duty as a Squad Leader has not been affected by this situation."

"Hasn't it though?"

"I fail to see how." Garrison kept his chin held high.

"What kind of example are you setting? It looks like you're taking advantage of the military benefits, playing the system."

Garrison winced. "We...we're not playing the system. I, I love the Army." His throat thickened, the accusation choking him. "If it looks like cheating the system, I apologize, but it's not. I love Lee. I can take care of her and Brie, and I'm thankful and proud that the Army can afford me that opportunity."

"You love her? That's what you're going with?" First Sergeant groaned and buried his face in his hands. He arched his back and let out a chuckle.

"I do love her. Very much."

"Does she love you?"

Garrison paused. His hand moved from his mouth to his chin. "It's complicated, but I love her."

"How many times have I heard that? And you? How many times have you heard the same thing from some young, crazy, dumb soldier meeting a chick at a night club, who then marries her two weeks later? How's that usually work out? Huh?"

Garrison swallowed. First Sergeant made a valid point. "But —"

"But what? You're different?" He folded his arms, widening his stance. First Sergeant cared. About all his soldiers. Garrison cared too. First Sergeant had been there for him, in war, in life, at backyard barbecues, and at his side after Tiff passed. They even moved duty stations to Fort Knox at the same time.

"I get you're worried, but Lee—" Garrison shook his head and smiled —"she's worth this very argument we're having."

"Remember Ramirez?" First Sergeant's fists balled at his hips. "Met that little *senorita*. She got insurance, housing, and access to his bank account. Cleaned him out when he deployed, then —"

"Disappeared." Garrison shook his head. "Yeah, I know." He cocked his head. "What if I'm the one using Lee?" First Sergeant pursed his lips in puzzlement as Garrison circled around. "I needed someone to look after Ez for me after all the provider plans fell through."

"Better reason to enjoy being on Rear D."

Garrison shook his head, a palm to his face. The man was impossible.

"And then you got the couples that marry to rack up the extra deployment money." First Sergeant motioned in the air with a wide sweep of his arm.

"C'mon. That's not us. It's not." Garrison placed a hand on the First Sergeant's shoulder and sighed. "I know you care about me and Ez. Tiff loved you and your family. You've always been there for us, so please, I'm asking for your support, again."

A somber sigh worked its way from First Sergeant's throat and out his mouth. "It's not up to me." His lips pressed together then pulled apart, as if the words forming in his mind caused him pain.

"I don't get a choice in this now?"

"Not anymore. You're not deploying, and that's final."

Garrison's head spun and a numbing heat climbed up his body. Not deploying. The news caused more fear than relief.

CHAPTER TWENTY-THREE

"NO, THE ARMY isn't always like this—er, for the most part." Garrison pressed his lips together, phone to his ear. "So it's like this more than I like to admit." He winced and held the phone from his ear as Lee huffed, her words increasing speed. Something about crazy Army life...

Crazy was right.

A day of cleaning toilets and all things grotesque at the soup kitchen, coupled with his news of a week in the field, had her in a tizzy. He suppressed a laugh. She continued to fill him in, voice alternating between high and low frequencies. "I know you've had a rough day, but I'm proud of you for helping them out so much." God knows the place needed all the hands they could get.

He nodded as she continued on about toxic fumes, tutoring, and resume writing. Was she happy or frustrated? Hard to tell, but on the topic of an unexpected week of training, definitely aggravated.

"You could have given me a warning." Her words spat at him through the phone.

"I didn't know." Garrison rubbed at his temple. How many times did he have to say that? "This is the Army. Plans change fast." Real fast. He twirled in his rolling chair and propped a leg on his desk.

"A week? In a field? Who does that?"

"Infantry soldiers. It's not a camping trip." He spun around, facing first the door, then back to the desk. Not much else to look at in the square box of an office. "Believe me, it's not like I'm looking forward to this."

"Right before you deploy?"

About that. Garrison held in the thought. He had so much more to say, but now? No. Deploying was a huge part of the reason they got married. Garrison swallowed and rubbed at his forehead. He'd have to tell her, but not now. Not over the phone.

She groaned. "I'm trying hard not to be upset."

Not hard enough. He lifted a brow.

"What about our date?"

He leaned forward, elbows on his desk. "Were you looking forward to crunching numbers, Mrs. Burke?"

Lee sighed and probably threw something. Humor hadn't assuaged the situation.

"I'm just as surprised as you, Lee." About a lot of things. Like not deploying. Like being forced on Rear D. "We just have to roll with it."

"I've been rolling with it and in it all day."

Garrison burst out laughing. "Toilet humor? You've got jokes now?"

"I'm not laughing." No, she wasn't.

"I'm not either." Not now. He sighed. "I know being away for a week is a long time. If Ez or Aunt Mary are a burd—"

"Don't say that. They're never a burden."

Garrison's heart thudded. He smiled. She cared for them. "Lee—"

"I was looking forward—I mean, we were excited to have you home this weekend."

His face warmed. "There's no place I'd rather be than with all of you."

"Then how about I call your boss and—"

"Wow. Ha." Garrison slid back in his chair. "That's the last thing you need to do."

"If I can explain to him why—"

"I'm going to teach you how the Army works when I get home." Garrison laughed. "Thank you for the kind gesture, but calling my superior wouldn't go well." He chewed on the inside of his lip, watching the time expire on the wall clock. Briefings and inspections coming up soon. "How's Ez? Everybody okay?"

"The kids love helping out at The Scoop." She made a popping noise with her mouth.

"Don't know why that surprises you. Brie practically grew up helping around there, and Ez has been there almost every weekend."

"That often?"

"Since we moved to Ft. Knox. They needed the help, and we were able."

Did her parents not tell her that, or was that information she dismissed? He imagined Mr. and Mrs. Wilson grew cautious of how much to talk about him.

"That's, well, that's really great of you guys."

Guess she really didn't know. There was something else she didn't know.

Garrison opened his mouth, but nothing came. *I'm not deploying.* Perhaps if she was excited to see him when he came home, the news of him not going overseas would cause the same joy?

The morning's disagreement with First Sergeant played through his mind and made his teeth grind. He scooped up a pencil and picked at the eraser.

"Guess I need to let you go. I'm sure you're busy." Lee's voice drooped. "Sorry I fussed at you."

"No worries." He smiled and tapped a pencil against the metal desk. "But I do have to get going."

"Will we hear from you?"

His smile widened. Oh, she was falling for him and didn't even know it, or ... Garrison sat straight. Maybe she did know. He fist-pumped the air and worked to contain a cheer. "Can't make any promises, but I'll try to call. Tell Ez I love him. Take 'em out for pizza and ice cream for me, will ya?"

"With a smile on my face."

"Lee, I love you too, you know?"

"Garrison—"

"You don't have to say it back. Yet."

"Talk to you soon." And then the phone fell silent.

Garrison closed his eyes and smiled, head resting on the back of the swivel chair. She loved him. He knew it.

But then...

There wasn't a deployment. No reason for Lee to stay married to him once she got back on her feet. They'd eventually figure out the financial mess, and Lee would surely land a job with benefits. His head throbbed. He leaned forward, elbows digging into his knees.

How could First Sergeant move him to Rear D like that? No warning. And then threaten his career? On what grounds? Garrison shook his head, pumping his knee. No, he'd been an outstanding soldier, thankful for the opportunity to serve his country and provide for his family.

The Army had given him a lot, cost a lot, but not deploying this time meant...

He stretched back in his chair and took a deep breath.

Marrying Lee provided a home, and a mother for Ez while away. Ez would be heartbroken if Lee left. Garrison ran both hands over his face. Ez wouldn't be the only one heartbroken. She already seemed on the edge of running, so reluctant to love him back. Just this morning...

Garrison held a palm to his forehead. He should've kissed her. He'd made his intentions with their relationship clear, but how clear? She'd made hers crystal, but Lee could never lie well. She cared. He knew it, but she was scared. Been hurt a lot. Lots of worries thrown on her shoulders.

He stood, lip tucked under his teeth. A stack of papers caught his attention. Weapons inspection at 1500. He'd better get through those forms fast before First Sergeant had something else to complain about.

"Knock, knock." Nelson stepped through the door.

"Can't do lunch today." Garrison shuffled the papers.

"Tacos at the DEFAC." His big head bobbed, a goofy smirk on his face. "Got lots to talk about before we hit the field, like how to make sure the Privates pack more than a few cans of Pringles."

Garrison grinned. Last time their men went to the field, one Private packed nothing but Pringles. Made for a cold night for the dude. "Sometimes they're like having a bunch of toddlers." Garrison pulled several sheets from on top the desk and held them out. "Here. Copies of the packing list. Should be enough for all our guys."

"You're so on top of it. This better help."

"I don't know what else we could do but pack their bags ourselves, and that ain't happening."

"They don't want me packing their stuff." Nelson slapped at his leg with a hearty laugh. Garrison laughed too. Nelson had a special talent for pranks, but all in good fun. The man had his back, like all the soldiers in his company.

Garrison divided the pile of papers. "How about you give me a hand with these, and we'll head to lunch before inspection?"

"Let's get busy." Nelson grabbed the pile and began to file. "Anything on your mind?"

"Really? You're gonna drag up my personal life right now?"

"Everyone needs to vent."

"I've done enough venting. I want to start making things happen."

"Ooh." Nelson held a fist over his mouth. "Macho man talk."

Garrison closed one filing cabinet and opened another. "I'm serious. Complaining doesn't get anyone anywhere. Yeah, bad things have happened, but I'm finally back on track." He shook his head. "I'm not going to let these little things derail me."

"Little things? We all heard your *little* conversation with First Sergeant."

"Nosiest people on the planet." Garrison shrugged and made a face. "So it's not all little things." Some were huge. Like losing Lee, not deploying, or getting kicked out of the Army. "That's not the point."

"Seriously though, man, we're all worried about you."

Garrison jabbed Nelson with an elbow.

"Dude. Can't believe I'm saying it, but First Sergeant makes sense."

Garrison folded his arms, jaw clenched.

"Don't get all defensive." Nelson held up both palms. "We know your story, but think about what it looks like to everyone else. To First Sergeant. And you have to admit some sloppy, quick decision making on both you and your new wife's part."

"I should punch you."

"But I'm right."

"I get why all of you are worried, but I'm thinking straight now, at least trying to. But First Sergeant's put me in a bind."

"Maybe staying off this deployment will help," Nelson said. "Give you more time to get to know your wife. Work on all the family things, you know?"

"Yeah, but..." She may leave.

"And another thing, if you're so ready to stop venting and make stuff happen, then why haven't you gone right to the Commander to find out what's up with this whole Rear D issue?"

"'Cause that's out of protocol."

"When has that ever stopped you when you're getting to the bottom of something?"

Garrison nodded, hands drawn to his hips. "No wonder First Sergeant said my career was in jeopardy."

"Ha. That's the one reason they'd be crazy to get rid of you." Nelson punched Garrison's shoulder. He dropped the last of the papers into its file and slammed the cabinet shut. "C'mon before all the tacos are gone."

Garrison wiped a hand over the back of his neck and over the chain of his dog tags. Lunch couldn't hurt. Clear his head and fill his belly.

Then time to make things happen.

CHAPTER TWENTY-FOUR

GARRISON KNOCKED AT the Commander's door and entered the office. He handed the family care plan over to Commander Jones who seemed to be expecting him.

"You again? Shouldn't you be getting ready to head out to the field, Burke?"

"Yes, Sir. I'm ready. Needed to stop by first." Garrison kept his chin high.

The Commander eyed the papers and flipped through them. "So it's true. You did get married."

"Yes, Sir."

"Guess I should say congratulations."

"Thank you, Sir."

"And that's your family care plan? Marriage?"

Garrison swallowed. "I'd like to talk about the Rear D assignment, Sir."

Commander Jones stood to his full height. "Some men don't realize they're running."

Running? Him? Garrison swallowed the thought, but it took root. "Come again, Sir."

"Life…family matters, well they can be as difficult as deploying. You're running."

"Sir, I'm ready—"

"I'm going to make this simple, Burke." His face grew stern. Garrison braced himself. "You'll stay back on Rear D and take care of your family situation, or it's time to make a career outside of the Army."

The words bit in the worse way. Garrison wet his lips, heartbeat throbbing in his ears.

"Do I make myself clear, Burke?"

158

Garrison managed a nod.

Was Commander Jones right? Had Garrison been running? Running from problems on the home front? The truth reverberated in ripples, waves louder than any explosion from a roadside bomb.

***

Dinner boiled. Well, part of it. Leanna stirred the angel hair pasta and added a pinch of coarse sea salt to the bubbling water. The skillet clanked on top of the range as she positioned it into place, then with a click, the burner flamed into life. Gas stoves were a bit tricky.

A drizzle of olive oil. In a few minutes and she could toss in the minced garlic and onions. She patted her hands on her patchwork apron— her mother's. As a little girl, Leanna had watched her mother move around the kitchen preparing dinner with such ease and grace, like a dance. Dad would sneak a bite, then twirl Mom in his arms before resting back at the piano.

Leanna dabbed at the corner of her eye. Could be the onion, the memories, or both.

She breathed in the fresh aroma of the produce perched on the counter and admired their varying hues. It made perfect sense why so many artists chose to portray fruits and vegetables in their artwork. Well, mostly fruit.

Her stomach grumbled and she popped in an apple slice to hold her over.

Laughter reached her ears and caused her mouth to lift. She glanced out the window over the kitchen sink. Had Momma done so as well, watching her play as a child? Surely so.

Ez and Brie took turns swinging on the tire swing, feet aimed for the sky. From this distance they almost passed as siblings, and in many ways, they were.

A beautiful thought.

Leanna tucked her lip under her teeth, her cheeks warming. She tossed the scene over in her mind. Friends, such as she and Garrison, with a jagged past, now family.

Funny. Wonderful even.

She gave the pot a quick stir and stole another glance out the window.

Garrison would be out there pushing them higher and vying for his own swing time, just like Daddy had with her and Brie. Leanna chuckled under her breath, then sighed. Garrison had been gone a week, and no word from him since his call about the field.

Such a strange thing to do. Did they actually stay in a field or was it a metaphor for some top secret location?

Military life seemed so ambiguous and quite honestly, mysterious, not to mention dangerous. Her arms pimpled with goose flesh. Though when she thought about it, her life contained its own danger. Its own mystery, like the unknown reason behind her parents' visit with Aunt Cindy the night they died. Leanna swallowed hard. She still hadn't pressed Aunt Cindy for answers. Why? She wasn't sure. Perhaps the truth would only further complicate her already complicated life.

No, Aunt Cindy was not the strung-out woman of her past. And she and Dale were kind enough to stay in Aunt Mary's home so Leanna could be near Brie. Still, Cindy wasn't someone who she completely trusted. Not yet. Then again, it wasn't as if she'd even had a real conversation with them yet.

"Are you sure you don't need me to help?"

Aunt Mary's voice startled her. Leanna dropped the wooden spoon. It clattered to the floor.

She turned. "I'm okay." Just lost in a million thoughts. Leanna picked up the spoon and plopped it into the sink. "You go on upstairs and get some rest."

"It's okay for you to rest too."

Leanna offered a slight nod. Her to-do list hung on the refrigerator, caught in her peripheral vision. She'd managed to mark off several tasks including submitting a request for an emergency teaching license, and even narrowed down a custody lawyer out of Elizabethtown, but the fee was astronomical. Maybe it was time to head on over to the Bullitt County Court House to see William's uncle, Judge Sinclair. It could be worth the fifteen-minute drive to Shepherdsville. Surely he wouldn't side or scheme with William. But wasn't he already? She crossed her arms, then let them hang, turning back to the stove. Dinner — a task she could manage with at least some success.

Aunt Mary pulled up a chair and sat at the table. She motioned for Ginger and the little fur ball jumped into her lap with a little push from Aunt Mary. "I thought about you during Pastor Jay's sermon on Sunday."

Of course she did. Leanna sighed, lifting both brows. She'd listened to the podcast: Pride comes before the fall. Not the best sermon to be connected with. She'd squirmed in the pew herself, but still. "I'll bite."

"You've been such a servant."

Was she joking? Leanna stood still, waiting for the knee-slapping laughter, but none came.

"I've been watching you care for those little ones. Bedtime stories. Dishes, laundry, working at The Scoop. Your parents trained you up well."

"Thank...thank you. That's the...the nicest thing anyone's said about me."

"Sometimes people need to hear the good. Know what I mean?" Aunt

Mary sat straight, appearing quite pleased with herself.

The scalding water spilled over the side of the pot. Leanna gave the pasta a quick stir, avoiding the steam. "Dinner's almost ready."

"Er." Aunt Mary's round face distorted. Ginger even groaned. "Tofu?"

"There's pasta too. I'm going to toss it in a garlic butter Parmesan sauce."

Aunt Mary laughed, and her high-pitched voice sounded much more like a child's than a woman closing in on seventy. Her smile kept her young. "It could be covered in chocolate and I still wouldn't touch it."

"That doesn't even sound good." Leanna continued to stir. "You can pick out the tofu, you know." She frowned and sighed. "You think the kids will eat it?"

"There's pizza in the deep freeze."

"Hmph." Leanna cracked a smile. "We'll see about that."

"Pretty sure there's casseroles too. A lifetime supply from the church ladies."

"That's nice of them and all, but it's not healthy to eat that stuff every day."

"Maybe not healthy, but not filled with tofu either."

"Har. Har."

Aunt Mary giggled. "Well, don't save me any leftovers."

Leanna grabbed another wooden spoon and shook it. "I traveled far and wide to find tofu in this area."

"There's a reason for that, but I guess my taste buds are always up for an adventure." Aunt Mary eased to her feet, and Ginger hopped down and trotted down the hall. Aunt Mary bent over and braced herself with mock horror. "I'm ready."

Leanna pinched a piece sautéed tofu between her fingers and passed it to Aunt Mary. She squeezed the cube, sneered, and then popped it into her mouth.

"Not bad, sweet girl." She chewed slowly and then swallowed, a curious expression on her face. "It's been a good day today." She kissed Leanna's cheek, and Leanna's heart warmed. "Interesting food, and the fog has lifted for now."

"The fog?"

"Those crazy bouts of me forgetting something."

Leanna nodded. In some ways she understood the fog and its departure. She smiled and kissed Aunt Mary on her cheek. "We're glad the fog has lifted too. We've missed you."

"Ha." Aunt Mary reached for an apron and slid it over the mound of short white curls atop her head. "I've missed me. Now give me something to do."

"Yup. Back to normal." Leanna laughed and pointed to the colander next to the canister set. "You can snap some peas."

"Fresh from the garden."

Nothing like produce from the garden.

Leanna tossed the garlic and onion into the skillet. It sizzled at first contact, sounding much like applause and smelling so much like...like...ah...her time in New York. She closed her eyes and grinned.

New York. Where she first learned to cook healthy meals. Those memories were nice, when life's problems could be solved in thirty minutes over dinner and drinks with a coworker.

Problems now, well, there were so many, and too many what-ifs. Not matter what choices she made, huge consequences awaited.

Even if they stayed married, wouldn't the Army have a different home for them? Moving from place to place every few years. Sounded tedious yet also appealing, but who would stay behind to care for the property?

So many things to consider. Her brain buzzed. She'd almost welcome a fog now. Oh, to forget.

"Honey, were you trying to cook Cajun food?"

"Huh? Oh. Oh." What water remained boiled over. The garlic and onions cracked and popped in the pan, resembling charcoal more than anything edible. Leanna grabbed a potholder and held the pan underneath the faucet. An angry burst of steam rolled upward. She and Aunt Mary stood amidst the heated cloud.

"Just like a sauna. Ah." Aunt Mary patted her face.

Leanna glowered at the scorched pan, then removed the pasta pan from the burner. She swished a fork down into the pasta. How long had she been standing there lost in her thoughts while dinner ruined? Apparently too long. Maybe part of the meal could be salvaged, but no, a lump of mushy noodles stuck to the bottom. Blackened underneath.

Ick.

"You let it boil dry, dear." Aunt Mary pursed her lips, a hand on her hip. "Frozen pizza or a casserole?"

Leanna huffed, throwing her head back with a groan. Dinner wasn't such an easy task to mark off the list.

"Leanna." Ez bounded through the screen door holding his nose. "What's that smell?"

"You're cooking dinner if you run through the house again," she shot back.

"Ooh, nice." Aunt Mary chimed in. "You're sounding more and more like a mother every day."

Ez lingered.

"What's up, Ez? Is Brie okay?" Leanna leaned over, glancing out the window.

"There's a man here with lots of boxes."

"Man?" Leanna squinted, trying to make sense of Ez's excited ramblings.

"He's got the biggest truck in world." His arms swayed back and forth, up and down, and moved as fast as his mouth. She wiped her hands on her apron and made her way through the kitchen.

"Can we keep the boxes for a fort?"

"Stay in here with me, Ez," Aunt Mary called from the kitchen.

Leanna rushed through the living room and out the front door, stopping on the front porch. A moving truck greeted her. Piles of boxes cluttered the front lawn. How had she not heard the ruckus?

Brie. Where was she?

On top a stack of boxes swinging her legs, eyes focused on the package handler.

"What's going on?" Leanna jumped down from the porch.

"Got my orders, miss." The man tipped his hat. His gray company logo shirt was drenched with sweat.

"Is this…?" Leanna hurried from box to box. Clothes. Shoes. Photographs. A chair. Her couch pillows. She shoved a box lid down. "Is this my apartment stuff?"

"Look, ma'am." The man paused. "I'm doing my job." He handed her an envelope, then continued to stack boxes along the front yard.

Leanna slid the letter open. William's writing scrawled on the lines of the paper: *Here's your junk back. Of course, I kept what's mine, which was most of it. You're welcome.*

Good.

More stuff to sell now.

***

"Remind me why I'm an Infantry soldier again?" Garrison's ears rang from a day of firearms practice. He carried his M-4 rifle, back aching from the weight of it, stalked through the woods mindful of the terrain beneath his boots. Breaking an ankle wouldn't be a good way to end battle tactics and navigation procedures.

Last duty of the day. Chow, then bed.

Nothing like sleeping on a mat under a canopy of trees. Minus the mosquitos.

"You could've shammed." Nelson followed at his side, two arms-lengths away. "Gotten out of this field problem. I mean, if I was in your situation, I'd be all about getting out of field training and a deployment."

"It's complicated."

"Duty. Honor. Your marriage. I get it." Nelson paused, hoisting the rucksack higher on his back.

"How do I convince her to fall in love with me?"

"We're all in love with you." Nelson made kissing noises.

"I'm for real."

"Why are you asking me? I'm no expert in marriage."

True. Nelson's marriage went down the tube several years ago. "Yeah, but figured you've learned a few things, even if it's what not to do."

Nelson punch at Garrison's shoulder, and Garrison smiled.

"I don't know, man." Nelson swatted at a mosquito. "What happened to the guy who was ready to make things happen?"

"Been wondering the same thing." These bouts of courage were great and all, but he'd need confidence that didn't waver. Where did that come from?

"Sorry to say it, but you two got married for all the wrong reasons."

Garrison nodded.

"Marriage is hard, man, and you made it harder."

"Thanks. Nice pep talk."

Nelson stepped over a fallen branch. "Hang in there. Divorce is a pain in the butt."

So much for that. Garrison nodded again, the chin strap of his helmet restricting his range of motion.

Did he dare pry further? Garrison braved forward. "How did your faith play a part in your marriage?"

Nelson took his time responding, the ground crunching beneath his boot. "It didn't. And that was the problem."

Garrison bit at his thumbnail. Nelson made sense.

"And if I may speak freely…"

"You always do."

"Faith doesn't seem to be playing a part in your marriage right now."

Ouch.

But Nelson was right.

He hadn't prayed about marrying Lee, only solving their problems, and righting wrongs. He'd prayed after. Garrison pushed the branches and twigs from his path.

When was the last time he'd opened his Bible? Pastor Jay encouraged him to do so. Maybe there was more to having faith then sitting in a pew for

Sunday service.

He shook the thought. "What happens to she and I when I deploy?"

Nelson lifted his head as if he were praying, then stopped for a moment. "Deployments don't have to separate people. Remember, man, love is a choice."

"I've told her that."

"It's a choice *you* make."

Wise words. He'd have to remember them, and keep them close.

Garrison wetted his lips. He stared past the underbrush. Trees as far as he could see. No end to the woods in sight, but they'd make their way out.

They always did.

CHAPTER TWENTY-FIVE

KIDS WERE IN bed. Not sleeping, but in bed. Huddled under a makeshift fort. Leanna swiped her hand across her forehead. Amazing what a few chairs, cardboard boxes, and blankets could create.

They'd each taken turns making up a story—the kind that ended with a happily ever after. Not always so true to life. Leanna struggled to piece together a tale filled with hope and joy, suitable for young ears. But the boxes, thanks to William, made great props for castles and caves. A damsel in distress, chased by an evil king. A hero to save the day— someone quite similar to Garrison.

Hushed giggles caught her ear and lifted the corners of her mouth. Leanna kept quiet, pressing herself against the wall. Her heart twinged at the possibility of hearing Brie's sweet voice again.

"Leanna makes the best forts." Ez's words managed to reach her past a mound of boxes. Leanna smiled to herself. Dad had excelled in fort building and storytelling. Late nights of serving at the soup kitchen. Gone most of the time, but he managed to tiptoe into her room most nights with a cookie outstretched in one hand and an adventure to share.

Leanna crossed her arms and squeezed. Those memories mattered. Not what Mom and Dad didn't do, but what they did. And they did so much. For many people.

For her. For Garrison. For Tiffany.

A lump rose in her throat. She swallowed it back and continued to listen.

"I don't ever want to leave this home." Ez sighed, and Leanna held her breath. No, she didn't want to leave either. But this wasn't a fairytale. Happy endings in real life, if any, were scarce.

Someone would leave this house. Perhaps all of them. Whether it had to be sold, or whether divorce ripped them a part, they couldn't stay. Not forever.

"I prayed for a mom, and God sent me the best one."

Leanna folded an arm over her stomach, the other on her mouth. Oh, how his words flooded her heart with dread and delight.

"And He gave me a sister too," Ez said. "A sister that likes to play in the dirt. How cool is that?"

What had she and Garrison been thinking? Did they ever once truly consider how the kids would be affected by their little deal?

The floorboard creaked, and Leanna startled. Just Aunt Mary.

Aunt Mary grunted, hunched beneath a stack flattened cardboard boxes — remnants of William's special delivery just hours ago. "Where should we put these?" Her voice was a whispered strain.

"Let me help." Leanna grabbed more than a handful. "Let's put 'em in the basement for now."

Her life and choices sat heavy on her shoulders, growing larger by the day. Something had to give. Something soon. But not yet. No, she wasn't ready to secede — to embrace a new dream, when maybe she could piece together the old one. An old dream that perhaps could include Brie, Ez, and Garrison.

They walked soft-footed down the hall until the airiness of the living room allowed Leanna to breathe again. For a moment, she was just a girl holding boxes and no other burden.

"I wish the trash people came out this far." A box slipped, and Leanna tucked it back into place as she reached for the doorknob. "You'd think recycling would've reached the end of this world by now."

"It has." The boxes hid Aunt Mary's face, but Leanna could feel a disappointed scowl.

She cringed. "Oh. Well. That's good."

"The Scoop does it. Your mom and dad —"

"Of course." A slight growl rolled from her mouth, but she couldn't be frustrated. "I'm really impressed at the place. I never expected..."

"Any good from the people in this area? We're all barefoot and pregnant, uneducated, no teeth, wallowing in poverty, and doing nothing to improve ourselves, right?"

"Geez." Leanna gulped. Her face warmed as she reached for the doorknob. "That's kind of harsh."

"I know what you think, 'cause those were my thoughts for a long time."

Leanna stood. How to respond?

"Are we just gonna stand here? Let's get these boxes put away." Aunt Mary shooed Leanna's hand from the knob and opened the door herself.

She continued down the stairs and was halfway near the bottom before Leanna followed suit.

Leanna hurried as well as anyone could holding a massive mound of boxes. "Well, for your information, I'm not thinking that now." Liar. "Not that much anymore." She smiled at the truth, at something good growing inside after years of decay.

"We know."

"We? Who knows?"

"Everyone you come in contact with."

"This town is so nosy."

"We know that too. Where do you want to put these?"

Leanna stretched her neck around the boxes, mindful of each step. A few of the boards were loose. Her pant leg snagged on a nail. Leanna gasped, then steadied herself.

"Please don't fall. Not tonight." Aunt Mary's nervous laugh resounded from the bottom of the stairs.

"We've had enough excitement, huh?" Leanna chuckled, placing each step with care, relieved to be at the bottom.

"Burnt tofu dinner, a special delivery, and forts."

"Dinner would've been great." Leanna scrunched her nose. "I think there's room over in that area." She directed with a nod of her head.

Aunt Mary placed her stack of boxes in the empty corner, and Leanna piled hers on top. That would work for now.

"I'm glad you took the kids out for pizza."

Leanna nodded and placed the stack of boxes in an empty corner. She dusted off her hands.

"Dinner was fun." She rested against the stair rail, arms folded. "You'd should've come." They'd taken turns playing Hangman and Tic-Tac-Toe on napkins while they waited on personal pans. Not gluten-free, nor void of carbs, but ... well, still delicious.

"Next time. Y'all need that time together. Family time."

Family time. Leanna sighed and dug her hands into the back pockets of her jeans.

Aunt Mary arranged the boxes neatly. "You've got enough of these things to make forts for the next ten years."

A laugh caught in Leanna's throat.

Like a time warp, the damp basement air swirled around her. Gooseflesh pimpled her arms and turned her head.

Memories poured from the walls, and just like that, she was six, building box tunnels with Garrison. She was eight, painting the horse mural on the far wall with her momma. She was twelve, lying flat-bellied near the old couch, making beaded friendship bracelets with Tiffany. Kool-Aid stains on the cream Berber carpet testified to their many sleepovers.

And their box. Wooden. Latched, but not locked. A slit on top. It still sat on a corner table next to an old lamp.

Dad made it for her and Tiffany when they were ten. That fall she and Tiff decided to follow Jesus – so long ago. When had she stopped following? Why? She squinted, sorting through blurry reasons. She eased her way to the table. Her fingers skimmed across the hodgepodge surface. Photos, magazines cut-outs, glitter, beads and quotes.

Their prayer box.

The latch released, and she eased open the lid. Small, folded pieces of paper filled it to the brim. Some torn. Some crumbled.

Prayer requests. So many. All hers? Not likely.

Leanna reached inside, but froze.

Why read these requests? She knew what many were. And how they hadn't been answered.

"He answers those things."

Leanna startled and jerked her hand from the box.

Aunt Mary placed a hand on her shoulder and squeezed. "He answers every prayer, though most often in ways we could never imagine."

"So I'm learning." She pulled back. "If I'm honest, I think that's what scares me most."

"That He doesn't do things in the way you want?"

Yes. Ugh. Her chest burned. Change the subject to anything. Leanna pursed her lips and rubbed her forehead.

"I'm surrounded by people who want to talk about their faith all of the time. There's other stuff in life too."

"Like burnt tofu dinners."

Leanna giggled, her frustration dissipated.

"Everything centers around God whether we like it or not. And He loves you, Leanna. And He wants the best for you, even if that means not answering the way you want."

"Even if His answers hurt me and others?"

"Ah." Her eyes lit up. "Even then, because He is good even when our situation is not. Even when we don't always make the best choices." Her words stung, but maybe that's what truth did sometimes. "Stay the course, and if you stray away, just get back on track."

She rolled her eyes, twisting her lips. "Just like that?"

"Simple as that."

Why did something so simple as trusting God have to be so difficult? Grr. Frustrating.

"I'll leave you to your box."

Leanna nodded, eyes already tearing.

"By the way, I'll make breakfast for the kids. Spare them something covered in broccoli."

"You're fired," Leanna teased as Aunt Mary disappeared up the stairs.

"Good thing. Been hoping for more free time." Her voice trailed off.

The box called.

The prayer box, she and Tiff called it. Filled with prayers of all kinds. Leanna knew all about those prayers, and why she'd stopped making them.

She sighed.

A time existed when her faith was simple and new. A sweet time. She smiled at the memories. Butterflies and rainbows as her Momma would put it. Yet, that faith had not been tested or tried, and when big trials came, well...

I'm sorry, Lord.

***

Leanna held her arms tight to her body, eyes clamped shut. She'd read only a few. Just two or three. No more.

Cross-legged on the floor, Leanna balanced the wood box on her knees. The lid hung open. Two envelopes, still sealed, stared back at her. From Tiff. Leanna swallowed, heart squeezing. *Not now. I can't read these, yet.*

Leanna pushed past the letters and pulled forth the first one that touched her fingertips. It was folded in fourths, and appeared newer than the others.

Dear Lord,

Momma's swift, elegant writing. A wave of warmth rushed over Leanna. Momma used the prayer box. Not surprising, but nonetheless unexpected. Leanna held the small piece of paper close, like a prized piece of artwork.

I ask for guidance for Lee. She's lost right now, Lord. Lost and hurting, and I can't help but feel her father and I have had part in that hurt.

Leanna's heart burned. Oh, Momma.

Forgive us Lord for putting our daughters to the side, and forgetting that they too are our mission field. Help us to be the parents you want us to be.

Leanna kissed the paper and held it to her chest. She let the tears come.

One more prayer request. All she could manage.

Dear Lord,

Her own writing this time.

Please give me a pony. A white one. Fast too. Rainbow colored hair.

Leanna laughed and wiped her nose. Crazy prayers of an eight-year-old.

That answer was no.

The next paper had sparkles on it. It screamed middle school.

Dear Lord,

Another in her writing.

Please help me do well on the test. I've studied hard. And help me beat Tiffany at the swim meet on Friday. Oh, and thank you for letting Garrison sit by me at the game. I'll keep you posted on how that goes.

Ha. She'd passed the test like a breeze, but the meet, well, Tiff was a pro. Leanna pulled her knees to her chin. Not that she'd ever want to relive middle school, but some moments, like sitting next to Garrison for the first time outside of church or the front yard, well, those were sweet memories.

She swiped a finger under her eye and grabbed another piece of paper.

More in her writing.

Dear Lord,

Help! I'm cramping so bad. Why did Eve have to eat that stinking apple?

Leanna laughed out loud, covering her mouth. Well, the cramps were just a part of it, 'cause they kept coming, right on schedule.

She'd read one more request. For real this time.

Another from her. Wow, she'd kept God busy in her youth.

Dear Lord,

Please help Tiffany find a home where people won't hurt her. She's had three homes this year, and that is way too many. She wants a good mom and dad really bad.

He answered. God didn't give Tiffany a good mom and dad, but the best. Her very own parents.

Wow. Leanna slumped, mouth open. They'd taken Tiffany in, no questions asked.

And please help Garrison. His dad hurts him too. I think his daddy is an angry person, so please fix him so he won't be angry anymore. It might take a long time, 'cause he's really mad all of the time.

Leanna swallowed, but her throat still restricted her airflow.

Another answer. The reason behind her parents' kindness toward Mr. Burke? A prayer request she made when she was eleven? No.

But maybe.

Maybe God cared about the people who hurt people too.

Leanna let the thought sink in, then continued to read.

I'm thinking about becoming a lawyer one day so I can help kids like my friends to find loving and caring homes. Do you think that's a good idea?

The reason, the real reason, she dreamed of a career in law slapped her in the face. Leanna winced and bit her lip. The tears kept coming.

It wasn't money. It wasn't status. It wasn't success. It wasn't even leaving this small town. Her dream began in a desire to help others and please God, but her hurts and hang-ups morphed that dream into something ugly, something like the person she had been.

No more. She was the new Leanna. The Leanna back on track.

She rolled to her knees and searched around through the art supply boxes scattered throughout the room. A blank sheet of paper and a marker. She popped the cap off, wedged it between her teeth, and wrote.

Dear Lord,

Please help me fix this situation, all of it, not my way, but your way.

And that meant taking the leap to commit to her vows. What would Garrison think? The thought brought fear and elation.

Leanna dried her eyes, climbed the basement stairs and tiptoed to the kids' room. She knelt, crawling toward the fort. Sound asleep. Books sprawled about, blankets thrown about, flashlight still on. She clicked it off, the light disappearing from the room, and kissed their cheeks.

Ez looked so much like Tiff, and Brie very much like Momma. Leanna touched a soft curl on her little head, then pulled the blankets over their bare feet. She'd spent time reading answers to prayers, and they were two answers to prayers she didn't even know to pray, until now. At this very moment.

"God, help me to look after them," Leanna said, head bowed, hands laid on their small backs. "Help me to be the person they need me to be."

Ez stirred and rubbed his eyes with balled fists.

"Shh." Leanna held a finger over her mouth. "Go back to sleep."

"Will you tell me a story?"

She smiled. Another story. Leanna sat on her bottom, and crossed her legs, careful to keep her voice low. "About anything in particular?"

"Would you tell me about my mom?"

Leanna winced, thankful the semi-darkness concealed her reaction. Most of it, at least.

"You knew her, right? Dad said you guys were best friends. All of you."

She wet her lips, breaths short.

"I remember her, but sometimes I can't." The moonlight shone across Ez's downcast expression. Leanna's heart ached for him. For Garrison. For everyone who lost Tiff.

Tears formed, and Leanna wiped them away. "Your mom was…" She kept her laugh quiet. "Was the prettiest girl in the whole school. She always wore something pink. Glittery, and loved bows in her hair."

Ez sat up, arms folded in his lap. "What were her favorite things?"

"Ha. Dancing. Makeup. Swimming. We'd stay up all night and make bracelets. When we weren't in school we were playing with kittens in the barn, or decorating the playhouse. We had a horse one time too."

"A real one?"

Leanna nodded. "Sugar. Evil horse."

Ez laughed, holding a hand to his mouth.

"Right after she moved in with us, Dad bought Sugar for us. Your mom tried to put sparkling beads all over the poor thing and it got to where the silly thing wouldn't come near us."

Ez's giggles were contagious, but then he grew serious, nervous even.

"Why did she live with you? Where were her mom and dad?"

Leanna held her breath. Had Garrison not shared this part of Tiff's life with him? Should she be the one to do so? She didn't even quite understand the whole story or who Tiff's real parents were.

"I only know your momma needed a family, and we gave her one."

"She lived with different families before you, right?"

Leanna nodded. Many different families. Tiff woke up often with nightmares from the experience, but that wasn't a story for bedtime. "It's late, buddy."

Ez yawned and wrapped his arms around Leanna's neck.

"I'm so glad you're my mom now."

Her shoulders sank, heart opening wider. "Me too, bud."

He tapped her three times. "That's our secret code for 'I love you.'" He pulled back, leaning close, voice still a whisper. "You tap back four times."

"That means, 'I love you too'?" Leanna tapped his nose four times. "Very clever. Now get some rest."

"Do you love my dad? He loves you."

Kids got straight to the point. "That's kind of complicated."

"Not really."

Leanna sighed. The kid was right. "Yes, I love your dad."

"I knew it." Ez grinned as he nestled into his pillow.

"Now get some sleep." She kissed them both again and left the room with a quiet sigh, pondering so much more than her mind could process during the length of a bedtime story.

It was true. She loved Garrison. Admitting it out loud was one thing, but showing it was something entirely different.

***

Late night shadows from the campsite stretched through the woods at awkward angles. Several of the soldiers hooted and hollered, acting more like boys than men. That was all right. Garrison's men had earned their right to a bit of fun. Land navigation went well, and at least now all the Privates could read a map well enough to survive.

Garrison placed his back to a tree away from the camp and held up his phone. No signal, no matter where he tried. He dialed again in hopes somehow Ez or Leanna would answer.

Still no connection. He sighed and swung the phone at his side. More than half finished with the field training, and he hadn't spoken a word to his family. Wednesday was too far away. He groaned and folded his arms. How much longer could he do the Army life? And where did that thought come from?

Commander Jones' words plagued him. Stay back on Rear D or get out of the Army.

And maybe getting out of the Army wasn't such a bad thing. Either way, he was being forced from this deployment.

For years the Army provided security for his family, but now it seemed to take him away, in a direction he wasn't heading. Strange. He'd never given much thought to getting out, but...

"Need some alone time?" Nelson hobbled over and took a seat on a fallen log.

"Better not let the Privates see you limp."

"That's why I'm here with you."

"Ha." Nelson took a long pull from his canteen and tossed it over to Garrison. "So, how is married life?"

"First week has been...eventful."

"You know I didn't mean to marry her, just date her..."

"Yeah, well."

Nelson stretched and moaned. Infantry life wreaked havoc on young bodies. Maybe it was time to consider a new path. Garrison scratched at his chin. Tiff had pushed so hard for him to finish that business degree online. Never thought it would come in handy, until now.

"Not sure if my body can take much more." Nelson's laugh broke.

"I've got three more years 'til my enlistment's up."

"You getting out?"

"I'm open to the possibility."

"You're open to a lot of things these days." Nelson bent, hands on his knees as he arched his back. "I like the new Staff Sergeant Burke."

Garrison slid his hands into his pockets and nodded toward the sky. "Me too."

Nelson yawned and scratched at his jaw. "By the way, First Sergeant ever buy Lee's car?"

"You interested?"

"Figured it's time to switch to four wheels instead of two."

"You?" Garrison quirked a brow, and took a drink from the canteen. "For anyone special?"

"I'm open to the possibility."

"Ha. Well I'm open to the possibility of taking your money." At least he'd have some good news to report to Lee before he dropped the 'not deploying' bomb.

CHAPTER TWENTY-SIX

THIRTY-FIVE PEOPLE. Could she feed that many? Hospitality was not a gift she possessed, so why had she ever invited the whole town over for dinner? Because Macy was kind. Because it's what her parents would have done. Because…because, she wanted so much to be different than the cold, selfish person she'd spent too long being.

Leanna pulled canned green beans and a variety of applesauces from the shelves in the stock pantry. Five casseroles, fresh salad straight from the garden, and a basket of rolls. Burgers. Hot dogs. Plenty of food. Too much, and more remained.

"Cindy, can you give me hand?" Leanna called from the pantry.

"She just left." Aunt Mary carried a bucket of warm soapy water and a rag through the kitchen. "Said she had a few errands to run."

"Errands." Hmm. Like a drug run? Leanna pushed the thought away, regretting the assumption as soon as it reared its ugly head.

Leanna carried as many jars as she could and placed them on the counter. "Still need help?"

She shook her head and popped the top from one of the Mason Jars.

"Holler if you need me. I'm gonna clean off the picnic tables. Rest of the house is in order."

"You mean, all my stuff is finally shoved in the basement?"

What would she ever do without Aunt Mary? Without Macy? Without all the wonderful people in Lebanon Junction who'd been nothing but kind. Funny how her perspective had shifted.

"I think there's a yard sale in your future."

"You think all fifty people in the town would come?"

Aunt Mary laughed as the screen door clanked shut behind.

"Ez. Brie." Leanna dug underneath the cabinet for one of those giant pots Momma used to prepare large portions. Feet hurtled down the hall, through the living room and into the kitchen. "You guys on your tablets again?"

No response was a pretty good answer.

"It's nice day outside." Leanna hoped the hint sank in.

"Can we swim?" Ez sounded hopeful.

Leanna bumped her head on the cabinet door as she lifted the pot with both hands. Brie and Ez waited, eyes dancing. "That's not a good idea, guys." Garrison may not be keen on it either.

"We'll do an-y-thing." He dragged out his words, crazy hair moving to the beat of his swaying body. Brie lowered her lashes. The last thing Leanna wanted to do was disappoint the kids. Swimming was fun. Being an adult, well, not so much fun. Brie and Ez needed to enjoy their childhood. Besides, how many times had she and Garrison, Tiffany even, jumped into the river?

But still.

Leanna emptied another jar of green beans into the pot. How many was that? "Let me get dinner going, then we'll make shaved ice."

The kids groaned, and Leanna placed a hand on her hip. "And when everyone gets here, we'll let all the kids swim." There'd be enough people to watch them. Ensure safety. "Deal?"

Ez held his hand in the air. Brie actually high-fived him. She improved every day— counseling had been a good idea. Leanna smiled and swatted at their hineys as they ran from the kitchen. "And go play outside. Stay off the tablets."

A faint "yes ma'am" floated from the hall.

"You've got mail." Aunt Mary's frail voice cracked as she entered the kitchen.

Mail this late? The time on Leanna's phone was ten after four, but there stood Aunt Mary, clinging to an envelope over her walker.

Leanna emptied another jar of beans into the pot and sat it in the sink. She took the envelope, turning it over once or twice. William's writing. She rolled her eyes but couldn't deny the shiver that wrapped itself around her body. This man couldn't take a hint.

"The nicest man delivered it."

"I bet." One of William's loyal subjects, no doubt. The man spent way too much effort trying to ruin her life. Moving on couldn't be that difficult, but for a man like William, who never lost, well...

"Handsome too, but nothing compared to my Garrison." Aunt Mary wheezed a happy sigh and found her spot at the table. "Don't just look at it.

Open it."

Broad daylight, birds singing, but her hands shook as she opened the letter. *Please no more bad news.*

He had nothing else to threaten her with.

Dear Mrs. Burke,

Leanna rolled her eyes. William was such a jerk.

Ever wonder what Garrison and Tiffany fought about the night she died?

You.

Her?

Garrison never mentioned that bit of information. But what did it matter now anyway?

She rolled her eyes. If William couldn't pry Brie away, he'd try chipping at her marriage.

Why did she read it? Why did she let his lies near her? Leanna wadded it in her hand.

"Keep everything you get from him." Aunt Mary raised a shaking finger. "That man is calculating."

Indeed. Leanna pinched her lips together, eyes stinging.

"And don't cry. Pull yourself together, prepare a great meal, and have fun with your friends— the people who love you, and your family."

"Yes, ma'am." Leanna offered a short nod. Despite her illness, Aunt Mary remained sharp in many aspects. "Where... where should I put this thing?" Leanna stumbled over her words, gripping the letter.

"This requires prayer. Where else would you put this but your prayer box?"

"Good idea."

"The only kind I have."

"Thank you. For everything."

"Honey, that's why I'm here, but tomorrow I may not remember any advice I've given." She giggled, veined hands resting on her knees.

If only Leanna had the option of forgetting. She'd start with forgetting William, forever.

***

Not quite thirty-five people, but close. Leanna finished the remainder of her salad, ignoring playful teases regarding her vegetarian, no-carb way of life. She'd have to choke down a burger and donuts to shut them all up, but the teasing was all in fun.

Honestly, she'd missed the way the folks in Lebanon Junction showed their affection. Much different than her time in New York spent with friends—well, acquaintances that helped her climb social ladders. Where were they now? She shuffled the greens on her plate. Was anything in New York real? Or did she not let it be? How many opportunities to be authentic did she miss out on while stepping on others to rise to the top, only to fall?

Aunt Mary patted her leg to the music as Pastor Jay and a few of the teen boys picked on their guitars. Brie sat close by, eyes rolled back in her head indulging herself with chocolate cake. But still no sign of Aunt Cindy and Uncle Dale. Leanna huffed and let the worry roll away. Tonight was about celebrating. Celebrating her parents' memory, good food, good friends, and good family. And not letting anything go to waste.

She listened to the chatter and laughter that filled the family grounds. Different from the silence of Central Park. Trees there formed in clusters, provided shade, a sense of wonder and solace, but were not able to replicate the fellowship she watched unfolding now. Something special, if not heavenly, in the way the moms made plates for their children and kissed boo-boos. In the way the men gave their seats for the women. They served one another, yet it didn't make them appear lowly. Leanna raised a brow, lifting her fork. In fact, they were the opposite of lowly.

And when she thought of her relationship with William... no. Leanna let the fork drop from her hand. She wouldn't think about William or any part of their relationship. He and their whole dilemma resided in the prayer box where it belonged, where she and others would pray about it. No, she'd wouldn't think about William. She'd focus on Garrison, her husband. On Brie. On Ez. Following the new path. The path God had for her.

Leanna stood, tossed her plate in the trash, hugged a few of the church members, and reached for a burger. The biggest one on the table.

"No way." Macy waddled over, hands over her mouth. "Y'all, look at this." Macy pointed a finger at Leanna.

The burger hovered inches from her mouth. Leanna closed her eyes, a laugh working its way from her throat.

"Do it," Pastor Jay called from the crowd gathering. Ez and Brie danced around her, their faces full, mouths wide.

"I'm so going to regret this." Leanna let her head fall back. But the crowd chanted. She doubled over laughing at the silliness of it all. Mom and Dad would love this. And they'd love watching her cut up, do something not serious, like the days before she allowed the world to slap her around. She bit her lip and balled a fist. It felt good to let go. To break free. "Here I go."

One solid bite.

Her friends erupted into cheers, claps, and deafening bouts of laughter. The meat should've repulsed her. But, oh, it didn't. Years without such goodness. How did she survive?

Grease dripped from the side of her mouth, and Leanna lopped it up with her forearm. Classy.

Another bite, and another. One more plug and she'd downed the whole thing, then licked her fingers. Even classier.

Pastor Jay and Macy gave her high fives, and the crowd patted her on the back.

"You looked like a T-Rex attacking." Ez swung on her arm. "Can we swim now? All the kids are here."

"Did you even eat?"

"Enough."

Leanna gave him a fist-bump, then rubbed his head. "Wear a life jacket."

"No one else is."

"Brie will. And several of the other kids too."

"Fine." Wow. Attitude for the first time. Ez frowned, nodded, and then ran alongside Brie toward the shed.

"I should go help them," Leanna said, pulling away from her friends.

"He'll be fine. The teens can help. Come chat with the ladies." Macy tugged her away to the nearest picnic table. "You can sit with all the meat eaters."

Leanna tried to smile, but was it the burger that turned her stomach and made her skin crawl, or something else?

She watched Brie and Ez through squinted eyes, careful not to look away for too long. Surely Garrison wouldn't mind Ez swimming. With so many people watching and all.

Leanna settled into an old wooden lounge chair next to Macy, where she could keep better track of the kids.

"Relax." Macy kicked back, crossing her ankles, and chatted with a few women from church.

Relax. Easier said than done.

The conversation was light. Accolades for a wonderful meal. Plans for the next gathering. A next time? Sweat beaded on her forehead as if the sun were not setting. The music continued. Several couples played Corn Hole, lobbing corn-filled bags at wooden boards, aiming for the hole top and center. Leanna never excelled much at that game, but Garrison had a knack for it. A few women swung on the porch swings, rocking infants, and Leanna couldn't help but go there in her mind. Children? Of her own? With Garrison? She played the entire scenario in her head, holding their child for the first time. The thought stole her breath.

"I can't believe he showed up." The lady next to Macy cupped her hand around mouth.

Who? Leanna scanned the grounds.

"I'm proud of him," Macy said.

"Who?" Leanna stretched her neck.

"Mr. Burke. Over there. Coming this way."

Leanna sat up, shoulders squared. There he was. The old drunk. The wife beater. The child abuser. She scowled.

He looked much like Garrison, long strides, broad shoulders. She clenched her jaw, and Macy placed a hand over hers.

"Just listen to what he has to say."

"He'll listen." Leanna moved her hand. "I have a lot to say."

"Not here. Not now."

"Who does he think he is, coming here?"

"You invited the church."

Leanna swallowed as Mr. Burke approached slowing his pace, head bowed. She turned her face from the other women, who made no attempt to hide their interest in the scene unfolding. "He really goes to church?"

Macy gave a soft nod accompanied by a smile. "People change."

Leanna scoffed. "Not him."

"Hello, Leanna." Mr. Burke extended a hand. She eyed the leather skin on those thick hands. How many times had he lifted those same hands to hurt his wife? His son? Leanna swallowed. Mr. Burke kept his hand out.

Her parents had cared for him.

And as a child Leanna even prayed for him.

This was it. The answer.

Her hand met his just as he lowered his.

"Hello, Mr. Burke. Thank you for coming." It wasn't much, but a handshake was a good place to start.

***

"Thank you for coming." Leanna gave Macy a hug.

"Sorry," Macy said, belly bumping Leanna. "Baby gets in the way. Praying this one comes before summer ends."

"You look lovely."

"So do beached whales." Macy chuckled at her own joke. "We'll stay and help out."

"We got it. Y'all are our guests."

"Got your accent back."

Huh? Oh. Leanna covered her mouth and talked through her fingers. "I said y'all."

They laughed, and Leanna gave Macy another quick hug.

"Hey," Macy said. "Is that Cindy and Dale?"

Leanna turned. Cindy and Dale stood near the end of the lot by the Oak tree exchanging what appeared to be heated words. Leanna tilted her head, eyes squinted. What were they saying?

"I'll see you later, Macy."

"Sure thing. Hey, when's Garrison coming back?"

"Tomorrow." Leanna didn't try to hide her smile.

Macy winked and hurried after her kids. Leanna directed her focus back to Cindy and Dale, debated on whether or not to approach, but decided it was time to have that discussion about 'family things'.

"Nice night," Dale called out as Leanna came close. "Nice party."

"You guys were here for it?" Leanna kept her tone casual.

"We got here late." Cindy glanced from Dale and back to Leanna. "Had a few things to do."

Leanna bobbed her head. They stood, and the silence grew uncomfortable. Leanna watched a few lightening bugs trail by.

"We're thankful for Garrison opening up his house to us," Dale said. He tugged at his beard eyes shifting from Cindy and back to her. Strange stares and silence. Leanna shifted her weight.

"It's good to have Brie so close." Leanna glanced over her shoulder. Ez and Brie were helping Aunt Mary and a few guests clean up. "Listen, um, you said you wanted to talk about 'family things', remember?"

Cindy and Dale shared a quick glance. Cindy paled.

Dale reached for her hand. "Maybe another night? We're both pretty worn out. Job searching, you know."

Cindy nodded along, and then they both turned.

"Wait." Leanna placed a hand on Cindy's shoulder. "I know."

Cindy spun, eyes wide. "You know?"

"That Mom and Dad visited you the night they died. Why?"

Something like relief washed over Cindy and Dale's face. *Peculiar.*

Dale stood tall. His scruffy beard shook as he cleared his throat, hands tight on his suspenders. "Cindy, it's not the time or place for this discussion."

"What discussion? Help me understand." But neither Dale nor Cindy replied.

Aunt Cindy's face pinched into a pained expression. "I am really tired." She stepped back into Dale's arms. "How about you and Garrison come over together. We'd like to talk to you both."

Dale ushered Cindy away.

"Wait. Please. Tell me more."

No response.

A thousand questions, perhaps more, hung in the air. Whatever 'family things' Cindy and Dale needed to discuss caused Leanna's stomach to clench.

CHAPTER TWENTY-SEVEN

LATE NIGHT. THE crickets serenaded him as he inched up the porch stairs. What a week. Garrison dragged himself inside his house and dropped the muddied duffel bag in the foyer. Commander Jones worked them dead, then released everyone a few hours early. Leave started tomorrow. He'd welcome the time off.

Garrison tossed the car keys in the glass bowl and flicked on the living room lights, careful not to wake Lee or the kids. He tugged off his Army cap, and pulled the check from his back pocket. Sold Lee's car. Half down —not bad. The rest would come when Nelson picked up the car. Garrison held the check and stretched, but lowered his arms. The smell. Ick. A shower would be glorious.

"Hey."

Garrison jumped back, and dropped the check. "Lee."

She smiled. "Didn't mean to scare you."

He smiled, and picked up the paper, now more awake. "Didn't expect you up this early."

She eyed him, curled on the couch, but didn't ask about it. "Couldn't sleep."

"Everything okay?"

"I've got so much to tell you. Your dad —"

"If he laid a finger on you—"

"Listen. Please."

Garrison sat next to her, steadying his breaths. He dug his fingertips into the cushion. "I'm ready." At least he was braced for the news.

"He's different. He's changed."

Garrison heard the words, but they made no sense.

"I'm not kidding. Everyone from the church came over for dinner—"

"You invited people over?"

"Listen. Yes. A bunch of people came and we sang and ate and played games and swam."

He focused, trying to translate the fast talk. "Did you say 'swam'?"

"You're not listening. Of course we swam."

"Ez too?"

Lee buzzed on, talking about the evening. He cut her off. "Lee, did you let Ez swim without me?"

"There were a bunch of people there. He had a life jacket on. I was watching."

"I can't believe you did this."

"I'm trying to tell you about your dad."

"I don't care about him. Never will." Garrison stomped to his feet, tone elevated. "Why did you let Ez swim? I didn't give you permission. You know how I feel about the water."

"I...I...it wasn't a big deal."

"Not a big deal?" He spun around. "You had no right."

"You were gone. He had fun. We all did."

"That's what you're going with?"

"Calm down."

"You're not his parent." He couldn't take the words back. Not that he wanted to at first, but after a second or two, yeah, he'd like a do-over. Garrison sighed. "Lee—"

"Don't. I know I'm not his Mom, but I do love him."

"Lee—"

"If you can't trust me to take care of your son, then why are we married in the first place? And don't think you can yell at me like that. I'm doing my best." Her voice broke. "I'm new to all of this parenting stuff, and Army life."

"Lee—"

She spun on her heels and walked away.

The woman was infuriating. But then, he'd jumped all over her, not giving her a chance to talk. No, he didn't care about his father, but the fact that Leanna seemed excited did pique his interest.

Still. He shook his head, grumbling as he gathered his belongings. How could she let Ez swim? What if something had happened? He would've been too far away to do anything. He'd be too far to do anything if he deployed. And how effective of a leader would that make him, worried about his family back home, paralyzed by fear of the unknown?

Years of keeping a close eye on Ez. Never letting him near any kind of danger, especially water. The fear of losing Ez never went away. Maybe he needed to talk to Pastor Jay about that.

So maybe he jumped too soon. He tossed his duffle bag over his shoulder and carried it the bedroom.

No maybe to it. He'd jumped, more like leapt, giving her no space to speak. What kind of husband material was he?

And asking her on a date? Ha. He rolled his neck. No way she'd go out with him now.

Garrison stood in front of her bedroom door. He'd sleep on the couch, but first, an apology was due. He sighed and rapped at the door.

"Go away."

"Lee, please."

The door flung open.

She shut the bedroom door behind her, eyes narrowed. Garrison shook his head and lowered his duffle bag onto the floor. He held up a hand in peace.

Even angry, wearing no makeup, hair all insane, she was beautiful. Full lips in a pout. Her eyes were red and swollen. He'd caused those tears, and it made his heart ache.

"Lee—"

"Don't. Don't come here and try to make things right after you jump all over me."

Garrison closed his eyes. All he wanted at this moment was a shower. A shower and a few hours of rest. Not a fight.

"I've been cleaning all week at The Scoop, serving meals, taking care of the kids, dealing with William—"

"He's been bothering you?"

Her eyes widened, her mouth opened, speechless.

"Wait." Garrison tilted his head. "Are you hiding something? 'Cause we're married. We don't keep secrets."

Her eyes narrowed. "Apparently we do. Why didn't you tell me what you and Tiff fought about me the night she died?"

Garrison stepped back. Ringing sounded in his ears. He shook his head and wiped both hands over his face. "Because it wasn't important. Is that what William's been up to? Stirring up junk?" The veins in his neck throbbed. That man had overstepped his boundaries too many times.

"What else are you hiding from me? You waited years to tell me about the twin Tiff aborted."

"Don't hold that against her. And you knew it all along. Just gave you reason to hate us more, but believe me, we hated ourselves more than you ever could."

Her brows pinched together. "I can't trust you."

"You don't want to trust me, because you're scared. How long will you punish me for the mistakes I made years ago? What do you want to hear? That I loved you when I married Tiff? Will that make you feel better?" He threw his hands up, then smacked them against his pant legs. "It's true. I did. But I made a choice to stop loving you when she became my wife."

Leanna dug her fingers into her arms, lips a fine line. "We should stick with the plan and divorce when your deployment is over." The coldness in her voice caused him to shudder. He shook the chill and straightened, refusing to back down.

She turned, and he reached for her arm, spinning her to him, their face inches apart.

"You want to know why Tiff and I fought over you?" He spoke in a hushed voice. She pulled away, but he held on. "Because she heard you got engaged. And she cried because she thought she'd robbed me somehow. But we robbed each other and still managed to find happiness. God blessed us even in the mess we made. He'll do the same for you and me, if you'd let him. Stop being this way. Stop fighting, and love me."

"If you think—"

His lips were against hers before he could think. Before she could utter one more fighting word.

He held her shoulders, their bodies pressed close together. No fighting, not even a fist raised at him. He held tight and she melted against his skin. He ran one hand through her hair and cradled the small of her back with the other. Her fingers, soft and warm, smoothed over the back of his head and skimmed over his shoulders.

No one around.

He should've kissed her a thousand times before this night. And he'd kiss her again, for the rest of his life if she'd allow.

A small sound called from behind them.

Garrison pulled away, and Leanna fell back to her feet, catching her breath.

Ez stared, tears in his eyes.

Leanna stared from Ez to Garrison, still in his arms, not pulling away.

"Did you and Momma kill my brother?"

Garrison sucked in a breath that caused his lungs to protest. Leanna held a hand to her mouth.

Ez searched their faces, but Garrison had no answer, and neither did she.

CHAPTER TWENTY-EIGHT

GARRISON SHUT THE truck engine off.

"We're talking here?" Ez scrunched his nose, a newly developed attitude showing itself. Not too surprising considering all Ez had been through.

"We haven't visited your momma's grave in a while." Garrison opened the heavy metal door and slid out. The morning dew dampened his boots. They walked through the rows, neither speaking.

Several new stones had been added. Patches of flowers lined sections of the cemetery, evidence of loved ones remembered. Those that bore no flowers gave testament to loved ones time forgot.

Tiff always had flowers. So did his mom. He couldn't forget her, no matter her faults. And there were many.

As a child he'd prayed for his father's death, not his mother's. Garrison lowered his head and kept walking.

A double mound of dirt covered Mr. and Mrs. Wilson's graves. Wilted greenery and silk ribbons faded from the sun lay lifeless on top. Sprigs of green grass shot up through clots of earth. Signs of life existed even amongst death. He'd seen it in war as well. Soldiers died, allowing others to live. But why had Mr. and Mrs. Wilson died? Tiff? And his mother? Why not those that deserved death?

But who deserved to live? With all his sins, not he.

Garrison sighed and slowed his pace. Cemeteries always made him introspective.

He kissed his fingertips, pressed them to Tiff's headstone, and sat on the ground. A few blades of grass folded over the bottom of her stone. Garrison plucked them away.

"Your Mom and I made some mistakes when we were younger."

Ez kept his distance but sat.

"And we hurt people we never meant to hurt. Even you, son." Garrison brushed his hand over Tiff's name. "We weren't married when we got pregnant with you."

Ez swallowed the news better than Garrison expected. His wide eyes blinked. "Moms and dads are supposed to be married first."

"That's God's intention. That's His plan. And it's the best plan for a whole host of reasons. Reasons we learned the hard way."

"I had a brother."

Garrison nodded. "Your momma was scared to tell me. To tell anyone. Afraid to be a mom."

"Because she didn't have parents?"

"That was a big reason."

"But Mr. and Mrs. Wilson raised her. They were like her mom and dad."

Garrison nodded.

"She tried to get rid of us anyway?" Ez's bottom lip hung in a pout, his eyes filling with hurt. If only Garrison could take it all away. He would. All of it.

"She was afraid."

"Do you want me now?"

Garrison heart wrung in his chest. He grabbed Ez, pulling him into his lap. He kissed his cheek and forehead, arms wrapped around him tight. Ez didn't fight, only sobbed.

"I miss Mom, and Mr. and Mrs. Wilson. Why did they have to leave? Everything would be okay if they were still here." Ez's body quaked, his shoulders hunching in short jolts.

No need to shush him. Garrison shared the same questions. He rocked his son and let him cry.

"Please forgive us, Ez. Forgive me and your mom. Forgive Lee. We're so sorry."

Cries hitched from Ez's throat. His arms reached around Garrison and clung tight to Garrison. "Please don't leave me too, Daddy."

Garrison no longer contained his tears. Thank God he'd been forced not to deploy this time. There would be other occasions when he'd have to go, but now, no. Now was not that time. First Sergeant, the Commander, and Nelson were right to urge him to put his family first. It was crumbling down all around.

"I'm right here." Garrison cradled Ez's head in his hand.

It took time, but Ez's sobs silenced. He pushed away, eyes swollen, fists balled tight. "Do you want Leanna to stay married to you?"

Garrison nodded, taken aback by his son's sudden anger.

"And you told her that?"

He'd laid it all out in the open with Lee but gotten nowhere. Still, he had to keep trying. Keep pursuing her. It's what God had done with him. With Tiff. It's the advice Pastor Jay gave, and Nelson. Loving someone who wouldn't return the love was painful, far from easy. But she'd kissed him back. She'd held on to him. A passionate moment. Heated. His thoughts began to drift, and he reeled them back.

"Then what's the problem?" Ez raised a brow. He looked so much like Tiff.

Garrison shook his head. "She's afraid too."

"Everyone around here is afraid." Ez scooted to his feet and kicked at the ground. "Can't swim. Can't say I love you. Can't stay married. Can't even tell the whole truth." Garrison flinched. Ez buffed his rounded cheeks with both hands, tears flowing. "We go to church every Sunday, and no one seems to remember that we're not supposed to be afraid."

This child oozed wisdom.

"Well, I'm not afraid." Ez stomped his foot, arms folded.

Garrison rose and placed a strong hand on Ez's shoulder. "I'm not either."

***

Breakfast was quiet. That awkward quiet when so much needed to be unsaid, or in Ez's case, unheard. Leanna eyed the bacon Garrison prepared, and her stomach threatened to empty its contents. The burger from the other night protested. Her body would revolt if she ate any more meat. Breaking free for the vegetarian translated into a dash for the toilet.

Ez still hadn't come from his room, and Brie refused to make eye contact with anyone. Leanna tapped her fork on the plate and slouched in her chair. Somehow she'd developed a serious knack for making life worse, even when trying to make the right decisions.

What's that about, Lord? She lifted a brow hoping He heard her prayer.

Aunt Mary shuffled about the kitchen with a smile plastered on her face, Ginger under her arm. "What a lovely morning." She raised her hands over her head in a long stretch. "No clouds. Blue sky. Beautiful. The good Lord knew we needed a sun-shining day around here."

Oh, to be oblivious. Leanna frowned and twirled her spoon in circles through the bowl of blueberry quinoa oatmeal. Delicious meal any other day, but after last night, her appetite may never return.

Garrison kept his arms folded. "I'll fix your plate, Aunt Mary."

"Sit, sit. Spend time with your wife." She let out a giggle, and Leanna covered her face with a hand. "I'll get my own plate and sit out on the porch. The birds are out. Got my Bible opened. I'm ready for the day."

Sounded like it. The woman literally losing her mind was the happiest in the room. Probably on the planet. Go figure.

Aunt Mary whistled a tune and made her way to the back porch.

Brie stood, silent as usual, emptied her plate in the trash and left the kitchen. Probably down the hall and into her room to talk with Ez about how terrible Leanna and Garrison were. Leanna stabbed at her oatmeal.

Garrison's chest rose and fell. He nudged the eggs on his plate with a fork. Yeah, they both needed to talk to Ez. "I had the opportunity to get out of the Army after Tiff died."

Where was this coming from? Leanna lifted her eyes to meet his.

"Didn't have to deploy for a while, but I missed it. Strange, huh? Everything felt out of place and abnormal with her gone, and going back to life as usual felt good...even if that meant deploying. Leaving Ez behind again. This time without a mom or me. Aunt Mary was more than willing to care for him while I was away, but then, well..." He bobbed his head. "My plans fell apart."

She understood that.

"I may not have ever laid a hand on Ez like my dad did to me, or stayed strung out like my mom, but I let him down."

Leanna blinked, hands falling flat on the table. "You're a good father."

"Yeah? I chose this deployment. So I could feel normal again, chase my own dreams, and when that fell through, I was going to leave him with you."

Was? As in he wasn't leaving Ez with her anymore? His tone bit. Leanna braced herself. Were they over?

Garrison tossed his napkin to the side. "Excuse me." He cleared his throat and left the kitchen.

Leanna sat, alone, unsure of her next move. Maybe there were no more moves.

***

Her next move needed to make her able to take care of Brie on her own, especially after the look on Garrison's face during breakfast. Better Job opportunities. Law Firms nearby. Teaching license requirements. Leanna laid sprawled over her parents' bed and chewed on her thumbnail, Google searching possible life scenarios. Most required time she didn't have.

Sigh.

She closed the computer with a clap and buried her head in the covers.

"Knock, knock."

Leanna startled and sat up, legs crossed. Garrison entered, one hand shoved in his pocket, the other rubbing the back of his neck.

"Any plans for the day?" He didn't come as close as usual.

Leanna pressed her lips together, feeling the distance between them, a distance she'd helped create. "Going to the The Scoop. Aunt Mary's coming —"

"We need to see William."

Leanna poked her tongue in her cheek. See William? For what? Draw up the divorce papers a year early? Talk about her parents' financial mess? Perhaps both. But yes, as much as she hated to admit it, they needed to see William. "If you'd let me finish, I was going to suggest that." Lie.

"Sorry." The words mumbled from his mouth.

Those lips. On hers last night.

Her cheeks warmed and she covered them with a palm.

It couldn't happen again. Not now. Not for a long time. Or ever.

Not after a fight like they'd had. Not after Ez's heart shattered. And not after Garrison had leaving written all over his face. She should've known he'd want to walk away. Nothing new there. Yet this time she'd been the one to push. But so had he. They'd hurt each other. That's what they did. And that's why they couldn't stay together.

God didn't like divorce, but He'd forgive them. He'd forgiven much worse before.

Garrison took a step closer. "What, um, why do you think we need to see William?"

She shrugged, face warming, mind drawing a blank.

"Well, uh," he continued. "I was flipping through the files last night. Couldn't sleep."

She knew the feeling.

"Wanted to see if he had anything we didn't."

"Doubt he'd share anyway." William was the last thing on her mind right now. Leanna cleared her throat. "Brie has counseling this morning."

"Can we both go?" His head shot up. "I mean…" Garrison took a step forward and then another. "It might help us too."

Help? He wasn't letting her go? But after last night…and his reaction this morning?

Leanna tucked her chin.

Soft footfalls neared the bed. Garrison sat on the edge. The fleeting scent of his aftershave, delicious and masculine, wafted past. "You've been through a lot. And so have I. We didn't have the best start, and by no means did this begin as a normal marriage, but it could be. It could be better."

Could it be? Leanna listened, eyes closed.

"We've got things that need to be discussed. Big things. Things more important than any financial mess, or all the wrong reasons we married."

Not too many things bigger than that. Leanna kept a tight lip as Garrison continued. "And I...I want to fix them."

Fix. Was it possible to fix their mess? With God all things were possible, right? Well, she'd tried to do what God wanted, and it didn't work out so well. Leanna sat back, crossing her legs at the ankle.

"Last night...," His hand touched hers, and she opened her eyes. "Don't tell me you didn't feel that between us. Feel it now."

She lowered her lashes. She couldn't deny it. The passion and longing, much more than lust, but a desire to be his wife, to love him back. But...they were both broken, and love was more than a feeling. Their marriage was a bust. A fake. All for show. For convenience.

"I know I've made it hard to love me in the past. To trust me. But I'm here, being honest with you when I say I don't want a divorce. I want you. I want us. And I want you to want the same thing."

"How?" How could they move beyond the past? And how could she ensure he wouldn't let her down again? Her heart throbbed, and his eyes pleaded.

"One step at a time." He drew in a breath and held it before the long release. "Counseling is a good step, but I'd like to take another first."

Leanna gave a sidelong glance.

"I need to tell you something."

What else? No more bad news. No more secrets to discover. She couldn't handle anymore. Tears bit at her eyes.

"I'm...I'm not deploying."

The words floated on the surface, and then sank deep. "You mean..." AWOL? They'd take him to jail.

"I mean, they gave me a choice, and I'm not going."

"If this is about Ez, I won't let him ever go near water again. I'm so sorry I —"

"I'm choosing to stay behind." He exhaled and rubbed both hands over his cheeks.

"Choosing?" Leanna curled the top of the bedspread between her fingers. Did this mean...? How long ago did he make this choice? Before they were married? "You... you tricked me into marrying you?"

"No. What? I would never trick you."

Blood pulsed in her veins. "How could you—"

"I have the choice now. Not then. Not when I married you."

"But you said it earlier. You said you chose to deploy. I should've known you— "

"I chose to deploy earlier in the year, before any of this. Made plans to go. And while I was at work this week, the higher-ups, well, they want me to stay behind. Gave me the option, well not really an option. It's a have to thing or they're pushing me out of the Army."

"And you're telling me this why?"

His face twisted, pained. "Because it changes everything."

She searched his face.

This did change everything... Leanna's jaw unhinged, lips twisting. "Then I'm, I'm free to go?"

He didn't need her anymore. Leanna gathered her knees to her chest. He didn't need her to take care of Ez. He didn't have to meet his end of their deal. She should've never trusted him or agreed to the crazy idea in the first place.

"You're free to stay. And we're free to work on our marriage. Grow as a family, and get over life's hurdles. We have plenty."

Free to stay. He wanted her to stay. Leanna cradled a palm over her forehead. "What about Brie?"

"I want to adopt her. We can do that. It takes time, but I know Cindy —"

"Cindy." The strange behavior from the gathering. What were she and Dale hiding?

"I know you don't fully trust her yet either, but she just wants to be included in your life and Brie's life."

Funny coming from the man who wouldn't even entertain the idea of his father changing. "Something's wrong there. I know it."

"Don't think about her. Or money. Or any other problem." Easy in theory. Garrison pulled her hand into his. "Think about where we're headed. Let's go to counseling."

Her mind raced.

Garrison touched her cheek. "Will you stay?"

He wanted her even after all the cruel things she'd said and done. Even when she was no longer bound to stay. He neared, the tip of his nose touching hers. The warmth of his body, the sincerity of the moment toyed with her logic. His lips skimmed against hers.

Leanna jerked away. She stared at Garrison. All he wanted was an answer. A commitment. Yet she couldn't bring herself to answer.

Why?

Oh Lord, help me.

She broke the eye contact. "You should go."

"I'll sleep on the couch tonight." Garrison rose from the bed, and made his way out the door. One word could have called him back, but her mouth wouldn't open.

CHAPTER TWENTY-NINE

How long would the counseling session last? It had already been an hour. And why did Brie not want her in there? Leanna slid pillows into their cases and folded blankets.

"Got a sec?" Macy's belly popped around the corner before her head. "I know you must be loving making beds today."

"Better than toilets, but anyone staying here should have to make their own bed."

"They do, but not on laundry day."

"Noted. Don't stop by here on laundry day ever again."

Macy chuckled, fanning herself with a Manila folder.

"So what's up?" Leanna took a seat at the round table near the front of the room.

Macy eased into a chair, catching her breath. Pregnancy looked exhausting. "We have a few things we'd like to discuss with you."

"We?"

"Well, Jay and I."

"I'm not ready to go on a double date yet. Garrison and I..." Leanna let the thought trail.

Macy bobbed her head, patting the folder on the table. "Not what I was going to say, but he's on your mind. That's a good sign."

"A good sign we're not doing so well."

"I'm all ears."

"You're all belly."

"Ha. You know there's no judgement here. Sure getting married like that out of nowhere qualifies as insane, but—"

"Thanks, Macy."

"I'm serious though. I'm here." Here smile was genuine.

"I'll fill you in later. Tell me what's up."

"Well, we need some help with decorating. The place needs work, and you have a knack for paints and prints and that kind of stuff."

Leanna took in the room around her. Yes, an accent wall would be nice. A few fresh paint colors would add a homey touch. "Count me in."

Macy jotted a note down inside the folder and grinned. "And we're kind of hoping you have professional clothing items you'd be willing to donate to our clothing store."

"From my closet?"

"And...maybe your mom and dad's?"

The room warmed. Leanna propped her head on her hand.

"Don't worry about it, just if you ever, well, go through things." Macy's face reddened. "Forget about that part. I'm sorry, I should've known—"

"It's okay. Just caught me off guard. I'll... I'll see what I can do." Her parents' clothes. She hadn't gotten rid of anything except food that would ruin if not used. Mom and Dad were gone, but giving their things away made it too real. They were leaving her piece by piece.

Leanna rapped her fingers on the table. "How much longer do you think Brie will be?" Did all counseling take that long? Goodness, she and Garrison would be in there forever working out all their problems. That is, if they went. Maybe one session couldn't hurt. Leanna scratched at her brow.

Macy pulled a granola bar from her purse and peeled the wrapper back. She chewed from the side of her mouth. "Got plans for the fourth?"

"Hadn't really thought about it." Leanna fluffed a pillow and placed it neatly on one of the bunkbeds before moving onto the next.

"Ft. Knox puts on a good show. Thought maybe that could be a fun thing for our families to do together." She nudged Leanna with an elbow and took another bite of her granola bar.

Leanna shot her a knowing look.

"What?" Macy shrugged. "It's not a date when the families are involved."

"Mmmhm."

***

While Leanna waited for Brie, she sat sideways on a sofa and sketched out room designs and color palettes on scrap sheets of notebook paper. The soup kitchen functioned as a business, school, and home for many in the community, and it needed design elements representative of those roles. The colors should be warm. Family portraits should hang in the halls and gathering spaces. She doodled away, sketch after sketch, until Pastor Jay's door opened.

"All done." He gave a nod.

"All done? Like she's talking again."

"Not quite, but she drew a really nice picture today." Pastor Jay held up the eight-by-ten piece of paper. "The people are smiling." And they were. "Good sign."

Pastor Jay knelt at eye level with Brie. "You can go find my kiddos and play for a while. I'm gonna talk to your sis, okay?"

Brie nodded and skirted off.

"A picture? That's it?"

"We can't force her to talk." Pastor Jay twisted his lips to the side. "Have a seat for a sec."

Leanna sat in a corner chair, and Pastor Jay pulled up a seat across from her. "Brie's experienced a traumatic event. You said she's sleeping okay now."

Leanna nodded.

"No nightmares or screaming?"

"Not anymore. She sleeps well. But how do I help her talk?"

"We know she's talking to Ez." He clasped his hands. "The rest will take time. Prayer. Love. Stop fighting with Garrison."

Leanna frowned.

"Brie needs to feel secure."

Yes, secure. Noted, and working on it.

"Here's another picture I want to show you." Pastor Jay slid a folded piece of paper from his pocket. "What do you think of this?"

Six figures. All labeled. Brie. Mom. Dad. Ez. Aunt Cindy and Uncle Dale drawn with a sad face and tears. The words 'help' written over Cindy's head. What was this? Leanna held the picture with little strength.

Pastor Jay's expression pinched together. "Do you know what it might mean?"

"I honestly don't know." But she intended to find out.

"Come back again next week, okay?"

Leanna tucked the paper in her purse, lips drying.

"And if it's okay, how about Garrison and Ez coming along too?"

"Huh?"

"You guys could benefit from family counseling." Pastor Jay extended a hand.

She shook it as her phone buzzed. "See you at church tomorrow."

Leanna left the office and answered her phone in the hall.

"Lee. Thank God."

"William? What number are you calling from?"

William huffed and the phone filled with static. "I need you to get every bill from your parents' house and bring it here to me as soon as possible. Today. Right now."

"Yeah. Sure." She rolled her eyes. "By the way, thanks for shipping all my stuff to me. I'll be sure to drop the key off to you. Real mature."

"I was trying to help."

"Sure."

"Lee, listen. Get the bills. Bring them here. Now."

"What's going on?" Leanna drew in her elbows, a fingernail between her teeth.

"Is Cindy or Dale with you?"

Leanna held the phone tight to her ear, teeth grinding. "Why?"

"Stop being difficult." William sighed, clearly frustrated. "I've been doing some digging, and things aren't adding up."

"If you're talking about the debt, I said that from the beginning. There's no way my parents had all that debt. My school was pretty much paid for —"

"Stop talking, Lee. Listen." His voice morphed into a hurried whisper. "After you see what I've found, you'll never have to worry about losing custody of Brie again."

"Why do you care? You're the reason she's with them in the first place."

"Look, I'm not that heartless, especially when I believe Brie could be in danger."

Leanna stood still, her heart pounding in her ears. Aunt Cindy and Uncle Dale. All those odd behaviors from their conversation and now Brie's curious picture. "Why should I trust you?"

"I don't know how to answer that, but your Aunt and Uncle aren't who you think."

What did that even mean?

Leanna bit her lip, trying to put pieces together. Nothing added up. "I'll be there as soon as possible.

***

"I don't know how long I'll be gone. I'll see if Garrison can drop Ez by too." Leanna sped-walked down The Scoop hall and fumbled in her purse for her cell phone. Impossible to find when needed.

She huffed and mumbled. Leaving Brie behind. Right after Pastor Jay said she needed stability. *Nice, Leanna.*

"It's just a few hours. Calm down. Brie and Ez love it here, and love being with the kids," Macy said, rounding the corner, keeping in step. "Call Garrison. Get over to William's, and I'm sure you'll be able to sort things out."

"I should've known not to trust Cindy and Dale. She's probably on the run from the law, just like old times. Back on drugs." Leanna threw a hand in the air. "She's probably dealing drugs from the house. I'm sure William is loving this."

"You don't have all the information."

"I don't need it. I know all about her. All about these people in this community. They never change."

"Listen to yourself."

Leanna bit her tongue, face hot. She stopped mid-step. "I… I'm sorry."

Why did she do and say the things she didn't want to do and say? Two halves, good versus evil warring within. Leanna's stomach knotted.

Macy offered a slight smile and squeezed her forearm. "It's all gonna work out. Keep the faith."

Sometimes keeping the faith felt like swinging from the bottom knot of a rope.

"Don't hurry back. You and Garrison need time alone too."

Leanna nodded, lips pressed together, and headed out the door, keys finally in hand.

CHAPTER THIRTY

"AUNT CINDY AND Dale are gone, Lee." Garrison bounded down the front porch steps.

"Gone?" Her face paled.

Garrison nodded. "She left this." Maybe Lee could make sense of the note. He handed her the small paper with scrawled writing.

Lee snatched it, eyes wide, frantic. "'We're trying to right what we've wronged. We love you all more than we can say. Please forgive us for everything we've done, and thank you for making us feel like family again.'" Lee shook the paper. "That's it? That's all she has to say? What does any of it even mean?"

Garrison rocked on the heels of his boots, one hand cupping his chin. He folded his arms. "Guns are all still in the cabinet. Nothing seems to be missing, and the kids are safe at The Scoop."

Lee bit her lip, looking off to the distance. Her eyes turned dark. "We have to find her."

"I don't know what this means, but we don't have time to hunt down Aunt Cindy over a note that makes no sense. I hate to say it, but William seems to have more answers than what they seem willing to give anyway."

"But can we trust him?"

"Ha. The devil you know..."

"Is better than the one you don't, yeah." And she hadn't known Cindy and Dale in years, not really. She nodded, lips making a fine line. "Let's sort through the file and get to William's before anything else happens."

***

Neither of them said much. Just filed through papers, sorting out what seemed important enough to take to William.

The monotonous work helped keep his hands busy, but didn't tame his mind. So much to process. Sort out. Much like the drawers and files stuffed with years of statements.

No deploying. Was he a coward for staying and not fighting back? No. Not a coward.

And Lee. Would she come around? Fall in love with him the way he tripped over her? Garrison stole a quick glance. Lee worked, eyes narrowed, brows close together. Lawyer mode.

He returned to his pile, setting out a credit card statement from three years ago, but his thoughts dragged him back. The way Ez looked at him earlier at the graveside tugged at his heart. He'd given his own father that look countless times. The similarity repulsed him. He shook his head and focused. Focused on the papers. One page after another slipped past his fingers.

The Wilsons kept detailed records of their personal finances. A lot better than he kept up with his own. Well, he did a better job now. Tiff had done all that stuff, and Garrison had to learn how to budget and balance a checkbook in a hurry. Took him a bit, but he got the hang of it, and enjoyed making the numbers in his account balance out. Felt good to make ends meet and be able to help others in need.

And there were lots of people in need in Lebanon Junction. Like Cindy and Dale.

Garrison scratched his head, letting his mind wander back through the years. He'd seen Mrs. Wilson cry over her sister's addiction and wild ways, praying that both she and Dale would find peace and choose the right path for their lives. Her prayers had been answered.

Or had Cindy and Dale slipped back into their old ways?

He steadied his breathing and dragged over a stool. "How long did you say Cindy and Dale had been clean?"

Lee lifted her nose from a stack of papers. "Right around three years."

"Hmmm."

"Hmmm, what?"

"Nothing, I guess. Just a lot of things happened three years ago."

A scowl folded across Lee's face.

He counted on his fingers. "Tiff passed away. You got engaged. Your aunt and uncle got clean."

She shrugged, but Garrison couldn't shake the connection. Maybe he was forcing it, but maybe not. What wasn't he seeing?

He flipped through the files in the cabinet. Yes, there was debt. Loan statements. Bank statements. Check stubs. Receipts. Homeowner's agreement, and...

"Look at this." He pulled a statement from the hanging file. "Paid in full."

Lee took the paper, turning it over in her hands. "It's their mortgage."

"And there's only one."

"And look at this loan paperwork. Here. Where your mom signed."

Leanna took the paper. "It's missing her middle initial. But that doesn't mean anything."

"It could." Garrison rubbed his temples. "We'll bring what we have."

"The whole filing cabinet?"

"It'll fit in the truck."

CHAPTER THIRTY-ONE

LEANNA DID HER best to keep calm, cool, and collected. Garrison lent her a hand to hold, but she declined with a small smile. No need to play with his emotions. Or maybe her own. She brushed her hair from her face.

William paced his office. "I don't know any other way to say this."

"Just say it." Leanna crossed a leg, tucking a hand between her knees. Her palms dampened.

"Your Aunt Cindy and Uncle Dale stole your parents' identity. Racked up an insane amount of debt."

Her mouth parted. She and Garrison shared a glance, and slid down into the leather seat.

It all made sense now. Why Cindy and Dale were gone. Their odd behavior. And perhaps why Mom and Dad went to see them the night they died?

"Mom and Dad found out. They must've confronted them." Her thoughts slipped out as words. "But why? Why did Cindy and Dale do this?"

"Drugs. Alcohol." Garrison stared forward, face draining of color. "Addiction makes people do things they never would think of doing under normal circumstances."

Wait. Leanna palmed her head, then stood. "How do you know all of this, William?"

His stammer raised her pulse. He cleared his throat and tugged at his tie. "I…I…was flipping through the files. Found some inconsistencies."

Inconsistencies. She watched Garrison from the corner of her eyes. His expression near unreadable as he peered at William, but he too must've been sensing the same thing. Something was up.

"The money is still owed," William said. He tossed a pencil onto his desk, and it rolled to the floor.

"We have to pay for their crime?" Leanna sat, and crossed her ankles. Fraud wasn't something she spent much time on in law school, but it seemed inaccurate to assume the victim of identity theft would have to pay back any of the charges in connection. He should know this.

"We may have been able to negate many of these charges if the issue had been reported earlier, but who knows how long this has been going on." William shrugged. "On the bright side, no need for a custody lawyer, Brie can be yours. We can probably even skip the court date coming up."

Something felt off. Leanna nodded and pried. "But we're still going to lose the house?"

William steepled his fingers over the bridge of his round nose. His shoulders lifted and fell, and Leanna lowered her head. They still owed. A lot. But the thought of paying for someone else's crime didn't hold in her mind.

Garrison cleared his throat. "We're not losing the house."

Leanna turned in the chair, knees facing Garrison.

"You're my wife. What's yours is mine and what's mine is yours...even the debt. We'll figure it out."

William appeared disgusted, working his jaw side to side. His expression darkened, and a shiver skittered up her spine. *Was all of this still a game to him?*

"Gar—"

"That house means a lot to me too, Lee. One day, I'd like to settle back down in this area, for good. Maybe even sooner than I'd planned."

Sooner than he planned? Was Garrison planning on getting out of the Army? Because of her?

He stood, and stepped close, too close, as if William wasn't in the room. "I'd love for that to be our home."

Our home.

"Where we build a life of our own."

Leanna swallowed, her feet planted. Why couldn't he let her go? Keep to their plan? They'd only hurt each other if they stayed together. That's what they did.

She hardened her jaw.

Was he really trying to do this here? They had more important things to discuss. Like finding Aunt Cindy and Uncle Dale and making them pay. Like anything other than their relationship.

William started. "You owe—"

"We know how much we owe." Garrison narrowed his eyes.

William kept his distance and behind the safety of his desk. He kept his arms locked behind his back. "At this point, honestly, you're looking at bankruptcy, or selling it all. Everything."

The land. The house. The Scoop. Where hungry children and families were fed. Tutoring services. Career building. A place that provided hope and possibility. Sold?

Her heart wrenched, but his words gave her pause. William was never one to be trusted. But should she continue to pry? She'd have Brie now. Wasn't that enough?

Leanna could make it on her own. Start a career. Raise Brie alone. Cut ties with this place once and for all. Headache gone. No William. No Garrison. No Cindy or Dale, no Tiffany's memory or anything else painful from this place.

Brie would be fine, right? A fresh start would do both of them some good.

William's desk phone beeped. He canceled the incoming call. "I've given you two a lot to think about."

Understatement of the year. Leanna nodded and picked up her purse, slinging it over one shoulder. If she could find Cindy and Dale, maybe something could be figured out.

Where had they gone? Was this the wrong she was trying to right? But how?

William knelt and unlocked the bottom drawer. "There's something else you need to know."

What else? Leanna held her breath, not sure if she could handle much more.

"I spent time researching. Trying to dig up what I could on Cindy and Dale." William scratched his head, and beads of sweat began to show on his brow as he pulled the file from the drawer. Was his concern genuine or all for show? Leanna couldn't tell. "They're more than con artists."

He handed the file to Garrison. Leanna folded her arms, neck stretching as Garrison opened the file and flipped through its contents. He sat, a shaking hand over his mouth, and drug a hand over his face.

William looked exhausted yet victorious, like he'd finally delivered some kind of fatal blow to her. His eyes filled with payback.

"Garrison?" Leanna knelt at his side, hand on his knee. He'd never lost composure like this before.

Tears formed in his eyes, but he swiped them away and wiped his nose. "Tiff."

Tiff?

He slid the papers into Leanna's hands, and her heart thudded in her ears. A deafening sound.

Her parents. No.

Aunt Cindy and Uncle Dale were Tiffany's biological parents.

The documents fell to her side.

Tiff was her cousin. Did Mom and Dad know? They must have.

And they never told Tiff. Never told her. Or anyone.

Garrison rested his face in his palms, elbows on his knees. "Ez has more grandparents."

That he did.

***

Memories from William's office earlier in the day felt like a distant memory. More like a dull, nagging headache. An ever present pain. Ez had grandparents. Tiff had parents. And William, he was lying, or at least not disclosing all the facts. Exactly how, Leanna couldn't be certain, but she knew it.

"Pretty good spot." Leanna helped set up makeshift easels, canvases propped against a log along the riverbank. She pressed the tips of her fingers against both temples, but the ache remained. Aspirin and an early bedtime for sure.

Ginger laid at Brie's side, appearing quite content to snooze away the day. Brie fluffed with Ginger's fur and then turned her attention to the buds of clover. She tied the buds together and hung it around her neck like a necklace. Maybe she'd join them and paint. Paint another picture like the one she'd drawn in therapy. Leanna twisted her lips and set out the paints, pencils, and markers.

Aunt Mary smiled at the wind as if it talked to her. Maybe it did. She seemed more at peace than anyone in the family. Her secret? She'd say God.

Leanna sighed. She'd prayed. Given everything, her whole situation over to Him, but it didn't help. If anything, the mess got worse.

"Show me how to paint a tree. Like that one." Ez pointed to the great oak bearing the tree house.

"Good choice."

How had Leanna missed the resemblance before? Ez to Tiff, Tiff to...Aunt Cindy.

Aunt Cindy. Her aunt. Her mother's wayward, drug-addicted sister gave birth to Tiffany and abandoned her. Left her at the mercy of the foster care system, bounced from home to home until Mom and Dad took over. But why had Mom and Dad waited so long to intervene? When Tiff was already close to being grown?

207

And when would Garrison tell Ez, if ever?

Her mind wandered as she helped Ez with each line of the branches, then the roots. "Good job, kiddo. Just like that."

"Is Dad gonna come paint with us?"

Leanna leaned to the side, hand pressed into the grass. She pursed her lips. "I hope so."

Garrison had stayed in the house most of the afternoon. Alone with his thoughts, and she was sure there were many. Much to process.

"What else should I draw?" Ez tilted his head, mouth in a pinch.

"Just draw, paint. See what comes out." The best advice Leanna knew to give. She'd heard it before from her professors.

Aunt Mary paused, holding her brush to the side. "Art helps to express what's on the inside. It helps put a picture to the words we can't seem to find."

Spot on. Leanna's heart leapt.

Aunt Mary brushed side to side and all around, humming a tune. Brie glanced over a time or two but stayed to herself, now working on a matching clover bracelet.

Leanna sat, grass folding beneath her skin. She picked up a clover and handed it to Brie. "I taught you how to make those, remember?"

Brie nodded, a small smile forming.

"You and I would make them for Momma." Leanna chuckled at the sweet memory. She crossed her legs, picking more clover. "When Tiff and I were younger, we'd make them for all the barn cats too."

Ez laughed out loud, and Aunt Mary wheezed out a giggle.

"They wouldn't keep them on, so one time we tried to tape them on. Didn't work too well. Gave up after a few tries." Leanna knotted together clovers of her own, letting the memories play across her mind. Open fields, climbing fences, hide and go seek in and out of the house. Her childhood was filled with many memories and moments, most involving Tiffany and Garrison. How could she ever have believed she could start over? Run from her past when it made up so many wonderful moments in her life? The good with the bad.

"We made mud pies too and tried to feed them to Garrison." Leanna tied the clover bracelet around her wrist and started a new one.

"Ewww." Ez threw his head back, holding his belly as he chuckled. Brie hid a laugh behind her small hands, and Leanna couldn't help but get excited.

"Did he eat them?"

"Once. Though he'd never admit it, I'm sure."

Everyone laughed.

When she focused, the earlier events of the day faded away, replaced by the sweet sight of those she loved sitting so close. The river coursed by in no hurry at all, and somehow Leanna slowed as well, soaking in the sights. Brie and Ez lost in their creations. A warm, safe place to be.

Aunt Mary painted nothing in particular, but the result was still eye-catching. Swirls and lines of various hues. It reminded Leanna of some of her own work.

She filled her lungs with the late afternoon air. This land was beautiful, as was their home. And now it had to be sold. Nothing else could be done.

To think one person could do so much damage.

She shoved Aunt Cindy from her mind. She chewed on the inside of her lip, eyes focusing on Ez and his painting. "That's a nice drawing, bud. Is that you and your daddy fishing?"

"Sure is." Ez continued to paint, tongue peeking between his lips. Had it only been last night that she'd watched his heart shatter? Now he appeared as calm as Aunt Mary and held no grudge. Had he and Garrison talked? "Now that he's not deploying, we'll have more time to fish together."

Brie paused, head turned. Had she not heard yet? Surprising Ez hadn't shared the news. Then again, the two of them hadn't had much time alone today.

Brie lifted her chin, small mouth turned down, and continued binding clovers together. If only Leanna could get into her sister's head.

"Where's Aunt Cindy?" Ez gazed toward the house, then back at his easel.

Leanna swallowed back the sting of the question. Aunt Cindy. Ez's grandmother. Dale—his grandfather. She folded her legs to the side, the grass bending beneath. "I'm sure she'll be back."

"She's probably with Lillian and Jimmy. They'll be home soon." Aunt Mary spoke, never missing a paint stroke, but Leanna stepped back from her canvas at the sound of her parents' names.

Brie stopped, holding the brush tip to the paper. Her eyes watered.

"Aunt Mary, Lillian and Jimmy are gone."

"Oh, no, sweet Tiffany," she giggled, a few drops of paint falling to the ground.

A cold tingling sensation ran down the side of Leanna's body. Aunt Mary called her Tiffany.

"They've only gone to the grocery store." Aunt Mary nodded her head, brush tipping from her fingers. "They'll be happy to see you and Garrison have come home to visit."

Ez and Brie watched Aunt Mary, their eyes unwavering.

What a terrible disease. Here one moment in sound mind, and the next, in a different time. The woman's eyes glassed over, and she blinked several times.

Leanna eased her way over, placing a hand on Aunt Mary's shoulder. "Momma and Daddy are gone. They passed a few months ago. And Tiffany passed away too."

The woman slumped, hand to her forehead. "I. I think I knew this." A small cry sounded from her throat. "So much sadness, but God will make this right. The joy of the Lord is our strength."

Leanna raised a brow. Aunt Mary's ability to recall Scripture from her ailing mind was an impressive skill. One she hoped she'd have if her mind were ever to fail.

"I never wanted to forget the important things." Aunt Mary's veined hand shook.

"You remember what matters most." Leanna kissed the top of Aunt Mary's head.

"You're Leanna."

Leanna nodded.

"And you're home now." She clasped Leanna's hands in hers. The frail skin was cool beneath Leanna's palms.

"And Lee's my...my mom now." Ez stood close, his eyes locked with Leanna's as if he'd chosen her. Approved of her. Even after he knew of the plan to divorce his father.

Leanna pressed her lips together.

"Let's get you inside, Aunt Mary."

"Let's eat first." Garrison walked toward them, picnic basket hanging in the crook of his arm.

He'd made dinner. A picnic meal for all of them. Even after the day he'd had, filled with an overwhelming amount of negativity.

He made dinner.

Leanna watched, mouth agape as he spread the quilt on the ground and served the family—his family. Their family.

CHAPTER THIRTY-TWO

WHAT PURPOSE WOULD it serve to tell Ez that Cindy and Dale were his grandparents? Divulging this information, considering all the upheaval, seemed unnecessary, and hurtful. Sure, Ez deserved to know, but at nine-years-old? All of it was hard enough for Garrison to process. Expecting a kid to get it? Garrison shook his head, and walked the grounds.

The sky, bright shades of sun setting orange, kept him company, while he kept alert, checking in and around the barn, past the shed and every corner of the house. Not that Cindy or Dale should be feared, but if either were struggling with an addiction and on the run, well, sometimes those people weren't always in their right mind. He'd seen it before with his mother.

He shook his head, but he could still hear her screams, the violent outbursts. As a child he'd climb onto the roof of his home, a place his father wouldn't find him, and look out over the hills, waiting for his mother to return. Days would pass before she'd come groveling back only to take another beating.

Had he ever had a normal childhood?

Aunt Mary blamed the war for his father's behavior, which led to his mother's choice method of coping.

Vietnam messed a lot of folks up in his family. His cousin, Collier, went through the wringer with his father, Garrison's uncle. But Collier turned out pretty well. In the military too, now. Got a wife and three kids.

A few stray cats skirted past. Garrison shooed them away and rounded the garden. He knelt, tugging at a few weeds, letting clods of dirt pass through his fingers.

There was a big difference between Collier's father and his own. Collier's father changed and worked to make things right in their relationship, but his father... well. His father was a liar. A man who'd probably sell out his own son for a few ounces of booze.

Garrison stood, dusting his hands on his jeans.

He lowered his head and made his way back to the house, past the tree house. Ez and Brie sat on the back porch, tablets in hand, taking turns showing each other something on their screens. Technology. Garrison snorted. It wasn't a bad thing, and since coming back to Lebanon Junction, Ez had put down the devices more often. Funny how this place seemed to help Ez thrive. He'd been lost since Tiff passed. Didn't quite fit in anywhere anymore. Garrison got that. He'd been out of sorts as well. But now?

Well, after they figured out how to make enough to save the home, and The Scoop, then, maybe they could start planning their future in Lebanon Junction, or at least in the area.

With Lee. If she'd stay.

He could use his business degree to help run The Scoop. Maybe start the survival training business he'd dreamed about years ago.

Lee had to stay, right?

The way she looked at him at dinner, sitting near the edge of the quilt. Garrison chewed on his thumbnail, then looped his fingers through his belt loops. She wanted them to be together, he knew it. Felt it. But she also wanted...wanted...

What else did she want?

Wow, they'd really complicated their lives by marrying without giving it much thought. But divorcing couldn't be the answer.

Garrison scratched at his head. Think. Think.

***

"There you are. Kids are in bed. Aunt Mary too." Garrison yawned, and ducked his head as he stepped down into the basement. Lee sat on the edge of the tattered couch, a wooden box in her lap. "You okay?"

"I should be asking you that."

True. The cool basement air caused him to rub the chill from his arms.

"Remember this box?" Leanna sat on the couch amongst cardboard boxes.

Garrison nodded. "Didn't think you were supposed to open it though."

She opened the lid, and grinned. "I've been opening a lot of things lately."

"Except for these, huh?" Stacks of cardboard boxes lined the walls. How much could one New York apartment hold?

"I think I'm ready to donate a lot of my stuff, and Mom and dad's."

"That's...wow, Lee. That's a big step."

She nodded. "May sell some of the bigger things. It may not cover what I owe—"

"We."

"But it'll help." She ignored his interjection.

"I'd hold off a bit. Garrison took a seat next to her. "Not sure that I'd trust everything William was saying."

"Figured you picked up on that too." She tapped on the box. "Just not sure what we're missing."

"I think it'll come out in time. William seems to have a knack for delivering life altering news." But when and how would it all come out? The soft lamp light shone on the dust particles lifting from the cushion. Garrison tucked the question aside for a later time.

"Thank you for making dinner. We all had a nice time." She offered a smile. The genuine kind.

"Peanut butter and jelly sandwiches are my specialty."

"It was thoughtful of you."

"It's been a bit hectic lately. Forgot to tell you Nelson wants to buy your car. Gave me half down."

Her eyes widened.

"Is that…is that okay?"

"Of course." She grinned. "That's great news. Thank you."

Garrison nodded. Good. Glad to see her smile. He leaned forward. "What are those?"

Envelopes tucked beneath her knee. Tiff's handwriting scrawled across the top. She didn't say much, only lifted the letters and held them close.

"Been a long day, huh?" Garrison sat back, shoulder blades sinking into the cushions. He blew out a burst of air. "In a lot of ways."

"I never opened any letter Tiff sent to me. I didn't care to hear what she had to say after, you know. So I stored them in here…my prayer box."

"So you're reading them now?"

"It's time."

Garrison jostled his leg, holding one hand over his knee. He thought through several possible replies but settled on none.

She held a letter out to him, and a lump rose in his throat. Could he read it? Garrison swallowed, heart panging inside his chest. He took the letter, and the memories flooded. The room squeezed around him. His eyes were a lens zeroed in on Tiff's writing.

Lee,

Asking for your forgiveness isn't good enough, and I don't deserve it, but I'll never stop wishing for it. You said that I was jealous, that I wanted your life, and family…

You're right, but I love you, and your family. I would be nothing without any of you.

We can't undo what we've done, but Garrison and I are trying to do what is right now. We've made so many mistakes, starting with hurting you, and I'm forever sorry. I pray one day we'll be friends again, and all will be well with us.

Love, Tiff

Lee cradled the box. "I wish I would have read these letters before tonight. I wish I'd made things right."

"She knew you loved her."

"She always felt like family to me. Guess that's because she really was." Her shoulders rose and fell. "Do you think she knew? That Cindy and Dale were her parents?"

Garrison shook his head, leaning forward over his bent knees. "If she knew, she never said anything."

"But Mom and Dad knew. Why didn't they tell us, or at least Tiff?"

"Maybe they didn't know." Garrison ran his nails over the top of his head and gave it a good scratch. "Tiff had been through so much already, how would it make her feel to know her real parents were druggies who didn't want her?"

"Maybe that's what Cindy meant by trying to right what she'd wronged?"

All he could do was shrug. No answers. More questions.

"You gonna tell Ez?"

Another shrug. "Eventually. We've hidden enough from that boy already." Garrison yawned and covered his mouth.

"You can have the bed tonight. I'll take the floor."

"So selfless, but we could share it?" He threw a wink in her direction. "We're married, you know." Garrison braced himself for a smack sure to come his way. He dodged her hand, and she laughed. "Afraid you won't be able to resist me?"

"Far from it," she said, but the glint in her eyes told him a different story. "Will you stay down here with me for a little bit longer?"

"And read some of these private prayer requests? Scandalous, Lee."

"We could play twenty questions. You go first." She balled fists under her chin.

Garrison stretched his legs, arms folded behind his head. Choose wisely. He cupped his chin, lips twisted. "Would you consider ending your vegetarian lifestyle?"

"If you'd reconsider your anti-vegetable lifestyle."

"So we're doing negotiations?" He laughed and bobbed his head.

"Not hardly. My turn. Are you thinking of getting out of the Army?"

"It's a possibility. Never gave the idea much attention 'til recently. Thought I'd retire. But..."

"Everything's changed, huh?"

"That it has."

"What would you do?"

"It's my turn to ask a question. No cheating."

"Make it a good one." She rolled her eyes.

"Don't you think it's weird to get an art scholarship but decide to major in history and then go to law school? Seems a little scatterbrained. Unplanned. And I know you like to have a plan." *Even if it's crazy.* He grinned.

"That seems like more than one question. And I'm the one cheating?"

"I'm being serious. What was your thought process for that?"

"Ugh." She cradled her hands in her face, then smoothed back her hair. "I don't know where to begin. I really am scattered, but have to force myself to focus and plan. When life gets, well, crazy, I tend to fall apart." She huffed and patted her hands on the box. "Going to New York, at first, was like getting revenge. Living the big city glamor life Tiff wanted." Her face reddened, and Garrison looked away for a moment. "I loved art, like Tiff loved to swim. But I did want to become a lawyer, and a history degree would get me there. I liked history more than the other options. So, there. Now it's my turn. What do you want to do when you get out of the military?"

"You'll laugh." Garrison leaned his head back against the back of the couch.

Leanna stuck out her pinky finger, and Garrison looped his pinky in hers. "Promise I won't."

"Iron clad deal you made there." He grinned, then sighed. "Tiff and I wanted to come back here and start our own thing. I wanted to create a survival training sort of business." He waited for Lee to laugh, but she didn't. Instead, she nodded, eyes on his. Really listening. "And Tiff wanted to run an event center, but off the land. Decorate barns for weddings and family reunions. Put together giant pumpkin patches with family-friendly fun things to do."

"Tiff wanted to do that?"

"I know. Totally different than city life, lights and fashion, but that's what she dreamed of. We talked about it a lot."

"I wish I could've known that Tiff."

"She changed. For the better. We both did."

"And I changed...but for the—"

"It doesn't matter now. It's in the past, and that's where it belongs. I like who you are now. You're stronger."

Lee tapped the envelopes on her knee, teeth dug into her bottom lip. "So what happens now?"

Garrison tilted his head.

"Now that you're not deploying?"

"Are we keeping track of the questions, 'cause I'm pretty sure it's my turn."

"I'm serious, Garrison."

"Talked to the First Sergeant earlier. There's a possibility of PCSing somewhere else after the guys get back from deployment."

"PCS?"

"Move to a different base."

"Oh. So like, leave Ft. Knox and Lebanon Junction?"

"Funny how that's all we used to dream of, huh?"

She nodded, thumbnail pinched between her lips.

"My turn to ask." Garrison cleared his throat. Would she answer this question? "What's William's issue? And what did you ever see in him?" So that was more than one question, and it may have come out a bit abrasive.

Leanna set the prayer box down beside the couch. She folded her hands in her lap, lips drawn tight. "I thought I knew him. I mean, he... he really was charming, and...accommodating. Generous in many ways. Though..." She wet her lips. "There was always something about him that made me a tad on edge. He never lost well. I thought maybe it was just his determination to succeed, never to fail, but it's more than that.

"Almost obsessive."

She nodded.

"Do you think he'd ever hurt you?"

It took her a moment to answer. "No." But her eyes said otherwise.

One thing was for sure, he'd never let William harm her in any way.

"It's getting late." Garrison rose, and yawned, but her questions followed him to his feet. "We've got church tomorrow."

"One more question?"

He'd love to, but his thoughts called. Thoughts of Cindy, Dale, Ez, Tiff, and William. "Let's say this game is to be continued." He offered a smile, kissed her on top of her head, then made his way upstairs.

CHAPTER THIRTY-THREE

BLUE EYESHADOW. LEANNA rubbed off as much of the stuff as she could. Aunt Mary, God bless that woman, insisted she wear it for church. Aunt Mary applied gobs of it on her own eyelids. At least the congregation would excuse Aunt Mary's appearance, knowing of her illness, but Leanna's? Ugh. Not likely.

Leanna rubbed at her eyelids and snarled at the snickers from Brie and Ez in the backseat.

"It's not that bad." Garrison pulled into the parking lot, keeping his voice a whisper.

Leanna eyed herself in the mirror. Okay, not as bad as it was before she left the house. "I'm washing my face when we get home."

"But you look so lovely, dear." Aunt Mary sat between the kids, legs crossed at the ankles, handbag in both hands. Her support hose had begun to slide down her knee. "Where are we going again?"

"Church," Ez said.

"Oh, I love church. We've been to this one, haven't we?"

"Every Sunday." Ez's tone held hints of frustration.

Aunt Mary paid no mind to Ez, but Garrison shot him a furrowed-brow glare.

Garrison helped Aunt Mary from the car, then opened the door for Leanna. Always a gentleman.

Aunt Mary patted Garrison's shoulder, straightening his tie. He looked nice dressed up. No ball cap. Leanna looked away.

Macy waddled down the church stair behind Pastor Jay, coming their way. She waved, and Leanna returned the gesture. Brie slid her small hand into Leanna's and they walked side by side.

"It's a great day for a miracle." Aunt Mary held her purse in the crook of her arm. Fellow church members ambled past.

"Let's hope she's right." Garrison leaned over, elbowing Leanna's arm.

Leanna hoped for a miracle. And soon. But perhaps the opposite of a miracle waited for them. Not even ten feet away.

Garrison's father.

Garrison must've seen him before Leanna had. He stopped in place, sheltering Ez with an open arm. Now if only Cindy and William would show they could have a real shebang. Some sort of a showdown in front of the church.

Leanna held tight to Brie's hand. She looped her arm through Aunt Mary's. Aunt Mary fumbled with her handbag, stretching to keep up. "Why are we walking so fast, dear?"

"You want to go talk to him?" Leanna whispered in Garrison's ear, hoping the kids couldn't hear.

Garrison sneered. "Not now."

Mr. Burke waved as if nothing was the matter, but neither she nor Garrison lifted a hand in return. His smile faded. He tucked his head and entered the church.

Garrison kept his focus straight ahead.

Leanna forced herself to move forward and pasted a smile on her face, nodding to the other church members as they walked through the parking lot. No need to burden others with her problems.

How many times had she sat smiling in church while crying on the inside? Pretending like she had it all figured out, but the whole town knew better. Leanna wasn't fooling anyone. Not anymore. Yet they still smiled at her. Hugged her neck. Sent food. Cards in the mail.

Everyone else looked so put together. Like they had life figured out.

She knew it wasn't true, but telling her heart to believe such proved impossible. Yes, mistakes had been made, but things were looking up.

Pastor Jay and Macy picked up their pace, shaking hands as they hurried through the church members. He clasped Garrison's hand and pulled him into a strong hug, and soon the service began.

The church band finished with an upbeat tune that had even Brie clapping along, and Pastor Jay encouraged everyone to greet one another. Garrison and Ez made their rounds greeting those to the front and side of their aisle. She shook the hands of those around her, some wrapping an arm around her neck for a quick hug.

"This is her, Momma, the woman I told you about."

Leanna tilted her head, trying to place the young girl.

"Oh. Mrs. Burke," the mother said.

Mrs. Burke. That name. Leanna smiled.

"Thank you for helping my daughter study," the mother reached for Leanna's hand.

"Study?"

"At The Scoop."

The young girl, perhaps a sixth grader, smiled wide at Leanna.

"That's right." Leanna held the woman's hand in hers. "I've been all over that place helping out lately." Recently the tutoring department kept her busy.

"Well, you made an impact. Jules aced her world history exam in summer school. You taught her with pictures?"

"Um, yes. Drawing pictures to reinforce a concept or fact increases the chance of remembering. Guess it worked." Leanna shrugged with a smile. Art helped in many ways.

"I'll bring my math homework in next time," the young girl said.

Leanna chuckled, a hand covering her mouth. "You may fail if I'm teaching that."

The band started, and the members made their way back to their seats.

"So nice to meet you, Mrs. Burke." The mother walked down the aisle with her daughter, but Leanna couldn't move.

She hoped she was smiling. That name again—Mrs. Burke. It caused her heart to jump for many reasons.

So many smiling faces, and while Leanna was sure several people were faking their joy, others had it. Real joy. The kind of joy not based on circumstances, but the unwavering kind. The kind her parents had. The kind she wanted. The kind she had once upon a time.

She scanned the crowd. So many people she loved and that influenced her life. Everyone from her childhood Sunday school teacher to the door greeter who'd slipped her a piece of peppermint before service.

Oh, she'd been to churches a time or two while in New York. Beautiful churches and cathedrals, but these four walls, a few tapestries draped near the front, were lovelier.

Pastor Jay took his place behind a small podium. Leanna opened her Bible, her parents' Bible—the one from their nightstand. She ran her fingers over the fine print. Notes taken on the pages of the Scripture they lived by.

"A collision with culture." Pastor Jay walked from behind the podium. "Those who live out the Christian faith will surely collide with culture, and we should. We live differently than society, or at least we should. For many of us, our faith has become a list of don'ts. Don't drink. Don't smoke.

Don't have sex before marriage. Don't cuss. Don't steal, kill, lie."

Leanna winced. She'd done a great job of keeping to that list.

Pastor Jay continued. "But living out our faith is more than a list of don'ts. It's not what we stand against, but what we stand for."

What did she stand for?

Leanna wriggled in her seat, face warming. Didn't this place have AC? August, and no air on. She'd talk to Macy about that first thing after church.

"Today in our collision with culture, I'd like to have a conversation about marriage."

Really? Leanna clamped her lips together. She eyed Garrison, but his eyes were locked on the preacher. Was that a bead of sweat on his forehead?

Brie leaned her head against Leanna's shoulder, and Ez drew some sort of a hero on the back of the church bulletin. They were all too close to the front to slip out unnoticed.

Leanna frowned. Stuck at church listening to a sermon that caused her legs to jitter and her stomach to twist.

"Marriage is a permanent union, created by God. One man, one woman, one lifetime."

Her chest burned.

Pastor Jay read from Corinthians. The love chapter, her parents called it. The verses, framed, hung in their bedroom. She'd read it often, knew it by heart.

Love is patient. Love is kind. It's not jealous or boastful or proud or rude. It doesn't demand its way. It's not irritable. It doesn't keep record of wrongs.

Love never gives up.

It never loses faith.

It is always hopeful...and endures...through every circumstance.

The words sank deep into a cavern in her heart she hadn't known to exist.

How unloving had she been?

Toward Garrison? Toward so many people.

Had she ever grasped the true meaning of love and its sacrifice?

Leanna whispered a prayer, and this time let it go. She'd written prayers before, stuck them in a prayer box, but never quite released them.

Music played. She lifted her head. Was Pastor Jay finished already? An hour had flown.

Pastor Jay rested his elbows on the podium. "You may have married for all the wrong reasons, but stay married for all the right reasons."

She would.

She would stay married.

***

Leanna reached for Garrison's hand, and they headed out the church doors. Things would be different for them, and she'd tell him so as soon as they were able to be alone.

Alone.

Her pulse raced at the thought. Her lips against his once more. And perhaps they could have a real wedding, and real honeymoon to follow. One they could both plan.

Yes, large obstacles lay in their path, more than perhaps the average couple, but they could handle them together. Leanna lifted her head to the sky.

A fresh start. She smiled at the heavens.

"What's up with you?" Garrison squeezed her hand.

Leanna opened her mouth, ready to reply, but a patrol car sped toward them and stopped in front of the church.

Chatter spread through the crowd exiting into the parking lot.

The sheriff stood from the car.

"May I help you, sir?" Garrison placed his body between the sheriff and Leanna. William had a hand in this, she knew it. Where was he? Leanna scanned the crowd, but found him nowhere.

"Garrison Burke?" said the Sheriff. "We're going to need you to come down to the office. Answer a few questions for us."

Garrison tilted his head. "What's this about, Officer?"

Leanna held her breath, hands holding Ez and Brie close. What *was* this about?

The officer drew back, posture rigid as a crowd began to gather. "It seems we've been given some information about Cindy and Dale Thorton, and we need you to confirm or deny a few things."

"What does he have to do with them?" Leanna stepped forward. "Garrison, don't talk to anyone without a lawyer present."

"Officer, perhaps we could do this later." Garrison's father pushed his way between Garrison and the sheriff.

"Step aside, sir." The officer lifted his chin, eyes stone.

Leanna watched. Mr. Burke was standing up for his son? The son he'd abused and betrayed?

"I don't need your help." Garrison splayed his hands wide, eyes like darts pointed at his father. Leanna stepped aside. His father remained close but silent. Poor man. At least he'd taken a stand. "I'll come," Garrison said to the officer.

221

Leanna clutched her hands, heels like stakes in the ground. Her stomach pinched. "Garrison, are you sure you want to go? This doesn't feel right."

"I won't be long." He cupped her chin, and ran a hand down her arm. "You guys go to Pastor Jay's and wait."

The situation felt off. It didn't settle well, and wreaked of William's involvement. Leanna twisted her neck relieving the building tension, but it remained until the force slammed against her chest. She covered her mouth and nose breathing in an out. No panic attacks. Not now. She spoke in between stalled breaths. "What…if…William…"

"Hey, Lee, we can handle him." Garrison said, and pried her hands from her face. "It's okay. Look at me. Breathe."

She lifted her face, gaze now lost in the green meadows of his eyes. So much peace, and the offer of a life of warmth, and love, and…and so much more. How could she have ever wanted to divorce this man? To hurt someone so true? Tears welled until her vision blurred.

Garrison held her face between his palms. He brushed a thumb over her cheek, and she fought back tears.

He needed to know, to hear her heart. "Garrison, I, I love you."

Garrison smiled, mouth parted, but she didn't wait for him to respond. Leanna leaned forward, pressing her lips to his, melting in the moment.

CHAPTER THIRTY-FOUR

SHE LOVED HIM. Of all the days for this to happen. Garrison finally heard it with his own ears. Lee loved him, but was it enough to make her want to stay?

Garrison pumped his foot beneath the table. The officer eyed him over a Styrofoam cup of coffee. Life seemed to grow more complicated by the moment. A few questions turned into countless. What point in his life led him here, sitting across from a police officer being questioned, and near accused for a crime he didn't commit? Cindy and Dale were the ones at fault.

When First Sergeant got wind of this— Garrison's stomach knotted. Word would pass up the rank structure—Garrison was sure to see an end to his military career quicker than he ever imagined. Even a possible court martial.

He dragged a hand over his face.

Ruined. In every way.

He'd failed.

Failed Lee. Failed Ez. Brie. Aunt Mary. Tiff.

Himself.

A failure—just like his father. Garrison swallowed back the bile threatening.

And Lee. She'd been through so much already, and now this?

The officer wrapped his fingers around the circumference of the cup. He leaned back in his chair mustache twitching. "We're talking fraud, and possible drug pushing. Serious stuff."

"I'm not involved." Garrison repeated for the hundredth time. But the officer looked unconvinced. Where was this nonsense coming from? And what if he was pegged for something he didn't do, for something he couldn't believe Cindy and Dale had done?

His thoughts raced. What if Lee didn't believe he was innocent? The thought turned his stomach, and panged his heart. He'd hurt her so much in the past, even let her down this summer, but he was no criminal. She had to believe that.

Even if he were set free, which the officer seemed intent on not allowing, he'd brought more shame to her. More heartache.

So much damage.

He loved her. Loved her too much to cause her anymore pain.

God forgive me.

Should he be the one to let go?

After everything they'd been through. His relentless pursuit of her heart. Over?

The question lingered burning into his very core.

No. Never. It couldn't be over. He'd made a vow, and how stupid of him to consider breaking it, even if for a moment.

"Officer, I'm trying to be respectful, but I'm not certain you have any incriminating evidence to hold me." Garrison straightened in the metal chair. "I've answered all of your questions. No, I had no involvement nor any knowledge until recently of the fraud or drug charges."

"These are your in-laws."

"It's a strange story, one I've told you, but we're all just now getting acquainted under the worst possible circumstances."

"Then why would a prominent lawyer in town feel you were somehow connected."

Garrison squinted. A prominent lawyer. A lump the size of his fist swelled inside. *William.* Had William planned this to get him out of the picture? To somehow get to Leanna? Well it wouldn't work.

Garrison crossed his arms, foot no longer working a pump. "I can think of a few reasons William Sinclair would drop my name. That is who you're referring to, right Officer?"

"Just a few more questions."

Yeah, that's all the confirmation he needed. After this little session was over, he'd be stopping in to confront William once and for all.

***

She ran her hands up and down her arms, but found little comfort even standing in Macy's home, a setting so inviting. Leanna focused on the floral rug, and then over to the baskets of toys, family portraits on the wall, and the stacks of books on the coffee table.

"Sit, child." Aunt Mary's voice was soothing, but Leanna couldn't bring herself to relax. What were the police questioning him about involving her aunt and uncle? Could Garrison have somehow been involved with the fraud? No. She shook the thought.

Pastor Jay placed a solid pat on Leanna's shoulder. "It's all going to be okay."

"And the kids are happy. We're about to pop in a movie," Macy said.

"And I'm about to take a nap," Aunt Mary said through a yawn. How could she be so calm at a time like this?

Nothing to do now but wait.

Being still, doing nothing?

Sheer torture.

Macy turned, and Leanna greeted her with a smile. "You smile like you might actually be okay. Your momma was good at that."

"My momma was the best at that." And she was. Smiling through the hard times.

"Is Dad gonna be all right?" Ez came down the stairs, Brie by his side.

Leanna pulled them close. "Don't you worry about a thing."

But Ez only looked down.

"Hey." Leanna bent on a knee, taking Ez's arm at the wrist. "We're gonna get through this." Whatever this was.

Ez sniffled and crushed himself against Leanna. His chin dug into her shoulder. Leanna took him into her arms. Brie stood to the side, and Leanna motioned her over and welcomed her into their embrace. If only she could make all their doubt and worry go away. If only she could make hers dissolve as well. She closed her eyes and sent up another prayer.

A couple of Pastor Jay's children called from the top stair.

"You guys wipe your tears and go play." Leanna managed a smile and dried their faces. "I'm gonna make sure your daddy gets home, buddy." Promise.

With a soft smile, Ez turned and walked away and up the stairs, head down. Brie stood for a moment staring at Leanna, as if sizing her up. Did Brie doubt her?

Brie's lips folded into a slight pucker, her eyes watering. What was this child thinking?

"You can talk to me, Brie. Tell me anything. Say whatever. I just want to hear your voice again."

But she turned and headed up the stairs.

"Sometimes we're not ready." Aunt Mary folded her hands in her lap, sitting on a living room ottoman. She'd been a quiet observer for most of the day's events, staring out the window in a world of her own.

Leanna wet her lips and stood to her feet.

Macy sat at the edge of the sofa, face drawn. "Strange, right? All of this. Does this stuff happen to anyone else or just your family?"

Leanna cracked a short smile, thankful for the small bit of comedic relief. "It's definitely movie worthy."

She glanced at the artwork overhead. Words written. A prayer of protection over the family, home, and all who enter. They needed that.

**

Still no calls or texts from Garrison, yet. How long did a 'few questions' take? Leanna plopped her cellphone on top of her purse. Maybe she should sort through the files one more time. But those were at the house. She puffed her cheeks, pushing back her hair. She paced the living room floor, considered calling William, but figured it would only feed into whatever game he was playing now.

"I'm so ready for this baby to be here." Macy arched her back. She looked miserable, but pushed on with a smile. "Anyone hungry?"

No one answered.

"I'll make the kids mac and cheese." Her smile was pleasant and helped to calm Leanna. Macy was too kind. A house full of kids, mouths to feed, and they'd opened their home to who knows what kind of drama.

Everyone sat. Still. What to say? Words didn't help.

Faint laughter and rattling of blocks sounded from the upstairs bedrooms. At least Brie and Ez were playing. It took plenty of convincing them all would be well. Convincing or lying? Leanna wasn't sure.

Aunt Mary had long since worked her way to the guest bedroom for a long Sunday afternoon nap.

Waiting was a horrid thing. Nothing Leanna could do. But there was someone who could. She outstretched her arms. "Can we pray?"

Macy took her hand, and Pastor Jay joined the circle of three. They bowed their heads, and Leanna started. Her voice cracked at first, but the words came, slow then flowing free.

The front door opened. Leanna snapped her head up.

Aunt Cindy and Uncle Dale stood in the entryway. Aunt Cindy's eyes were red and puffy.

The prayer circle broke apart, and Leanna fought the urge to lash out at Cindy. Leanna's eyes filling with tears she couldn't stop.

"Why?" Leanna's question fell out in a near whisper. The tears came. "How could you do this to us?"

"I...I heard Garrison was with the police."

"And you came back for that?"

"He's my..."

"Son-in-law. I know. I know it all." Leanna scowled, voice rising. "I know how you stole from my parents. Your own sister. What kind of a person are you?"

"Call the police." Pastor Jay's tone was stern. Macy reached for her phone.

"Don't call them yet, Macy." Leanna shot her arm like an arrow toward Macy. "I want answers."

"Why?" Leanna seethed. "Why did you do it? All of it? Try to take Brie from me. Rack up a lifetime worth of debt? Abandon your own daughter? And now you're concerned that Garrison is with the police?"

Dale spoke up. "We don't want Garrison blamed for something he had no involvement in."

"That's the most nonsensical thing I've ever heard." A tight laugh slipped through Leanna's lips. She shortened the space between her and Cindy and Dale. "Garrison has nothing to do with your fraud."

Cindy continued. "We know, but, William..."

William. Leanna stiffened at his name. She knew it. Somehow, he was involved. What was his problem? And when would he stop? The answer caused her insides to tremble. He wouldn't stop. Not ever. Until he got what he wanted. Her.

Leanna wet her lips. "William what?"

Macy tucked herself under Pastor Jay's arm, both watching and listening to the private components and conundrums of her life splayed out before them. A vulnerable, naked feeling, yet there was no judgement or condemnation in their expressions. Leanna swallowed and embraced the transparency.

Cindy rubbed at her hands, and shared a glance with Dale. Her sigh was heavy. "William said he'd pin it on Garrison somehow too if we didn't...if we didn't do what he wanted."

"What he wanted?" Leanna arched a brow.

Cindy continued, face pained. "He wanted us to take Brie."

Macy covered her mouth, Pastor Jay keeping his arm tight around her.

The news was repulsing, but not surprising. "And he knew about the fraud?"

Cindy and Dale nodded.

"He knew you were Tiff's parents?"

Another nod.

"He knew this for a while?"

"Before your parents died," Dale said.

William—that liar. Her heart beat like a drum in her ears. Heat rushed from her neck to her face. He'd played them, each bribe tying them to him like string to a kite. No more, and never again. The urge to attack in order to defend her family caused her pulse to shoot throughout her body.

"Leanna." Cindy's voice was frail. "I never would've taken her from you. That's why we took Garrison up on his offer and moved. We only wanted to be a part of this family again."

"A family? Ha." Leanna folded her arms. "Families don't do what you did."

"We're here, now, trying to make this right," Cindy said, eyes pleading. Her face was streaked with tears. She hung her head, swinging it side to side.

"What did you do with the loan money? Still using drugs?"

"No. No. We've been clean for three years." Who was this woman before her? A stranger. Though, Leanna too had once been a stranger to her own self. Leanna swallowed the bile rising in her throat. "Then what?"

"We're felons," Dale said, and rubbed a palm across his forehead. "Job opportunities are pretty bleak for us, so, we used the money to buy drugs, small arms, and sell them different places."

Leanna raised both brows, limbs going numb. Was she hearing this correctly? No one interjected. Aunt Cindy and Uncle Dale built a case against themselves complete with a jury.

"We wanted out. Wanted a new start. Both got jobs working a factory in Louisville until they laid us off." Cindy said. "So we were working to pay back your parents, a little at a time. They were going to help us get a better place to live —"

"Mom and Dad knew?"

Cindy nodded.

The air fled from Leanna's lungs. She stepped back until her shoulders found a wall. "The second mortgage." It made sense now. Leanna stooped, head low. Her parents' ability to forgive and extend grace and mercy knew no bounds.

"But then, they…they…"

"They died." Leanna hunched over, hands clasping her knees.

"And William bribed and blackmailed you both." She stood, heart aching. "You should have come to me. Told me right away." Should-haves. What-ifs. Mistakes that could've been avoided. Oh, didn't she understand those well enough. Fear keeps people from doing the right, and often the most logical thing. Fear. It's what William wielded so well. It's what kept her down for far too long.

The facts remained. Ez lost a mother, and Tiff lived her whole life feeling abandoned because of Cindy and Dale. They'd sold drugs, and committed fraud.

"Have you confessed to the police yet?"

"We went to William." Cindy's voice quaked. "Told him we were going to the police."

"He went crazy, Leanna." Dale waved a hand. "Talking outside of his head."

"Because he's guilty." Leanna jerked her arm out to the side. The movement caused her elbow to pop. "This is obstruction of justice."

He knows it. The thought held her captive. He knows it, and he's scared. William is scared. If she could take the files to Judge Sinclair, coupled with all of their testimonies, William could be stopped, and Brie—Brie would be with her and Garrison forever. Yes, with Garrison forever. She'd tell him as soon as he came through the door, but for now, she'd have to catch Judge Sinclair. On a Sunday afternoon, he'd more than likely be lounging at home.

"I've got to go." Leanna skirted across the room, swooping down for her purse and throwing it over her shoulder in one quick motion.

"Where are you going?" Macy caught Leanna by the wrist.

"I've got to grab files from the house." Leanna dug through her purse pulling out her keys. She grabbed her cell. "If I can show Judge Sinclair, tell him everything, then William—"

"What if Judge Sinclair is in on it too?" Pastor Jay said.

Leanna paused, but not long enough to change her mind. "For too long, I've made many decisions in life for all the wrong reasons. It's time to start making the right choices." She drew in a breath, and the tension rising in her chest dissipated. "And I'm okay if the right thing isn't easy."

Macy nodded, and gave Leanna a quick hug. "Your parents would be so proud."

Leanna smiled, Macy's words were soothing to the soul.

Pastor Jay gave Leanna a solid pat to the shoulder. "We'll keep the kids, and Aunt Mary." His laugh was short.

"Coming with me?" Leanna turned to Cindy and Dale.

Dale slipped a hand in Cindy's. "We need to talk to the police first, and then go from there. Pastor Jay, will you call them for us?"

"How about I take you guys down to The Scoop? We'll call from there, and keep the kids away from anything that may, um, transpire." Pastor Jay twisted his lips.

They all knew what would transpire. At least part of this mess had an ending, even if it wasn't the happiest. Cindy and Dale would serve time for their crimes, perhaps decades. Yet, they were still willing to confess, and make things right. How selfless. How brave.

Leanna drank in the thought. "Aunt Cindy. Uncle Dale. Thank you."

"Hurry back." Macy called as Leanna jetted out the door. If all went well, William would be on his way to jail, and Garrison would be home. Her family—all of them, safe, living out their new dream.

CHAPTER THIRTY-FIVE

THE FILES. WEREN'T they on the counter? Leanna brushed her hair to the side, bent as she searched, hands fumbling past vitamins and receipts.

There. Next to the fridge. Right in front of her. Garrison would've made some comment about her lack of observation. Leanna smiled and laughed at herself.

"Hey Ginger." Leanna stooped and rubbed Aunt Mary's dog on top the head. Ginger kissed her hands, tongue wagging to the beat of her jingling collar. "We'll be back home soon."

Leanna slid her phone from her back pocket and sent Macy a quick text.

Got the files. Headed over to the judge's house in a sec.

She headed from the kitchen ready to leave, but flickers of light caught her eyes. Leanna huffed. Aunt Mary must have forgotten to blow the candles out. That woman. Leanna smiled and worked her way down the hall snuffing out each one with a quick pinch.

Leanna turned, and closed the bedroom doors, but paused in front of Brie's. She peeked in, and stared. Brie's teddy bear lay on the bed, fuzzy bottom up.

The room, though once hers, had been taken over by toy cars, unmatched socks, and broken crayons. Brie and Ez had made it theirs, even decorating the walls with their art.

How had she not looked in sooner? Their drawings, impressive for their age.

Leanna walked in, and scanned the room.

Colorful drawings hung alongside her posters, paintings and pictures. Most cheerful. Leanna smiled, and then...notes. Letters of sorts.

She eased forward, chin quivering.

Post-it notes pressed around her college graduation picture. The last picture she had of her family together.

'I miss you, Mommy and Daddy.'

'I love you.'

'Please come back.'

'I talk to God, but he doesn't answer me. Did he answer you?'

Leanna sniffled. Her eyes burned.

The notes and letters were like a conversation to Mom and Dad. Brie struggled with her loss. Was this how she was coping?

"Brie." Leanna sat on the edge of the bed. She scooped up the bear and cradled it close. How could Leanna help her? Help give answers to the unanswered.

At some point in life it was trust that propelled a person onward. Blind faith. And learning to live with the unanswered questions while believing in the end, it was all worth it. But how did one teach a child such a lesson? Leanna had only began to learn. And probably would continue to learn it throughout her life.

She stood, head swirling. Time to leave for sure. Leanna exited her room.

Ginger barked and gave her a start. That dog rarely barked.

"Hello, gorgeous." William leaned against the hall wall, one leg out. He grinned and tilted his head.

Her voice. Gone. She dared not open her mouth.

"Nothing to say? No apology? Leaving me with nothing, and now you've got it all?"

His breath wreaked of alcohol, his eyes dark orbs that caused her to cringe. Leanna kept still, and steadied her rising nerves.

"You've been drinking."

"Smart one. What's the point of being sober if you're not coming back to me?"

"There are plenty of reasons to stay sober."

"Yeah? Like money. Power. Ha." He reeked, and his words slurred. "None of that satisfies." He beat his chest.

"Go home. Get some sleep." She lifted her chin, but her insides shook.

"I really thought we could've been a great team."

Leanna backed down the hall. She'd seen him roaring drunk before, even angry, but not like this. Not this desperate. She swallowed. Nowhere to run. He'd catch her anyway.

"Come back to me, Leanna." He fumbled forward and she stumbled backward, the wall catching her back. Nowhere to go. His chest pressed against hers. Oh, he reeked of booze and smoke. Leanna choked and turned her face away. "I'm so sorry, Lee. I'll do better. Promise. Please come back."

"William." She kept her voice calm. "We have to move on."

"Because of him." He punched the wall and a few pictures shattered on the floor. "Garrison."

"You're unhappy. We can get you help."

He wiped tears. "I only wanted to love you."

"And we had good times."

"We did, didn't we?" His laugh sounded manic. "But you still want him."

Leanna was firm. "I need to go."

He laughed again, his warm breath smothering. "You still haven't made the connection yet, have you?"

"You're drunk."

"They've turned against me."

"They're doing what's right."

"But everyone will know soon, and that's it—I'm done. I've only got you left." His face, unshaven, scraped against hers. "Stay with me."

She flinched. Her mind raced. Leanna had to get free, but William kept her pinned to the wall. A beast hid behind those eyes. How had she not seen it before?

William pressed his lips to her neck, hands around her waist leaving just enough room for Leanna to send her knee to his groin.

He wailed and fell back, arms flopping against the hardwood.

He gagged and gasped, and she pushed past him, willing her legs to move down the hall.

William lunged forward and clutched a fistful of her hair. She screamed, falling backward, grabbing at the table in the hall and sending a mix of glass and candle wax into the air. She cried out when her head smacked against the wooden floor. A metallic wet sensation flooded her mouth. Her head ached, vision blurred.

William turned her over, pining her down with his legs.

She flailed her arms, clawing at his face, but he held her wrists.

"I love you, Leanna. Why are making me do this?" He gritted his teeth, sweat falling from his face onto hers.

"I love you," he said as he worked his palms around her neck and pushed.

She gasped, clawing at the wooden floor, mind blanking. Her head throbbed, vision blurred. Leanna willed her arms and legs to move, but they refused and became weights too heavy to lift. The walls spun, and darkness stretched like a night sky overhead. Tears seeped from her eyes, before her lids closed.

"I'm so sorry." William repeated the drunken phrase through sobs.

His footsteps staggered close by her body and then grew distant. A rustling of sorts sounded from the kitchen. The clatter of metal. A clicking, and then a low hiss.

What was happening?

And what was that familiar smell?

Was that smoke or death, or both? Darkness hovered closer. Leanna relaxed, giving in, no longer able to fight. Did this pain have a purpose? If she were going to die, then God, please make it quick.

Like her parents.

Leanna closed her eyes.

She prayed. *Take care of Garrison. Of Brie, and Ez.*

CHAPTER THIRTY-SIX

"WHAT DO YOU mean, she's not answering?" Garrison tried not to raise his voice at Macy. To let Lee leave the house, especially since he couldn't find William anywhere. He'd vanished, leaving only empty bottles of hard liquor on his deck.

"She was going to see Judge Sinclair. Said she was on her way back, but that's been…" Macy Stiffened.

"I need to get to her." To know she was okay. And she was okay, right? Garrison ran outstretched fingers over the top of his head.

Aunt Mary swallowed and tried to smile, but no one else in the room did. Not Macy or Pastor Jay. It wasn't like Lee not to answer her phone. One missed call, maybe two, okay. But ten. Now fifteen. No.

"Dad." Ezra flew into the room and collided with him. Garrison lifted his son, kissed his face. His father watched Ez with wide eyes—a hopeful expression. If a reunion were to happen, it wouldn't be today, not when Lee could be in trouble.

"You're back." Ez held tight to Garrison's leg. "I thought they were going to keep you."

They tried hard enough. "Nah, bud. We got it all worked out."

"So, you're free?" Ez raised a fist in the air with a shout.

"Free indeed."

Brie peeked around the corner and inched her way into the room. Garrison smiled, and Brie waved.

Garrison held Ez's hand and bent to a knee. "It's okay, Brie. Lee will be right back. I'm gonna go check in on her." He smiled, hoping to convince himself of her safety as well, but his stomach twisted.

Garrison stood. "I'll be back."

Pastor Jay nodded. "We'll be waiting."

"Got your phone?" Macy asked.

Garrison tapped on his back pocket.

"Please bring back my sister." The urgent voice came from behind. Tiny but powerful.

Garrison spun on his heels. "Brie?"

She rushed toward him, tears streaming. "Please bring her back. Don't let her leave me too."

Garrison knelt, her arms wrapping around his neck, hair tangling up in his face. He gasped, perhaps from shock or perhaps from the strength of her hold. "You're talking."

"She's been talking to me..." Ez mumbled, a smug smile creeping onto his face. Garrison pulled him close, and planted a kiss on both their cheeks.

"I'll bring her back." Garrison landed another kiss on their faces, then headed out the door, pulse pumping in his ears.

***

Smoke billowed from the Wilsons' house. Flames smacked at the window panes. Garrison's heart thudded in his throat. His truck couldn't go fast enough.

A black car pulled from behind the house and took off down the gravel drive, headed his way.

William.

Garrison pressed the gas pedal to the floorboard. No way was William getting away this time. Garrison gritted his teeth. Gravel spit from the sides of his wheels. A head-on collision would take him out. But it was no time to play chicken. He could kill him. Or worse — get himself killed.

And where would that leave Ez, Brie, and Lee? Getting himself killed would tear them apart. Garrison slowed, but William did not. He yanked the wheel to the right, but clipped the front driver's side of William's car. The truck jolted to a stop, and Garrison bolted from his seat, darting toward the house. Lee had to be all right. Was she even in there? Small cries competing against the crackling flames confirmed his fear.

Garrison wrenched the shirt from his body, soaked it in the bird bath near the porch, and wrapped it around his nose and mouth, then kicked down the front door. Flames licked at his arms and legs.

"Lee." He cleared the living room, keeping low as he maneuvered down the hall. "Lee. Answer me." He coughed, working to defend his lungs. Smoke billowed past his head. No sign of her in the hall.

A cry.

But from where?

He went from room to room. The moisture from his shirt began to evaporate. His time would run out soon. Too soon.

Garrison coughed, his throat dried then burned. He guarded his face with his forearm. The heat. Intense. From the hall, back into the living room, and then the kitchen. There, in the doorway of the back screened-in porch. Hanging partially out.

"Lee." He rushed over, hands swiping over her face. "Oh God, help us."

With what energy and air he could muster, Garrison lifted her into his arms and stumbled out the door and off the back porch. He carried her as far from the flames as possible before collapsing to his knees.

Garrison leaned over her body, ear close to her nose. No breath. He checked her pulse. Faint, but there.

He yanked his phone from his pocket, dialed 911, and put it on speakerphone. Fingers interlocked, he placed his hands over her chest and pushed down.

One. Two. Three. Four. He pumped his hands counting each chest compression.

"Nine-one-one, what's your emergency?"

Eight. Nine. Ten. "There's a fire. I'm doing CPR." Garrison continued the compressions careful not to lose count. "Get someone here now. Possible arsonist nearby."

Fifteen. Sixteen.

The operator continued to talk.

"Can't respond. Doing CPR. Send help."

Twenty. Twenty one. His arms ached but Garrison continued to push down. Lee's body jolted with each pump. He'd stay on the line, but the operator would have to hold.

Thirty. And then Garrison tilted her head, chin up. He pinched her nose and covered her mouth with his, pushing his breath into her body. Her chest rose, then fell. He gave a second breath, then checked again. Still not breathing.

He checked her pulse once more. Still there. Still faint.

"Stay with me, Lee. Don't you go." The sun set and darkness swept in. He started the chest compressions once more counting off. "Brie's talking. She talked, Lee. You hear me?" Eleven. Twelve. Thirteen. "Stay. You have to stay." His eyes burned from smoke and tears. "For her. For Ez. For me." Tears fell. Garrison let them. "Stay for me."

Her chest caved with each thrust of his hands, eyes closed, lips cracked. A thin layer of ash coated her body. "Lee—"

A force struck his back, shoving Garrison forward. He groaned, jaw clenched as he caught himself, palms dug into the cold earth. Another blow to his side, and Garrison leapt to his feet in time to catch the solid slab of wood blazing toward his head.

William gritted his teeth, eyes aflame. They glared at one another, strength in a stalemate. Cuts and mounds of bruises plagued William's face. He'd been in a battle of his own. With Lee? Garrison hoped she'd given him a fight to rival them all, but with marks like those, Garrison's father must've done the damage.

Garrison grunted, yanked the piece of wood toward his body and jabbed William in the gut with a solid punch. William doubled over, a croak forced from his mouth, and Garrison threw an elbow, but William dodged, rolling to the ground. He coiled back, then pounced before Garrison could regain his footing. William swung, his fist making contact with Garrison's jaw, and then another punch.

Blood oozed from his lip, his head ached, and Lee lay close by, still not breathing. Garrison barreled into William, slamming him to the ground. He grabbed him, fists full of his collar.

Blood outlined William's teeth. He smiled, twisted, and gurgled in his own blood. "You won't win."

"It's never been about winning. Or the money. Or whatever else you've been living for."

William laughed. A quick swipe of his hand sent Garrison reeling backward. Shiny and stained red, William held the small blade in his hand.

Garrison stood and stumbled. His side pierced. The blood poured freely.

William rolled to his knees, picked up the 2X4 and limped toward Lee. He raised the weapon. Garrison cringed, the veins in his neck tightened as he shouted, but his shouts couldn't reach her.

God help me.

Two shots rang out. Blasts from behind.

William dropped the piece of wood, swayed in place, and then crumbled to the ground.

Judge Sinclair stood behind the gun, eyebrows drawn.

Sirens sounded in the distance.

Garrison inched forward, hand pressed against his side, blood bubbling through his fingers. Each breath was labored, but he had to get to Lee. A sigh passed through his bloodied lips.

"Stay put." Judge Sinclair held him up.

"She needs CPR."

"You're in no condition."

"I have to save her."

An ambulance and EMTs rushed onsite and hurried into action.

"They'll take care of her," Judge Sinclair said.

A team of men and women began working on her, and another team surrounded him, tending his wounds. He tried to fight them, keep sight of Lee, but she was lifted and whisked away.

Garrison's body went limp, tired and worn. Red lights swirled against the backdrop of the night sky and vanished in the distance.

CHAPTER THIRTY-SEVEN

THROAT DRY.

No, sore. And dry.

Painfully sore. And her nose too. Leanna tugged at the plastic tubes in her nostrils.

"Leanna."

The tiny voice brought instant tears to Leanna's eyes. "Brie." A raspy sound worked its way out of her mouth.

Brie ran to her side, arms careful with their hold. Leanna winced under the slight pressure, the pain still raw. Images of the attack followed. Then the flames. The smoke. She banned them from her mind.

"I love you, honeybee." Leanna's voice sounded almost foreign even to herself. The words painful to a throat that had been filled with smoke and worn from screaming.

"Don't try to talk," the doctor said. It was their doctor, their primary care giver. The one who she'd taken Brie to earlier in the summer. He jotted something on his clipboard and watched the monitors next to the bed.

"Two broken ribs. Another cracked." The doctor grimaced, shaking his head. "Smoke inhalation."

"I didn't know you work in the hospital too."

"Today I do." He grinned. "You are lucky to be alive."

"Not lucky." So much more than luck.

"I told you before, I've only seen a handful of miracles. Guess I've seen another." He smiled. "No talking."

Leanna nodded but dismissed his orders as soon as he left the room.

"You're safe now." Leanna cupped Brie's face in her hand and dried her tears.

"I couldn't lose you too." Brie's cheeks were red, rosier than Leanna remembered. More beautiful than any flower that had ever grown in Momma's garden.

"I'm here, honeybee." Leanna lifted Brie's small hand to her lips and planted a soft kiss. "We can all be together now."

Brie's mouth turned down, her head bowed. "Garrison..."

Garrison what? The heart monitor raced. Leanna remembered. He saved her from the fire. Worked over her, making her breathe, and she wanted to, but...but her body wouldn't, couldn't.

And then William. He'd attacked Garrison too.

Oh, no. Please no.

"Brie, where's Garrison?"

The door opened. Macy walked in.

"Garrison?" Leanna searched Brie's face, then Macy's.

"Garrison is resting just down the hall." Macy's smile was warm. "He's okay."

Leanna sank her head into the pillow, heartbeat steadying. Thank God.

Macy patted Brie on the shoulder. "Brie, baby, could you step out in the hall for a bit? Pastor Jay has a few games you can play on his phone."

Brie nodded, kissed Leanna, and walked toward the door. She paused, glancing back over her shoulder.

Leanna smiled. "I'm okay, Brie." Leanna's voice still sounded odd. Would it ever return?

Brie blew a kiss, then eased away.

"What day is it?"

"Tuesday." Macy took a seat in the chair next to the bed. "You haven't been out long."

Two days seemed long enough.

Macy folded her hands in her lap. "You remember what happened?"

Leanna nodded. She closed her eyes, but the images returned. "Most of it." Some things were a blur. A few things. "William? Is he..."

"He'll survive."

Relief washed over her. Though he'd been cruel, there'd been too much heartache already.

Macy place a hand over Leanna's. "And he'll be gone for quite some time, I'm sure."

It hurt to swallow. Like sandpaper on an open wound. "I never wanted any of this to happen."

Leanna wet her lips with what saliva she could muster. Her hand trembled as she lifted it, covering her mouth. The tips of her fingers fell to her chin, then to the white knit blanket laid across her torso. "So it's over?"

Macy nodded.

"And Cindy?"

"She and Dale have been taken in."

Leanna swallowed. She'd visit them both as soon as possible.

"The house." More of a realization than a question. Tension in Leanna's chest rose.

"Don't worry about that right now."

"It's gone, isn't it?"

Macy paused, then nodded. "Not much could be saved."

The memories. Her parents' belongings. All were mere things, but they still hurt to lose. Her home may have went up in smoke, but the truth remained— love, in all its facets, matters most.

Leanna pressed back tears. "And Garrison is gonna be okay? Really?"

"He is. Asking to see you right now. The doctors won't be able to keep him from you much longer." Macy giggled.

Leanna rocked her head. That man. He'd fought for her, nearly died fighting. Still fighting to see her. "I don't think..." She swallowed, voice fading. "I'll ever be able to keep him away."

"That's a good thing." Macy winked and stood. "Get some rest. You and Garrison have whole lot of talkin' to do, and Lord knows your voice needs to heal. You sound like a man."

Leanna tried to laugh, but it came out as a strange rumble.

Taking a beating and going through a fire...losing everything—all worth it if it meant keeping her family together. She worked to pull her scattered thoughts in some kind of order.

"Rest." Macy crossed her arms and leaned against the hospital bed. "I'll make sure we check back in before we go."

"Thank you."

Macy grinned and made her way out the door.

Friends. A comforting thought. Leanna nestled down in the pillow, heavy eyelids closing. She could rest now.

***

He'd talked to First Sergeant and Commander Jones. Both were relieved to hear he was okay.

Nelson and the rest of his crew had come to visit. Good buddies. Took their personal time from leave to come out. Garrison slid a hand into his jeans pocket, the other rubbing across his twenty-four-hour scruff. He shook a chill away, and the heels of his boots echoed in the hall of the hospital.

It was over. Part of it, at least.

Lying in a hospital bed gave a man plenty of time to think, and Garrison thought. Prayed. Considered plans for the future. Good things.

William was no longer a threat.

Cindy and Dale had made things right.

And his father—well, he'd work on forgiving him. He'd get there.

Now it was time to start over. Start new. With Lee.

What did it matter what anyone else said about their relationship, how they met, married, or the little deal they struck up? In the end, he and Lee were accountable to God for their marriage. With their faith, friends like his Army guys, Pastor Jay and Macy, he and Lee had a shot. A real shot at making a life for themselves.

He rounded the nurse's station too fast and held his side. Bandaged and stitched, but still not fully healed. The doc said it could be weeks. *"Take it easy,"* he said.

Sure.

Garrison slowed his steps, a line of sweat forming over his brow. He took a deep breath, eyes squinting. Maybe he should opt for a little bit of pain meds after all, give Nelson something to razz him over.

He nodded to a few nurses and a patient in the hall, and then stopped in front of Lee's door.

He chewed at his thumbnail. He hadn't seen Lee since the other night. His throat tightened, stomach coiled in knots at the memory of her bloodied, beaten, and pale. Too close to death.

Only out of concern for Lee did he heed to the doctor's advice to let her rest.

This was it. He swallowed, hand readied.

But how would she look?

As if it mattered. Garrison shook his head. Burnt or scarred, he'd love that woman until the day he died, and if God allowed, longer.

***

Leanna kept still, back pressed against the hospital bed. Garrison walked forward, the door clicking shut behind him.

Jaw bruised. Eyes slightly sunken, perhaps from exhaustion, yet there he stood at the end of her bed. Strong as ever. Her husband.

Leanna smiled, lifting her hand. He moved forward as if the gesture pulled him, yet he didn't hesitate.

"We made it." Leanna's lips, dry as they were, pried apart. She curled her fingers around his hand, the warmth as soothing as his presence.

"How you holding up?"

"I should ask you the same thing. A knife wound?"

Garrison shrugged. He smoothed a thumb over her wrist, his dark brows lowered as if too many thoughts prevented them from rising. "We made it."

Her eyes watered. She blinked away the tears. "How…how did William…"

"With the gas stove. He lit it, then, well…"

"I never wanted it to end this way…for William…and the house…"

"William made his choices."

"I can't believe how stupid I was to ever—"

"He was the stupid one. For not seeing how amazing you really are. For underestimating you. For thinking you would never see through him."

Leanna lifted her chin, letting Garrison's words sink deep. He loved her.

Garrison eased close, sitting on the bedside. "I've had a lot of time to think—"

"Me too. The house, and the debt—"

"About more important things."

His words silenced her. Yes, there were far more important things. Like the man sitting at her side.

Garrison brushed her hair, hand cradling her cheek. "I know you're worried about this debt, but don't be."

Leanna listened.

"Some of it we'll have to pay for sure, but you were right about not having to pay a lot it. The sheriff says since this a case of fraud and identity theft, he's sure most of it can be canceled. Make payments on the rest."

"Payments?"

"Probably less than what that Lexus of yours was worth."

She smiled and winced.

He gathered her hand in his. "We can rebuild your parents' house if you want."

Her breath caught, and the tears came.

"Breathe." Garrison laughed, holding his side.

"I can't believe this. Any of it."

So what's next? Leanna lowered her hands, fidgeted with her fingers.

The room grew hot. Garrison needed to hear the words again. Needed to know she would go anywhere with him. But where to start? How to say everything he needed to hear? Maybe begin with an apology, or skip the words and kiss him. That could say a whole lot of things, no words needed.

"So." Garrison scratched at his neck and tugged at his dog tags. "Brie's talking. That's new."

Opportunity gone. Leanna hid her frown. Brie, talking, yes. Thank Jesus for that. "And hasn't stopped much."

"Talked to Ez." Garrison coughed, one hand on his knee. "Hard conversation to have, but he's kind of pumped to have grandparents."

"It's good he knows about Cindy and Dale. Tiff would've wanted it that way."

"He forgave them. No questions asked. The boy amazes me. Made me promise we'll visit them in jail." Garrison wheezed a laugh, then held his side for a moment. "How redneck is that? Visit Grandma and Grandpa in jail."

"This is Kentucky." Lee cracked a smile, and the skin around her mouth pulled. She swallowed, and winced as she drew in a breath. "Kids have this incredible capacity to forgive and move on. I think they're rubbing off on me." She too needed to forgive Cindy and Dale...and William.

Garrison nodded. "I think I'm going to let him meet my father."

Words too many to ask and questions too large to fathom filled her mind. Leanna blinked.

"That's...that's a big deal." She loosened her hold on his hand, but he tightened his with a gentle grin.

"Figured we'll take things one step at a time."

"The best way."

***

Leanna waded through the ash still wet from the firefighters attempt to put out the flames. Macy had been right. Not much of the home could be salvaged. The scent—unforgettable. The sight—unbelievable. Part of the house caved and sank into the basement, and the roof of the front porch folded into a frown. Was it only days ago she'd rested beneath comforts of this home? Her parents lived and loved within these walls, raised a family, and now...it was gone. All gone. And perhaps it was best—a push to start new, and shake the memory of how William had attacked.

Leanna breathed in, the tinge of smoke burning her throat. It reminded her of that night. When she thought her life was over. She shivered, and thanked God for another chance at life, and love.

Brie crossed the yard, a bucket in hand. Ginger bounced at her side. No one was more thankful than Aunt Mary to find out Ginger had survived the fire.

"What's that?" Leanna called out. Brie ran her way, ponytail swinging side to side.

"Look." She lifted the bucket, and Leanna peered inside. Coins, silverware, and...

"Mom's jewelry?" Leanna lifted the melted mound, turning it over in her hand. Broaches, earrings, necklaces, once individual pieces were now one, inseparable. Ash lined the crevices, but only accented its beauty.

"The fire did that?" Brie said, eyes full of awe.

Leanna nodding, the simple truth speaking volumes to her core. Fire can unite, refine, even create. She'd been through a fire. Garrison too. And they'd survived. Now they could thrive.

"Can Ez and I dig around for more?"

"I'll help." Leanna scanned the remains. Garrison pillaged near the kitchen. Aunt Mary fussed over Ginger by the shed who had no intention of sitting let alone staying. Leanna smiled, heart full.

She knelt, hands in the soot and pulled out the remnants of a hardbound book. It crumbled in her hands. The firefighters had managed to pull out a chest from her parents' bedroom, and several photos from the walls. Treasures. But most of the rest, gone.

Leanna watched where she walked, bent, eyeing the ruins for signs or items capable of salvage. She stood where the living room once was. The piano, keys now resembling more ebony than ivory, remained upright even covered with singed rafters.

"I found a few plates." Garrison stepped over debris, his Army T-shirt now looked more black than gray. He carried the plates in his hand. "Keep or toss?"

"Keep," Leanna said.

"What about these?" Ez lifted what looked like bent knitting needles.

"Toss," they all said in unison.

Gravel cracked and caught her attention. A truck, not much older than hers, pulled up the drive.

Judge Sinclair.

He ambled from his car. They still had a couple of weeks until their court date, but given the current circumstances…

"Thought I'd stop by," he said.

Leanna dusted the soot from her hands and onto her jeans. Garrison kept pace at her side.

"Figured I'd go ahead and make things official. Brie's yours." He tapped the envelope in his hand and then handed the papers over.

She held it. It weighed much less than it cost. "Should've come to you the moment I came back home."

"Who knows why William did what he did, or why he ever did what he did."

She'd wondered the same. Leanna squinted blocking the afternoon sun. "I'm sorry you had to…" Even though William survived, It couldn't have been easy for Judge Sinclair to shoot his nephew. "I'm grateful. Thank you."

"He came to see me. I knew he was drunk the moment he staggered up my stairs. Tried to get him to sleep it off, but he kept raving on about seeing you." Judge Sinclair crossed his arms resting them overtop his stomach, eyes focused on the gravel. "Then he left. Said he was going home, but I couldn't reach him. When Garrison called, I knew." He exchanged a knowing glance with Garrison and continued. "I knew where William was, and afraid of what he was going to do. I'm so sorry, Leanna. I didn't know. I didn't know any of it."

She tilted her head. From this angle, Judge Sinclair appeared more like a brokenhearted old man, not a judge.

Garrison extended a hand and the two men shook.

"There's no need for a court date now. Take good care of Brie." Judge Sinclair bobbed his head. He gave the remains of the home a once over and made his way back to the car.

Leanna tucked the envelope in her back pocket and reached for Garrison's hand. He squeezed three times, and she returned with four quick pulses—*I love you too.*

"Look what I found." Ez's voice called from behind.

She and Garrison turned in unison. The prayer box.

Leanna yanked at Garrison's hand. "It survived. How?"

"Guess that means we'll always have prayer requests."

Leanna laughed, voice still rough. She pushed her hair back. They made their way back to the ruins.

Garrison smoothed a thumb over top her hand. "You know, Lee, we never finished playing twenty questions."

"That's what you're thinking right now?"

He shrugged. "Ladies first."

Her face warmed, pulse beating a rhythm in her neck. What did she want to ask? Not so much ask, but say. "You've had some time to think."

He nodded.

"Been thinking of future plans?"

He nodded once more.

"Well? What are they?"

"That's another question. My turn." He grinned.

Leanna shot him a look, chin tucked. "Fine."

"What's the dumbest thought I've ever had?"

"There's too many for me to answer." She raised a brow, tilting her head.

"Funny. Figured you'd say that. Naw." Garrison leaned forward and slid one hand under her head. Leanna let her grin fall at his serious expression.

"Right before all this, while I was sitting in the police office, for a moment, a split second, I thought I should leave to keep from hurting you anymore."

She searched his face. "That is the dumbest thought you've ever had." She kept her voice low, afraid any sudden sound or movement would ruin this moment. "I've been thinking what a good team we make. Maybe good enough to start our own business. Something to do with a survival camp, and maybe a pumpkin patch."

"I'm thinking Ft. Knox makes a great place for a family to live while we rebuild here in Lebanon Junction. You can start your own firm here, or teach, or stay home. Whatever." His lips skimmed across hers.

Her body melted, and the corners of her mouth turned up. "We're starting to think a lot alike."

"That's what married folks do." Garrison's nose brushed the tip of hers.

She grinned. Fireworks crackled in the distance. Some kids setting off leftover fireworks from the 4th. "We missed it."

"Huh?"

"Macy invited us to watch the fireworks at Ft. Knox."

"That's totally not what I was thinking about right now."

Leanna watched the smoke trail in the sky until it cleared.

"You know," Garrison said. He placed a hand on her hip. "Where there's smoke…"

"I love you." Leanna blurted out the words. Garrison needed to know, for sure, for certain and forever.

"Say it again."

But before she could utter the words, his lips were against hers, gentle but fierce. He kissed her, standing in the ashes.

THE END

VISIT HANNAH

www.hannahrconway.com

JOIN THE *LETTING FREEDOM RING*

NEWSLETTER

Like *Up in Smoke*?

Show the Love & Share the Love

Show the love and leave a review on Amazon, Goodreads,

Barnes & Noble or anywhere this book is sold.

Share the love and tell a friend either face to face or on the

web.

ABOUT "UP IN SMOKE"

This novel takes place in Lebanon Junction, KY, a real town near my hometown of Elizabethtown, KY. Lebanon Junction is a quaint , yet quite friendly place. I love small towns, always have, and I hope you'll fall in love with this wonderful town and the people. Though many of the places that pop up in this novel, like The Scoop, are fictional, the restaurant, Little Rick's Neighborhood Bar & Grill is very much a real thing, and if you're ever in Kentucky, check it out.

Leanna and Garrison have been a part of my life for many years now. In fact, their story first emerged close to a decade ago when our family was stationed in Colorado. My husband and I heard of a couple who met and married within two weeks of meeting each other for the sake of financial convenience with the intention of divorcing after a period of time. I wondered what would happen in that marriage if they both discovered the value and sanctity of their vows, and Leanna and Garrison's story began to unfold in my mind. This story began as "The Deal", morphed into "Meant to be Broken," and finally my agent and I decided on "Up in Smoke". I believe it's a perfect fit for this novel, and I hope you agree.

AUTHOR NOTE

Dear Reader,

Thank you so very much for taking the time to pick this novel, and read it! Out of all the books in the world, you're holding this one—that means a lot to me, and it feels like we're on this novel journey together.

This novel has been a long time coming. It's been "finished" for some time, and we've been sitting on it waiting for the right moment to release. Looking back over the course of the past couple of years, I'm so very thankful that we've waited.

Life is full of challenges, obstacles, time of growth and drought. It seems our family has been through all of those seasons in a short time, yet, it was necessary that I go through those personal challenges. Without them, I believe this novel would lack depth. There's something about living and learning that allows us to communicate and relate better with the world around us.

It is my prayer that this novel speaks to you in ways that I may never have intended. Ultimately, I pray you find themes of redemption, grace, and mercy in abundance to be present in this novel, and in your life.

Again, thank you for sharing this journey with me.

Love,
Hannah R. Conway

MORE READS FROM HANNAH

Wedding a Warrior, FREE ON EBOOK! WHITLEIGH HAYNES, a college student, plans her future with precision, and no intention of ever leaving her Kentucky home.

After the attacks of September 11th, her longtime boyfriend, COLLIER CROMWELL, puts his plans aside to join the Army in order to serve God and country, at any cost—even if it means losing Whitleigh.

Collier proposes unexpectedly, and an old boyfriend comes calling, Whitleigh is left to wrestle with choices she never wanted to make. Her faith is stretched, and her once planned path is blurred. There's much to consider, and saying yes to either man would change the trajectory of her life.
Which path should she take?

Whitleigh turns to God, but is she willing to listen when the answer may mean a future marked with plans she can't pencil in on a calendar, or worse–control?

The Wounded Warrior's Wife. WHITLEIGH CROMWELL dreamt of a happy life with her newlywed husband. Army Private First Class COLLIER CROMWELL loved God, his wife, and his country, though the military demanded he pay a high cost.

When an unexpected deployment during the height of the Iraqi war sends Collier away for another year, their lives tumble down a path marked with struggles and fatalities. War weary and faith crippled, Collier brings home a war of another kind leaving Whitleigh staring at the pieces of their shattered marriage.

Are some wounds too deep, and marriages too broken, that fall beyond even God's ability to restore?

www.ingramcontent.com/pod-product-compliance
Lightning Source LLC
Chambersburg PA
CBHW071138260626
47162CB00003B/837